A NOVEL

CHRONICLES OF NICKY SPADE

BOOK 1: RISE TO FAME

A NOVEL

CHRONICLES OF NICKY SPADE

BOOK 1: RISE TO FAME

JANICE WILLIAMS
AND TRACEY SCHUMANN

PRIMIX PUBLISHING

THE WRITE CHOICE

Primix Publishing
11620 Wilshire Blvd
Suite 900, West Wilshire Center, Los Angeles, CA, 90025
www.primixpublishing.com
Phone: 1-800-538-5788

Published by Primix Publishing   03/23/2022

ISBN: 978-1-957676-03-6(sc)
ISBN: 978-1-957676-04-3(e)

Library of Congress Control Number: 2022904506

CONTENTS

PROLOGUE

Nicky lit his third cigarette of the evening as smoke permeated the quaint bar. Patiently waiting for Cameron, his son, to walk on stage, he glanced at his watch. It was almost 8:00 p.m. With trembling hands, he raised a glass of bourbon to his lips. Nicky no longer resembled the famous rock icon his fans knew and loved. Yet, sitting here unbeknown to others around him sat a *living legend* who had greatly influenced the world of music. Nicky's long career in the music industry had seen him perform in front of dignitaries and royalty. His albums had sold into the hundreds of millions worldwide. There had been numerous books and movies detailing his remarkable career. Tonight, he was again experiencing those same emotions that had driven him to the pinnacle of fame and fortune. However, this time it wasn't about him.

As the band began their warm-up, the sounds resonating from backstage sent chills throughout his body. He could easily relate to the nervous tension which he knew Cameron felt. No matter how many times he had performed, the sheer terror of going on stage in front of an audience never left him. It had been the one constant in his career which had given him the edge to perform at his best. It only disappeared when he saw the excitement reflected in the faces of his adoring fans that he could relax and lead into his first song of the evening. After the initial jolt of fright, he would begin to feed off the energy and passion of those who came to watch his performance. At this instant, he always became a true artist in every sense of the word, destined to be the legendary performer his audience had come to see. Now, it was Cameron's turn. Cameron was young but well on his way to making the world take notice.

As the curtains opened, the audience came alive with enthusiasm. Nicky knew those who had come this evening would not leave disappointed. Cameron reflected his father's younger appearance. He was tall and thin with wavy black hair. In addition to inheriting his father's handsome appearance, Cameron, with his strong vocals, could deliver any song with magnetism.

His talent for singing was easily discernable. Cameron carried within him the genes of a rock star. Looking at his son, Nicky felt many different emotions. He knew in his heart that Cameron's life was about to change in ways he never thought possible.

After finishing his first song, Cameron gave recognition to someone of importance in the audience. Little did they know the significance. No one could have kept Nicky Spade from being here this evening. He had lived a remarkable dream. This evening Cameron Spade, or Ace, as he lovingly referred to his son, seemed destined to be on the same path. Memories flooded Nicky's mind. Wiping tears from his eyes, he reflected on his rise to fame.

CHAPTER ONE

The early years

A pristine white blanket covered the small rural town of Middleton, Michigan. Snow had fallen relentlessly for days. Unbelievably, the spring of 1970 was proving to be harsh. It had set records for the coldest temperatures in over a decade, which inevitability left the residents dealing with the aftermath of a massive snowstorm.

"Hey Nicholas, the front sidewalk is buried in snow. I need you to get the shovel and clear the walkway before your father gets home, and don't forget to throw down some extra salt."

His mother's voice wasn't the first thing he wanted to hear walking in from school. Nicky was still reeling from the shocking news circulating at Middleton High. Everyone was devastated to hear the Beatles had just disbanded via a press release from England. Unfortunately, he had missed his opportunity to see them perform. It was the turning point that catapulted Nicky further in the direction of his dreams. Middleton held nothing for him, and he knew that remaining in this insipid town would dissolve any aspirations of pursuing his dreams. Hoping to get the sad news off his mind, all he wanted was to change clothes and go to Larry's for band practice.

Why was he the only one who knew how to shovel snow? Why wasn't Tony, his older brother, asked to clear the sidewalk? He could have quickly done the job. Tony had remained at home attending the local vocational school after graduating from Middleton High. His ambitions had always been to become an auto mechanic, a fair trade for someone born and raised in Middleton. Tony, from birth, was destined to follow in his dad's footsteps.

Their father, Joseph Spade, worked at the Ford Plant. He had always thought his sons would someday follow him into the auto industry. However, Nicky had no interest in cars or anything related to them. He was a dreamer, and his dreams had never included Middleton. He was always trying to devise a plan that would take him far from his hometown after graduation.

Nicky reflected his father's handsome Italian profile. His sculpted facial features, olive complexion, black hair, and deep blue eyes were evident. However, this was where the similarities ended. Nicky had never been close to his dad or shared his desire to become an auto mechanic.

Nicky had inherited his mother's natural talent for singing. He was the lead vocalist and played guitar in the small band he formed with his friends. At this time, it was more of a hobby than a serious effort. However, the other band members were unaware of Nicky's aspirations. He knew one day soon he would get his ticket out of Middleton.

Hurriedly finishing the sidewalk, Nicky was anxious to get inside and out of the frigid weather. The only thing on his mind was getting together with the boys in the band and rehearsing. Middleton High had more than its share of boy bands in the seventies. However, theirs was unique. It had Nicky on guitar singing lead vocals.

Borrowing his mother's car, he drove the few short blocks to Larry's parking in front. Then, grabbing his guitar, Nicky quickly ran up to ring the doorbell. He was freezing and needed to get inside and out of the relentless snow. Hopefully, the snowplows would clear the street before he left.

"Hey, man, come on down to the basement. Everyone's already here," Larry remarked, opening the door.

Larry was more of a jock than a serious musician. He was the star quarterback for the Middleton High football team. Nicky thought Larry didn't par up with the rest of the band members as far as his musical abilities were concerned. However, Larry was a cool guy, and his parents allowed them to use their basement for band practice. They tolerated the noise level, along with the ever-constant parade of young men coming in and out of their house. Nicky was sure the band could have easily used a more talented guitarist if not for this fact. Still, Larry was a decent musician, and no one was about to oust him from the band, at least not at this moment.

Walking downstairs and entering the large basement, Nicky could see the other band members had already arrived and were ready to practice.

"Hey, where have you been? That was shocking about the Beatles, wasn't it? Bet you had your face glued to the television watching the news, or did Aunt Joan have you busy doing chores again?" Jerry laughed.

Jerry and Nicky were cousins. Their mothers, Joan and Joyce, were twins and had always remained close as sisters. Joan had turned down a career in music to marry Nicky's dad. The boys shared a strong family resemblance between them. However, unlike Jerry, Nicky always seemed to catch the attention of all the girls at school.

"No. I just finished a huge plate of lasagna before coming over."

"Oh yeah, and you didn't bring us all some," Justin teased.

Sitting behind the drums was a young guy who was short and chubby. He was by far the best drummer at Middleton High. The boys were lucky to have him as a member of their band.

Then, all at once, an amp cord was thrown in Nicky's direction.

"Good catch. I hope you enjoyed the lasagna," Jerry grinned with a bit of sarcasm.

"Hey, Bro, I'm not that late. You could have easily stopped by and picked me up."

"Oh, I had to run over to the Ford Plant and drop Dad off at work. His car is in the shop, and he's working the late shift."

Middleton offered its residents no higher education opportunities outside trade schools. Instead, Middleton doomed them, for the most part, to a fate of spending their entire life working at the Ford plant. Except for the lucky few, who happened to own and operate the small shops located on Main Street.

"Well, are you going to stand there, or are you ready to warm up?" Jerry asked, grabbing his bass. Jerry was good, and he could hold his own with any group of musicians. However, he was quite the showman, and most of the time, his antics were too outrageous for Nicky.

"Let's do, *Wild Thing*," Nicky suggested picking up his guitar.

He was talented and often felt frustrated being a member of their small band. He knew he was destined to become a solo artist. After finishing their first song, Nicky found himself dreaming of one day being on stage in front of thousands at a sold-out arena.

The boys would spend the entire evening practicing popular hits, including *Under My Thumb* by the Rolling Stones, except when Larry's mom would bring down pizza and soda for the boys. She would sometimes sit in, listening to them practice. Glancing at his watch, Nicky discovered it was almost 11:00 p.m., and on a school night, it was time to stop.

"Larry, I know football practice was canceled for Wednesday afternoon, so would it be alright to get together for rehearsals, say about 6:00 p.m. on Wednesday?"

"Sure, that's cool."

The weekends were always out due to sports. If you weren't seen at the Friday night football games, you were nobody in Middleton. With nothing more to do in town except the movies, the game was the highlight of the week.

"Jerry, don't forget to have your mom call mine in the morning. I think they're going to the flea market tomorrow."

"Okay. See you later," Jerry answered, closing the door.

Reaching for his jacket, Justin looked over at Nicky.

"Hey Nick, can you give me a ride home?"

"Sure. You're on my way. Let me get my guitar."

Stopping in front of Justin's house, Nicky couldn't help but let him know what a talented drummer he was.

"Man, if I ever make it to the big stage, I'm taking you along for the ride."

"Oh yeah, call me when that happens," Justin laughed, getting out of the car.

Walking in, it was 11:15 p.m. Nicky hoped to get upstairs and into bed before his mom discovered the time.

"Nicholas, do you know it's almost midnight? What did I tell you about being home by 10:00 p.m.?"

"Oh, Mom, it's not midnight. It's only a little after 11:00 p.m."

"Whatever, Nicholas, you know the rules," his dad yelled up the stairs.

Nicky's parents were not strict, but they kept a close watch on their two sons. Nicky and Tony had an older sister, Annie. She had long since moved away from home when she married her high school sweetheart, Joey Morgan, at the young age of eighteen. They now lived in upstate Michigan, where Joey pursued a law degree. With Annie no longer at home, it left Nicky and Tony striving to live up to Annie's reputation. She had been the perfect child if you were to believe his parent's side of the story. But, didn't his parents realize they were now left with two boys at home? Shouldn't they be allowed a little room for getting into trouble? Joseph and Joan were good parents. However, Nicky dreamed of the day that he too would leave Middleton, just as Annie had done. Nicky's last thoughts as he jumped into bed were that his dreams were too big for this place. Nicky Spade was getting out one way or the other.

Nicky was awakened by the sounds of the train whistle, which blew each morning just like clockwork as the train routinely passed near the edge of town. Looking over at his alarm clock, it was 7:00 a.m. Another day in the middle of nowhere, he moaned. Deciding to skip breakfast, Tony waited to give him a ride over to Middleton

High. Tony and Nicky shared their father's handsome Italian profile as brothers but were completely different in personality. Tony was content to live and die in Middleton, but Nicky would rather die than live in Middleton.

"Bro, you better get a move on. You're not going to make me late for my class on engine repairs," Tony ranted as he walked downstairs.

"Cool your wheels, Tony. You're not going to be late."

Taking a seat in first-period Algebra, Nicky couldn't help but notice the stares from the new girl sitting across from him. Her name was Jenna. Her dad had just accepted a new job at the Ford Plant, and as a result, they had relocated from Quebec, Canada. Middleton was a small town. It had to be a hard place to wind up, Nicky thought. However, she was amazing. Jenna was tall and slender with long blonde hair, pulled back with hair clips. She also had the most beautiful green eyes he had ever seen. Nicky thought she was stunning, sitting at her desk wearing bell-bottoms, a pink sweatshirt, and sneakers.

"Hey, I'm Jenna," she smiled, reaching down to pick up her pencil as it rolled under his desk.

For once, Nicky was almost speechless.

"Yes. I know. My cousin, Jerry, has Chorus with you. He mentioned you just moved here with your family from Canada. How do you like living in the United States?"

"Oh, I'm used to being on this side of the border. Most of our family lives here."

"Well, maybe I'll see you around sometime."

It would be sooner than he thought, as she also shared his next class, English Literature.

After the Algebra class ended, they walked down the hall together in deep conversation. They were now carrying on a lengthy discussion about how they both detested homework—sensing an instant connection, maybe he should ask her out, he thought. Staring into her eyes with her long dark eyelashes and sculptured brows, she was gorgeous. If he didn't act quickly, he was sure Jerry would have no problems asking her to the game Friday night.

"Are you going to the game on Friday?"

"Yes. My parents figured it would be a great way to make new friends."

"Well, why don't I pick you up? We can go to the game and get pizza afterward. How does that sound?"

"Okay. That sounds like fun."

"I'll introduce you to some of my friends."

"Awesome. I can't wait until Friday," Jenna smiled, taking a seat in the lit class. "Oh, here's my phone number. Call me later tonight, and I'll explain how to find my house."

"Thanks," Nicky answered, quickly taking the number as the teacher walked into the room.

He couldn't wait to find Jerry and let him know that he had finally met Jenna. Friday evening couldn't come soon enough for him. He was anxious to spend more time with her.

Game night had finally arrived. Nicky parked in front of Jenna's house and quickly ran up the steps to ring the doorbell. As the door opened, Jenna looked cute, wearing her hair in a ponytail and jeans with a red sweater.

"Wait for a second while I grab my purse."

Jenna returned to the porch and stopped for a second while Nicky helped her into her jacket. She looked stunning, and Nicky couldn't wait to be seen with her at the game.

Arriving at the high school, they held hands while walking to the stadium. Then, making their way to the top of the bleacher, which offered the best views of the game, they sat close watching as loyal fans of the Middleton Eagles filled the empty seats.

"Hey over here," Nicky yelled, noticing Jerry making his way up the bleachers.

"Hi Jenna," Jerry smiled, taking a seat on the other side of Nicky.

He wasn't exactly surprised to see Jenna with Nicky. He always seemed to attract the cutest girls at the high school.

"Hey Jerry, nice to see you again," Jenna answered, returning his smile.

It turned out to be an exciting game, sitting in the stands watching the Eagles play their rival school, the Bull Dogs. Nicky put his arm around Jenna to keep her warm as the evening air became cooler. As the halftime performance began, Nicky and Jenna walked down to the refreshment stand with Jerry to get a drink. Nicky felt incredibly lucky to have her by his side at the game. Even though he wasn't an athlete or even the star quarterback, he knew the guys would be impressed to see Jenna with him. So, as promised, he proudly introduced her to some of his friends, who had also grown up in Middleton.

"Nicky, who's the hot blonde?" Bobby asked, being obnoxious.

"Jenna Jones, her family just moved down from Quebec."

"Hi, Bobby, nice to meet you," Jenna smiled.

Jerry went back to his seat in the bleachers. At the same time, Nicky and Jenna continued down to the fifty-yard line, where Nicky introduced Jenna to Dovey. She was the cheer team captain, your typical, cute and energetic cheerleader. Nicky knew everyone at Middleton High. Afterward, they made their way back up the bleacher to their seats next to Jerry with halftime almost over. It seemed the second half of the game flew by quickly. Finally, Larry scored the winning touchdown of the evening. The Eagles had beat the Bull Dogs, 35 -17, and it was time to celebrate with pizza.

"Hey Jerry, Jenna and I are going over to Vinnie's Pizza Palace. Do you want to go with us?"

"No. But thanks for asking. I'm going to play pool with some of the boys later on," Jerry yelled, running down the bleachers making a fast exit.

"Okay, man, see you later."

As they hurried back to the parking lot, snow flurries began drifting down from the night sky. The temperature seemed to be plummeting. Nicky put his arm around Jenna to keep her warm. Then, quickly getting inside the car, Nicky turned on the heater.

"How did you like the game this evening?" Nicky asked.

"Well, to be honest, I'm not much of a sports fan. But, I'm

glad that our team won. Thanks for taking me to the game and introducing me to your friends." Jenna shivered, putting her hands up to the warm heat.

"Okay, so you're not a sports fan, but you do like pizza, right?"

"Yes. Definitely," she smiled.

"Good answer," Nicky winked.

Parked in front of Vinnie's, Nicky opened her car door and held her hand as they made their way through the snow, which was beginning to cover the sidewalk. Once inside, they walked up to the counter to order.

"So, what's your favorite?" Nicky asked, handing her a menu.

"Oh, I'm pretty particular. I like pepperoni and black olives with extra cheese."

"That's not hard to remember. I like all the toppings."

After placing their order, they found an empty booth. Taking their drinks, Jenna snuggled in beside Nicky.

"I'm starving," Nicky remarked, inhaling the delicious aroma of the pizza as it was brought to their booth. Enjoying several slices of pizza, the conversation between them seemed effortless as they discussed school projects, friends, and family. Finally, looking down at his watch, Nicky discovered it was almost 11:00 p.m.

"Wow. I should get you home. It's getting late."

Driving back to Jenna's house, Nicky knew once again that he was sensing a connection between them. Walking her up to the door, Nicky stopped for a moment. Then, against his better judgment for a first date, he quickly gave Jenna a gentle kiss on the cheek.

"Thank you for going to the game. It was a fun evening," Nicky smiled.

"Thanks for taking me to the game and the pizza. I had a great time."

"Jenna, before I leave, the boys and I are getting together on Wednesday for band practice around 6:00 p.m. would you like to go and meet them?"

"Yes. I'd love to."

"Great. I'll stop over and pick you up around 5:30 p.m. on Wednesday."

"Thank you. I can't wait."

Monday morning seemed to arrive early, and the weekend was over. It was another school day at Middleton High. Walking down the hall, Nicky could see Jenna in the distance. Quickly catching up to her, he grabbed her hand as they walked into first-period Algebra.

"Would you like to go over to the A & W Drive-in after school and get a root beer?"

"Sure. That sounds like fun. But first, I'll need you to take me home. I need to let my mom know."

"Great. I'll take you home after school." Holding hands, they continued their walk through the halls. Everyone who saw them thought they were the perfect couple.

It wasn't long before Wednesday evening arrived. Jenna agreed to drive over to Nicky's house and ride with him to Larry's. Walking up to the door, Jenna looked pretty in black corduroy jeans, a gray sweater, and knee-high boots.

"Hi. Come in. You must be Jenna?" Tony inquired as he opened the door.

"Yes, nice to finally meet you. I've heard a lot about you from Nicky."

"Well, I hope it's all good. Have a seat. I'll let Nicky know you're here."

Walking upstairs to Nicky's room, Tony knocked on the door.

"Hey Nicky, Jenna's downstairs."

"Tell her I'll be right down."

Nicky had to have every hair in place. He found himself for once paying attention to his appearance. Before he met Jenna, he would have easily gone out with his hair tousled, wearing faded jeans. Jenna was beautiful. He knew she could easily have any guy at school on her arm, so he needed to look his best.

Running downstairs, he saw Jenna sitting on the sofa.

"Hey Jenna, are you ready to go meet the boys?"

Jenna's parents, even though strict, had finally allowed her to be out late during the week. As a result, she accompanied him to a band rehearsal.

"Yes. Let's go. You've told me so much about them that I feel like I already know them. However, you and Jerry seem more like brothers than cousins."

"Well, we've always been tight. Italian families are known to be close. We do everything together, especially holidays," Nicky mentioned grabbing his jacket from the closet.

"You're so lucky to have Jerry."

Jenna had been an only child. She had always felt deprived and lonely not having siblings. Having met Nicky, she felt like a stage three clinger, hanging on to him for dear life. He had quickly become the most important thing in her world, her everything. Jenna knew how vital the band was to Nicky, and she was anxious to meet the boys who were so close to him. You didn't get to know Nicky without first knowing his aspirations to leave Middleton. He had a burning desire to one day become a famous rock star, writing and performing his songs before millions. Jenna wasn't sure she shared his dream, but she liked him enough to support any crazy idea he might have.

It wasn't long before they parked in front of Larry's. Then, with his arm wrapped tightly around her petite waist, they walked up to the front porch.

"Hey man, come in," Larry grinned, opening the door.

"Hey Larry, this is Jenna."

"Hi Jenna, wait till the boys see you. Follow us down to the basement."

"Thanks. Nice to meet you. I already know Jerry. But I don't think I've met Justin," Jenna smiled, carefully descending the stairs.

Walking into the small room, Justin came over to meet her.

"Hey, Nicky, who's the cute blonde?"

"Jenna, please meet Justin, our drummer. He's really talented," Nicky mentioned, walking over to get a chair.

"Nice to meet you, Jenna. I've seen you two together at school. Jerry told me a lot about you. How do you like living in Middleton?"

"It's great. Especially now that I've met Nicky," Jenna replied, noticing all the band equipment.

"Hey Jenna, finally glad to see that you two could make it tonight. Nicky always drags in late for practice," Jerry laughed.

"So this is where you boys hang out," she smiled.

"Yep. You've got it. Glad you're here. Take the chair from Nicky and have a seat."

Jenna felt like a fish out of water. However, she was excited and thrilled to finally meet the boys, getting a glimpse of the world that Nicky so loved and talked about. The room seemed to get outrageously noisy as Justin began his warm-up on the drums. Even though Jenna was not musically inclined, it was incredibly easy to notice that Justin was a terrific drummer. He was every bit as talented as Nicky had said. Nicky grabbed his guitar and strummed out the music to *Wild Thing,* looking straight in her direction as he sang the lyrics, *you make my heart sing.* Jenna got goosebumps, feeling herself blush, almost embarrassed, hoping the guys didn't notice. Nicky had a great voice. Nothing could have ever prepared her to hear him sing. After finishing his first song, Jenna was very impressed. She knew he was exceptionally talented.

Sitting in her chair, she was mesmerized as Nicky, and the boys delivered one hit song after another. He was right. Jenna began to understand and share his desire to make it big in the music industry. The time seemed to fly by quickly. She felt as if she had just been at a rock concert starring Nicky.

"Hey boys, it's getting late. Let's do one last song."

Nicky had other things on his mind, which didn't include music or the band. Instead, he wanted to spend time with his girl. Little did he know that Jenna was already beginning to feel a strong attachment to him as well? She felt as if the stars must have all aligned the day she met him. How could she have been so lucky to have moved to Middleton and met him?

After finishing their last song, Nicky helped Jerry put away the guitars and equipment. He then walked over to give Jenna a gentle kiss on her cheek.

"Well, boys, it's a wrap. Jenna and I are going to get a pizza before calling it a night."

"Okay. See you at the game Friday night," Jerry replied.

"Justin, do you have a ride?" Nicky questioned.

"Yes. You and Jenna go ahead and get pizza. Jerry is giving me a ride home," Justin answered, putting on his jacket.

"What?" Jerry frowned. "Oh, what the hell. Come on, Justin, I guess I'll drop you off on my way home. Aren't your parents ever going to get you a set of wheels?" he added, grabbing his keys.

"Yes. As soon as I can pay for it," Justin laughed.

It was cold as Jenna stepped inside the car.

"I'm freezing," she shivered.

Nicky leaned in her direction and put his coat around her giving her a quick kiss.

"Thanks for coming to the band rehearsal and letting me introduce you to the boys," Nicky said, turning up the heater in the car. It'll warm up soon. It's just a short hop over to Vinnie's," he added.

He was right. It was only a few blocks from Larry's house. Parking in front of Vinnie's, Nicky opened the car door and held her hand tightly as they walked inside.

"Is it going to be your usual pepperoni, black olives, and extra cheese?"

"Oh, you remembered?"

"How could I forget any of the details of our first date," he admitted squeezing her hand.

Placing their order at the counter, they quickly found an open booth.

"It looks amazing," Nicky grinned as the pizza was brought over.

"Seems like I always work up an appetite after rehearsing with the boys."

After Nicky had finished eating, he reached over, taking Jenna's hand.

Looking down at his watch, "Let's get out of here, it's still early, and your parents aren't expecting you home till 11:00 p.m. Why don't we go over to Lincoln Park and walk out on the pier?"

"Isn't it too cold tonight for a walk down by the lake?" Jenna hesitated.

"Hey, I'll keep you warm. It's my favorite place to go. Clears my head after rehearsals."

"Oh, alright, but if I get too cold, I'll be the first one back to the car."

Leaving Vinnie's, it was only a short drive to the park. Parking the car, the lights on the pier were still on, and it seemed others must have had the same idea. Walking along, they noticed that all the vendors along the dock had closed early.

As Jenna looked up, the bright stars were amazingly out in abundance. They seemed endless on a cold clear night, appearing close enough to reach up and touch.

"Are you warm?" Nicky asked, pulling her close.

"Yes. As long as you keep your arms around me."

Stopping at a bench near the end of the wooden pier, they sat silent for a moment listening to the waves gently roll inland.

"Okay. Let's make a wish on one of the stars," Jenna suggested.

"Well, which one?"

"See the bright star directly overhead. I think it appears lucky."

"Oh, so you know the lucky ones, do you? Alright," Nicky smiled, squeezing her hand as they gazed upward at the night sky.

Giving her a kiss for luck, they both looked up, making their wish.

"Jenna," he said, stopping to kiss her. "I can't explain it, but it feels like we've known each other forever. From the moment I first saw you in Algebra, I've not been able to think about anything except you."

"Nicky, it's weird, but I also feel like I've known you forever," Jenna whispered.

Sitting on the bench under the stars, what they could have never known were the wishes made this night would not only bring them closer together but also pull them thousands of miles apart. Jenna no longer felt the coldness of the night as they walked back to the car.

"Well, I don't suppose you're going to tell me what you wished for?"

"You're right. You know what they say about wishes. If you divulge your wish, it won't come true."

"Thank you for such a wonderful evening," she smiled.

Nicky and Jenna would later spend many romantic and intimate evenings together before fate intervened.

CHAPTER TWO

The Costs of Wishing On a Star

Three months later, as Nicky walked through the corridors of Middleton High, he heard someone shouting his name.

"Hey Nicky, slow down, man. I've got some awesome news," Jerry yelled, almost out of breath.

"Oh yeah, well, it better be good. I just flunked a huge finals test in Chemistry," Nicky snapped with a bit of an attitude.

"Well, maybe today is your lucky day," Jerry stated enthusiastically.

"Whatever, man, this better be good. I'm in a hurry. I've got to run some errands for my mom after school."

"Well, if you'll slow down long enough, I'll tell you what happened today."

"Okay. What's going on?"

"I heard the music department is going to sponsor a local high school band competition to raise money."

"That's nice. But how does that affect me?" Nicky asked impatiently.

"Well, you've got to hear this. Our teacher, Mr. Hollenbeck, has personally invited a talent scout to judge the competition. I overheard him telling some of the boys in our class that it was his friend, and he's connected to some of the large recording studios. He's also possibly looking for someone whom he considers to have a huge amount of natural talent. Nicky, that's you. The competition could be your big break in the music industry you've really wanted. So I was hoping you and the boys would want to enter our band. What do you think?"

"Okay. It's probably a long shot, but I guess we have nothing to lose. Have you told Larry or Justin?"

"No. I just found out today."

"Well, what are you waiting for? Give them a call. Find out if we can meet tonight and discuss the idea of entering," Nicky agreed, hiding a smile. Trying not to act too overconfident, Nicky knew this might be the golden opportunity he was looking for.

After his encounter with Jerry, he couldn't wait to get home and finish the errands to the deli and bakery. The only thing on his mind was the upcoming competition. Later that night, the boys decided to meet over pizza and discuss the possibilities. After gorging on pizza, they were all in agreement. They would enter their band. What did they have to lose? Before leaving, everyone agreed that extra practice would be needed. They started rearranging their schedules to fit in the hectic practice schedule required. Middleton did not lack great high school bands, and the competition would be tough. Nicky was their ace in the hole, and Justin was a competitive drummer. Jerry was a great guitarist. Even though Larry wasn't quite as musically talented, Nicky was sure they could hold their own against other bands. He thought they might stand a chance at winning. However, what he wanted was to be noticed by the talent scout. The next step was to tell Jenna about the competition and his parents. Undoubtedly they would all be excited for him.

Walking up the front steps to Jenna's house, Nicky was sure he heard screams and angry voices coming from inside. He almost hesitated to ring the doorbell. When Jenna answered the door, it was apparent she'd been crying.

"What the hell, Jenna? What's going on?"

Gently pushing him off the porch and back down the sidewalk, she whispered in his ear. "It's not a good time for you to be here."

"Well, I'm not leaving until you tell me what's going on?" Nicky replied, holding Jenna by the arm.

"It's my dad's job. He's being transferred back to Quebec," she cried, wiping tears from her face.

"This can't be possible. Your father just took the job over at the Ford Plant where my dad works," Nicky replied, extremely frustrated.

"Guess there's going to be some downsizing within his office, and my dad has low seniority. So his office will be transferring him back to Quebec," she explained with tears welling within her eyes.

"Jenna, I love you. You can't leave. Well then, you can move in with my family. You can finish your senior year here with me."

"Oh, Nicky, I only wished that could happen. But you don't know my parents. They would never allow me to do that."

Jenna could hardly speak as she threw herself into Nicky's arms. Tears ran down her cheeks as she held onto him tightly, afraid that by letting go, she would lose him forever.

"Babe, there's got to be an answer. We'll figure this out. Please don't cry. I came over to give you some good news. Our band is entering a competition, and I think we might have a good chance at winning this thing. Jerry called and said the first prize would be a thousand dollars. So the boys and I have decided to sign up.

"What do you think?"

Jenna hesitated for a moment, wiping the tears from her cheeks with the back of her hand.

"Oh, that sounds nice for you guys, but don't expect me to be excited. I'll be leaving soon."

"Jenna, go inside and grab your coat. I hear your parents. They're still fighting, and I'm getting you out of here. Let's go down to the pier and get something to eat. How does that sound?" he asked, trying to lighten her mood.

"Okay. Wait out here. I'll go inside and let my parents know."

It wasn't long before Jenna returned.

"Alright, we can go. My mom said it would be fine. She's so upset with my dad. She doesn't blame him, but she doesn't want to move back to Quebec."

The drive down to the lake was quiet. Jenna was still emotional from the news she'd just received. Then, sliding an arm around Jenna's slender waist, they slowly walked down the pier.

Approaching a hot dog stand, Nicky stopped.

"How does a hot dog with sauerkraut and a soda sound?"

"You know, I'm not hungry," she answered quietly.

Nicky pulled her closer to his side. Glancing down, Jenna seemed worried and distracted.

"Jenna, please don't worry."

Nicky could see their favorite bench was empty as he looked down toward the end of the wooden pier.

"Let's go sit on our bench."

"Okay," Jenna agreed, trying to smile.

"Remember that night we sat here in the cold and made our wishes on your lucky star?"

"Yes."

"Well, do you think they're going to come true?"

"Maybe. But I don't feel so lucky right now."

"Jenna, I don't know how to explain it, especially after this evening at your house, but I feel like something big is about to happen."

"Yes. Something big is about to happen. I've got to move back to Quebec," Jenna said with tears streaming down her face.

"Oh Babe, don't cry," he pleaded, wiping the tears from her face.

As they sat in silence contemplating their future together, maybe wishing on a star was just a stupid naïve thing to do. It was child's play, and he was old enough to know the difference. Nevertheless, he couldn't live without her. He felt as if his life was being torn apart at the seams.

"Jenna, does your dad know how much longer he will be in Middleton?"

"I think I overheard mom saying we would be back in Quebec before the end of this month."

"The band competition is just about two weeks away, and I need you there for support. So I was counting on you being in the audience."

"Nicky, your boys, as you call them, will be on stage with you. They are your support. I believe in you. You can win this competition. I know it," she answered, laying her head gently on his shoulder.

"Oh, did your star confirm that for you?"

"Nicky, you don't need any star for good luck. You're very talented. The band is lucky to have you singing lead vocals," she added. "You guys will win, hands down. Oh, I've never asked, what's the name of your band. Isn't that funny? I've never thought to ask."

"We're called *The Underground*. We came up with the idea for the name one night. We were being silly because we spend so much time down in the basement," Nicky laughed.

"Well, that definitely sounds original."

"Let's walk back to the vendors. I want to get some cotton candy."

"Okay. You're craving something sweet?" Nicky smiled.

Jenna stopped Nicky as they were walking down the pier. Then, suddenly, she gave him a huge hug and kiss.

"Nicky, what am I going to do? Tears were streaming down her cheeks, "I can't live without you. I can't leave Middleton and move back to Quebec."

"Babe, don't worry about this now. Let's just see what happens and take it one day at a time. So, stop crying, and let's go get that cotton candy."

Getting back into the car, Jenna became restless again as she thought about going home. Why had fate brought her to Middleton? Why had she fallen in love with Nicky, only to be ripped away from him? She would soon have her answers, but they would come as quite a surprise and in a most unexpected way.

The following month flew by quickly. Nicky was busy with the boys at band practice, so Jenna talked with Nicky daily by phone. They spent weekends together going to movies, trying to get the worries of the competition and the move away from their thoughts. The rigors of daily practice were driving Nicky crazy. He wanted to spend every moment with Jenna, knowing she would be moving back to Quebec. All this stress was starting to push him over the edge. How would he ever be focused enough to win the competition when his whole world was falling apart around him. His only thoughts were of spending more time with her. She was the only thing that mattered to him at the moment.

The weekend before the competition, Jenna and Nicky spent each day together and most evenings. They needed each other now more than ever. However, the pressure of the upcoming band competition and Jenna's relocation was stressful. After their Saturday night marathon of movies, Jenna dreaded the thoughts of going home.

"Nicky, let's take a drive down to the lake. I'm not ready to go home, and we need to talk."

"Okay, Babe, what's on your mind?"

"Oh, it's the thoughts of me having to move back to Quebec."

In reality, Jenna kept a secret, which even her parents were unaware of, a secret that would change their lives forever. Jenna wasn't sure about telling Nicky, at least not yet. She needed to talk to him. But, she wasn't sure if the timing was right, especially with the pressure of the upcoming competition.

"Nicky, where do you see your life taking you, next month, next year?"

"Well, that's a mighty serious question, Jenna. Where did that come from?" he asked, leaning over to give her a quick kiss.

"Nicky, I know your heart. I know you won't give up your pursuit of becoming a solo artist one day. You're very talented, and no one deserves a break more than you, but have you ever thought about getting a steady job after graduation? Maybe trying to get on at the Ford Plant where your father works?"

She was fishing for answers, which would help her decide whether or not to divulge her secret—solutions which might encourage her to stay in Middleton.

"Babe, that's not me. I don't fit into that mold. I'm not my father. You know how bad I want to get out of Middleton. I've got this burning desire to pursue my music career, and I will not stop until I make it happen. Being traditional in any sense of the word, it's just not me. That's not who you've fallen in love with. I'm restless, Jerry will tell you. I know my mom's stories of giving up her dreams of becoming a solo artist to settle down and marry my dad, but that's not me. You know me, Jenna, and you know my dreams. So why would you even think I would be happy staying in Middleton working at the Ford Plant?" Nicky asked, a bit confused.

"Well, Nicky, I just needed to hear what your plans were after graduation. Knowing my dad is being transferred back to Canada has given me some serious thoughts about my future."

Deep inside, Jenna knew she had her answers, and it was breaking her heart. Nicky was indeed restless. He would never stay in Middleton, never fit into any traditional role and never stop pursuing a music career no matter what happened in his life. As tears rolled down her face, she would never be able to tell him. She would take her secret with her back to Quebec. Nicky was not father material, at least not at this point in his life. The thoughts of not telling him were killing her.

"What's wrong, Jenna?" Nicky asked, wiping the tears from her eyes.

"Oh nothing, it's just the thoughts of leaving Middleton and leaving you. I love you and your crazy ambitions," she answered, leaning over to kiss him.

This kiss turned into much more in the back seat of Nicky's car that night. Jenna knew that moving away from Nicky would be the hardest thing she would ever do.

It was the night of the band competition, and everyone's nerves were on edge. They were the third band in the lineup to perform that evening. Looking out from the side stage, Nicky could see Jenna. He was surprised to see her sitting next to her mom and dad. They had never seen him perform, and Nicky knew very little about what Jenna might have told them. He was proud nonetheless to realize they had taken the time to come out this evening with her. He could also see Tony sitting in the front row with his steady date, Ashley. His mom and dad sat directly behind them along with Jerry's parents. The first two bands were good, and the audience seemed to love them. The heat was on as they were announced.

"Tonight, we are pleased to have as our third entry a local group from Middleton High, *The Underground*, Mr. Hollenbeck said. "Please make them welcome with a huge round of applause."

The boys were finally on stage. Over the next four and a half minutes, Nicky was living his dream. Looking out to make eye contact with Jenna gave him the courage and determination needed to perform at his best. He once again belted out the lyrics of *Wild Thing*. Nicky was unbelievably good. As Jenna sat in her seat, she knew the boys were at their finest on stage tonight. Once again, she caught Nicky directly glance her way when he sang out, *and you make my heart sing*. That moment of eye contact with Nicky sent chills down her spine. She could have never been more in love with him than at this moment. He was definitely in his element, and she no longer doubted his ambition to become a solo artist. The audience went crazy as Nicky and the boys walked off stage. She was emotional, quickly wiping tears from her eyes before her parents noticed. Jenna knew Nicky was right. He was destined for greatness. However, in her heart, she also knew there would be no room for three people. She knew Nicky was on the verge of greatness, no matter what he had to do to get there. She would not stand in his way. Deciding to bow out gracefully, she would take a part of him with her back to Quebec. Jenna couldn't stay in her seat another minute. She told her parents she needed to go to the ladies' room and quickly found her way backstage. She had to see Nicky. However, she first caught sight of Jerry.

"Hey Jerry, where's Nicky?"

"Oh, he's talking with Justin and the boys."

At that moment, Nicky glanced her way and came running over.

"Hey Babe, what did you think? Think we have a chance to win this thing?"

"Nicky, you were brilliant. I'm so proud of you," she smiled as he scooped her into his arms. He squeezed her so tight she thought her ribs would break.

"I couldn't have done it without you," he whispered lovingly into her ears.

Kissing her ever so gently, he found her face moist.

"Hey Babe, don't cry. What's with all the tears lately? You know how much I love you, don't you? Let's get out of here," he suggested.

"But aren't you going to wait to see if you've won?"

"Nope, the boys are going to hang backstage until the winner is announced. I've given it my best. But, it's no longer up to me and besides, waiting here makes me nervous," he added.

"Well, okay, but I need to go back inside the auditorium and tell my parents. I'm sure they're going to stay until all the bands have performed."

"Let them know that I'll bring you home early tonight. You've been acting all teary-eyed and weird lately. You must be coming down with something."

"No. I'm fine. Don't worry," Jenna lied, turning around to go back inside.

"Hey gorgeous," Nicky yelled, "I'll be waiting for you by the exit door," he winked.

"So, what do you have in mind?" Jenna asked as she was getting into Nicky's car.

"Let's get pizza. How does that sound?"

"Actually, pretty good. I'm starved."

"I hope you don't mind, but I told the boys to meet us over at Vinnie's after the competition is over. Figured the sooner I knew, the better."

"That's okay. No problem," Jenna answered, knowing she had wanted him all for herself this evening.

All too soon, the boys arrived and not with happy faces.

"Okay. Let's have it. What happened?" Nicky questioned.

"Well, let's just say that we didn't win," Jerry frowned.

"You're kidding. Right, Jerry?"

"No, man, I'm telling you the truth. We didn't win," Jerry reiterated.

Grabbing his face in his hands, Nicky was distraught, looking defeated.

"Hey man, it's only one small band competition, not the end of the world."

Jenna reached for Nicky's hand, pulling it close to her.

"Hey Babe, you were great. Jerry is right. What do they know about talent anyway?"

"Jerry, you told me Mr. Hollenbeck was inviting his friend who happened to be a talent scout. So you did tell me that, right?" Nicky ranted harshly.

"Yes, but Nicky, don't take this so hard. Who knows, maybe he didn't even show up," Jerry countered, trying to ease his cousin's worries.

"Yeah, Babe, calm down," Jenna said, excusing herself to the bathroom, hoping to get there before she threw up.

"Guys, now you've gone and got her upset," Nicky fumed in anger.

"Nicky, Jenna knows how hard it is to get a break in this business. She can take the heat. She's with you, right?" Jerry laughed with a quirky smile.

It wasn't long before Jenna returned to the booth where they all sat, trying their best to put Nicky in a better mood. But, unexpectedly, Jenna had just sat next to Nicky when another wave of nausea overtook her again.

"Excuse me. I'm not feeling very well tonight. Be right back."

Seeing her walk out of the bathroom, Nicky met her at the door.

"Jenna, I'm taking you home. You look pale."

"Okay. I think that's probably a good idea. But are you going to be alright?"

"Babe, you're the one sick. The boys and I are going over to the pool hall and shoot some pool later. So don't worry about me."

It wasn't long before they were once again parked outside of Jenna's house.

"Babe, are you sure you're alright?" Nicky asked again.

"Yes. I simply need to get a good night's sleep. I'll be fine in the morning."

Helping her out of the car, he walked Jenna to the front door. She was just about to step inside when he pulled her closer to him. Putting his arms around her tightly and kissing her passionately, he whispered into her ear.

"I love you, Miss Jones. I'll call you in the morning."

Back in the car, Nicky was more than ready for a night of playing pool with the boys. They were right. Tonight was a small thing. It's not how you start a career but where you wind up that matters.

The next few weeks seemed to race by. It wasn't long before a moving van was parked in front of Jenna's house. Driving by, Nicky couldn't find the courage to stop. He would see Jenna later that evening. Only two more days and Quebec would hold the only person in the world that ever mattered to him. Nicky decided to go home, shower, and get dressed early for his date with Jenna later that evening. Walking in the front door, he could hear his mother calling out from the kitchen.

"Nicholas."

"Yes, Mom, what's up?"

"Jerry called and said it's important that you call him as soon as you got home."

"Okay, thanks, Mom."

Wondering what it was all about, he decided to run upstairs and call Jerry. "Hey man, what's up?"

"Well, you're not going to believe this. Are you sitting down?"

"Yes, Jerry, what's going on?" Nicky demanded.

"Mr. Hollenbeck called me over to his desk today in Chorus and gave me a phone number. He knows we're cousins, and he wanted me to make sure that you gave this guy a call."

"What's it about?" Nicky asked impatiently.

"I don't know, but he made it sound like you needed to make this call."

"Okay. Let me write down the number. I'll call you right back if I reach him."

"Okay, Dude, make sure you call me back," Jerry insisted.

"No problem," Nicky replied, hanging up the phone. It would only be minutes before Jerry's phone rang.

"Jerry, you're not ever going to believe this."

"Believe what?"

"There was a talent scout in the audience the night of the band competition," Nicky said with his voice trembling. So I'm being given the opportunity to join the rock group, Black Tie Affair. They have an open position for a standby lead guitarist on their world tour. He thinks I would be perfect for the job," Nicky screamed into the phone.

"Say that again, Dude. I almost thought I heard you say you might be joining the rock group, Black Tie Affair."

"Yes. That's right,"

"Nicky, what did you tell him?" Jerry eagerly questioned.

"Calm down, man. What do you think? Of course, I told him I was definitely on board for this gig. I'm not crazy, you know. I've waited my entire life for a break like this. He said I have a powerful voice and would be a tremendous asset on tour. So he is sending a limo over tomorrow to take my parents and me to Rosetta's Restaurant. We're going to go over a contract," Nicky added.

"Who is this guy? What's his name?"

"Didn't Mr. Hollenbeck tell you? His name is Mr. Weber. He's the manager for Black Tie Affair on their upcoming world tour."

He couldn't believe what he was saying.

"Man, you've made it, really made it," Jerry screamed excitedly.

"Well, I wouldn't exactly say that. Remember, this is just a temporary position as a guitarist," Nicky hesitated.

"But you never know. You just never know where this might lead. At least I'll be on stage doing what I've always loved to do while I work on becoming a solo artist. My dream is to own that stage with a band of my own on a world tour."

"Well, Nicky, don't knock a gift horse in the mouth. I think this is the lucky break you've been dreaming of. Congratulations, man. Can I call the boys and let them know?"

"Sure. I'm getting ready for a special date with Jenna tonight. So you can make all the calls you want."

Hanging up the phone, Nicky almost had to pinch himself to make sure this wasn't a crazy dream. Then, running downstairs, he couldn't wait to tell his mom.

"Hey, mom, you're never going to believe this. There was a talent scout in the audience the night of the band competition. I just spoke with him over the phone. He's sending a car tomorrow to pick us up around 3:00 p.m."

"Nicholas, what are you saying?"

Screaming from excitement, Nicky danced around the kitchen floor.

"I've been asked to join the rock band Black Tie Affair on their world tour as a guitarist."

"Nicholas, what did you say?" she asked again, hoping she'd misunderstood the implications.

"Mom, sit down for a minute. I've got the opportunity to tour with the rock band Black Tie Affair. Mr. Weber, their manager, was at the band competition the other night. I guess he thought they just couldn't go on tour without me," Nicky answered hysterically.

"Oh Nicholas, what does this mean? What about finishing school? You're a senior this year, and more importantly, did I hear you say the words, *world tour*?"

"Mom, stop being a mom for a moment and let me enjoy this."

Before she could say another word, memories of the years she had spent hoping to become a background vocalist came flooding into her mind. She had given up her dreams to marry Nicky's dad. Did she want the same for her son?

"Nicholas, you're so young. Are you sure this is what you want?"

"Mom, is that a question you even have to ask? I just need you and Dad to support me. So please go figure out what you're going to wear tomorrow and make sure Dad's suit is pressed."

"Okay, Nicholas, but you know your dad doesn't always share

or understand our dreams. I'll talk with him as soon as he comes in from work tonight and tell him how important this is to you. I'll do my best," she promised.

"Thanks, Mom, but I'm going. I'm going do you hear me," he persisted, not wanting to look her directly in the face. "Jenna and I are going out for dinner tonight, so I'm going upstairs to get dressed," he yelled, running back up to his room.

He quickly forgot about his lucky break as he was getting dressed. Jenna was the only thing on his mind. She would soon be back in Quebec, and he would be thousands of miles away. How was this going to work? How was she going to react when he gave her the news? Certainly, she would be happy for him, he thought. Jenna was the love of his life. How were they ever going to make it apart? His hands trembled as he dressed. Tonight he had made special plans to take Jenna to dinner. Wanting to look his best, he decided the occasion required dress attire. His hands shook so much that he could hardly button his shirt. Glancing at his watch, it was 6:00 p.m., and Jenna was expecting him at 6:30 p.m. Splashing on her favorite cologne, Nicky raced for the door. Almost forgetting the bouquet of red roses, he grabbed the flowers and ran out to his car.

Parking in front of Jenna's house, Nicky stopped for a moment before walking up the steps. Tonight was the last evening they would spend together before Jenna returned to Quebec. What was happening? Tonight was surreal. He had just gotten the best news of his life, and he was losing Jenna at the same time.

Stepping onto the porch, Nicky was about to ring the doorbell as Jenna opened the door. She was stunning. Jenna was wearing the sexiest black strapless dress he had ever seen. He was speechless, and guys never got speechless, especially Nicky Spade. She took his breath away.

"Jenna, Babe, you're stunning," he said, almost tripping over his own words.

"Wow. You rock that dress?"

"Oh, do you like it?" she smiled seductively.

"Like it? It's sexier than hell. Doll, you're gorgeous," he winked.

"I wanted to let you see what you're going to be missing."

"Babe, it doesn't take a dress like that to let me know what I have with you. Are you ready to go?" he asked, handing her a bouquet of red roses.

"Thank you, Nicky. They're beautiful. Thanks, Babe," she said, giving him a quick kiss.

"Well, let's go. I've made dinner reservations for 7:00 p.m."

Nicky put his arm around her as they walked down to the car.

"Where are we going?"

"Oh, it's a surprise, but I think you'll like it," he answered, putting in a tape of her favorite songs.

"Nicky, you sure know how to impress a girl," she smiled.

It didn't take long before they arrived at the Hilton Hotel. It was beautifully located down on the shores of the lake.

"Geez, Nicky, the Hilton. Really what did you have in mind?"

"Jenna, it's just dinner, nothing more. Besides, I've saved a little money from my part-time job at the car wash, and I can't think of a better way to spend it.

Nicky proudly escorted Jenna inside.

"So, what do you think? Hope you like seafood?"

"Yes. You know I do."

"Good evening, I'm Nicky Spade. We have dinner reservations for two at 7:00 p.m.," Nicky stated to the maître' d.

"Good evening Mr. Spade. Please follow me to your table."

The maître d' led them to a reserved candle-lit table overlooking a beautiful terrace. Nicky felt every eye was on Jenna as she walked over to their table.

Pulling out her chair, he gave her a quick kiss.

"Babe, I hope you approve of my choice for dinner tonight."

"Oh, it's wonderful," Jenna smiled, picking up her menu. Then, after a glance, she looked up at him. "Nicky, are you crazy? Have you seen the prices on this menu?"

"Jenna tonight is not about prices. This is our last evening together before you leave for Quebec. I have some news big news," Nicky grinned, reaching across the table to hold her hand. "Jenna, there was a talent scout, Mr. Weber, at the band competition, and I was given his number this evening by Jerry and told to give him a call."

"Jerry?" Jenna asked, puzzled.

"Yes. Mr. Hollenbeck knows that Jerry and I are cousins. So he gave the phone number to Jerry and told him to call me. He wanted to make sure I made the call that it was imperative. Well, that number was Mr. Weber's."

"So, what did he want?"

"Jenna, he's the tour manager for the rock band Black Tie Affair. He told me that he was looking for a great guitarist, someone who was naturally talented. He has offered me the opportunity to perform with the band on their upcoming world tour," Nicky stated as his hands started to tremble. "Babe, do you know what this means? I've been practicing for years, hoping to get an opportunity like this. Jenna, this is our dream come true," he added.

"Nicky, this is not our dream. It's your dream. But I'm happy for you. Really, I am very happy for you," she answered, forcing a smile.

Jenna knew this would happen. Nicky was talented, and it was inevitable. He was gifted, and she had always known his dreams would come true. She just didn't think it would be this soon and the timing of everything. But, wow, this was unbelievable.

"Oh Babe, congratulations," she said, pulling him across the table for a quick kiss. So what did you tell him?"

"What do you think I told him?"

Well, that was a stupid question, she thought.

"I jumped at the chance. In fact, he's sending a car tomorrow to pick up my parents and me so that we can go over a contract."

"Well, what about school? This is your senior year. What are you going to do about graduation?"

"Well, I'll somehow finish later, probably after the tour is over."

"Sounds like you've already got it all worked out," she shrugged.

"Let's order. What would you like?"

"I think I'll have the salmon with Broccoli." Jenna wasn't sure she could even eat after hearing Nicky's news. "Oh, and I'll have a glass of iced tea with that."

After Nicky ordered lobster, they sat in silence.

"What's wrong, Babe? Aren't you happy? Aren't you excited?"

"Oh Nicholas, I'm very excited."

"Nicholas, is it? Where did that come from? You're beginning to sound like my mother."

"Nicky, I always knew this day would come. You're truly talented. You would be an asset to any rock band. But wow, Black Tie Affair is huge, and you mentioned a world tour. Congratulations," she said, crying.

"Jenna, for heaven's sake, what's the matter? This is our last night together, and you look beautiful. It's taking all the power within me, not to grab you into my arms and hold you here forever, not ever letting you go. Do you know how much I love you?" Nicky asked, leaning over the table to wipe away her tears.

"Yes. Nicky, I do know how much," she answered softly, crying. "You're my entire world, and now we're being pulled apart."

At that point in their conversation, the waiter brought out their meals.

"Looks good. Let's eat," Nicky suggested trying to change the subject.

Jenna had hardly taken one bite when nausea started to return. How was she ever going to get through this evening? Wasn't he going to suspect something? Wouldn't he start to make a connection between her bouts of nausea and food? Maybe not. He was too heavily distracted from the news he had received this evening. After two more bites, Jenna had to excuse herself for a quick trip to the ladies' room. He was waiting for her when she came out. Seeing him standing by the door, she panicked. So this was it. Nicky was surely going to suspect what was going on.

"Babe, how are you feeling? Are you still having lingering effects from being sick the other day?"

"No. I just wanted to freshen up my makeup," Jenna lied, trying not to look up at him."

"Well, I was concerned, and I wanted to walk over and see if everything was okay."

"Yes. I'm fine. Let's go and finish our meal before it gets cold."

Nicky once again pulled out her chair as she sat down. Trying to act hungry, she was struggling to finish her salmon.

"Thank you for this evening. The food is delicious," Jenna said, barely eating anything. It wasn't long before Nicky had finished his lobster.

"Well, are you ready to go? I have one more surprise."

"Oh, what could that be, Nicholas?"

"Here you go again, calling me Nicholas. You're acting strange. Believe me, Babe, when I tell you, tonight you are not my mother," he winked.

After pulling out her chair, Nicky kissed her once more in front of everyone. His kiss left her weak in the knees. How could she have been so lucky to have met him, and now in only a few short hours, she was leaving?"

"So what's this next surprise?" she asked, getting inside the car.

"Oh, you'll find out soon enough."

As they started to drive further down Lake Shore Drive, she leaned over and whispered in his ear, "So where are we going, Nicholas? What wild schemes have you come up with now?"

"Hush, with the Nicholas," he smiled, leaning over to kiss her. "My mother has no place here tonight," he reminded her once again.

"Whatever, Nicholas," she laughed.

"Hey, I think I missed the turn. Well, maybe not."

He drove a little farther down the road.

"Ah, we're here," Nicky said as he parked in front of a beautiful cabin that overlooked the lake. All the lights were on, and it was stunning.

"Okay. What's going on?"

"Well, Larry took care of us tonight. His parents own the cabin, and he got the keys for us. Call it a present from the boys in the band."

The entire first floor was filled with flowers and lit candles as they walked in. Jenna had never seen so many candles, no wonder the cabin was illuminated as they parked out front. There were flowers and even more candles glowing outside on the balcony.

"Nicky, who did all of this?"

"I told you, the boys have taken care of us tonight," he grinned.

"Oh, Babe, this is gorgeous."

Taking her hand, they walked out to the balcony.

"Look up, they even gave us all these beautiful stars tonight," he winked, giving her a gentle kiss.

"Well, I'm not sure I believe that one, but be sure to thank them for me."

The moon casting its glow over the lake was mesmerizing.

"Wow. Nicky, this is spectacular," Jenna exclaimed.

"Just for you, Doll, just for you." Nicky grabbed her, pulling her tightly to his chest, and kissed her ever so softly. At that moment, Jenna could have stayed there forever.

"Oh Nicholas," she attempted to say as he stopped her short with another kiss.

"Shush," he whispered, kissing her ear. "Let's go inside. The boys made dessert."

"Wow. They cook too?" Jenna smiled.

"Well, I don't know about that, but guess we'll find out."

Walking into the kitchen, the boys had left a note on the fridge which read,

Dessert if you need it.

"Man, now that's funny," Nicky laughed. "Let's forget dessert for now and go sit by the fireplace.

Walking over to feel the warmth from the roaring fire, the guys had left extra wood nearby on the hearth for their use. The heat from the fire made the room warm and cozy. Taking some large fluffy pillows from the couch, they tossed them on the floor. Nicky pulled Jenna down to him.

"Oh, Nicky, is this romantic or what?"

"Yes. But only because of one thing, Doll, you," he whispered.

"Nicky, you always know just what to say." But before she could even finish her sentence, Nicky interrupted her once again with a passionate kiss, and she wasn't about to stop him. Jenna thought she must certainly be in a dream. This guy in her arms, surrounded by the candles and the smell of fresh flowers, couldn't possibly be real.

Nicky had been right. The idea of dessert had been funny. Lying here in his arms, she never wanted to wake up. They used every second of the night to share and explore the passionate bond between them. The seconds turned into hours, making love as much as was humanly possible between two people. She knew he was and would always be her one true love. She also knew this would be the last night she would ever spend with him. It would have to carry her for a lifetime. She felt that dying tonight in his arms would be a better fate than trying to live without him.

Jenna woke before Nicky. She wanted a few minutes for herself. She just needed to watch him breathe, to know that he was truly hers. Jenna tried to impress into her memory every detail of the night. She needed to carry with her enough love for three people, one of which he knew nothing about.

"Hey Doll, you're still here?" Nicky teased as he woke up and rolled over to kiss her. "What a night," he winked.

"Yes. It was quite a night," she answered, trying to hold back tears.

"Well, Sweetheart, guess you may be in a whole heap of trouble, not going home last night," he whispered in her ear, kissing her again.

"Nicky, home doesn't exist for me anymore. You were my safe place," she reminded him as tears streamed down her cheeks.

"What's with the waterworks, Doll? This is only a temporary separation. I'll call or write as soon as I get settled with the band. I'll let you know where I am. Okay, Babe."

"Sure, Nicky, you promise? You can always reach me through my grandmother's address in Quebec for the time being until we get settled. You know that, right? You do still have the address, don't you?" she asked again.

"Jenna, what's with all the questions? You're not getting away from me that easy," he said, pulling her closer for a kiss.

The candles had all burned out, and all that remained was

the scent coming from the fresh flowers. Jenna could see the sun beginning to peek in through the curtains.

"Hey, Babe," she smiled, grabbing his hand.

"Oh, you need some more of Nicky Spade?" he winked, gently running his fingers through her hair.

"No. I need some fresh air."

"Boy, you sure know how to hurt a guy's ego."

She was beginning to feel symptoms of nausea returning.

"No. You silly goof," Jenna remarked, throwing one of the pillows at his head. "Walk with me out to the balcony. I can see the sun coming up. It looks beautiful."

"Sure, Doll, if you're positive that's all you want?" he asked, giving her a wicked grin.

Pulling the blanket around them, they walked out to the balcony. The sun coming up over the lake was incredible. Jenna was sure she had never seen a more spectacular sight in all her life. The bright golden rays of the morning sun reflected off the lake. Its brilliant hues appeared to make the water sparkle as if it was dusted with a fine layer of diamonds.

"You're right. It's gorgeous. Do you think the boys arranged this too?" he asked, laughing.

"Nicky, be serious."

Standing together in a tight embrace, they watched as the sun vividly bathed the sky in shades of golden orange.

"Nicky, no matter what happens after today, please know that my love for you will go with you wherever your dreams take you," Jenna reminded him with tears flowing down her face.

Nicky held her even more tightly, trying to kiss away each tear.

"Babe, please, you're killing me with these tears. But, Jenna, you're not getting rid of me that easy. How many times do I have to tell you?" he whispered into her ear. "Now, let's go back inside. I have a huge day ahead, and you need to get home and finish your packing."

"Well, if you say so, but can't we just stay here forever?"

"Sorry Doll, life doesn't work like that," he said, kissing her once again. "It's going to be okay. Everything is going to be fine. You trust me, right?" he asked.

"Yes," she said, knowing in her heart the truth. But this was Nicky Spade, and he would always be chasing dreams.

"Let's go in and make sure all the candles are out. I've got to get home and make sure my parents are on board for today's meeting."

Jenna was overwhelmed with sadness as they got in the car to leave.

"Please thank the boys and Larry for the wonderful night at his parent's cabin," she asked.

"No problem, Babe."

Sitting in silence on the drive back into Middleton, there were no more words to be said.

As Nicky entered the street where Jenna lived, he could see the enormous moving van parked out front again. Trying to maneuver around the truck, he looked for parking.

"Just park across the street. You're coming inside, right?"

"No, Babe, you're on your own this morning. I think the last thing your parents would want to see today is my face, especially since I didn't bring you home last night."

"Well, I guess this is it," she sighed. "Nicky, I can't do this, I can't. I need you more than you know." Reaching over to grab his jacket, she was holding on with all her strength, not wanting to let go.

"Jenna, Jenna, it's okay. I love you. You're going to be fine. Call me when you reach your grandparent's house in Quebec. Oh hell, Jenna, I'll call you after the meeting with Mr. Weber today if your phone is still connected. Come over here and give Nicholas a goodbye kiss," he smiled. Jenna climbed over the car console. Then with both hands, she caressed his face, staring deep into his blue eyes.

"Nicky Spade, I love you," she cried, kissing him with so much passion, he for once got emotional.

"Now look what you've done, you've made me cry, and I never cry."

"Well, I wouldn't think you were human if you didn't."

"Okay. Babe, you've got to go now," he whispered gently, trying to pull her off him with tears in his eyes.

"Okay. Okay," Jenna sobbed. "But I'm not looking back after I get out of the car. I can't."

"All right, if that makes it any easier," he answered, wiping his face. Closing the door, Nicky watched as she slowly walked up the sidewalk to her house. Then, rolling down his window, he yelled loud enough for all the neighbors to hear.

"I love you, Jenna Jones. I love you."

To his surprise, she never turned around but yelled loud enough for the whole world to hear.

"I love you, Nicky Spade. I love you."

As Nicky drove away, his heart was breaking into a million pieces. How would he ever get through the meeting today with Mr. Weber?

Parking in front of his house, he had to sit for a few minutes. He had to regain his composure before facing his parents. He reached into the glove box and pulled out a pack of cigarettes. He needed a smoke to calm his nerves. It might not be easy trying to convince his father to let him drop out of high school in his senior year, but he was eighteen years old and could make his own decisions.

"Hey, Mom, where's Dad?" Nicky asked, walking into the house.

"Oh, he's outside on the porch smoking a cigarette." Wasn't that funny? He had just finished a cigarette in his car.

"Hey, Dad," Nicky smiled, taking a seat next to him.

Joseph Spade looked older than his age of forty-five. The years of hard work at the Ford Plant had not been kind to him. With his grey hair and wrinkles, he appeared tired. However, he'd always been a very loving father and husband.

"Nicky, what's this talk about you dropping out of high school?"

"Well, I'm being offered an unbelievable opportunity," Nicky smiled.

"What's so awfully important about it? Son, are you crazy? You've got good grades, and you're just a few weeks short of graduating. Are you going to throw it all down the drain to follow some idiots around the world?" he asked angrily.

"Dad, I wouldn't exactly call them idiots. Do you know how

much money those guys are making? But it's not even about money. It's about my dream to one day become a solo artist."

"Oh, you and your mother and those stupid dreams of yours. You are both alike. She probably wouldn't have amounted to anything if she hadn't married me—no telling what would have become of her. I've worked hard all my life making a darn good living for her, you, your brother, and Annie, but you know what the worst part of it is?" he fumed.

"What, Dad?" Nicky answered.

"She has never let me forget that I was the one who caused her to give up her ambitions of becoming a background singer. She blames me for all of her so-called dreams not coming true. So now she wants me to make things right by letting you go finally."

"Damn, Dad, that's a lot of guilt Mom put on you. But Dad, I'm honestly here to tell you that I want this more than I want air to breathe."

"Well, Son, I guess that leaves me with no other choice. Your mother will make the rest of my life a living hell if I don't let you go. So you better go in the house and thank her."

Thanks, Dad. Mr. Weber is picking us up in about an hour. You're going to be dressed, right?" he asked, giving his dad a huge hug.

"Yes. Go inside and see your mom."

Jumping up, Nicky ran inside to find her.

"Hey, Mom, you're an angel," he said, scooping her into his arms as he twirled her around the kitchen floor.

"Well, Nicholas, I don't know about that, but you remember one thing, if this doesn't work out for any reason, please come home. Oh, and one more thing, you've got to promise to finish high school, do you understand?" she demanded.

"No problem, Mom, that's a promise. I told Dad the car would be here for us in about an hour. Can you be ready?" Nicky beamed.

"Yes. Nicholas, don't worry," she smiled, continuing to dry the dishes.

Later they all stared out the front window watching as the limo parked in front of their house. "Wow, guess he wasn't kidding about the ride," Nicky laughed.

As the doorbell rang, Joseph went over to answer it.

"Hello, Mr. Spade. I'm Mr. Weber."

Bruce Weber was very distinguished. He wore a black suit and tie and appeared very professional in his attire. Nicky figured Bruce was probably in his mid-fifties. He had grey hair with a receding hairline and was a little stout.

"I guess you know why I'm here. I was at the local band competition a few days back and noticed your son, Nicky. You've got a talented son, Mr. Spade, very talented. He's just the young man I've been looking for," he smiled. "I've come by to take you, your wife, and Nicky out to dinner to discuss the possibility of bringing him on board with our band. Have you heard of the rock band Black Tie Affair? Guess, from your expression, probably not. Well, if you and your wife are ready, I would like to go and discuss a potential contract with you. How does that sound?"

"Don't guess there's any harm in hearing what you have to say," Joseph replied.

"All right, let's go. Shall we. I have a car out front," Bruce grinned.

"Oh, this is my wife, Joan."

"Nice to meet you, Mrs. Spade."

"Nice to meet you too."

"Nicky, are you ready to take these fine people to dinner?"

"Yes, sir, Mr. Weber."

"Just call me Bruce. No need to bother with Mr. Weber anymore."

"Great. Then, Bruce, it is."

Walking out to the limo, Nicky missed Jenna for the first time. She'd always been a tremendous support and comfort to him. Now, he was flying solo without her. Nicky thought getting into the limo seemed surreal, but something he could quickly get used to. Arriving at the restaurant, Bruce asked for a table near the back.

"We need a quiet place to talk. So why don't you folks go ahead and order while I get all the paperwork out of my briefcase."

The waiter came over and took their orders. Coming back shortly, he set piping hot plates of lasagna in front of Nicky and his parents.

"Well, that looks good," Bruce said to the waiter. "Might as well go ahead and bring one out for me too," he suggested. "Let's eat first. Sure wouldn't want to let a fine meal like this get cold, now would we?"

Nicky was the first one to finish eating.

"Well, one thing is for sure, you've sure got a fine appetite," Bruce laughed, looking at Nicky's empty plate.

After they had finished eating and the waiter had cleared the table, Bruce looked over at Nicky.

"Okay, folks, guess we better get down to business. Does anyone care for a cup of coffee before we get started?"

"Sure. That sounds wonderful," Joan smiled.

"How about you, Joseph?"

"Yes. Please."

"Nicky, are you alright, or would you care for something more to drink?"

"No, thank you, I'm fine."

Passing out several papers that were stapled together, Bruce handed them each a copy.

"Well, this is what our band Black Tie Affair is currently looking for, and I think we've found our person in your son, Nicky. As you can see, the position being offered is that of a lead guitarist, or I should say, stand-in guitarist. He will travel with Black Tie Affair throughout their upcoming world tour. He will play on an as-needed basis, to begin with, meaning that he will not necessarily be on stage during each concert. However, I'm keenly aware of his vocal abilities. I think he would be a tremendous asset to our band permanently if a position should open. We will pay him five hundred dollars per night for each night he's on stage. Now it isn't a lot of money. You must understand that extras are not on the higher end of the scale. We only pay for the nights he performs. However, the band will cover his boarding, the cost of all meals, and travel expenses. Let's just say that it will give him the chance to get his feet wet, so to speak, if he does as well as I expect. In that case, if a position should open, there's always the possibility of Nicky finding a more permanent position with the band. The contract is a two-year agreement, which simply means that Nicky is signing to travel with the band throughout their two-year tour. It will take him into over thirty countries. How does that sound, Son?" Bruce asked, looking directly at Nicky.

Before Nicky could even respond with an answer, Joseph jumped in.

"Bruce, I have some questions. Nicky is only eighteen and will give up graduating to take this position. What about his age, and are there any provisions for him to finish school while on tour?"

"Well, to answer your first question. Nicky is indeed old enough to sign the contract, but we always like to have the parents' approval when Nick's age. For your second question, we don't normally hire teachers to tour with the band. However, suppose Nicky wants to enroll in a correspondence class of any type. In that case, he is more than welcome to do so," Bruce mentioned. "Now, there happens to be one more important question I need to ask," Bruce said, looking over at Nicky. "Son, I have to be in London by tomorrow night, and I've been asked to bring you along. Now you need to know that if you're not available to leave this early, it will probably cost you this position, do you understand? I cannot negotiate this part of the deal, and I hate to spring this bit of news on you at the very last minute. Would you all like to step outside and discuss this as a family?"

"No. I don't think that will be necessary," Joseph replied.

"Oh, most importantly, do you have a passport?"

"Yes. It just so happens that I do," Nicky answered.

"That's a relief. I almost forgot to ask," Bruce paused, rubbing his forehead.

It seemed as if fate had stepped in to play a role in her son's future that afternoon, Joan thought.

"I got a passport last year when the boys in the band and I were thinking of going over to London to do some sightseeing. But we never made the trip," Nicky mentioned.

"Well, Son, it appears tomorrow is your lucky day. London

happens to be our first concert on this tour, and it's sold out. So, Nicky, what do you think? Are you ready to leave Middleton as early as tomorrow?"

Those were words that Nicky had been waiting his entire life to hear. Middleton had never been more than a birthplace to him. He'd been looking for ways to get out of Middleton for years, and now he had his chance. But, with Jenna leaving in the morning, Middleton offered him no reason to stay.

"Yes, sir, where do I sign?"

"Great. All I need are just a few signatures from Nicky on each paper, and you have your ticket out of here, Son. Okay, I guess my job is finished here, Joseph," Bruce said as he picked up the signed papers. "Oh, and one last thing, don't worry about Nicky. Our band, Black Tie Affair, has a great reputation. Check us out if you like," Bruce grinned.

"Well, Nicky, are you ready to go and travel the world with a rock band?"

"You bet," Nicky answered, reaching across the table to shake hands with Bruce.

"Great. I should get you, good folks, back home. But, Nicky, before I forget, I will be sending a car around to pick you up at 4:00 a.m. I have a private jet at the airport, so I'll be waiting for you early in the morning," Bruce stated, shaking hands with Mr. and Mrs. Spade. "Let's walk out to the car, shall we. This boy's got an early ride in the morning and a long flight over the pond."

Wow. Nicky could hardly breathe. Stepping inside the limo, he couldn't wait to get home and call Jenna, hoping that her phone was still connected.

As the limo parked out front of the Spade's home, Bruce looked over at Joseph, "Guess this is your stop," he said smiling. "It was very nice to meet you all this afternoon. I know it will be hard on the family to let Nicky go sooner than expected, but he's in good hands. He's a talented young man and extremely lucky to have a chance to work with Black Tie Affair. Son, I'll see you early in the morning. The car will be around by 4:00 a.m. Again, it was nice meeting you folks. Take care. Nicky see you tomorrow morning, don't forget and sleep in," Bruce laughed.

"Not a chance Bruce, not a chance," Nicky grinned as he shook hands with Bruce.

Running straight inside to call Jenna, luck would be on his side again. The phone in Jenna's house was still connected. Hopefully, she would be the one to answer. He didn't relish hashing out the details of the previous night with her parents. He was sure her parents were not fans of his at this point. Hell, he could easily understand. Nicky was sure he wouldn't want any eighteen-year-old daughter of his out all night with anyone, especially a musician with fantasies of becoming a rock star. Nicky was nervous as he dialed Jenna's number.

"Hello."

Thank God she answered.

"Hey Babe, we just returned from our meeting with Bruce."

"Who's Bruce?"

"Oh, Mr. Weber. He asked me to call him by his first name, can you believe it?"

"Sure. It makes sense. You will be spending a lot of time together," she replied.

"Jenna, you're not going to believe this, but I have to leave tomorrow morning."

"Well, guess that makes two of us."

"Jenna, there's a private jet out at the airport owned by the band. It will take me to London tomorrow morning. The limo picks me up around 4:00 a.m.," he said, not believing his own words.

"Wow, Nicky, today a limo and tomorrow a private jet. It seems like your life is moving pretty fast," Jenna said, fighting back the tears. "Congratulations, Babe," she added, almost choking on her words. "So you said you're leaving about 4:00 a.m.? So are we. My dad wants to get an early start on the drive tomorrow. Nicky, I miss you so much, and we haven't even been apart for more than a few hours," Jenna cried softly into the phone.

"Jenna, you're my girl, my one and only. It's just distance. Our love is strong enough to conquer whatever life throws our way."

"Yes. I know," she sighed, knowing in her heart that fate was pulling them apart.

"Jenna, I've got a lot to do before tomorrow morning. I haven't started to pack. Please be strong for me. Please, Babe, I'll write as soon as I can. I love you."

"Okay. Nicky, I love you too."

She had to quickly hang up the phone with Nicky before a small part of her tried to sabotage his plans by revealing her secret. Running into the bathroom, she sat for what seemed like an hour. She cried rivers of tears. Life wasn't fair. It just wasn't fair. So much had happened to her since moving to Middleton. She had found everything she'd ever wanted, and now she was losing him. In a twist of fate, she would leave with only a small piece of Nicky growing safely near her heart.

It was early morning as the limo arrived to pick Nicky up. He hadn't slept at all. How could he sleep when so much was happening? It was hard to leave his parents behind. Watching as his mom wiped tears from her eyes, he walked over to say goodbye.

"Mom, I love you. Thank you for everything. Dad, please take good care of yourself, Mom and Tony," he said, kissing them goodbye. Then, before turning to leave, he gave his mom one last hug as he gently wiped the tears from her eyes.

Tony hadn't even bothered to come out and wish him a safe flight. He was hurt that Nicky would have even considered leaving Middleton. Tony was not the type to ever leave home. Knowing this, Nicky held no animosity towards his brother.

"Mom, please don't cry. I love you," Nicky smiled, walking down the steps to the limo.

His parents stood silently and watched as the limo pulled away, carrying their young son inside.

Arriving at the airport, Nicky could see Bruce waiting at the bottom steps of the Lear Jet.

"Well, Son, are you ready for the ride of a lifetime?" Bruce asked as they slowly ascended the steps to the cabin.

"Yes, sir," Nicky smiled, turning around to take one last look at

Middleton. Once inside, the doors were closed, and the plane taxied over to the runway. The sun was just beginning to peek through the clouds as the private jet lifted off. Nicky stared out his window. The cars below seemed to get smaller and smaller. Nicky's eyes were fixated on each one. His heart was breaking knowing that the love of his life was possibly a passenger in one of the tiny vehicles.

As Jenna's dad entered the freeway leading out of Middleton, the sun was just barely coming up over the horizon. Wasn't it only a few hours ago that she had stood with Nicky out on the balcony with her arms wrapped tightly around him, watching the sun come up over the lake? Sitting in the back seat of the car with tears rolling down her face, she placed her hand softly over her stomach. Soon, she would feel the first gentle movements of the new life she carried. In another strange twist of fate, she found some comfort in leaving Middleton. Wiping the tears from her face, maybe she had been given the best part of Nicky Spade. Jenna couldn't help but wonder if the wish made on the star that night on the pier had cost her everything.

CHAPTER THREE

A Whole New World...
London

I t was going to be a long flight to London, England. Would Nicky be prepared to handle what lay ahead of him?

"Hey, Son, I'm going to be sitting in the back. Lots of paperwork to get done before we land," Bruce informed him. "How are you holding up so far? Bet you didn't get a wink of sleep last night."

"Yes. Bruce, you would be right about that. Things are happening too fast for sleep right now."

"Well, Son, then try to get some rest if you can. There are blankets and pillows on board, so make yourself comfortable. Oh, there's a fridge in the back which is completely stocked with drinks and snacks if you get hungry. It should be a pretty smooth ride today, according to Capt. Dave. I'll come to check on you in a while. Try to get some sleep," Bruce suggested as he walked toward the back of the plane.

Looking around, Nicky couldn't fathom the idea the band made enough money to fly one of their private jets over the Atlantic with only two passengers on board. He took a blanket and pillow from the seat next to him. Hopefully, he could get a few hours of sleep before they arrived at Heathrow International Airport. Nicky shifted in his seat, trying to find the perfect sleeping position. His only thoughts were of Jenna. Had he done the right thing by letting her slip so easily out of his life? He was madly in love with her. Why hadn't he proposed and made Middleton their home? He could have easily gotten a job at the plant where his dad worked. Nicky was sure Jenna would have said yes, and their lives would have forever been spent in Middleton. As the plane hit a little turbulence, it was almost a wake-up call. He wasn't Tony, and that town was sucking the life out of him. Settling down and thoughts of raising a family, even with Jenna, was not going to happen, at least not now. Wow. He'd come too close. He felt like a fish that was almost hooked and then somehow miraculously managed to free itself. That was a close call, he thought, finally drifting off to sleep.

He must have been asleep for several hours when Bruce began gently tapping him on his shoulder.

"Hey, Son, we're only about two hundred miles out from the airport. You might want to go back to the bathroom and freshen up before we land. I'm sure you'll want to be fully awake when we arrive. You'll be meeting some of the boys soon, and even though I told your parents we're a mellow group to work with, well, that wasn't exactly the truth," Bruce admitted with a grin. "Hell, there isn't a rock band alive that I know of that could make that a true statement. Heck, Son, if I told the truth or even close to it, no parent on earth would ever let me sign their son up for a two-year world tour. You seem pretty independent, and you're very talented. You've got nothing to worry about. Tomorrow you'll meet the boys in the band. There are a few of the guys who've let their status as members of Black Tie Affair go to their heads. So no worries, you'll do just fine. We should be on the ground soon. I have a car waiting to take us downtown to the hotel. We always try to stay as close to the venue as possible. As I said before, it's opening night, and we're sold out," Bruce reminded him.

As the jet touched down on the runway, there was still enough light left from the day to catch his first glimpse of this exciting city.

"Hey, they do drive on the wrong side of the road," Nicky exclaimed.

"Son, welcome to England. You're about to see a whole new world over the next two years. In fact, your entire life is about to change."

As the plane came to a stop near one of the large hangers, Nicky gasped. The hanger contained another Lear Jet, which also carried the band's logo. Bruce could tell from Nicky's reaction that he was shocked to see the other jet.

"Wow." Nicky was at a loss for words.

"Son, welcome to a new circle of affluence called Black Tie Affair," Bruce smiled.

As they descended the jet's steps, a limo drove up to the plane.

"Looks like our ride is here," Bruce said, putting on his coat.

Quickly getting inside the car, it sped away, taking them into the heart of London. Before they even entered the motorway leading into town, Nicky began to see tall billboards advertising the concert. Gigantic advertisements for Black Tie Affair and their upcoming concert were everywhere.

"Man, it appears you've bought up every billboard in town."

"Well, we try," Bruce said, opening a small bottle of Smirnoff from the fridge and mixing it with orange juice. "Just a little something to revive me from the flight," Bruce stated. "Would you like a coke? I would offer you something stronger, but being in a management position with the band, I can't. So I'll leave that for the boys," he said, taking a sip of his drink.

Even though it was beginning to get dark outside, Nicky sat back in his seat, trying to take in the sights unfolding around him.

"Maybe some of the boys will be able to give you a quick tour of the city before we leave on Thursday. We're just here for the next four days, and three of those are going to be extremely busy. As I told you, we're sold out for every night of our stay here. Our next venue is in Glasgow, Scotland. We open there on Saturday night."

"Did you say, Glasgow?"

"Yes, Son, that's right."

"I guess my next question is, are you sold out there also?" Nicky asked.

"Only the first two nights, but there's still almost a week left for ticket sales, and I highly suspect by the time we arrive, the other two nights will be sold out as well. So I've asked the limo driver to take a detour by the convention center. Thought you might want to get a quick glimpse of the place before I drop you off at your hotel."

"Thanks, Bruce."

"You will be staying with some of the crew at the Hilton Hotel. Randy and the other band members will be down the street at the Carlton. It's just a little closer to the venue."

As the car made a sharp left turn, Nicky could see the enormous auditorium coming into view. Nicky sat back in disbelief as the car slowly drove past. The building seemed to take up the whole block. The entire front of the steel structure was enclosed with glass and lit up like a Christmas tree. The marquee seemed to wrap itself around the length of the upper structure and was brilliantly glowing, not to be missed. Nicky was stunned as he read the huge lettering, *Black Tie Affair*. It also displayed the dates and times of the concert, and just underneath were the words, *sold out*.

"What do you think, Son?" Bruce asked, noting Nicky's curiosity.

"Oh, I can't wait to get inside."

"Well, tomorrow morning will come soon enough. It will be a beehive of activity. We always hire a few locals to help set up equipment. Good for business, and we always want to be invited back. I'm leaving you under the care of Todd Stevens for now. You'll like him and the boys."

It wasn't long before the limo parked under the portico of the Hilton.

"I'll walk you inside and introduce you to Todd. He's the one in charge of the sound crew. I called him yesterday before we left the states and told him all about you. So he knows that you were flying in with me tonight."

As they walked over to the elevator, the door slowly opened, revealing a middle-aged man with salt and pepper hair.

"Hey Todd, just the man we came to see. This is Nicky Spade."

"Glad to meet you, Todd," Nicky smiled, reaching out to shake his hand.

"Nice to meet you too. Welcome to London," Todd replied.

"Nicky, you're in good hands now. Todd will help you get your suitcases upstairs. Well, goodnight, boys, I'm out of here. See you at the convention center in the morning," Bruce said, turning around to leave.

"We're up on the sixth floor," Todd said as he grabbed one of the bags. "Let's get you upstairs and settled. I'll introduce you to some of our crew. So what do you think of Bruce?" Todd inquired.

"Oh, he's great."

"Yes. Bruce is a nice guy. He's been managing Black Tie Affair for about six years now, and everyone really likes him. He's a great asset to the band," Todd added.

As the door to their suite opened, Nicky saw three guys sitting on the sofa by the massive front windows watching television. They each appeared to be in their early twenties, and it was evident they hadn't shaved in days. There was no clean-cut appearance amongst the group. In fact, he was pretty sure they must have spent days in the same clothes.

"Hey guys, this is Nicky Spade. He just came over with Bruce tonight. He's the temporary lead guitarist for the band. Nicky, please meet John Anderson, Michael Stone, and Pete Hamilton, our sound techs. They look worse than their bite," he teased.

"Hi guys, nice to meet you," Nicky grinned.

"Hey man, welcome to London," John said.

"No man, welcome to Black Tie Affair," Pete added.

They all laughed. Michael, sitting at the end of the couch, got up and walked over towards Nicky.

"Boy, Bruce keeps bringing us kids," Mike implied as he reached out to shake Nicky's hand. "Just a joke, kid."

"Hey Mike, be nice," Todd scolded.

"Oh, don't worry, we're just one big happy family over here, and we'll take great care of you," Mike said, jabbing him to the arm.

"Hey kid, you want to go out and see ole London town tonight?" Pete inquired with a laugh.

"Yes. Sure," Nicky hesitated, not knowing what else to say.

"Don't worry, Nicky. No one comes over here on their first night and goes to sleep. The boys will make sure of that. Call it a sort of initiation into the family," Todd mentioned.

"Hey boys, grab your jackets and let's take this young man down to Paddy's," Mike suggested.

"Wait just a minute, Mike, I'll call for a cab. I know you guys too well, and no one is getting into trouble tonight. No telling where you'll wind up before the evening is over. When I think you've had enough, I'm throwing your butt into a cab and bringing you back to the hotel," Todd sternly informed them.

"Okay. Dad," Mike laughed.

"Come on, boys, let's go downstairs," John said, walking over to the door.

"Hey, don't just stand there, kid, that means you too," John smiled.

"What time is it?" Nicky asked, getting into the elevator.

"Oh, it's about 10:30 p.m. local time," Todd answered.

"Kid, one thing you should know, the faster you can adapt your body to our schedule, the easier it will be on you. So first stop, Paddy's," Mike grinned.

The cab let them off at the corner of Wellington and High. Walking across the cobblestone street, a fine mist of rain was falling, and the light from the street lamps cast an eerie glow on the wet street. Having never been to an English pub before, Nicky found it much as he would have imagined. It wasn't a large place. Instead, it was very quaint in appearance with small mottled window panes that looked like they'd been there since the beginning of time. The typical British pub sign hanging out front read, *Paddy's*. It was rather busy this time of night as they walked inside. Mike headed directly to a small corner table over in the back of the pub.

"Is it a pint of New Castle Brown Ale for everyone tonight?" Mike grinned.

"Sounds good," Todd mentioned.

Nicky was becoming a little intimidated. This was a new experience. He had never been inside a pub before or tasted New Castle Brown Ale. Hell, he was only eighteen and back home, not legally old enough to drink. However, five tall mugs were put on the table with no questions asked. Nicky was just one of the guys tonight. He seemed worlds removed from Middleton. All the guys were watching as Nicky took the first sips. Wiping the foamy brew from his mouth, he smiled.

"Okay. This is awesome."

What else could he have done? He was at the point of no turning back. No matter the look of the dark ale or the taste, he was Nicky Spade. Not a kid, as Mike had called him. After he downed the first few sips, he found it easier and easier to down the dark brew. It seemed as if they'd been in the pub for about an hour. But, of course, he couldn't have known for sure at this point.

"Okay, boys, let's head over to the White Horse. Oh, that's another pub," Mike laughed, glancing at Nicky.

So with that being said, they were out of Paddy's and back inside the cab. Todd asked the driver to take them over to the White Horse Pub near the Thames River. The scenario was quite the same as earlier. The cab dropped them off outside the pub. Walking inside, this time, they all took seats at the bar.

"What will it be, this time, boys?" Mike questioned.

"Guinness," John announced.

It seemed like only a few minutes before the heavy glasses of dark beer were placed on the bar in front of them.

"Nicky, here's to you," Pete toasted as he took his first drink.

"Yeah, Nicky, welcome to the family," Todd added.

Taking his first sip, Nicky wasn't quite sure if he liked it as much as the New Castle, but he had no other choice than to finish it at some point. Looking over at John, he seemed to be having no problems. A young girl, who reminded him of Jenna, brought out the next round of drinks. Nicky almost fell off his barstool when he saw her walk out from behind the bar. For one second, he almost asked himself what he was doing here. But instead, Nicky just downed what was left of the beer and then asked for another. He no longer wanted or wished to be sober at this point. Had he just left behind the best thing which ever happened to him back in the states, he wondered?

"Damn," Mike stated as he ordered Nicky another beer. It looks like you're going to fit in just fine," he laughed. Nicky didn't remember much about walking back to the cab, except for the few minutes bending over a garbage bin, throwing up enough beer to almost fill it. He now smelled like a brewery. Nicky was too wasted to care what the guys thought of him at this point. Todd and Pete helped him into the back of the cab.

"Well, let's get this kid back to the hotel. Bruce is going to kill all of us if this kid shows up wasted tomorrow morning," Todd said, calling it an early night.

The guys arrived back at the hotel and helped Nicky out of the cab and up to the suite. Once they got him inside, they laid him down on the bed and covered him with blankets.

"Don't think he's going to feel so well in the morning," John said, turning off the light in Nicky's room.

Walking back into the lounge, Mike was sitting in front of the television with a beer and a cigarette in his hands.

"Poor kid," he remarked, taking a sip.

"Well, tomorrow is going to come early, so think I'm going to bed. See you guys in the morning," Todd yawned.

"Yeah, that sounds like a great idea," Pete agreed, walking down to his room. Mike and John were left behind watching television with their beer and smokes. The guys were hard-core drinkers. They could drink all night and then show up at the venue sober the following day.

Nicky's head was pounding the next morning as the light filtering in through the curtains woke him. Wow, he had managed to survive his first night out with the guys. As Nicky lay in bed, the loneliness of not having Jenna lying next to him almost sent him in the direction of another bottle of ale. God, he missed her so much. Maybe today, he could find a postcard and drop a line to let her know he was alright. Slowly getting out of bed, he tried to make his way into the bathroom to clean up. There was no way he was walking out to the lounge letting the guys see him in this condition. Standing in the hot shower felt like heaven. Finding the soap, he quickly cleaned up, shaved, and dressed. He was anxious to get over to the convention center. After all, this was his reason for being here. The guys were sitting on the sofa drinking coffee as he walked into the lounge.

"Good morning, Mr. Spade," Mike said with a grin. "Quite a night last night, wasn't it?"

"Oh yeah," Nicky answered.

"We took the liberty of ordering breakfast for you this morning. Hope you don't mind bacon and eggs?" Pete asked.

"Sounds good. I hope you ordered lots of orange juice to go with that," Nicky mentioned.

"Yeah, there's plenty of orange juice in the fridge. Please help yourself. As soon as we're all finished with breakfast, I'll call for the car to take us over to the convention center," Todd mentioned.

"Sorry about last night, guys," Nicky apologized as he hurriedly finished his eggs.

"No problem, man, "Mike grinned, lighting a cigarette. "You actually hung out with us longer than I would've expected. So you're alright, kid."

"Okay, guys, we've only got thirty minutes, and the car will be downstairs," Todd reminded them.

"Are you excited?" John asked, looking over at Nicky.

"Are you kidding? I can't wait."

"By the way, if you have any dirty clothes which need washing after last night, grab one of those white laundry bags from the closet. We always leave our dirty clothes out by the door every morning. Although, as you can tell, some of us don't," Todd laughed, looking directly at Mike. "Okay, guys, let's go. The car is waiting downstairs."

Closing the door, they walked over to the elevator. Once inside, Todd looked over at Nicky.

"If the boys show up early enough tonight, either Bruce or I will introduce you to the members of the band. But, of course, we never know the exact time they'll arrive. It usually depends on what kind of night they've had, but they are always here in time to rehearse and for sound checks."

As the car drove by the convention center, Nicky could see street vendors already in front setting up their stands with souvenirs and programs. Finally, the driver went around to the back entrance of the convention center. The guys jumped out without saying a word and seemed to disappear except for Todd.

"Don't worry, kid. I'll show you around. Just stick by my side. You'll be working with me today. When you're not on stage with the boys, you'll just be helping set up equipment with Mike and Pete. I'll give you a quick tour."

Walking in, it was an extensive labyrinth of concrete walls with long hallways leading off like trails in several directions. There were huge pipes and wiring that ran above the long corridors.

Opening a door, Todd mentioned, "Here's where the band hangs out before they go onstage."

There were two large green sofas against the back wall, and over to the side near the dressing area was a rack of men's suits. In addition, there were long racks of white shirts and black ties. A fridge sat in the corner, next to a small bar and a television. Setting on the coffee table was a large vase of red roses.

"Later this evening, before the guys arrive, catering will show up and set up a small feast in here. So let's go out into the auditorium."

Walking behind the stage and around huge crates of equipment, it was hectic as the guys were busy moving amps and speakers.

"It takes a crew of about fifty people depending on the size of the venue to set up. I've got to run backstage and check on something. I'll catch up with you in a few minutes. In the meantime, go ahead and check the place out."

Nicky felt like he had an out-of-body experience walking out to the center stage. He stood frozen, unable to move as he took in the view. The auditorium was vast. It held several hundred rows of seating. Nicky found it hard to believe they were all sold for the next three nights. Taking in the enormous space, he got goosebumps dreaming about his chance to perform on stage with the band. Box seats encircled the upper portion of the auditorium, and a fine mist could be seen settling near the beams of the extremely tall structure. Wow, this place must have its own ecosystem, he thought. The sound equipment was immense. Huge speakers and lighting were hanging from the massive steel structures. Nicky stood there for minutes taking in the impressive view. He almost found himself getting emotional as thoughts of Jenna came out of nowhere and began racing through his mind. If only she could see this place and be standing next to him.

At that moment, he was pulled away from his thoughts of Jenna when he saw Bruce walking across the stage toward him.

"Well, Son, what do you think? Are you're prepared to walk out on a stage like this and perform with the boys?"

"Oh, you have no idea. It's surreal. I've dreamed of this my entire life. Except for one thing, Bruce?"

"Oh, yeah, what's that kid?"

"I want to walk out on a stage like this one day with my name on the marque. I want it more than the air I breathe."

"Well, Son, that sounds pretty serious, but for today I just need you to hang with Todd and get a feel for what goes on. Then we'll work on getting you involved with some rehearsals with the boys. How does that sound?"

"Great," Nicky answered, hugging Bruce.

"Okay, kid, let's try not to get too emotional. I'll leave you here to your thoughts. I've got work to do. Oh, by the way, I've asked Todd to introduce you to the boys in the band when they show up later this evening."

"Thanks, Bruce." As Nicky stood on the stage, he knew in his heart one day he would perform in an auditorium just like this, but with his band. Call it fate or Deja Vu, staring at the rows of empty seats, Nicky no longer doubted his dreams were coming true. Then, just at that moment, Todd walked up.

"I just saw Bruce backstage, and he asked me to introduce you to the boys tonight."

"Yeah, I know. I just talked with Bruce."

"Well, let's get to work. Mike wants you to help him set up extra speakers for tonight."

"No problem," Nicky said, following Todd backstage.

The rest of the day was spent helping the guys set up for the concert. He could have never imagined the amount of work required to prepare for an event as large as this one. But, he also knew he would have great respect for his crew one day and treat them with the dignity they would deserve.

"Hey Nicky, the catering truck just arrived. Food has been set up in the back for everyone. Stop and get yourself something to eat," Todd smiled.

"Sounds good," Nicky replied. "Guess I did work up an appetite."

Walking backstage, he looked down the long hallway. Against the concrete wall, a long table was filled with everything imaginable. Mike and John had beat him to lunch. So they were standing against the wall, already eating.

"Hey Nicky, where's Pete?" Mike questioned.

"Oh, I don't know. I haven't seen him."

"Well, come on over, get yourself something to eat," Mike said, taking a bite of his roast beef sandwich.

"Oh, don't worry, I intend to."

Getting a plate, he filled it with fruit and enough cold cuts to make a giant sandwich.

"You better have enough to last you until later tonight. We always go out to eat after the concert, but you'll be starved by then," Mike mentioned.

Walking over to where the guys were standing, Nicky began devouring his sandwich.

"Hey, Pete," Mike yelled. "We're over here."

"You guys got here ahead of me today. Todd had me working on the sound system. Unfortunately, one of the speaker wires came loose, and we had to reattach it to the rigging. Let me grab a plate of food, and I'll be right back."

"Damn, I'm hungry," Pete said as he walked back over to the boys. Kid, how are you holding up today? I was a little worried about you last night, but you seem to be working pretty hard today," he added.

"Oh, don't worry about me. A little hard work never hurt anyone."

"Well, guess it's time for a cigarette before I get back to work," Mike grinned, searching his pocket for a lighter.

"Yeah, can I bum one off you?" John asked.

"Sure," Mike replied, handing him a smoke.

"Okay, boys, back to work," Todd demanded as he walked by.

It was now late afternoon, and the convention center was a beehive of activity, just as Bruce had described. Nicky walked out to the front doors of the auditorium. There were already long lines of people waiting to get inside. However, the doors wouldn't open until about an hour before the concert started. The noise level inside from the sound checks was almost deafening. Nicky could feel an energy in the air. It almost felt like an electric charge which made the hairs on his arms stand up. As he stood briefly trying to take it all in, he almost had to pinch himself. It wouldn't be long before all the narrow, long rows of seats would be filled. The concert was scheduled to start at 7:00 p.m., and it was already 6:00 p.m.

Remembering Todd was supposed to introduce him to the band members, he thought he should try and locate him just in case Todd had forgotten. He didn't want to miss his chance. Finally, Nicky saw Todd in the distance. He was standing in a row of seats midway through the auditorium talking with some men. Nicky had nothing else to do at the moment, so he figured he would walk over and remind him.

"Hey, I was just wondering if it was still on to meet the band members tonight."

"Yes. Charlie just heard they're on their way down to the convention center right now. Their limo should be arriving shortly. I'll give them time to get changed, and then I'll take you in to meet them. How does that sound?" Todd asked.

"Great. I can't wait."

It wasn't long before the doors were opened, and the auditorium began filling up with people. They were streaming in like ants. Nicky was excited by what he saw. What a life to get to perform in front of so many people. No wonder Bruce said some of their egos were out of control. He could easily understand how that might happen.

"Hey Nicky, are you ready to go meet the boys?" Todd asked as he walked up.

"Yes. Let's go."

Nicky began to get nervous. In his mind, he had built an image of the guys. He hoped he wouldn't be disappointed. Walking backstage to their room, the excitement and noise level in the auditorium was overwhelming. Goosebumps covered his arms. It was just a short walk back to their dressing room. As Todd knocked on their door, Nicky held his breath. What if they didn't like him or had a problem with him playing lead guitar? They didn't know anything about him. All kinds of crazy scenarios began running through his mind. Then he relaxed, seeing Bruce open the door.

"Hey Bruce, didn't think you were going to be back here tonight," Todd inquired.

"Well, I had to run over to the BBC and set up an interview with the guys for tomorrow, and I got back earlier than expected."

As Nicky walked in, the guys were still getting dressed. The room was filled with people busily getting a few band members ready to go on stage. You could hardly breathe from the smell of cigarettes, and the large coffee table was cluttered with open liquor bottles. Two girls, who looked questionable, were sitting on the green sectional. They were clearly groupies by their demeanor.

"Nicky, come over here. I want you to meet Randy, David, Jeffry, and Alex," Bruce said, walking over to where the boys were still dressing.

"Hey man, I'm Randy. I'm the lead vocalist. Nice to meet you," he smiled, reaching out to shake Nicky's hand. Nicky was sure he could smell pot. Randy was tall, medium build, and sporting a five o'clock shadow. He had long black curly hair with a chiseled facial profile. Nicky was sure Randy would have all the girls screaming when he appeared on stage. The next member of the band Nicky met was Alex.

"Welcome aboard. I'm Alex," he stated as he lit up a cigarette, not even bothering to shake hands. I'm Randy's wingman onstage." Alex was also tall, with blonde hair pulled back in a ponytail. He had an incredible physique. This guy must live at the gym, Nicky thought. Alex was also sporting a day's growth of facial hair. Next, Jeffrey walked over.

"Hey, man, welcome to the family. I'm Jeffrey, but the boys just call me Jeff. I'm the drummer for the band." He wasn't as tall as Randy and Alex. Jeff had long, sandy blonde hair which hung loosely below his shoulders. He was the only one not sporting a five o'clock shadow. He seemed to be the most down-to-earth and friendliest, Nicky thought.

"Hey, Nick, welcome to Black Tie Affair, I'm David, and I play lead guitar." Nicky was sure he could smell pot again. David appeared to be in his early thirty's, he guessed. David was definitely older than the other band members. One of the girls, whom he figured wasn't David's wife as there were no rings, walked over and began hanging all over him. David was tall and seemed to be quite the lady's man. He was sure the girls considered him to be extremely handsome. David had a tan complexion with wavy black hair, the profile of an Adonis. He was also sporting the manly unshaven look. After meeting Nicky, David walked back over to the couch, poured himself a drink, and sat down with the girls. After meeting the guys in the band, Nicky thought their suits were the only clean-cut thing about them, except perhaps for Jeff.

"Well, guess we better get back on the floor," Todd stated. "There are several boxes of T-shirts with the band's logo on them, and Bruce wants us to have them ready for the guys to throw out to the fans standing in the front," Todd added.

"Okay. I'll just follow you," Nicky replied, closing the door.

"After we put the boxes of T-shirts up on the stage, we'll grab us a cold drink and go see if we can find Mike and the guys.

Nicky was amazed to hear the girls in the audience already starting to scream out the band members' names. The noise level was so loud you had to yell to be heard. Walking back to get a drink, they found Mike, John, and Pete standing next to the water cooler smoking cigarettes.

"Well, only a few minutes left. After that, I have to go backstage. Bruce will have Mike take you to a great place to watch the concert. Since it was your first night, he figured you should just enjoy the concert and have fun. Pete and John will be with the other stagehands and me. See you after the show."

"Well, are you ready to go watch the boys perform?" Mike inquired.

"Are you kidding? I can't wait."

After Mike put out his cigarette, he looked at Nicky, "Okay, kid, follow me. Bruce always keeps a few seats open in the auditorium for friends or family who might happen to show up unannounced. You're lucky, there's no one here tonight, so those seats are ours, thanks to Bruce."

Nicky was ecstatic. Looking around, he couldn't believe he was here. The day before, he was in Middleton, and tonight he was about to watch Black Tie Affair perform.

The audience was going crazy. The noise level was deafening. Then, all at once, the girls standing down front started screaming.

"Randy. Randy. Randy."

Wow. No wonder the boys in the band had ego problems, he thought. Nicky shifted in his seat, catching a glimpse of Jeff walking on stage to take his place behind the drums. As Jeff began playing, it only made the noise level from the fans grow even louder, if that was even possible. Jeff seemed to play for several minutes, building the momentum for the arrival of the other band members. Then, as Randy walked on stage, the audience went wild, out of control. Alex followed close behind him. They both walked to the front of the stage. Then kneeling, they handed roses to several girls who rushed toward them. It was pure chaos at the moment.

As David made his appearance on stage, the roar was deafening.

Nicky thought they definitely considered him a rock god from the sound of the screams coming from the fans. However, seeing the boys on stage in their black suits and ties, Nicky had to admit, it was a great look. No wonder the girls were going crazy. It was pandemonium, but it was brilliant.

"Hello, London," Randy yelled as the fans went out of control once again.

"How is everyone tonight?" Alex screamed, sending all the fans into a frenzy.

"Hello, London town," David yelled into his microphone as he began playing guitar.

"We're thrilled to be here with you tonight," Randy said just before opening with one of their biggest hits, *Without You*. You could hardly hear the lyrics over the noise level.

As the boys finished their first song, they began loosening their ties and throwing them to the girls in front, except for David. He knelt on one knee, gently wrapping his tie around the neck of a beautiful young girl. Pulling her toward him, he softly kissed her on the cheek. As David walked back from the edge of the stage, he turned around to watch security as they lifted the young girl and carried her away due to fainting. The act of tossing their ties into the crowd of screaming fans sent all the girls into a hysterical frenzy. Girls would stop at nothing as they desperately tried to catch one of the boy's ties. Security worked hard as they managed to lift each girl who fainted out of the crowd before being trampled. Man, these guys had their act together, Nicky thought. What girl wouldn't want to leave the concert with one of their ties as a souvenir? Unbuttoning the top buttons on his white dress shirt, Randy looked out at the audience and screamed.

"Hey, London, are you ready to party tonight?"

It was an uproar at that point in the auditorium. The fans went wild. Randy held the audience captive as the crowd continued going crazy from the band's gesture of throwing their ties. Next, Alex, Randy, and David walked closer together to jam on their next single, which had made it into the top ten on the London Billboards, *Black of Night.* As Nicky sat in his seat, he had difficulty controlling his emotions. He was born to do this. Looking around the auditorium, catching the fans' reactions, he could feel his skin tingling from the electricity in the air. He was watching his future unfolding in front of him. As Black Tie Affair launched into their next slow song, *Colors of Love*, Nicky's thoughts began to consume him. The rest of the concert flew by him in a state of unreality. Nicky sat motionless, soaking up each second mesmerized throughout the band's hour and a half performance. Mike had to ask him twice what he thought of seeing the boys perform for the first time. All Nicky could hear was Randy, Alex and David screaming.

"Goodnight, London. Goodnight. We Love you. Thanks for having us."

"What did you think?" Mike asked him again.

"Oh, it was truly an out-of-body experience," Nicky said, finally beginning to snap back into reality.

Mike could never have known Nicky's desire to be on the stage. Standing up, they watched the boys on stage throwing the rolled T-shirts to their fans in the front. The fans were going crazy as the boys left the stage.

The noise level was too loud to talk, so Mike motioned that he was going backstage to find Todd and the boys.

"Wait. I'm coming with you," Nicky shouted.

"I need to find Todd and see what he has on the list for us to do before leaving tonight," Mike yelled over the noise. "I want to get out of here early. There's a New Castle out there with my name on it. Come on, Nicky, the night isn't over yet," Mike motioned, nudging him.

Trying to fight their way through the crowd seemed like quite an obstacle. Finally, they needed to get down the aisle and backstage to find Todd. Nicky was grateful that Bruce had allowed them to use the seats for tonight. Bruce seemed to be an alright guy. He wanted to ask him now more than ever when he might get his first chance to practice with the band members. Now that he had sat through his first concert, Nicky was like a horse at the starting gate, which couldn't wait to be let out onstage.

It seemed as if Bruce must have been able to read his mind. Nicky had just walked behind the stage curtain when he heard someone calling his name.

"Hey, Nicky," Bruce said loud enough to be heard. "So, what did you think of the boy's performance?"

"Oh, it was awesome. Thank you so much for the use of the seats tonight."

"Well, I'm glad you enjoyed yourself. I needed to see you before you left to go back to the hotel. I will be stopping by tomorrow morning to discuss a few things with you, say about 10:00 a.m. I don't have time to go over it with you now, so tomorrow will have to do."

"Oh, sure, Bruce, no problem," Nicky answered.

After watching the guys perform, Nicky could only hope it was to discuss the possibility of starting rehearsals with the band.

"See you in the morning, Son," Bruce said, slowly walking away in the direction of the boy's dressing room.

"Over here, Nicky," Pete yelled. "Todd has a few things for us to do. We should be out of here in about an hour if we hurry, later the boys and I are going down to the White Swan for drinks," Pete added.

"That sounds good. Does the White Swan serve pizza?"

"Well, I'm not sure about that. You're not in Kansas anymore, Dorothy," he laughed.

After helping Todd with the equipment, they finally went to the White Swan. Getting in the cab for the drive down to the pub, the guys were tired.

"Long day, kid. How are you holding up?" Todd asked.

"Not bad. Sure takes a lot of work to put on a concert."

"Yeah, but you sure pulled your weight being a newcomer," Mike grinned.

"Gives me a new appreciation for the roadies and the crews," Nicky admitted.

"Yeah, most of them work pretty hard," Todd added.

It was only a short drive from the town center to the White Swan.

Once again, the cab driver dropped them off. As he walked across the street to the pub, Nicky began to think that all pubs looked very similar even though it was dark.

"Hey boys, let's grab that table in the back corner," John said as they walked in.

Sitting down, they soon had menus in their hands.

"Boys, Nicky wants pizza," Pete said, laughing.

"Well, I think you're probably going to have to settle for meat pies," Todd chuckled.

"Is it our usual?" Mike asked.

"Sure," John answered.

"Okay. Five New Castles, please," Mike said as a young man came over to take their order.

"Here's to your first Black Tie Concert," Todd toasted as they all lifted their glasses of beer.

"Well, it may not be pizza, but there's a lot to say for these meat pies," Nicky laughed.

Mike grinned curiously, looking at Todd, "Heard some interesting rumors today."

"Oh yeah. What did you hear?"

"Well, I heard through the grapevine that Bruce is seriously thinking of sending Romeo to rehab or ousting him from the band. Is there any truth to that?" Mike questioned, looking at Todd.

"Okay. Guys, since you've brought it up, I guess it won't hurt to let you know. Bruce is going to give David a choice of either rehab or leaving. He's not been happy with David's performance since he signed on with the band, and he hasn't been the asset Bruce hoped for as lead guitarist. In addition, rumor has it that David is pretty heavy into cocaine. Bruce could have gotten past his use of pot, but he draws a line in the sand regarding the use of hard-core drugs.

"Man," Nicky said. "I thought I smelled pot when I met him this afternoon. He sure seems to be quite the womanizer."

"Why do you think we all call him Romeo?" Mike laughed.

"Well, kid," Todd said smiling, "Looks like you may be moving up pretty fast. Now, this has to stay just between us. Bruce is going to let him play Glasgow. But if he hasn't voluntarily offered to go into rehab by then, he will never play Dublin."

Fantastic, Nicky thought to himself. Evidently, this had to be the reason why Bruce said they needed to talk in the morning. He would be replacing a rock god. Wow. Now that was a role he was born to play. After another couple rounds of New Castle, the boys seemed to be falling asleep in their beers.

"Well, are you guys ready to get out of here for the night and go back to the hotel?" Todd asked.

Walking over to the cab, Nicky felt quite proud of himself. It seemed he was beginning to build a tolerance to strong English beers and acquire a love for meat pies.

Arriving back at the hotel, the boys seemed to trail off in the direction of their beds without further cigarettes or drinks. Nicky was tired as well. What a day. His life was still moving fast. He'd just finished his first day with Black Tie Affair, and he might be getting his promotion to lead guitarist quicker than he could have ever imagined. As he lay in bed, not able to sleep from all the excitement of the day, he began to think of Jenna. He wondered what her day might have been like. Grabbing his pillow, he had to find a way to sleep. Morning would arrive early, and he had an important meeting with Bruce. Turning out his light, he found himself whispering.

"Good night, Babe."

Waking to a knock at his door the following day, Nicky stumbled over to answer it.

"Nicky, Bruce just called and said he's on his way over," Todd informed him.

Looking down at his watch, it was almost 9:30 a.m.

"Okay. Be right out."

Man, he had overslept. No time for a shower or shave. He quickly got dressed and splashed on cologne.

"Good morning Nicky. The guys are already downstairs in the car. We've had breakfast, and we've ordered for you as usual. You'll just have time to eat if you make it fast. Bruce is on his way over. He said he would give you a ride over to the convention center.

"See you in a few," Todd grinned.

"Okay. Thanks for saving me this morning." Nicky hadn't adjusted to the vast time difference, and he couldn't afford to jeopardize his career.

"Oh, no problem, but you might want to think about an alarm clock," Todd added.

It wasn't long before there was a knock at the door.

"Hey, Bruce, come in. There's hot coffee on the buffet table if you would like a cup," Nicky offered.

"Sounds good. Let me get myself a cup, and then I'll tell you why I'm here," Bruce smiled, pouring himself a cup of coffee.

Nicky was trying to remain calm and not indicating that he was aware of the reason for Bruce's visit.

"Well, Son, let me get down to business. I wouldn't say I like to beat around the bush when something needs to be said. I don't know how much you know or have heard about David. But he's left me with no other choice than to force him into rehab or replace him permanently. I'm aware that you just met him for the first time yesterday, but I've had my eye on that boy for quite a while, and now my suspicions have proven themselves to be true. He's heavily addicted to cocaine. Now I know that drugs are against the band's policy, but hell Son, I would have kept him on as lead guitarist if his addiction was simply weed. Now he's left me with no choice other than rehab or replacing him. He's a little older than the other band members, and they've made it quite clear that he's become a handful when he leaves the venues. We've already had some bad publicity regarding his antics. His name has been spread across every rag tabloid around. I can't have him out of control and showing up on the front cover of every newsstand. It's just bad publicity for the band. It's just a matter of time before he gets himself into so much trouble that I won't be able to help," Bruce explained, taking a sip of coffee.

"I'm in the business of selling tickets. Now I know our venue in London is sold out, but Son, it won't stay that way for long if he continues on this path and gets arrested for drugs. That's why I'm giving him no other choice than rehab. Hell, that's even too lenient if you ask me, but I'm going to stick by the band's policies and offer him a chance to clean up his act. Well, anyway, Son, you start practicing to take his position as soon as we hit Glasgow. He'll be in rehab for several weeks. If he gets clean, only time will tell. I'm not a betting man, but I'd say the odds are heavily stacked against him getting his act together at this point. However, I'll have to offer him his position with the band if he does. Kid, what I'm here to tell you is that we're going to need you onstage by Dublin. I think you've shown me enough talent that I'm not worried about you getting up to speed with the boys in such a short time. So my question to you this morning is, are you ready to rock and roll? I know I said I would give you some time to get your feet wet, but I need you on stage within the next two weeks. So what's your answer?" Bruce asked, smiling.

"Oh, I thought you'd never ask." Nicky stood, giving Bruce a huge hug. I'm not going to disappoint you, Bruce. I promise."

"Okay, kid, you can skip the formalities. So, let's get down to the convention center," Bruce grinned, setting his cup down.

The following two concerts in London went by in a blur as Nicky watched the boys of Black Tie Affair perform each night in front of sold out crowds. Soon he would be where he had always dreamed of, onstage. His only thoughts now were of Glasgow and replacing David as lead guitarist.

Postcard from London: *Hey Babe, leaving London today. We play Glasgow next. Things are happening fast. Miss you, Doll. Love you forever, Nicky.*

CHAPTER FOUR

Rehearsing in *Glasgow*

Once the band was in each country, Bruce provided a bus to shuttle the roadies and extras to each venue. It was overcast and raining as the bus pulled onto the motorway leading north. Today they were traveling from London to Glasgow. As Nicky sat in his seat, the thoughts of starting rehearsals with the boys in the band were consuming him. Glasgow would be the catalyst that brought him closer to his dreams.

"Hey Nicky, want a beer?" Mike asked.

"Yeah. That sounds good," Nicky responded, walking to the back of the bus. Nicky owed a huge debt to the guys. They'd taken him under their wings and introduced him to the world of Black Tie Affair. Once they arrived in Glasgow, Nicky would spend much less time with Todd and the other roadies. However, the bond of friendship they shared would never diminish.

"Nicky, how are you at cards?" Pete asked, lighting a cigarette.

"Pete, that's a dumb question. His last name is Spade, isn't it?" John laughed.

"Oh, I can hold my on," Nicky replied.

Sitting in the back of the bus playing cards with the guys of the sound crew made the ride less grueling. It was almost noon as the smoke-filled bus arrived in Glasgow. Parking near the back entrance to an older brick building, they had arrived at their destination, Brighton Hall. It was bitter cold as the guys stepped off the bus. The venue was smaller than London. Mike and the guys waited outside for Todd. The other roadies rushed past them getting inside out of the cold. Finally, Todd walked down the steps of the bus as he lit up a cigarette.

"Well, let's go inside and check the place out."

"Oh, we're staying down at the Creighton Hotel. It's across the street from the Fox and Hound Pub," he added.

Entering the corridors of the antiquated building, it looked gothic in appearance. Photos of past performers and artists who performed at Brighton were everywhere. The interior was dark and foreboding as they walked through the dim corridors. The band member's dressing room wasn't as nicely furnished as the one at the convention center. However, a fully stocked bar sat against the brick wall, with a lighted vanity and a small worn sofa in the corner.

"Okay. Let's check out the auditorium," Mike mentioned, closing the door.

The auditorium was large enough for a rock concert as they walked out to the center stage. However, the ornate ceilings were low and held antique chandeliers. Unlike the vast open space of the convention center with its technical equipment exposed from steel rafters, Brighton Hall felt enclosed and comfortable. Red tapestry curtains lined the sides of the vintage auditorium, making the décor and ambiance appear more suitable for plays and solo acts.

However, Nicky felt energized standing at center stage, knowing that he would start rehearsals with the band tomorrow. He etched every detail of the auditorium into his memory. It wasn't long before Bruce walked over.

"How was your flight?" Todd inquired.

Along with the band members, Bruce never traveled by bus with the crew.

"Fine. The boys and I got in last night. We're staying down the road at the Crestview Hotel. Nicky, everything is set for you to start rehearsals with the band tomorrow afternoon," Bruce mentioned.

"Oh, I'm ready. I can't wait."

"Great. Well, I've got to run. I've got an appointment to meet with the local press. Todd, I trust that you and the crew will have the venue set up and ready by tomorrow evening."

"No problem. As soon as the other bus rolls in, I'll have the lighting and sound crews go over their checklists. Don't worry. My boys will get started right away."

"Oh, do you need me to hire any locals for this venue?" Bruce questioned.

"No. The venue is small. We've got it covered."

"Alright then, I'm out of here for the afternoon. I've got some free tickets to give away at the local radio station. Also, don't forget, I'm staying at the Crestview Hotel. So you can reach me there if you were to need anything," Bruce reminded, walking backstage.

"Okay. Thanks."

"Well, guys, let's get busy. Have the trucks carrying our equipment arrived?" Todd asked Mike.

"No. Not yet. But they should be rolling in any minute."

"Okay. Guess you boys can go take a smoke break before they arrive."

Looking around the quaint auditorium, Nicky couldn't help but wonder about the other artists who had performed here.

"Okay. Nicky, I suppose this venue is the last time you'll be working with our crew, so hang with Mike for this afternoon. There's a lot of equipment which needs to be connected before tomorrow," Todd said.

"Alright," Nicky replied, running backstage to catch up with Mike and the boys.

It wasn't long before the trucks carrying the equipment arrived. It gave Nicky and the boys enough work to keep them busy until late evening. It was about 9:00 p.m. when the boys finally finished for the night.

"Hey Pete, have you seen Todd?" Mike asked.

"No. The last time I saw him, he was backstage talking with one of the guys on the lighting crew."

"Well, I think we're all done for the night. Let's try and find Todd and get out of here. I'm ready to call it a night and walk over to the pub. What did Todd call it?" he questioned.

"Oh, the Fox and Hound," Pete answered.

"Yeah. That's it. I'm starved," Mike said.

"Okay. Let me see if I can find Todd and round up the rest of the guys."

Finally, Mike saw Pete walking up with Todd, Nicky, and John.

"Okay. We're done for the evening. I heard you guys want to go over to the Fox and Hound," Todd grinned.

"Yeah. That's right," Mike answered as he lit up a cigarette. "I'm starved," he remarked, taking a drag on his smoke.

Walking into the Fox and Hound, Nicky again discovered that most pubs were alike. Only the signs hanging outside changed, and this time it was conveniently located across from their hotel.

"How convenient is this?" Pete smiled, opening the door.

The quaint Scottish pub was busy, so the guys took a seat at the bar until a table became available. Looking around, Nicky thought his life had just become one endless line of pubs and setting up venues at the moment. He was tired, and once again, memories of Jenna flooded his mind. He felt himself needing her in so many ways. So how did the other guys do it? There was never any mention of past or present girlfriends. Certainly, these guys hadn't gotten this far in life without meeting someone special.

Seeing a table cleared, the guys walked over and sat down.

"Guess I'll have those meat pies again," Nicky said, laughing.

Heavy pint glasses of New Castle were set on the table as the boys ordered large platters of fish and chips.

"Hey kid, why don't you give those meat pies a rest and try this."

Pouring on the malt vinegar, Nicky thought it was the best thing he had ever eaten.

"Man, this stuff is great," Nicky grinned.

As the guys consumed their beer and fish, Nicky inquired about relationships they might have left behind in the states.

"So let's have it, are you guys presently involved with anyone?" Nicky asked half-jokingly.

"Are you kidding? We're not monks, you know," Mike laughed. "Todd is divorced. This damn band cost him everything."

"Yes," Todd answered, lighting a cigarette. "Distance doesn't exactly help a marriage," he said, gulping New Castle.

"Oh, I'm sorry to hear that," Nicky frowned.

"Oh, that's okay, kid, it happens."

Pete put down his beer, "I was married, but unexpectedly, my wife passed. We were only married for five years. Fortunately, we had no children. So I jumped at the opportunity to travel with the band. It sure beats loneliness," he added.

"I'm sorry to hear that. What's your story?" Nicky asked, looking at John.

"Well, I've never been married. Guess you could say I'm still looking for that right one to come along," John answered.

"Okay, Mike, what's the deal with you?" Nicky questioned.

"Well, Mike smiled, "I've got a girl living in Frankfurt, Germany. We've been together for over seven years now. She tolerates my addiction to the band and allows me to travel. So guess, you can say that I can't wait till we play Frankfurt," he winked.

"Wow. That's great," Nicky smiled.

"Okay, kid, with all the questions, so what's your story?" Mike inquired.

"Well, I left behind the best thing that ever happened to me. Her name is Jenna. She had to move back to Quebec. In fact, she left the same day I flew out with Bruce. It was so hard leaving her and even harder on Jenna. I believe we would have married shortly after graduation, but fate seemed to have other ideas. So now it seems we are a world away and an ocean apart, and I have to say, it's killing me honestly."

"Oh kid, you're young, too young," Mike replied, handing him a cigarette. "Just wait, you're about to have so many girls falling at your feet. Of course, as lead guitarist with Black Tie Affair, you don't have girl problems," Mike laughed.

"Okay, girls, therapy is over. We better walk over to the hotel, check-in, and get our rooms for the night," Todd mentioned, glancing at his watch.

Finishing their smokes, the boys left the Fox and Hound and walked across the street to their hotel.

The Creighton was a timeless, two-story stone building. From its outward appearance, it resembled the Fox and Hound. Ivy had overtaken the front of the hotel, leaving only the stained glass mottled windows exposed. Entering the lobby, the warmth of a roaring fire in the massive stone fireplace felt inviting. The boys walked over to warm themselves while Todd went over to the reception desk, checked them in, and got the keys to their rooms.

"Well, boys," Todd explained as he walked over to where they sat, enjoying the fire. "Here's the deal. We all have separate rooms upstairs. There's a shared bath at the end of the hall upstairs, and there's no room service," he laughed.

"Oh hell, how many nights are we stuck here?" Mike complained.

"Three nights," Todd laughed.

"What was Bruce thinking when he booked this hotel?" Pete questioned.

"Well, I'm not sure, but probably the fact it's the closest hotel to the venue. We're only here for a few nights. I'm sure you'll survive," Todd mentioned. "Just be sure you get up early. Then, we'll run across the street to the pub and eat breakfast. The pub is owned and operated by the hotel, so they open at 8:00 a.m. I'll have the car pick us up after breakfast and drive us down to the hall."

"Okay, If there's no other choice," John shrugged reluctantly. "But if this place is haunted, I'm out of here," he laughed.

"Oh, I don't think you would even notice, after all the New Castle I just watched you put away," Todd laughed.

"Okay. Here are your keys." Todd handed them each a key as they walked upstairs.

"See you in the morning. Let's meet down in the lobby about 8:00 a.m.," Todd suggested unlocking his door.

"Whatever," Mike answered. "I may head back to the pub for a bottle of Guinness before it closes tonight," he ranted.

"This place gives me the creeps," John reiterated with a laugh.

"You guys are a bunch of wimps," Todd laughed, opening his door.

As Nicky tried to sleep, the discussion at the pub had left him missing Jenna more than ever. Thoughts of her and their last night together were killing him. How was a guy supposed to sleep after having those thoughts? As he lay awake, staring at the ceiling, he could only imagine Jenna having sleepless nights as well.

It appeared the boys managed to make it through the night as slowly, one by one, they walked downstairs the following day.

"Glad to see you girls survived," Todd smiled.

"Yeah, well, I've sure slept in better places," Mike insisted.

"Only two more nights," Todd replied.

Walking over to the pub, they consumed a substantial Scottish breakfast consisting of square Lorne sausage, fried eggs, streaky bacon, with sides of baked beans and black pudding. Even though Nicky found the food interesting, he had no problem devouring his meal with several cups of hot tea. Hurriedly finishing breakfast, they were soon on their way to Brighton Hall. Once again, giant billboards sprang up along the route advertising the concert.

"Man, are we sold out tonight?" Nicky asked.

"Yes. I believe we are. The last time I spoke with Bruce about ticket sales for this venue was last week in London, and it was almost sold at that time."

As the car arrived at the back of the large hall, Nicky was getting genuinely excited. He would have his first rehearsals with the band today. Nicky had hardly made his way inside when someone loudly yelled his name. Turning around, he saw Bruce walking up the dark hallway.

"Nicky, just the person I wanted to see this morning. I've talked with David, and thankfully, he has agreed to rehab. He knows this is his last gig before he has to clean up his act. He's not exactly happy about the idea, but he knows he has no other choice. So practice is set for about 3:00 p.m. this afternoon. The guys in the band should be arriving about 2:30 p.m. They know it will mean long days for them over the next three days, but it's the price they have to pay for David's bad behavior. So I'll need you on stage and ready to rehearse by 3:00 p.m."

"No problem," Nicky agreed.

"Okay. Thanks, Son. I've got to run."

Nicky worked odd jobs helping Mike set up sound equipment as the day seemed to drag.

"Stop looking down at your watch. They're not going to start rehearsals without you, kid. So let's take a break. I need a smoke. Besides, I think the food truck has arrived, and you can grab something to eat."

"Alright," Nicky answered, following Mike backstage.

"Hey Nicky, good luck today rehearsing with the boys," Pete smiled, walking past.

"Thanks, Pete."

Nicky could see fish and chips on the long table, so he hurried over to get a plate. As he was eating, Bruce walked over.

"Say, Nicky, I almost forgot something. The boy's suits have just arrived in their dressing room. I'll need you to go down after you eat and try one of them on. I have a tailor waiting for you. If you can't fit into one of the suits on the rack, I've instructed the tailor to take your measurements and get a couple of suits made to fit. I need you to do this before the guys arrive. So please get this done right away. David knows he's on his way to rehab, but until he leaves, I don't need him creating a scene if he were to see you being fitted for a suit."

"Thanks, Bruce. I'll go down after I finish eating."

"Okay, Son, then I'll see you when the guys arrive."

Quickly finishing the fish and chips, Nicky ran over to the boy's dressing room. Opening the door, it didn't seem real. It was now his dressing room. There was a large vase of red roses on the bar, racks of suits and dress shirts, just as before.

"Hello, I'm Tim. I've been asked to come down and fit you into one of these suits," the young man informed him.

"Hi, Tim. I'm Nicky. Nice to meet you," he smiled, reaching to shake Tim's hand.

"Let's try on one of these suits, shall we?"

As luck would have it, the very first one fit him like a glove.

"Well, you've sure made my job incredibly easy," Tim smiled. "Looks like you and Alex wear the same size, except perhaps I'll shorten the sleeves and the pants. This is great. Bruce was worried we might need to have new suits made. Congratulations, I heard you're the new lead guitarist."

"Oh, thanks."

"Well, if you'll hand me those pants, I might just shorten the length about a quarter of an inch. I'll get them hemmed and be out of your way. Again, congratulations," Tim said, hurriedly leaving with the pants.

Nicky walked out to find Mike. He was almost too excited to keep his mind on anything but the upcoming rehearsal.

"Sorry about that, Mike. Bruce stopped me and asked me to go down to the boy's dressing room and try on a suit before they got here."

"Oh, no problem. If you can just lend me a hand with this speaker, I think we'll be done for the afternoon. After helping Mike, it was almost 3:00 p.m.

"Well, Nicky, think you better stop and go find Bruce and the boys. I'll finish up. Good luck, kid, and by the way, congratulations."

"Oh, thanks, Mike."

Nicky walked up the aisle of the auditorium toward the stage. He could see the boys walking out. Holding his breath, this was it. Hopefully, they would welcome him as David's replacement.

"Hey man, welcome," Randy smiled.

"Yeah, Dude," Alex added, putting out a cigarette with his shoe.

"Hi Nicky," Jeff grinned.

"Yeah, whatever," David sneered. "I suppose you're my stand-in for a while. But I'll be back, kid. You can bet on it. Do you hear me?" David fumed with a look of disgust.

"Hey," Randy smiled, seeing Bruce step on the stage accompanied by a distinguished-looking man.

"Nicky, meet Robert. He's the musical producer for Black Tie Affair.

"Hello. You can call me Bob," he replied, reaching out to shake Nicky's hand. "Glad to have you. I've heard a lot of good things about you from Bruce."

"Oh, thanks. Nice to meet you too."

"Well, with the formalities out of the way, why don't we all just run through some of the songs you'll do for tonight's show," Bob suggested as he handed Nicky an extra guitar.

The boys picked up their instruments as Jeff took his position behind the drums.

"Okay. Nicky, join in as you get a feel for the music. The sheets of music are on the stand if you need them. Jeff, why don't you hold off on the drums, so we can just get a feel for the music with guitars only for now. Nicky, how are you at just hearing a melody and being able to pick it up instantly?"

"Well, what if I run through a few songs and show you."

Bob was pleasantly surprised after hearing Nicky cover the songs needed. Nicky was gifted and undoubtedly a great asset to the band as lead guitarist.

"Okay, Jeff, why don't you bring in the drums on the next song?"

Bob sat in the front row with a huge smile on his face. They had finally found their boy. Nicky was just the person they'd hoped to discover.

"I've got to give you credit, Bruce. You've found an extremely talented guitarist. But, David, I need you to stop playing on the next set, so I can just hear Nicky and the boys. So, guys, once more, go back over your opening song for tonight's concert," Bob instructed.

As the guys started to play, there was no room for doubt. Nicky was a natural and, most importantly, destined to become a solo artist.

"Damn," Bob exclaimed. "Bruce, this kid is great," he whispered, hoping David wasn't able to hear their discussion. We're lucky to have him."

The boys rehearsed for over an hour, running through one song after another. Soon, David began to realize what was happening. He knew his replacement was not only good but might easily replace him permanently if given the opportunity. There was no room for doubt, and he was pissed. Not only was he upset, but he was facing rehab as well. David stormed off the stage in a rage.

"Hey David, I need to talk with you in the dressing room," Bruce yelled. "Now," he added.

Following David into the dressing room, Bruce cornered him.

"I need you to complete your contract by playing the remaining three nights here in Glasgow, but, Son, if you give me a reason, you'll be done as of right now," Bruce demanded angrily. "You're the one who messed up here, not your replacement. Do you hear me? Do you understand? I don't even have to offer you rehab. It's truly my call at this point."

Realizing the tone and seriousness in Bruce's voice, David sat down on the couch.

"Okay. I'll finish the three nights here in Glasgow," he replied, rubbing his forehead.

"Look, Son, I'm trying to help you get your life back together. You've got potential. The ladies love you, but you've got to get into rehab and get your life cleaned up," Bruce compassionately stated, putting his hand on David's shoulder. "There's not any need for you to show up for the rehearsals with Nicky if that makes it any easier on you. However, I'll need you here for sound checks and on stage every night until we finish our concert dates in Glasgow."

"No problem. You've got my promise," David reluctantly answered, lighting a cigarette as he got up to pour himself a drink.

"Okay, Son, I'll leave you to your drink. I've got things to do before the concert tonight," Bruce said, walking out of the dressing room.

As Bruce walked back into the auditorium, the rehearsals couldn't have been going any better. He was astounded at Nicky's abilities. After the rehearsals ended, Randy walked over to Nicky.

"Well, there's no doubt you're going to be quite an asset to the band."

"Yes. No doubt," Alex reiterated. "You're really talented, man," he added, lighting a cigarette.

"Oh, I'm amazed at how easy it was for you to transition into David's position as lead guitarist," Jeff agreed.

Nicky thought Jeff was the most approachable and likable band member. He seemed to have an instant rapport with him.

"See you tomorrow at rehearsals," Jeff nodded.

"Okay. See you then," Nicky replied.

There was only about an hour and a half before the doors would open, so Nicky figured he would find Mike and the guys. But instead, he saw the guys standing against the back wall smoking while walking backstage.

"Well, Bruce came by and said you are a natural kid. He said you were great and picked up the routine easily. From the sounds we heard coming from the stage, it sounded unbelievably good," Pete said.

"Now, don't go letting your ego give you a big head and forget us, wee folks," Mike said, laughing.

"Not a chance Mike," Nicky smiled. "So, are any of you going to be watching the concert from tonight?"

"Hate to disappoint you, but it's sold out. Todd's going to need extra help. So we'll all be busy tonight. Why don't we go and grab something to drink before the concert starts," Mike suggested.

It wasn't long before the auditorium began filling up. People began rushing in through the two large doors in the front vestibule.

Finding John by the water fountain, "Todd said he'll meet us in a few minutes to let us know what needs to be done before the concert."

Seeing Todd walk up, the boys were ready to get busy.

"Hey guys, well, I guess you heard some of the stagehands are sick and won't be showing up tonight. So I'll need three of you backstage, but one of you can hang back after the concert starts."

"Okay. Nicky, you can just stand by if needed," Todd stated. "I know you would be the one most wanting to check out the show," he smiled.

"You're right. I will find an inconspicuous spot and see how the boys perform tonight. Thanks," he added.

Finding a great spot by an exit door at the rear of the auditorium, Nicky was ready to watch the boys perform. The noise level grew into a loud crescendo as Jeff came on stage and began the warm-up. Finally, Randy and the remaining band members walked onto the stage.

"Hello, Glasgow," Randy yelled as the fans went wild.

"How are you tonight?" Alex yelled.

Then David walked out, as the girls went crazy.

"Wow. Glasgow, you have the most beautiful girls," David shouted, making every girl in the house scream.

The boys were great at getting the attention of their fans right from the start. As usual, they approached the edge of the stage and handed out red roses to a few girls standing in front. Then, walking back to take their places on stage, Nicky thought the boys' appearance wearing suits and ties could not have given them a better stage presence. It was brilliant, just brilliant. He couldn't wait until Dublin when he would be on the stage. His dreams would soon become a reality. Opening with one of the songs he had rehearsed earlier in the afternoon, the roar of the fans was deafening.

Next, as always in their performance, the guys walked down to the edge of the stage removed their ties and tossed them into the crowd. Immediately, the act of throwing their ties into the crowd sent the girls into a wild frenzy as they tried to capture one of the guy's long black ties. David's usual ritual including kneeling and placing his tie around the neck of a young girl with a kiss on the cheek. Wow. Nicky wondered if he would continue David's tribute to the girls. It was a sexy thing to do, and evidently, the girls loved it. The girls were roaring chants. "David, David," as Randy and the boys took their places back on stage.

Nicky was mesmerized watching their performance. Randy, as always, slowly unbuttoned his dress shirt and yelled.

"Glasgow, are you ready to party?"

Nicky couldn't tell which the fans loved more, the guys handing out the roses, throwing their ties, or Randy unbuttoning his white shirt. The noise level was off the Richter chart. It didn't matter, the guys were terrific, and the fans loved them. Nicky again found himself captivated and so looking forward to Dublin, where he would finally get his chance to live out his dream of being on stage. Unfortunately, the concert went by way too fast as always. The fans were held captive for over an hour and a half by the boys of Black Tie Affair. It was amazing, especially now since he knew most of the songs in their routine. The concert was over way too soon.

"Damn. That was great," Nicky found himself saying out loud.

The fans continued to scream long after the boys left the stage. Today had been the first small milestone in Nicky's career. But, rehearsing with the band of Black Tie Affair was only the beginning. Watching them perform for the next two evenings was enough to get him excited for his debut. He was ready and eager to take his place on stage. Next stop on tour Dublin, Ireland.

Postcard from Glasgow: *Hey Babe, rehearsed with the guys in Glasgow. We're on our way to Ireland. I'll finally be on stage with the boys as the lead guitarist. Miss you terribly. Love you forever, Nicky.*

CHAPTER FIVE

Taking the stage in *Dublin*

Nicky's life had been upgraded. He was on his way to Dublin as the lead guitarist of Black Tie Affair. As the jet cleared the runway, he relaxed in his seat. He was now flying with the band members on another private plane owned by the band. Having replaced David, he was one step closer to his dreams becoming a reality. However, Nicky soon discovered that while making his way to the top, some of the close relationships formed along the way would suffer. He missed the close connection he shared with Todd and the guys. The members of the band now replaced the time spent with them. Nicky felt a cold distance between himself, Randy, and Alex. However, Jeff was more welcoming. Jeff didn't seem to suffer from the ego problems which so afflicted Randy and Alex.

The smell of pot permeated the air, but he was not about to question the actions of the other band members. Being the new member, Nicky was determined to fit in. Bruce was undoubtedly aware of the guys using marijuana. How could he not? He was aboard the plane. However, Bruce seemed lenient regarding their pot use unless pushed beyond his ability to cover such actions, as with David.

It was only his second flight on one of the corporate jets. Yet, it held every possible comfort one would expect. The band members lacked for nothing while in the air. Bruce made sure they were completely comfortable. Traveling with the band members of Black Tie Affair was now a luxury to which Nicky could quickly become accustomed.

"Nicky, would you like a Guinness?" Jeff asked.

"Sounds like a good idea."

Taking the seat next to him, Jeff handed him an opened beer.

"Man, I'm glad to have you with us. David was becoming a loose cannon. I was surprised Bruce even gave him a chance at rehab."

"Yes. Bruce filled me in about his problems with David. I've waited my entire life for an opportunity like this. So it may be David's loss, but I'm more than excited to take his place," Nicky added.

"To tell you the truth, you're one heck of a guitarist. You're going to fit in just fine as Romeo's replacement," Jeff grinned, taking a sip of beer.

Sitting near the back of the aircraft and not close enough for Randy and Alex to be privy to their discussion, it offered Nicky and Jeff a chance to discuss the band. It also gave Nicky time to ask questions.

"So Jeff, what's it like working with Randy and Alex?"

"Well, now that's a whole different conversation and would take too long to tell on such a short flight. But, just let me say, the guy's actions will speak louder than words," Jeff laughed. "They're a very tight unit, and you'll be just a third wheel as far as they're concerned. David and I always tolerated their big egos. But, becoming a member of Black Tie Affair will propel your life in an entirely new direction. You seem to be a pretty grounded individual, so you'll do just fine. Bruce would have never brought you on if he didn't think you could stand the heat."

Nicky would soon find out the significance of becoming a band member. As the plane began its descent into Dublin, Nicky was about to face his first day as a celebrity. Safely on the ground, the plane taxied over to a huge hanger. He could see a limo awaiting their arrival. Quickly getting into the car, their luggage was stowed in the trunk, and they were on their way downtown.

Passing billboard after billboard advertising the concert in Dublin, Bruce never failed to make the public aware of the arrival of Black Tie Affair and their upcoming concerts.

"Hey, where are we staying?" Jeff asked as he took in the scenery passing by outside.

"Oh, we're booked into the Kilgore Hotel. We have the entire top floor. Bruce and some of his team will be staying on the same floor, but don't worry, we all have our own suites," Alex whispered, noting that Bruce had fallen asleep.

As the limo pulled into the circular drive, Nicky gasped when he saw the impressive hotel. He was happy to know that he wouldn't have to share his sleeping quarters with the boys, at least not initially. The Kilgore was an older building but grand in scale and appearance. The front entrance accentuated an elegant rounded blue canopy covering revolving glass doors. Crowds of screaming fans, mostly girls, waited for their arrival and surrounded the car.

"What the hell," Bruce instantly bolted upright.

"Oh, someone definitely leaked the name of the hotel," Jeff implied, staring at Randy."

Randy waved to the girls blowing kisses in their direction. Then, stepping out of the limo, it didn't take Alex long before he joined in the fun. His attempt to sign autographs soon became chaotic, quickly evolving into a mob scene. Bombarded by fans, security guards worked feverishly, holding back the crowds as they desperately attempted to rush the band members inside to safety. Once safely inside the lobby, Randy and Alex laughed, staring at the mob through the large glass doors.

"Looks like we're dining in tonight," Jeff laughed.

"We'll be discussing this later," Bruce stated vehemently, staring at Randy and Alex. Their antics often resulted in uncontrollable situations and could easily endanger their lives and those of their fans. Bruce often thought if they were not vital to the band, he would easily replace them.

"Yes, from the looks of that crowd, I'd say we're staying in, at least for tonight," Alex smirked.

Walking over to the reception desk, Bruce checked in and picked up room keys.

"Here are your keys," Bruce said. "No one leaves the Kilgore without first checking with me. I'd suggest you plan to stay in tonight from the looks of that crowd," he strongly suggested.

"Guess we'll go upstairs and order room service," Randy grimaced as they entered the elevator.

Nicky would no longer be pub-hopping with the roadies. His circle of friends had changed, and Bruce would scrutinize his every action.

Unlocking the door to his suite, Nicky could smell the aroma of fresh-cut flowers. Alarge vase of red roses sat on a baroque bureau. The suite featured floor-to-ceiling windows, and a beige leather sofa centered the room—a fruit basket set on a large marble table. The suite was sheer elegance as he surveyed the room, much nicer than anything he had experienced with Todd and the guys. Nicky knew he could easily adjust to the band's opulent lifestyle. After all, wasn't this how all rock stars lived, he thought? Then, answering a knock at his door, it was Bruce.

"Hey, kid, I guess you've realized from the mob scene downstairs that going anywhere tonight is out of the question. So, I've asked Randy and the boys to order room service. I'll have a car sent around tomorrow afternoon to take you over to the venue at the Dublin Town Center. Have a great night. Tomorrow you'll get your first experience as a member of Black Tie Affair on stage. Hope you're ready."

"Oh, I'm ready, and I promise not to disappoint you."

"Great. I'll see you tomorrow afternoon," Bruce grinned.

Lounging back on the sofa, Nicky lit a cigarette. He needed to unwind from the events of the day. Suddenly, hearing another knock at the door, he walked over. Man, he wondered who else needed to speak with him tonight. Opening the door, it was Jeff.

"Hey man, just thought I'd come over, and we could have a few drinks."

"Sounds good, come in. Since we're in for the night, we might as well order up some food. I've been eating at the local pubs with the guys from the sound crew, but guess those days are over."

"Yes. You won't be going into many public places without Bruce previously arranging it. However, he usually reserves restaurants late at night for all of us, so we can unwind before going back to our hotel for the evening."

After ordering room service, Nicky sat down on the sofa and opened a bottle of Guinness for himself and one for Jeff.

"So, what's your story, and how did you become a member of the band?" Nicky inquired.

"Well, there's not much to tell. Not a lot of people are aware, but Bruce is my uncle. Bruce is my dad's younger brother, and if you know much about siblings, you can only imagine the pressure he put on Bruce to take me on the road with the band. I've always been a good drummer, and after college Bruce finally took notice and gave me a chance."

"Oh, I didn't know Bruce had a relative in the band?"

"We don't make it known. Almost no one knows our connection. It just works better that way."

"Well, you're secret is safe with me."

"So, how did my uncle discover you?"

"I had formed a band with some of my high school buddies, and we entered a competition. The band didn't win, but Bruce was in the audience that night. I was given his number. I made the call, and the rest is history."

"You're a great guitarist. No wonder you caught my uncle's attention."

Lighting up another cigarette, Nicky shifted further back into the sofa to relax.

"Yes. It has been my dream to perform on stage for as long as I can remember. However, it cost me the love of my life, my girlfriend, Jenna. She's in Quebec, and it was so hard leaving her behind," Nicky added as he finished off a Guinness.

"Damn, that has to be a hard trade-off," Jeff replied, opening another beer. "Can't say that it has been that hard on me being away from home, but then again, with my Uncle Bruce being the tour manager, it's like I never left home," Jeff smiled.

"He's a great man. I've got a lot of respect for him. I sure owe him a huge debt for taking a chance on me."

"Bruce only hires the best. Trust me. You're going to be a great addition to the band." Jeff looked down at his watch. "It's after midnight. I should walk back over to my room and get some sleep. Tomorrow is going to come early enough."

"Thanks for the conversation and beers. See you tomorrow."

Now he was alone with only his thoughts of Jenna to keep him awake. How he wished she was here tonight to share this elegant room and to warm his bed with her body close to him. Thoughts of their last night together at the cabin on the lake were haunting him. Hadn't she asked him to stay forever? Nicky would always regret the fact that he'd let her slip away so easily.

It was late afternoon when the knock on the door came, letting Nicky know the car was waiting downstairs to take the band members to the venue. Walking down to the lobby, it didn't take long to notice there was still a crowd of fans waiting for them to exit the hotel.

"Okay, boys, security is going to keep the girls at bay. So please get inside the limo as quickly as possible. I'll be right behind you," Bruce instructed.

"Can't we just sign a few autographs?" Randy questioned.

"Not tonight. I've got a photographer waiting to take new photos of the band with Nicky as lead guitarist."

As the car approached the auditorium, there was already a long line of fans waiting to get inside. Nicky for once got nervous as the limo parked at the back entrance. This was it—the chance to finally be on stage with a band as famous as Black Tie Affair.

The auditorium was well lit, nothing like Glasgow. Instead, it had high cement walls and long corridors, which were more like tunnels, trailing off in every direction.

"This way, boys, the dressing room is only a short hike down this hallway," Bruce gestured, leading the way.

Finally, they arrived at the end of the long hall. Opening the door, Nicky held his breath as he stepped inside the rather large room. Quickly surveying his new digs, he saw the familiar vase of red roses sitting on a marble table in front of a long sectional. The room contained a fully stocked bar, and catering had set out a spread that looked more like a banquet. Near the back wall hung the familiar racks of black suits, white dress shirts, and black ties. In addition, there was a lit dressing area with four chairs, each positioned in front of tall ornate framed mirrors.

"Oh Nicky, your suit is on that last rack. I'm sorry, I forgot to introduce myself. I'm Kaitlin, your personal assistant while on tour, but everyone just calls me Kate. I will also be doing hair and makeup for you as well."

Kate was tall with long curly black hair, which she wore pulled back in a ponytail. Upon taking a closer look, she was gorgeous with the most beautiful brown eyes he had ever seen.

"Well, nice to meet you, Kate," Nicky smiled.

What a surprise. No one had mentioned an assistant of any kind, and he was sure he hadn't asked for one.

"Oh, I see you've met Kate," Bruce said, walking into the dressing room. "She's brilliant, and the boys just love her. Kate's the greatest at hair and makeup. You'll be seeing a lot of her, especially before you go on stage. She's like family to all of us."

"She's the kid sister I never had," Randy smiled, sitting down to have his makeup applied.

"Yes. Well, nobody ever had a kid sister like that," Alex teased, making Kate blush.

"Boys, I'll need you in your suits and dressed for photos within the hour," Bruce informed them before leaving the dressing room.

Alex poured himself a tall drink and sat down on the sofa when Bruce was gone, lighting a cigarette. Alex and alcohol were old friends.

"Hey man, you better lighten up with that before the concert," Jeff suggested noticing how fast Alex finished his drink.

"What's that, Dad?" Alex replied, giving Jeff a seething look.

"Just saying to take it easy, man," Jeff added.

"Nicky, you're next for makeup," Kate said, motioning him over to her chair. "So you're the new lead guitarist? You replaced poor David, right?"

"Yes. That's right."

"So, where are you from?" she asked, styling his hair.

"Middleton, Michigan or the middle of nowhere," Nicky replied, checking out his profile in the mirror. "Great job never thought of styling my hair like this before. I like it. Thanks."

"Well, that's why I'm here, to make you guys look your best. We're finished, so you can get your suit and take it over to that small room in the back and try it on."

"Okay, Alex, you're up next," Kate said, adjusting the chair for him.

Kate let out a whistle as Nicky walked out dressed in his suit.

"The girls aren't going to miss David when they see you walk out on stage tonight," she smiled.

"Oh, thanks."

"No. Just giving credit where it's due."

It wasn't long before Kate had finished with Alex and Jeff.

"Okay. I'm done here. See you guys after the concert," she said, opening the door to leave.

Stopping, Kate glanced back at Nicky, making eye contact.

"Oh, good luck," she smiled.

Nicky thought he felt a connection for a brief instant as he looked into her beautiful brown eyes.

Walking out to the center stage, Nicky stopped for a second to take in his surroundings before the photos were taken. The auditorium was large and held four thousand seats waiting to be filled. The ceilings were extremely high, surrounded with enclosed box seats, much like London, and tall riggings held the speakers and the lighting system.

Nicky was about two hours away from making his first appearance with the band. As the light bulbs flashed from the camera, Nicky thought he was going blind. The photos were taken in every possible stance, with guitars, with Jeff behind the drums, but mostly group photos.

"Think that does it," Bruce informed the photographer.

The band was finally ready for sound checks. As Nicky picked up his guitar to run through some of their songs, he couldn't help but think of all the band practices in Larry's basement. Damn, he was a long way from Middleton. Nicky wished some of the guys could be here tonight, especially his mom and dad, not to mention Annie and Tony. He remembered the night Jenna had sat in the front row during the band competition watching him perform and how she had run backstage to find him afterward. So many emotions and memories were beginning to overtake him.

"Okay, boys, we're about to open the doors to the auditorium, so take a quick smoke break now or whatever, and good luck tonight," Bruce mentioned.

Walking backstage, Nicky almost walked straight into Mike.

"Hey Nicky, almost didn't recognize you in the suit. Guess this is your big night."

"Hey. How are the guys?" Nicky asked.

"Oh, they're all fine. Maybe one of these nights, we can all get together for a couple of beers."

"Yeah, that would be awesome."

"Well, good luck tonight. You'll do great."

Nicky walked back into the dressing room to pick out a rose for the concert. He again smelled the familiar smell of pot as he saw Alex sitting on the sofa with another drink in his hand. Randy had just finished a sandwich and was lighting up a cigarette. Jeff was reading a book.

"Hey Nicky, did you get a chance to eat yet?" Jeff asked, looking up from his book.

"No. I'm too nervous to eat anything now."

Bruce poked his head in the door for only a second, "Okay, boys, ten minutes till showtime. Best of luck, Son," Bruce grinned.

Quickly putting his book down, Jeff had to hurry. He was always the first one on stage.

Nicky could feel his forehead beginning to sweat, hearing the roar of the fans at their anticipation of seeing the band. His heart was racing wildly out of control. Finally, it was almost time to leave the dressing room and make his way out to the stage.

"Okay, girls, let's go," Randy laughed. "Oh, Nicky, don't forget I'm going to introduce you to the fans tonight."

The boys took a rose and walked down the long corridor toward the stage entrance. Jeff could be heard on the drums, as he always entered first and played an intro for the boys. After that, there was no turning back. This was it. Nicky was about to be on stage for the first time. He walked out with the boys as a member of the band, Black Tie Affair.

The fans were going crazy as they made their appearance on stage. Nicky felt energized as the screams from the crowd grew louder and louder.

"Hello, Dublin," Randy screamed.

"Dublin, are you ready to party?" Alex yelled as the fans went wild.

"Tonight, we're proud to introduce our new lead guitarist, Nicky Spade," Randy grinned. "Dublin, please make him feel welcome."

"Hello Dublin, I'm so glad to be here tonight," Nicky yelled as he held his guitar high in the air.

Wow. Nicky could feel the electricity coming from the fans. He was born to do this. He was in his element. You only had to look at him to see he was living in the moment, as only a rock star could. Nicky was brilliant. He fed off the energy of the fans. The crowd went insane as the boys walked down to the front of the stage and gave out the roses. Nicky felt out of touch with reality, as he led into the next song. The audience appeared as if it was a real live breathing entity, and Nicky took in every breath. The chants of the girls screaming, "Black Tie, Black Tie," reached a crescendo as the boys walked down to the front of the stage, removed their ties, tossing them to the girls standing in front. Nicky handed his long tie to a young girl, who reminded him of Jenna. Wow. He felt like a rock god. Maybe next time, he would kneel and wrap his tie around the neck of a beautiful girl, gently pulling her toward him for a quick kiss to continue David's ritual.

As Randy unbuttoned his shirt, the girls were going crazy.

"Dublin, are you ready to party tonight," he screamed. "What? I can't hear you," he teased, feeding off the frantic screams of the fans.

Staring into the audience, Nicky felt that time was standing still. There was no way to describe his feelings that night on stage. For the next hour and a half, Black Tie Affair held their audience captive as they performed one hit after the other. Nicky Spade, the rock star, was born that night on stage in Dublin, Ireland.

As the concert came to an end that evening, the fans continued with their screams.

"Goodnight, Dublin," Randy yelled.

"Dublin, thanks for coming out tonight to party with us," Alex screamed. "We've had a blast."

"Thank you, Dublin," Nicky shouted. "Honored to be on stage with you tonight."

As the boys left the stage, the screams grew even louder. Damn, how do you unwind after being on such a high, Nicky wondered? Feeding off the energy from the audience that night was like an addict shooting up with his drug of choice. It was surreal.

Walking back to the dressing room, Nicky felt the energy from the audience still coursing through his veins as he entered the room. He needed a drink to calm himself. Lighting a cigarette, he sat down and opened a bottle of Guinness. It wasn't long before Jeff walked in and grabbed a cold bottle of Guinness as well."Wow, man, was that incredible tonight or what?" Nicky grinned.

"Yes. Every audience is different, but tonight the fans were wired."

At that moment, Randy and Alex both walked in with girls draped around them like arm candy.

"Has Bruce called for the limo?" Randy asked.

"Yes. I think he reserved a restaurant downtown called, The Boar's Head.

"Okay, boys, ready to go eat and unwind for the night?" Bruce asked as he opened the door to the dressing room. Let's go. The limo is waiting."

Filing through the door, they were out of the building, including the girls who now seemed to be a part of the night's activities and on their way downtown.

Entering the restaurant, it resembled a hunting lodge. Bruce had chosen to eat here because of the varied menu, primarily wild game. On the walls were life-like renderings of wild boar, deer, rabbit, and fox, which had been restored to their living state by a taxidermist.

"Bruce, you sure picked a unique restaurant," Nicky remarked, looking around.

"Well, you're going to love their menu."

The Boar's Head was now closed to the public and reserved privately for the band's enjoyment. Food and drink flowed easily for almost two hours as the boys kicked back and reminisced about how intently the audience had enjoyed the concert that evening. Randy and Alex seemed impervious to anything happening around them except for the girls holding their attention.

"Well, it's getting late. So we should close this party down for the night," Bruce suggested as he finished his Guinness.

As the limo drove them to their hotel, it seemed the girls were along for the rest of the night as well. Bruce wasn't about to tell the boys who they could or could not have in their rooms. He figured they were all adults, and as long as things didn't get out of control, he kept his opinions to himself.

"Goodnight, boys," Bruce said as the elevator reached the top floor.

Randy and Alex, along with the girls, disappeared, entering their suites.

"Goodnight, Jeff," Nicky said, unlocking his door.

"Yeah, great concert. See you tomorrow."

Waking up the following day as sunlight streamed into his room, it seemed as though Nicky had slept forever. His body had finally adjusted to the life of a musician. He was awake all night and slept in each day until early afternoon. Being a band member no longer required him to show up early at the venue like Todd and the sound crew. Nicky's life had changed forever. Glancing at his watch, it was almost 2:00 p.m. He was starved as he quickly ordered room service. Hopefully, they still served breakfast even at this late hour.

"Yes, sir, it will be right up. Would you like coffee with that as well?" the voice on the phone inquired.

"Yes. Please."

Nicky needed tons of caffeine after last night. He had just finished his last piece of toast when there was a knock at the door.

"Hey Nicky, it's Jeff. The limo is scheduled to arrive at 4:00 p.m. Just wanted to let you know."

"Come in. We still have a few hours before we leave for the venue."

"Okay. Do you have any Guinness?"

"Yes. Open the mini-fridge and grab yourself one."

"Oh, you're just finishing breakfast. But, man, isn't it a little late for breakfast?"

"No. I was starved, and I was craving breakfast."

Lighting a cigarette, Jeff sat down on the couch by the window with his beer. Bruce called the rehab down in London where he sent David, and it seems as if he's being the model citizen right now."

"So, what are you saying?" Nicky questioned. "Are you saying it's beginning to look as if he'll be coming back?"

"Oh no, not at all. David's got a long way to go. Nothing is for sure yet. But, hell, I know my uncle, and if he can get around it somehow, he won't be bringing him back at all. So, don't jump to any conclusions."

Finishing his beer and cigarette, Jeff walked over to the door. "Guess I better get back over to my room. The limo will be downstairs in about an hour, and I need to shower and shave.

"Shave," Nicky laughed. "I think the five o'clock shadow is working great for Randy and Alex. Maybe you should give it a try," Nicky grinned, rubbing his day's growth of facial hair.

"Sorry, I'm not a fan. See you downstairs in a few," Jeff laughed.

It wasn't long before they were all in the elevator heading

downstairs. It seemed as if the girls were becoming a permanent fixture with the guys at this point.

A large crowd of fans could be seen loitering near the hotel entrance as they walked into the lobby. There seemed to be more people outside today than last night when they arrived.

"Okay, boys, you know the drill. If the girls want to ride with you down to the venue in the limo, it's your responsibility to get them inside the car as quickly and safely as possible," Bruce insisted.

Arriving at the Dublin Town Center, once again, the line of fans waiting to get in appeared to wrap the entire complex. As the limo pulled into the back entrance, the boys made a fast exit into the auditorium.

Walking into the dressing room, Kate was the first person Nicky saw.

"Hey, you were awesome last night. You were great, and the fans loved you," she added.

"Thanks."

"You're a natural and such a great guitarist. David will never be missed with your talent. Come on over, and we'll get started with your hair and makeup."

Sitting in the chair that afternoon, Nicky began to feel an attraction to Kate.

"Oh, so you're going for that five o'clock shadow look, are you?" she teased with a smile.

"It sure seems to work for Randy and Alex," Nicky replied with a grin.

"Oh, I'm not so sure that's what the girls have on their mind," Kate laughed.

"Okay. We're done here."

"Next," she motioned for Jeff to take a seat.

It wasn't long before all the boys were dressed and waiting to go on stage. The girls left only moments before the boys were about to perform. Alex had managed to put away his two drinks before leaving the dressing room, and Randy had just finished smoking like a chimney.

Walking out to take their place on stage, Nicky always had an initial moment of stage fright until he locked eyes with the fans, at which point he shed all his inhibitions. The fans seemed as excited as the night before, with their loud, boisterous outbursts. However, tonight their screams were focused toward Nicky.

"Nicky, Nicky," the girls shouted as he walked on stage.

Wow. He couldn't believe his ears. It was only his second night on stage with the band, and they had remembered his name. He felt goosebumps running down his arms as he yelled back.

"Hello, Dublin. Thank you. Thanks so much."

The hour and a half seemed as if it were only a few moments in time, as Nicky relished every second. Living life at center stage was the only place he wanted to be. Nicky felt the love from the fans that night. He would never forget Dublin. The two concerts in Ireland had changed him forever. Now they were set to play Amsterdam.

Postcard from Dublin: *Hey Babe, My dreams are coming true! Two nights on stage, and they remembered my name. Love you forever, Nicky.*

CHAPTER SIX

Love Affair No Ties Required.
Quebec

Arriving back in Quebec, Jenna had somehow managed to ease back into her normal routine. However, the day she left Middleton, she had carried away with her a small precious piece of the person she had so madly fallen in love with. Jenna carried close to her heart a new beginning. A new heart beating, reminding her forever of the one she had loved and lost. It would be weeks before she would be ready to tell her parents about the extra cargo she had brought back home to Quebec. Time was on her side, at least for a few short weeks. She desperately needed to find a way to tell them. Jenna knew her parents had never been fans of Nicky Spade, and she wasn't ready to sit through any lectures. She couldn't bear the thought of hearing them tell her how foolish she had been falling in love with him.

"Jenna, when are you ever going to finish unpacking those boxes in your room?"

"Oh, I'm working on it, Mom."

"Well, seems like since we've gotten back to Quebec, you've not been yourself."

"I'm okay. Can I borrow the keys to the car? I need to run down to Benton's Hardware. There's some shelving I would like to get for my room. It will help me organize my things and clear out the boxes faster."

"Alright, but don't be gone for long. Your dad is going to need the car.

He has a union meeting tonight at the factory."

"Okay. I'll be right back. I promise."

Jenna needed to run down to the local newsstand. She wanted to look through the tabloids to see if there was any news about Nicky. Anything which had been written about the band, Black Tie Affair. She had received no postcards from Nicky, and this bothered her tremendously.

Luck would be on her side as she glanced at the racks of tabloids. An article about the band was on the front cover of the weekly tabloid. It appeared that Black Tie Affair was losing their lead guitarist, David Simmons, to rehab. Jenna skimmed through the news article as quickly as she could. There was no mention in the article who would replace him. However, Jenna instantly knew it would be Nicky. Quickly buying the tabloid, she couldn't wait to get home and read it more carefully in the privacy of her room. Driving back, she was anxious to read the article in its entirety.

"Mom, I'm home," Jenna yelled, running upstairs to her room. Closing the bedroom door, she took the news article and ran over to her bed to sit down. Devouring the information as quickly as she could, it seemed the band had just performed in London. The band's manager, Bruce Weber, had decided to replace David. So, why didn't it give the name of a possible replacement? Why was there no mention of Nicky yet, she wondered? Carefully she placed the tabloid in a box under her bed. These past few weeks had been hard, not even knowing if Nicky had arrived safely in London.

"Mom, has Grandma received any postcards for me since we've gotten back to Quebec?" Jenna yelled down to her Mom. "How about phone calls? Has anyone called for me or left a message for me over at Grandma's house?"

"No, Jenna, who were you expecting to hear from? Please, don't let me hear the words Nicky Spade coming out of your mouth," she replied angrily. "That boy was nothing but trouble. I'm telling you. I've told you repeatedly that your father and I never liked him."

Jenna would never know the extreme hatred that her parents felt toward Nicky. However, many years later, she would discover Nicky's postcards sent to her grandmother's address. Her parents had even involved her grandmother in their exploits to keep Nicky out of her life. Their evil plan was working at present. But, soon, a twist of fate would keep him involved forever in their lives, in a most unexpected way.

Jenna was still experiencing bouts of nausea. However, they were now becoming more frequent. She knew for her sake and that of the life she carried that she would need to see a doctor. She could no longer wait to tell her parents the secret she had been keeping since leaving Middleton.

One afternoon after coming in from high school, she asked her parents to sit down in the living room. She told them she was worried about something. They had presumed it was about her transferring back to the local high school and classes required for graduation.

"Okay, Jenna, what is it that's so important?" her dad, Frank, inquired as he sat down in his favorite chair in the living room.

"Could we wait just a minute until Mom comes in?"

"Sure," he answered as her mom came walking in.

"Alright, Jenna, what is it? Is it about graduation? Don't worry. You can always take summer classes if needed so that you get enough credits to graduate this year."

"Mom and Dad," she said, hesitating.

"Jenna, for heaven's sake, what is it? I don't have all day to sit here," Frank replied, lighting a cigarette. He was a hard worker and strict father who had very traditional beliefs. He believed the woman's place was in the home, no questions asked. Jenna had always felt intimidated by him, which caused their relationship to be strained.

"Well, I really don't know how to tell you," she paused again, starting to cry. "I'm pregnant and almost two months along."

"Oh Frank, I knew it. I just knew," Jenna's mom, Audrey yelled. "Jenna, how could you do this? How could you let something like this happen? How could you?" Audrey shouted.

"Well, I didn't exactly plan this, but to be truthful, I don't regret it either. I love Nicky. Love him. Do you understand?" Jenna answered, sobbing bitterly.

"Oh hell, then you can just have an abortion," Frank suggested, not even considering the impact of the statement he had just made.

"No. I'll never do that. Never. Do you hear me?" Jenna screamed.

"Frank, do you even know what you've just said? We're Catholics, and we don't believe in abortions," Audrey replied, becoming emotional.

Audrey was a mild-mannered woman who had always been submissive to her husband. Living with Frank had never been easy. It was evident in her prematurely grey hair, which she kept pulled back in a bun. Nevertheless, she loved Jenna enough to fight for her, and this was one battle she didn't intend to lose.

"Jenna will have the baby. It's our flesh and blood. We will help her as much as possible. But, Frank, I will not hear of anything else. Do you understand," Audry demanded. "Jenna, I will call Dr. Peterson and get you an appointment. Stop crying. Oh, does Nicky know anything at all about your situation?"

"No. That's the way I want it. He's traveling with a band overseas, somewhere in Europe, and I don't ever want him to know about this."

"Okay. I agree. That's the most logical thing I've heard. I think it's best to leave that boy out of this," Frank recommended. It was the only good piece of news that he'd heard come out of his daughter's mouth. He detested Nicky Spade.

After hearing Jenna's news about the baby, Audrey was now convinced more than ever that she had done the right thing hiding the postcards from Nicky. Jenna would never know about the messages left on her Grandmother's phone. Audrey would go to any lengths to keep Nicky out of her daughter's life.

Over the next few weeks, Jenna's pregnancy became more noticeable. Jenna loved Nicky more than ever. However, she would spend the rest of her life focused on the baby she now carried. Nicky was no longer a part of her world. She was determined to finish school and provide the best possible life for herself and her unborn child. Jenna hoped that Nicky would find love again. She did not wish him anything but success. In some small way, she felt fate had played a significant role in separating them. They were now oceans apart. There was nothing that she could do that would ever change things. Jenna knew her love for Nicky would easily be given to their young son or daughter. Her life would no longer include Nicky Spade.

Jenna would closely follow Nicky's career in the tabloids. She would save the news articles so that one day their child would have some connection to their father. A father they might never know. Finally, Jenna sat down to write a letter to Nicky. She knew he would never read it, but somehow it gave her closure and helped her let go of him. Emotions and memories began overtaking her as she poured her heart out to Nicky on paper.

> *Babe, I know you may never read the letter I'm writing today, but there are so many things to say. I love you more than life itself. You were the best thing that ever happened to me. I'm sorry for not telling you that you were going to be a father. I tried to tell you, but fate had other ideas. I wish you love, and I wish for every dream of yours to come true. In another lifetime, maybe things would have turned out differently. Love, Jenna.*

CHAPTER SEVEN

Fallin in love…
Amsterdam

It was cold and raining as the boys walked off the plane in Amsterdam and over to the limo. All that Nicky knew about Holland was wooden shoes and drugs. As the limo drove through Amsterdam and along the canals, the city was beautiful despite cloudy skies and falling rain. Their hotel was located within a large sports complex, the venue for the concert. It was going to be an easy two nights, according to Bruce. Once again, the venue was sold out.

"Okay, boys, I'm going to drop you off at the hotel. I've got to go down to the public television station and arrange for an interview with their personnel tomorrow. I promised the band would appear in the morning and give a press interview for the local news channel. So there will be no sleeping late in the morning. Set your alarms," Bruce suggested.

As the limo pulled into the enormous hotel and sports complex, the large marquee headlined the upcoming Black Tie Affair concert.

Parking under the massive covered entrance would be extremely useful at keeping everyone dry today.

"Oh, one last thing before I leave you, you'll be sharing rooms. Randy and Alex, I have you both in one suite. Nicky and Jeff, you will share the other. Sorry about the inconvenience, boys. I'll have the limo pick you up around 8:00 a.m. to bring you down to the news station. Have a great evening. See you tomorrow."

Walking into the foyer of the giant complex, it was very modern and entirely enclosed with glass. It was beautiful with a large indoor fountain, which cascaded water from the tall ceilings into a small pool. Randy walked up to the reservation desk, checked the guys in, and picked up room keys.

"Okay, here's your room keys," he said, handing them to Nicky. "See you both in the morning."

Randy and Alex walked over to the elevator.

"Well, Jeff, let's go up and check out our accommodations," Nicky suggested.

"Sounds good."

Opening the door to their suite, Nicky and Jeff were pleasantly surprised. The décor of the suite was modern and spacious. It overlooked one of the many canals. The large windows appeared like a postcard revealing views that depicted boats filled with tourists, houseboats, and a colorful array of row houses. A long narrow sofa covered in a pattern of bright blue swirls sat in front of the tall windows. A steel coffee table with a glass top sat in front, holding the usual fruit basket and a large vase of tulips sat on top. Nicky bent over to smell the fresh flowers.

"Oh, I forgot, Holland is famous for tulips," Nicky stated.

"I think you're suffering from jet lag," Jeff laughed. "You're acting weird."

"Yeah, come to think of it, I do feel tired. Why don't we order some food? I could use some coffee," Nicky replied as he stretched out on the sofa and lit a cigarette. "Wonder if they have fish and chips?"

"Well, there's only one way to find out," Jeff replied, calling room service. "Okay, we've got fish and chips. I also ordered six bottles of Heinekens, figured that might hold us over for the night."

"You're kidding, right," Nicky smiled, removing his shoes. "Six bottles will hardly get us started," he complained. "Wonder what Randy and Alex are up to?"

"Oh, there's no telling with those two, but I'm sure whatever they do won't include staying in for the night," Jeff replied, joining Nicky on the large sofa. "I've heard legendary stories regarding the nightlife in Amsterdam. Ihope they manage to stay out of trouble. Uncle Bruce doesn't take kindly to bailing out band members. With the press interview scheduled for tomorrow morning, it sure wouldn't be the type of press Bruce is looking for," Jeff laughed.

A knock at the door announced the arrival of the fish and chips along with the beer. After eating, they relaxed on the couch, knocking back a few beers. "How's that girl of yours back in Quebec?" Jeff inquired, lighting a cigarette.

"Well, I haven't heard anything at all from her since I left Middleton. I've sent postcards and even called her grandmother's house and left messages. So I guess it's probably safe to say at this point that she's probably moved on with her life. Hell, if I were her, I sure wouldn't become a nun and wait forever on Nicky Spade," he laughed.

"I thought you were madly in love with her?"

"Yes. I've never stopped loving Jenna. I always thought I was lucky to have found her. Some guys live a lifetime, never finding the right one. Jenna was that special someone, one in a million. But we live in the real world, and it can be cruel. With an ocean between us and no way to contact her, I need to move on with my life. That's what I would wish for her. I'm sure she would want the same for me. But fate can be cruel, and sometimes getting what we want in life comes with a costly price tag," Nicky explained as he reached for a cigarette.

"So Jeff, what's your story?" he asked, taking a sip of Heineken.

"Well, guess I'll just put all my cards on the table and be honest for once. I'm not attracted to girls. It's not like I'm trying to keep it a secret. Hell, all the guys in the band are keenly aware that I'm gay," Jeff said, sitting back in his chair as he lit up another smoke.

"Man, I respect your honesty. However, I've never understood why some people seem to have a problem with an individual's sexual orientation. I've never had a problem with that."

"Yeah, well, that's another reason Uncle Bruce finally brought me on board as the drummer for Black Tie Affair. My mother was never able to come to terms with my homosexuality. So it was a lot easier for her to send me away on tour with Uncle Bruce than deal with my sexuality," he added as he finished his beer.

"Well, that must have hurt. Your mother not wanting to deal with you?"

"Yes, little did she know that by pressuring Uncle Bruce to take me on tour, she had given me everything I had ever wanted. But, of course, the joke was on her," Jeff smiled, putting out his cigarette.

"Well, Jeff, you're a great guy and an awesome drummer. So I would definitely say the joke was on her," Nicky agreed, finishing his Heineken. "You're an asset to Black Tie Affair, and thank goodness Bruce had the good sense to bring you on tour," he added.

"Oh, thanks, man. Fate can deal some amazing cards. I've never wanted anything more than to become a drummer for an awesome band. So here I sit tonight. My dreams have come true. I'm traveling the world with Black Tie Affair, all because my mom couldn't face the fact that I happened to be gay."

"Damn, what a story. But I have to tell you I'm proud to go on stage with you, man," Nicky said, getting another beer.

After their long conversation, Nicky knew it was finally time for him to move on. Jenna was no longer a part of his future but rather a part of his past.

"Well, I'm going to try and get some sleep. Good night," Jeff smiled, turning in for the night.

"Sounds like a great idea. Bruce will be sending the limo around early tomorrow morning for the press conference. See you in the morning," Nicky said, putting out his cigarette. As Nicky went to sleep, he realized the significance of the conversation he had just had with Jeff. Tomorrow would be a new day.

Waking early, Nicky showered and dressed for the press interview. Now that he was a band member, he decided against a shave. Maybe the girls did like a hint of growth, he thought, looking in the mirror. Then, splashing on some cologne, he walked out of his room and sat down on the couch as he lit up a smoke.

"Good morning Jeff. Have you ordered breakfast?"

"No. But we should hurry. It's almost 7:00 a.m., and the car will be here at 8:00 a.m."

After Nicky ordered room service, there was a knock on the door.

"Hey man, Bruce wants us dressed in our suits for the interview. Guess he also promised a few photos of the band this morning, so he's sending Kate up to do hair and makeup. Oh, the concierge will be bringing up a rack of our suits. I just wanted to give you and Jeff a heads up," Alex informed them.

"Okay. Thanks," Nicky replied, closing the door.

It wasn't long before there was another knock at the door.

"Think our breakfast has arrived."

Jeff was surprised to discover Kate at the door.

"Oh, I know you both were probably not expecting me. Bruce demanded that I get over here to your hotel and do hair and makeup before leaving for the press conference. Have your suits arrived yet?"

"No," Jeff answered.

"Well, they should be right up," Kate added, leaving the door ajar.

"Room service," the service attendant announced.

"Oh, something smells delicious," Kate smiled.

"Have you had breakfast this morning?" Nicky asked.

"No. Not yet. After I got the call from Bruce, I quickly got dressed, grabbed my makeup bags, and made it down to the lobby just in time to catch the limo."

"Well, let's see what we have here."

We've got eggs, bacon, and potatoes," Nicky announced, lifting the silver tops of the serving trays.

"Okay. We only have a few short minutes to eat," Jeff remarked.

Nicky took a small plate and shared his breakfast with Kate.

"Well, we can't let you starve, can we?" Nicky grinned, handing her the plate.

"Thanks. I never came to eat breakfast, but it smells good," Kate replied, tasting the eggs and bacon.

Answering another knock at the door, "Valet," the guy announced.

Opening the door, the valet pushed a rack of suits inside the room.

"Well, I hate to rush you guys, but I promised Bruce that I would have you looking your best this morning."

Quickly getting hair and makeup out of the way, Kate rushed next door to Randy and Alex. She felt like a dorm mom, trying to get all the guys ready. Walking down to the elevator, Kate was amazed at how great the boys looked this morning. The elevator smelled of men's cologne.

"I know you guys never see this side of morning. So I suppose you turned in early last night or did you?" she asked, looking over at Randy and Alex.

"Amsterdam, are you joking?" Alex answered, staring at Randy. He laughed

"You better not let Bruce hear about your escapes," Kate reprimanded as she left the elevator.

It wasn't long before they arrived at the local television station. Bruce was waiting. He was talking to an older gentleman, probably the station manager, Nicky thought.

"Hey, boys, glad to see that you all could make it at such an early hour."

"Nice to meet everyone this morning. I'm James Dennison, the station manager. Follow me."

The lights were very bright as they walked into the studio.

"Please, just have a seat on the sofa. This won't take long. We are going live this morning with the interview, and I'll be asking you a few questions. Bruce, why don't you take a seat on the sofa next to the guys?

"Okay. First, what a great look for a rock band. You look incredibly handsome in suits and ties. It sure isn't the expected style, but it's a brilliant idea. Alright, we're almost ready. When you see the green light above the camera go on, it means we're live. Are you ready? Okay, counting down from five….five, four, three, two, and one. Good morning. I'm happy to be sitting here this morning with the band members of the rock group Black Tie Affair. Welcome to Amsterdam."

The interview only lasted about fifteen minutes. However, the photoshoot seemed to drag on forever. Before leaving the news station, Bruce never failed to give out free concert tickets to the managers and the crew. With the press interview and photos over, the guys were anxious to get back to the hotel and out of their formal attire.

As the limo drove them back to their hotel room, Nicky found himself wondering if Kate had any plans before the concert. There was only one way to find out. So Nicky called her hotel room.

"Kate, would you like to come up for coffee when we get back to the hotel?"

"Sure," she answered.

Bruce looked at Nicky and smiled. He couldn't help but think that Nicky reminded him of David. The young confident David he had first met before his downfall with drugs. Bruce knew that Nicky was an asset to the band. He would never forget how he had discovered him in the small rural town of Middleton, Michigan. Nicky had quickly transitioned from an obscure artist to lead guitarist with Black Tie Affair. Bruce boasted to himself like a proud father.

The limo dropped off the boys at the hotel as Bruce continued to the radio station. He constantly promoted the band, maintaining a sold-out status for each venue.

A light knock on the door indicated Kate's arrival.

"Hey, come in. I think the coffee is still warm," Nicky smiled, pouring coffee from the insulated pot from breakfast. Then, walking over to the mini-fridge, he grabbed two cold bottles of Heineken.

"Hey Jeff, catch," Nicky said, tossing a beer in his direction.

Taking Kate's hand, he pulled her over to the brightly colored sofa. Lounging back, Nicky lit a cigarette and opened his beer.

"Hey, I've got a great idea. Why don't we rent bicycles and ride along the canals?" Nicky suggested.

"Oh, that sounds like fun. I would love to," Kate agreed.

"How about you, Jeff? Would you like to come?"

"No. You two go ahead and have a good time. I'm still pretty tired. Think I'm going to get a long nap before the concert tonight."

"Alright. If you're sure, you don't want to get some fresh air?"

"Oh, I'm sure. There's a bed in the other room calling my name," Jeff yawned.

"Okay, Buddy, see you later this afternoon."

The sports complex was situated close to downtown Amsterdam and the market area. So, Nicky and Kate decided to walk to the nearest bike rental. Nicky felt confident he wouldn't be recognized wearing his favorite baseball cap and sunglasses. The fact that he was new to the band would also help to hide his identity.

After renting bikes, they found themselves riding along a path that followed the canals. The grey skies were beginning to clear, and the sun finally made its appearance as it peeked from behind the few remaining clouds. Amsterdam was gorgeous. Colorful boats filled with tourists passed beneath the small bridges. Continuing their bike ride, they passed a small bakery. The aroma of fresh-baked bread heavily infused the air.

"Let's stop. The smell of bread is overwhelming."

"Okay. That sounds good."

Stopping to pick up a loaf, they decided to park their bikes at a bench by the water and enjoy the taste of their warm purchase.

"Wait here," Nicky said, running across the street to a small market where he picked up a bottle of wine.

Sitting on a bench in the afternoon sun, Kate began feeding ducks who managed to walk up for a handout. Staring at Kate, Nicky felt drawn to her. She was gorgeous—the complete opposite of Jenna. Jenna was naive and inexperienced in matters of the world. Kate had a career and traveled the world with a rock band. Nicky instantly felt a connection between them as Kate looked up at him and asked for more bread for the ducks.

"Wow. The ducks must be starved," Kate laughed.

After enjoying their bread and wine, they continued their bike ride, following the narrow paths around the canals. Stopping on one of the small cobblestone bridges, Kate smiled, taking in the impressive views.

"Amsterdam is a beautiful city, but Paris is by far the most beautiful. I spent a lot of summers in Paris with my parents," Kate stated. "My dad works for an international insurance brokerage, and one of their headquarters is located in Paris. So we always came over with him in the summer. I'm in love with that city, so when you guys play Paris next month, I'd love to show you the sights."

"Okay. I'm going to hold you to that," Nicky smiled.

Nicky found himself leaning over to kiss Kate while watching the boats pass under the bridge. She eagerly returned his kisses and afterward laid her head on his shoulder. Together they stood on the bridge, taking in the ambiance and beauty of the old world city.

"We should return our bikes and walk back toward the sports complex. It's almost 3:00 p.m., and I've got a concert to do, and you've got hair and makeup," Nicky winked.

It was only a short ride back to the bike rental, where they returned their bikes. Walking the short distance back to the hotel, Nicky looked at Kate.

"Would you like to come up and hang out until we walk over to the venue?"

"I should get back to my room. I have things to do before the concert, and I told Todd and the boys I'd meet them in the lobby of our hotel for a drink, but thanks for the wonderful afternoon," Kate smiled.

It was only about two hours before the concert. As Nicky entered their hotel suite, it appeared Jeff was still sleeping. Lighting a cigarette, Nicky got a drink from the mini-fridge and sat down to have a smoke. Hearing Nicky return, Jeff walked out of his bedroom.

"How was your afternoon?" Jeff questioned.

"Oh, it was fun. Amsterdam is beautiful, and I would highly recommend renting bikes to ride along the paths by the canals."

"No. I meant with Kate? How did that go?"

"Well, it's too early to tell, but I'm very attracted to her at this point. I can't say for sure, but I think it's mutual on her part as well."

"Oh, that's great, man. Kate is a wonderful girl, and you two look good together," Jeff remarked, lighting a cigarette.

After a second cigarette and beer, it was getting late.

"We need to get ready for tonight's concert. Our suits are already here, and it won't take long for hair and make-up."

The arena was located inside the sports complex. So security had been arranged to walk the boys over. A knock on the door made them aware that someone had been sent to escort them.

"Security," the man stated. "Are you ready to walk over to the sports complex?" the burly security guard asked.

"Yes. But there are two other band members next door."

"Oh, my buddy already escorted them over."

Fans tried to get as close as possible and yelled for autographs as they made their way through the narrow corridors with security. Wow, Nicky felt like a celebrity. He loved it. The life of a rock star definitely could give you an ego problem.

It seemed like they'd walked for quite a distance when finally they reached the dressing room at the end of the long hallway. Opening the door, Kate was already inside and styling Randy's hair. Alex was sitting on the sofa with a new girl wrapped tightly around him, smoking a cigarette with one hand and holding a drink in the other. He never seemed to change. The room seemed typical of the other dressing rooms, except for rugby teams and other sports-affiliated photos. A long table covered with fruit platters and cold cuts of every description sat against the back wall. Nicky felt a bottle of Heineken would be the perfect cure for the stage jitters he was experiencing. So he opened a bottle, sat down in one of the chairs, and lit a smoke.

"Hey, you're next for hair and makeup. So either finish your cigarette or put it out," Kate demanded, glaring at him.

"No problem." Nicky glanced in her direction, putting out his smoke.

"Jeff, next chair. Please."

Kate was working fast tonight, trying to get all the guys ready.

"Okay, boys, time to go," Bruce yelled, opening the door.

The fans went wild as the guys walked on stage this evening. The sports arena was vast, and every seat was filled. Even the nose bleed seats were completely packed.

"Hello, Amsterdam," Randy yelled as usual.

"Amsterdam, how are you this evening?" Alex shouted.

"Hello, thanks for having us tonight," Nicky yelled.

The fans went crazy as the guys walked down to hand out the roses. When they opened with their number one hit single, the fans were so loud you could feel the vibrations from the floor as everyone danced to the music. There were shouts of "Nicky, Nicky," which made him feel welcomed.

After the band performed their first song, Jeff continued on drums as the boys started their ritual of loosening their ties to throw to the girls in front. Just as Nicky was about to throw his tie into the crowd, he couldn't believe his eyes. Kate was standing in front. No wonder she had been trying so hard to get out of the dressing room early. He couldn't even fathom how she had made her way through the crowd of fans and was standing directly in front of him. There was only one thing for him to do. Kneeling, he placed his tie gently around Kate's neck and pulled her close for a passionate kiss. The crowd went wild, never knowing the connection between the two of them.

Walking back to his place on stage, he noticed Jeff's expression. He was laughing. Wow, had that really happened, he thought. Nicky was wired for the rest of the concert. Randy did his usual skit of unbuttoning his shirt and shouting.

"Amsterdam, are you ready to party," which resulted in complete hysteria from the girls. The rest of the concert was a riot as the fans just worshiped Black Tie Affair.

Nicky was in his element. Time didn't exist onstage. He felt like he was in a weird hypnotic trance as the band ran through song after song, including their number one hits. Nothing on earth could ever compare or even come close to the feeling of being on stage in front of thousands of adoring fans.

What a privilege, he thought. Music was in Nicky's blood, and he loved nothing more than performing. The hour and a half seemed to fly by as Nicky led into the last song of the evening. He felt as if he could have remained on stage forever. He was meant to do this. He was born to be a rock star.

"Goodnight, Amsterdam," Randy shouted.

"Amsterdam, thanks for coming out to party with us tonight," Alex yelled.

"Thank you, Amsterdam. We love you," Nicky screamed.

At that point, the fans started shouting.

"We love you, Nicky, we love you." Their shouts gave him goosebumps.

Man, he was living his dream, except for one minor detail. He wanted to be front and center on stage. He dreamed of replacing Randy as a solo artist. Nicky knew it was going to happen. He didn't know when or where. He just knew that it would.

Walking back to the dressing room, he saw Kate wearing his tie.

"How the hell did you manage to get down to the front so easily?"

"Oh, I had help. Mike got me through the crowd. Remember this afternoon. I told you I was meeting Todd and the boys. Well, I asked Mike for help. Guess you want your tie back," Kate laughed.

"Now, that wouldn't be right. It's what you wanted, wasn't it?" Nicky grinned with a wink, grabbing the tie around Kate's neck once again and pulling her close to him, kissing her passionately. At that moment, Bruce walked in.

"Okay, boys, the limo is waiting. I've reserved a restaurant for us tonight on Canal Street. Are you boys ready to eat? Oh, Kate, darling, that includes you too," Bruce smiled. "By the way, great job tonight. You were superb. Let's get out of here. I'm starving," he added.

Randy and Alex had their usual arm candy hanging on for dear life as they stepped inside the limo. Nicky sat with his arm around Kate. Randy, Alex, and their girls lit cigarettes before the limo even left the complex. Jeff smiled at Kate, observing Nicky holding her in his arms. It wasn't long before the limo parked at the entrance of a beautiful restaurant that sat at the edge of the canal overlooking the breathtaking waterway. It appeared to be glowing from within as candles lit each window.

"This place is gorgeous," Kate smiled, holding Nicky's hand as she exited the limo.

The restaurant, as usual, was closed to the public and reserved for the band members and their dates. As Bruce walked in, the maître d' escorted them over to a long table near a wall of windows that revealed views of the canal. Nicky pulled out a chair for Kate, quickly kissing her cheek. Soon wine was being poured, and menus were handed out.

"So, what are you going to have?" Nicky asked, looking at Kate.

"Oh, I'm thinking about pheasant and wild rice."

"Well, that sounds good. I think I'm going to have the braised beef and potatoes with cabbage," Nicky smiled, putting down his menu.

It wasn't long before huge platters of food were brought out. The aroma was enticing. Nicky and Kate enjoyed dinner. The ambiance of the wrought-iron street lamps reflecting through the windows, along with the candles and soft music playing in the background, made the evening romantic. It seemed as if they had been there for over two hours. Finally, after dessert and wine, Bruce stood up.

"Well, boys and girls think we should call it a night. Tomorrow is another day, and we still have one more concert in Amsterdam. Nicky placed his arm around Kate's petite waist as they walked back to the limo. It was only a short drive back to the sports complex. Nicky gave Kate a quick kiss as they exited the limo.

"Oh, and by the way, you look cute in the tie," he winked.

Black Tie Affair played one more sold out concert in Amsterdam. Every night was simply amazing. However, Nicky was looking forward to Paris.

Postcard from Amsterdam: *Hey Jenna, we've just*

performed in Amsterdam. I hope you are well. I haven't heard from you. I suppose you've moved on with your life. I wish you the best.

Always, Nicky.

CHAPTER EIGHT

The City of Lights...
Paris

As their private jet circled the vast city of Paris, Nicky got a bird's eye view of the Eiffel Tower. It would be one of the places he would have to visit before the tour moved on to its next venue. He knew just the person to take with him. She was sitting next to him. Kate loved Paris. She had visited there numerous times with her parents, and she was thrilled about the possibilities of showing Nicky the City of Lights as she always referred to it.

The plane taxied over to the hanger as Nicky sat in his seat, reflecting over the past few months of his life. He felt as if everything around him had been put on warp speed. It had been two short weeks since he had stepped on stage in Dublin. After that, the band toured Amsterdam, and now they were scheduled to perform in Paris. After Dublin, Nicky was finally beginning to make a name for himself as the lead guitarist with Black Tie Affair. The fans adored him, and it seemed his position with the band was secure since David never made it through rehab. Bruce had been right regarding David. At first, his chances of getting through rehab seemed to be a certainty, but when his girlfriend left, it seemed to be the straw that broke the camel's back. He spiraled downward so fast that no one even knew his whereabouts at this time.

Besides becoming an integral member of the band, fate had given Nicky another surprise. He was falling in love with Kate. They had become inseparable. Nicky's feelings towards Jenna still tugged at his heartstrings. However, the distance between them had given him reason to rethink the possibility of their relationship ever continuing. There had been no way to contact her. Even the postcards he had sent seemed a futile attempt at trying to stay in contact with her. Also, the phone messages he had left on her grandmother's phone never made their way to her for some odd reason, or so he assumed. At this point, Nicky was sure Jenna had moved on with her life. Apparently, he was no longer a part of her future but rather a part of her past. Time and distance were enough to destroy any relationship, and he was finally ready to put aside his feelings for Jenna and move on. After all, what was a rising rock star supposed to do? No guy in his right mind would become a monk when his life had been so quickly catapulted into the limelight of lead guitarist with one of the world's most famous bands. Girls were everywhere, and no band member of Black Tie Affair lacked arm candy, definitely not now and definitely not Nicky Spade. Kate seemed to enter Nicky's life at just the right moment, and he wasn't about to let her slip away.

Two limos were waiting for the arrival of the private jet, which carried the band members into Paris today. Nicky had managed to persuade Bruce to allow him a chance at some semblance of privacy. At the same time, the band played the venue in Paris. He needed downtime, but more importantly, he wanted to spend time with Kate. Bruce had not loved the idea and Nicky's risks being recognized without security. Still, after strongly being persuaded by him, he had reluctantly given in. Nicky, in return, promised to be on time each night and ready when the limo arrived at their hotel each evening, taking them to the venue. Bruce and the boys were staying at the

Ritz Carlton. Bruce reserved a quaint hotel on the Champs Elysees for Nicky and Kate. It was more private and offered them the best chance of not being seen.

"Okay, Nicky, I guess this is where you and Kate go your separate ways, Bruce said, getting into the limo with the other band members. I'm taking a big chance on you, Son. If you're late or worse yet fail to show up in time for the concert, well, you don't even want to know the repercussions. Kate, I need you backstage in the dressing room before the other band members arrive. Do you both understand?" he demanded, scratching the top of his head. "I must be crazy, Son, to allow such lunacy, but you've done one hell of a job replacing David. I'll trust you on this hair brain scheme of yours," he added before the door to the limo shut.

Nicky winked at Kate, giving her a quick kiss as they stepped into their limo.

"Wow. I can't believe Bruce actually allowed us to get away with this."

"Well, he thinks of you as a son, you know. You've done a great job replacing David, and no revenue was lost in the transition, so guess he figures you've earned his trust."

Lounging back in his seat, Nicky took in the scenery as the limo drove them to their hotel.

"Don't worry. You're not going to miss anything. I know Paris very well, and I'm looking forward to showing my city to you," Kate said, leaning over to kiss him.

As the limo arrived at the side entrance of their hotel, it was stunning. It sat nestled into a side street, just off the busy Champs Elysees, and was covered with Ivy. The cobblestone street leading into the hotel turned into a circular drive which encircled a small charming courtyard at the hotel's front entrance.

"Wow, this is stunning and hidden from the busy street and traffic," Kate smiled. The limo parked near a beautiful three-tier fountain that centered the courtyard. The old-world appeal of the hotel was inviting.

"Welcome to the Courtyard," the doorman greeted, opening the door to the limo.

"Thank you," Nicky smiled, helping Kate out of the limo.

The hotel sat secluded enough so no one would know their whereabouts, and Bruce had made their reservations under anonymous names.

Walking inside the lobby was breathtaking. Its charm was appealing. It felt like a comfortable cottage inside, with low ceilings, exposed stone walls, and heavy wooden beams which crisscrossed the ceiling. French doors led outside to another courtyard.

"Oh Nicky, this is so charming," Kate remarked, walking up to the reception desk.

"We have reservations under the name of Adams. That would be Mr. and Mrs. Adams," Nicky informed the staff.

"Yes. We have you listed for the next three nights? Is that correct?"

"Yes. That would be us," Nicky answered.

"Just one second, and I'll have the concierge take up your luggage. The hotel was small, only three floors. Their room was on the top floor, with a balcony overlooking the courtyard.

Opening the door to their room was much like the décor in the lobby.

"This is wonderful," Kate said, sitting down on the edge of the bed.

It was covered with a heavy floral duvet that matched the tapestry swag hanging above it. Nicky walked over to open the tall French doors leading to a small wrought-iron balcony.

"How do you feel about dining in for the evening?" he questioned, looking at Kate.

"Oh, that sounds nice. Fortunately, we don't have to be at the Seine Auditorium untiltomorrow afternoon."

Calling for room service, Nicky ordered beef stew along with root vegetables and a bottle of champagne. It wasn't long before a knock at the door let them know their dinner had arrived. Popping the cork from the bottle of champagne, Nicky poured them each a glass.

"Let's take our food and drinks outside to the table on the balcony," Nicky suggested. "I think we could use some fresh air."

Kate followed Nicky outside. Sitting down in a wrought iron chair, she reached up and untied her hair which had been pulled into a ponytail.

"Oh, this feels much better," Kate smiled, shaking loose her curly black hair. "The hotel is simply stunning?" she mentioned, taking a sip of champagne.

"Kate, we should talk," Nicky smiled, pulling her onto his lap. "Sweetheart, you have to know that I've fallen in love with you. I've wanted to tell you, but I was waiting until the time was right. I love you, but I feel I can't continue with our relationship until I've explained someone important to me until recently, a few months ago. I was very much in love with her," Nicky continued.

"Stop. You don't have to explain. I know about Jenna. I could never have allowed myself these feelings for you if Jeff hadn't explained everything to me. I know she was a huge part of your life before you left Middleton. I know that you once loved her, and maybe in some ways you still do, but Nicky, this world that now revolves around you doesn't include her any longer. It can be a very solitary existence traveling with Black Tie Affair. I know. I've experienced what it's like to live in hotel rooms with no one there each night. But, the day I met you in the dressing room, call it fate or whatever, I knew we were destined to be together. I couldn't imagine her life now."

How do you fall in love with Nicky Spade and ever let him disappear out of your life, she wondered?

"I'm so lucky to have met you, and I love you," Kate smiled with tears in her eyes, kissing him passionately. Thanks for being considerate of my feelings enough to tell me about Jenna. Oh, but just one thing before we close the door on this subject, just remember I'm Kate and not Jenna," she said, looking deep into his eyes.

"Kate, I would never want you to be anyone other than yourself," Nicky answered, pulling her even closer to his chest in a tight embrace.

Nicky felt that fate had once again stepped into his life. Now being on stage as the lead guitarist with a world-famous band and having Kate in his life, Nicky was ready to conquer the world of rock and roll. His dreams and desires of one day performing with his own band as lead vocalist was still alive and strong.

Kate was beginning to feel the cold of the evening as she suggested they go inside and start a fire in the fireplace for the evening. It was now summer in Paris, but the evening air could still be quite cool.

"Well, we better call it an early night. I've got a lot of beautiful places to show you starting tomorrow morning, and we'll only have a few hours each day before the concert."

Feeling the heat from the fireplace, Nicky jumped on the bed motioning for Kate to join him. Lying there with Kate in his arms, he still had difficulties removing Jenna from his mind.

"Hey Babe," he found himself saying, endearing words which had only been reserved for Jenna until now. "I'm a lucky guy to have you in my arms tonight. I love you, Kate," Nicky whispered as he brushed back her hair. "I love you."

The intense feelings shared between them as they snuggled in a tight embrace naturally led to hours of passionate romance. The night didn't seem long enough to express the love that now connected them.

Waking up to sunlight streaming in from the balcony doors, Nicky looked over at his watch. It was almost 9:00 a.m.

"Hey Doll," he said, kissing her awake. "We better get ready if you're going to show me this city of yours. We only have about six hours this morning before the limo will pick us up and take us to the auditorium."

Quickly getting dressed, Nicky put on a baseball cap, turning the cap's brim around to the back of his head. Hopefully, this would work as a disguise.

Watching as Nicky put on his cap, tight blue jeans, and a sweatshirt, sporting a five o'clock shadow, Kate almost melted at the mere sight of him.

"Well, Sweetheart, I don't know about a disguise. But you may have every girl in Paris glancing your way today. Of course, they'll never suspect you're the lead guitarist for Black Tie Affair," she smiled, giving him a lengthy kiss.

"We better get out of here before I'm tempted to pull you back into bed," he teased.

Once they were in the lobby, Nicky called for a taxi.

"I want to show you Paris the way I remember it. I have a surprise for you."

"Oh yeah, and what could that be?"

"Just wait. You'll see soon enough."

The taxi drove them further down the Champs Elysees, stopping at a Moped rental.

"You're kidding, right?"

"Catch," she said, tossing him a helmet.

"Now, get on the back, you silly thing. You're not driving, remember I'm the tourist guide," she said, putting on her helmet.

"Damn, you look sexy in that helmet," Nicky grinned, leaning in to give her a quick kiss.

"Now hold on," Kate laughed as they sped away down the Champs Elysees. "This is the only way to see Paris."

The Champs Elysees had beautiful street lamps on each side of its tree-lined motorway with various shops along its path and cinemas. It wasn't long before they were driving past the Arch of Triumph.

"Napoleon Bonaparte built this to honor his victories," Kate said loud enough for him to hear.

Nex,t she drove over to the left bank of the Seine River, where she parked the Moped.

"How do you feel about a walk along the banks of the river today?" she questioned.

"Great," he smiled, taking off his helmet.

They walked for what seemed like miles along the banks of the Seine. The sun glistened off the water as long glass-covered boats filled with tourists went past. Hand in hand, they strolled past charming open-air cafes. Stopping to eat ice cream at one of the small shops, they sat outside under a bright red canopy taking in the ambiance of the quaint buildings. Later stopping on one of the bridges which crossed over the river, Nicky grabbed her in his arms and kissed her softly.

"Well, this city of yours is very romantic," Nicky smiled.

"Tomorrow, I'll pack us a picnic lunch, and I'll take you to the Eiffel Tower. We can spend the entire morning there." Kate suggested.

Looking down at his watch, Nicky noticed it was almost 2:00 p.m.

"Doll, I hate to end such a lovely afternoon, but we've got just a few hours before the limo picks us up this evening."

Holding hands, they quickly walked back to where the Moped was parked.

"Oh, I've rented the Moped for the next two days, so there's no need for us to turn it in now."

Putting on their helmets, they swiftly sped away. Once they were back at the hotel, they quickly showered and dressed. It would be less than an hour before the limo picked them up. Kate needed to be at the venue early. She had promised Bruce to arrive before the members of the band. She had hair and makeup to do. Racing down to meet the limo, they were soon on their way to the concert. Sitting in the back of the car as it drove through the City of Lights at dark was exhilarating enough. Still, as Nicky held her in his arms, Kate knew she was the luckiest girl in Paris this evening.

As the limo parked at the back entrance of the Seine Auditorium, Nicky was beginning to get nervous. It would be the first time he performed in Paris with Black Tie Affair, and he couldn't help but wonder how the fans would accept him as the new lead guitarist. Paris was one of the larger venues for the band and had a huge fan base.

Walking with Kate through the maze of concrete corridors, it wasn't long before Nicky heard Bruce's voice.

"Hey Son, sure happy to see you made it on time. But Kate, I wanted you here before the boys arrived, and they are already in the dressing room. The guys needed to be dressed a few minutes early this evening. I've given away free tickets to the concert, and I promised photos with the boys in the band."

"Sorry, Bruce. No problem. It won't take me long at all."

Walking further down the corridor, they quickly found the

dressing room. Opening the door, the smell of cigarettes and pot permeated the air. It was by far the largest dressing room the boys had ever shared. The back wall was covered in mirrors, and there were rows of chairs sitting in front. The buffet this evening was a smorgasbord of the finest French Cuisine. Kate got to work styling hair and applying makeup. Jeff was the first up this evening.

"So, how was your first day back in Paris? Did you show Nicky all your old haunts?"

"Well, we kind of got off to a late start this morning," Kate said, blushing. "We're going to the Eiffel Tower tomorrow," she added. "Next," Kate announced, motioning for Alex. "Please, put out that cigarette. Really, Alex, you think I can style your hair and put on your makeup while you continue to smoke. I may be an artist, but I'm not Houdini."

"Okay. Calm down. I thought you'd be all relaxed staying with Nicky in a private hotel."

"Well, it's not like you and Randy don't have your share of girls and private places, too," Kate snapped.

The boys felt Kate was their kid sister and a member of the family, so to speak, which naturally included sibling rivalry. Thankfully, with Bruce hovering over her, it didn't take long before the boys were ready for photos to be taken with a few lucky fans. The fans chosen were excited and eagerly waiting backstage to get their pictures taken with the band. Nicky again felt his celebrity status posing with his fans while the light bulbs from the cameras flashed in his face. He was indeed a long way from a small town called Middleton and once again about to go on stage, this time in Paris.

The noise coming from the auditorium was deafening as the boys walked out to the center stage.

"Hello, Paris," Randy screamed.

"Paris, how are you this evening," shouted Alex.

"We love you," Nicky yelled.

It was by far the largest auditorium Nicky had performed in so far. As the guys walked down to hand out the roses for this evening's concert, it was almost overwhelming to look out over a vast sea of people who filled every seat. Nicky couldn't imagine where Kate might possibly be in such an enormous crowd, but he thought perhaps Mike or Pete had taken her to an obscure place where she could watch the band perform. The fans screamed as they opened with their first song, and Nicky was sure he heard fans shouting, "We love you, Nicky."

As the boys began their ritual of tossing out their ties, the girls in front, as usual, became hysterical. Several of them fainted, and security had to carry them out of the crowd. Nicky singled out one of the girls in front and knelt, gently wrapping his tie around her neck, giving her a quick kiss. Randy walked back to center stage and began his usual act of unbuttoning his dress shirt as two of the girls in front tried to scramble onto the stage. Security worked quickly to remove them.

"Okay, Paris, are you ready to party?" Randy screamed.

As the fans yelled out their love for the band, the noise level could once again have been registered on the Richter scale, Nicky thought. However, he loved every minute of it. Nicky felt a strong bond between himself and the fans. He would make sure that no one left disappointed. The lights were lowered as the band sang one of their slower songs, and the fans lit cigarette lighters, swaying with the rhythm of the music. It made the vastness of the immense auditorium come alive with flickering lights. Nicky found himself again screaming before their next song, "We love you, Paris." Naturally, the fans went out of control, screaming back their love for the band. Never before had Nicky felt such a strong connection with the fans. He was where he always wanted to be, with fans who adored him. The concert continued for the usual hour and a half, but Nicky always felt time stood still while on stage. It was simply irrelevant.

"Good night, Paris," Randy yelled.

"Thank you for coming," Alex shouted.

"We love you, Paris. Thanks so much for coming out to party with us," Nicky yelled.

Security was working overtime at tonight's concert. Several girls attempted to climb up on the stage as the guys waved goodbye. Nicky was hyped. It was by far one of the largest crowds he had ever seen. He was sure they left the concert extremely excited because they had just spent an hour and a half with Black Tie Affair.

As the guys walked backstage to their dressing room to rid themselves of their suits for the night, Bruce came over to share his excitement regarding the concert.

"Damn, what a great group of fans you boys have here. The concert was unbelievable. It seems safe to say that Paris loves you. Well, boys, the limos are already at the back entrance. I've reserved a great French restaurant located on the Champs Elysees.

"Bruce, if it's okay, Kate and I will pass on dinner with the boys tonight. Since we'll only be in Paris a short time, Kate has a restaurant that she loved eating at with her parents, and she can't wait to go back there."

"Okay, kids, go have fun. After all, it is Paris. But remember, keep a low profile. I don't want to be called away from dinner tonight to rescue you, and as I told you before, don't be late for tomorrow's venue. You've begun to feel like family, Son, so don't disappoint me."

"Don't worry, Bruce, I hear you loud and clear, Dad," Nicky smiled.

As the limo drove near the banks of the Seine River, the numerous ornate wrought-iron street lamps scattered along its streets and over the many stone bridges were romantic. Kate thought she loved Paris even more after dark as she held onto Nicky in the back of the limo.

Finally, the car stopped at a small French restaurant on the banks of the Seine. It was beautiful with its old-world charm. The restaurant had detailed baroque trim, which outlined its architectural features. Bathed in the darkness of the night, it was breathtaking. The copious lights coming from inside the restaurant cast a reflection on the water.

"So, what do you think?" Kate questioned as the limo parked in front.

"It's beautiful. Now let's hope they serve great food. I'm starved after tonight's concert."

"Well, I can promise you won't be disappointed."

Walking inside, the ambiance from the lighted candles sitting on each table gave it a warm glow. The maître d' ushered them to a small table in the back corner which overlooked the Seine.

"Isn't this romantic?"

"Well, I can honestly say it's much better than eating with Bruce and the boys tonight," Nicky admitted.

As the waiter came over to their table, Kate ordered Ratatouille, eggplant casserole with tomatoes, zucchini, and onions. Nicky ordered Boeuf Bourguignon, beef stew. The night seemed to fly by as they sat, enjoying the romantic atmosphere of the restaurant. Then, they watched again as glass-covered boats slowly passed, taking tourists for a beautiful evening cruise on the Seine.

"I love Paris even more at night. It appears bathed in lights. So tomorrow, I will take you to my favorite place," Kate said, finishing her dessert.

"Great, I can't wait, since I've got the perfect tour guide sitting next to me. Let's get out of here."

Nicky's life had significantly changed from the nights spent with Todd and the boys. However, nothing could have ever prepared him for life as lead guitarist with Black Tie Affair.

Arriving back at their hotel, Nicky ordered another bottle of champagne. Tonight was not over, and a few nights remained in Paris. However, the champagne would help drown out his memories of Jenna and their night spent at the cabin on the lake. He didn't want that night to take precedence over this evening with Kate.

After pouring the champagne, Nicky and Kate walked out to the balcony. The night sky was clear and scattered with an abundance of stars. Kate was captivated by the beauty of the evening sky.

"Wow. Have you ever seen so many stars before?" Kate asked, holding Nicky close to keep her warm.

"Well," Nicky paused, staring at the sky. "I've been told that if you find the brightest star and make a wish on it. It will come true."

"Really, then I guess we should give it a try."

Looking overhead, they found the most brilliant star and made their wish. Nicky thought back to the night when he and Jenna had made a wish on their star on the pier in Middleton. He couldn't help but think his wish had been granted. However, he would never know for sure what Jenna had wished for that night and if her wish had possibly come true.

"It's getting cold. Let's go inside where it's warm."

Walking Kate back inside, it appeared that she had a little more to drink than her body could handle. Nicky just managed to sit Kate on the bed when he noticed she was out for the night. There was only one thing he could do, cover her with a blanket and let her sleep.

Waking the following day, Nicky leaned over, kissing Kate awake.

"What happened?" she smiled.

"Well, Babe, I think you had a little too much champagne," he winked, giving her another kiss. "So, how do you feel? Are we still on for seeing the Eiffel Tower this morning?"

"Are you kidding?" Kate answered, jumping up then racing into the bathroom. "Just give me twenty minutes, and we'll be out the door. Don't forget we won't need the limo. We have the Moped downstairs. I'll be done in a flash," she yelled out from the bathroom.

Kate wasn't about to miss her opportunity to show Nicky her favorite place in the city. Nicky could hear the water running in the bathroom as he sat on the edge of the bed. He wasn't sure what Kate had wished for last night, but his wish was in the next room anxiously getting ready to show him Paris.

"Nicky," Kate yelled from the shower, "Can you fold up the blanket from the bed. We'll need it today."

"Okay. But you've been in there forever."

Walking out of the bathroom, Kate looked stunning. She was wearing a baseball cap with her long black hair tied into a ponytail and pulled through the back. Along with denim capris, she was sporting a white tee shirt with the band's logo on it.

"Hey Doll, your T-shirt, really," he laughed. "Do you think that's a good idea?" "You do know that I'm the lead guitarist, right?" he winked with a smile.

Walking over, he handed her his jacket.

"Here, I think you may need this," Nicky grinned, kissing her passionately. "The last thing we need today is to get recognized."

"Okay. But that's my favorite T-shirt. Of course, Todd and the boys keep me supplied with them."

"Well, Babe, let's just try and keep a low profile today," Nicky smiled, reaching down to pick up his baseball cap and the blanket from the bed.

Walking out to the hotel's courtyard, they walked over to where the Moped was parked.

"Alright. I'm driving today. Give me directions as we go," Nicky said, stomping out a cigarette with his foot before he strapped on his helmet.

"I'm not sure about this. Do you have any idea how to get there?" Kate questioned.

"Well, we're about to find out," Nicky laughed, driving out of the courtyard of the hotel and onto the Champs Elysees.

Kate held onto Nicky as he swerved dangerously in and out of traffic along the busy streets of Paris. Finally, after missed directions and a few wrong turns, they arrived safely at the Eiffel Tower.

"Geez, Nicky. No more driving for you. I'm taking your keys," Kate laughed.

"Well, I got you here. Now, let's see this tower of yours," he teased.

Parking the Moped, Nicky grabbed the blanket. It was breathtaking, just as Kate had said. Seeing it from the plane the day they arrived gave no hint of the size of this majestic steel structure. The massive behemoth towered overhead, giving thought to those who had erected such a monumental structure.

"Wow. You have to see this for yourself to appreciate its size and beauty," Nicky exclaimed.

"I knew you would love coming here. Why don't we get something to eat?"

Walking over to one of the vendors, they bought sandwiches and drinks.

"I see an open spot. Quick, let's run over and put down our

blanket. I'm starved since we skipped breakfast this morning," Kate added.

Spreading the blanket on the ground, they made themselves comfortable and opened the sandwiches.

"This is my favorite place. I've always loved coming here, watching the tourists, and simply taking in the sights."

The sun was warm, and the day was beautiful. Nicky thought there couldn't have possibly been a better time to see the Eifel Tower, and seeing it with Kate was perfect. As people wandered about the surrounding gardens, it was a microcosm of every age, the old, the young, and the lovers.

"This is the Paris I love," Kate smiled proudly.

Lounging back on the blanket, a young family with small children sat down nearby. Suddenly, a ball was accidentally thrown in their direction. Catching it, Nicky quickly tossed it back.

"Have you ever thought about marriage or having a family one day?" Kate questioned.

"Can't say I've ever given it much thought. My focus is entirely wrapped up with the band. I'm right where I want to be at the moment. My dream is to become a lead vocalist and have a band. It's safe to say that I'm not going to stop until I get what I want out of life," Nicky stated, lighting a cigarette.

"Oh," Kate hesitated. "Well, you're a great guitarist, and I'm sure nothing will stop you short of your dreams." Kate's expression turned serious as she sat up quickly. "There's one thing you should know, Nicky Spade," she said, calling him by his full name.

"Oh yeah, well, this sounds serious."

"I just want to remind you that I'm falling in love with you, and I'm not Jenna. She wasn't ever going to share this part of your world with you. Fate seemed destined to see to that. Nicky, I'm not going anywhere. I share this part of your world. I travel with Black Tie Affair. It was my dream to be part of something huge. Something that would take me away and that I could feel connected to. I love traveling with the band. Bruce has been good to me, and the boys, well, they come with their own set of problems. But they feel like my brothers. I love the world of Black Tie Affair and everything that comes with it. Nicky, I will be at each venue. I will be wherever you go. I'm part of your dreams. Do you understand what I'm trying to say?" Kate asked, becoming emotional.

For once in his life, it was probably the truest statement he had ever heard. Perhaps Jenna was only destined to enter his life for a short time. Many years later, Nicky would discover the complicated repercussions of his love affair with Jenna. But, Kate was right, she wasn't going anywhere, and for once, he could feel safe falling in love again. Putting out his cigarette, he reached over, pulling her close to his chest, kissing her more passionately than ever should've been allowed for a public place.

"Alright, Doll," he smiled. "Are you ever going to take me to the top of that tower of yours?"

Finally, reaching the top of the Eiffel Tower, Nicky held Kate in his arms. He felt like he owned the world today, feeling the wind on his face and observing the panoramic vistas below. It couldn't have been a more poignant moment in his life. Holding Kate in his arms, he knew in his heart that he had one piece of his life now with him, and he wasn't going to stop until he had the last piece.

"Well, Doll, as wonderful as it is standing here with you in your special place, it's getting late. We both have work to do. So let's get going."

The traffic was terrible. Nicky again wove in and out through the traffic, trying to dodge the other cars with their Moped.

"Wow, that was quite a ride. I think we're both lucky to be alive. You came close to getting us both killed."

Walking into their room, Nicky pulled Kate down to the bed, and for the few hours remaining before the concert, they simply shut out the world.

It seemed all too soon the limo arrived. Nicky and Kate were on their way to the Seine Auditorium. The concert was sold out. Paris had indeed been the perfect place to fall in love.

Over the following six months, the band performed in numerous locations throughout Europe. Finally, however, the guys were anxious to play Frankfurt.

Their next stop on tour was Germany. Nicky was looking forward to meeting Mike's girlfriend, Michelle, and enjoying more time with Kate.

CHAPTER NINE

Nightlife in *Frankfurt*

Kate was sitting next to Nicky as their private jet touched down on the runway at Frankfurt International Airport. Although after being on tour for months, the guys were excited to be performing in Germany. They were looking forward to some downtime afterward before touring in Italy. In addition, Nicky was hoping their fans in Germany would be thrilled to attend a Black Tie Affair concert. As the plane came to a stop near the large hanger, Nicky could see the limo waiting to take them downtown to their hotel.

"Hey, kids," Bruce said, exiting the plane. "I've got both you and Kate booked into the InterContinental Hotel along with the other band members. But we've had to tighten our security for this venue."

"Why? Are there problems?" Nicky questioned, escorting Kate down the steps of the jet.

"Well, none specifically, but we've had reason to hire extra security for Frankfurt. Don't worry. We're on top of everything."

Exiting onto the autobahn, Nicky began seeing the billboards advertising the concert. As usual, Bruce was on top of his game. Arriving at the hotel, he was always busy with the press and media.

"Well boys, here's your stop," he announced, arriving at the hotel. I've got the usual promotional meetings in the morning. So, I'll see you tomorrow evening at the Frankfurt Sports Arena. Oh, by the way, I've promised some lucky fans another photo opportunity with you. So I'll need you at the sports arena dressed and ready for photos before 5:00 p.m."

"Alright," Randy said, reluctantly exiting the limo.

Randy walked up to check the boys into their rooms.

"Okay, we've each got a private suite, except for you two love birds. So you'll be sharing as usual. Here are your keys, have a great night," he winked at Kate.

Agitated by Randy's snide implication, Kate frowned. "Thanks, Randy. You guys have had plenty of wild nights."

Nicky thought the sibling rivalry between Kate and the boys was quite amusing.

"By the way, Jeff, Kate and I are going out with Mike and the guys tomorrow night after the concert. Why don't you consider coming along? Mike is going to introduce us to Michelle, his longtime girlfriend."

"Well, that sounds like fun. See you tomorrow," Jeff replied, stepping out of the elevator.

Walking into their room, it was impressive. The bright city lights of Frankfurt filtered in through large windows, bathing the room in a soft glow. There was a beautiful vase of flowers and a typical fruit basket sitting on the large credenza. Walking over to the sofa which sat beneath the tall windows, Nicky pulled Kate down next to him and lit a cigarette.

"Doll, is this the life or what?"

"Yes, Babe, I can honestly say that my touring with the band has taken on a whole new perspective. It was lonely at best before you came into my life. Every night I came home to an empty hotel room and watched the boys with their never-ending supply of girls, which shared their evenings. Jeff seems to be the only one who isn't bothered by not having someone special on tour."

"Well, I wouldn't say he's not lonely. Perhaps it's more like he just hasn't made that special connection with someone yet. Did you know that Bruce is Jeff's uncle?" Nicky asked, opening a bottle of Bitburger from the mini-fridge.

"Yes. It's common knowledge among the band members, but Bruce definitely shows no favoritism toward Jeff. He pulls his weight around here just like the rest of us," Kate mentioned.

"Oh, I know. Jeff's a great guy. I like him a lot," Nicky added.

"Okay, are you going to share that beer or what?" Kate asked.

"So, you drink beer. Do you Doll?"

"Well, what do you think? Working around all of you guys?" Kate laughed, taking a sip of Nicky's beer.

Sitting together on the couch sharing a beer, he knew he never wanted to come home to an empty hotel room after a concert. Kate was right. She did share his dream in more ways than one.

"Well, Babe, let's move this party over to the bedroom, shall we?" Nicky grinned, quickly putting out his cigarette. Kate smiled as she took Nicky's hand and followed him. Jumping onto the bed, Kate grabbed Nicky and pulled him down next to her. They were like two playful kids who were having their first sleepover. However, the night quickly turned from playfulness into one of romance. Nicky would no longer share his nights with thoughts of Jenna.

Waking up, Nicky rolled over to kiss Kate awake.

"Hey Doll, so what country are we in this morning?" he teased.

"Germany," Kate answered with a laugh returning his passionate kiss.

Lying in bed with Kate in his arms, Nicky couldn't believe he actually got paid to live such an opulent lifestyle. Spending the morning hours with Kate was more than anyone could ask. However, looking over at the clock, it was noon.

"Babe, it's noon. I think we better get up and get the day started," Nicky smiled, sitting up in bed to light a cigarette.

"You order room service. I'll get a shower and get dressed," Kate said, running for the bathroom.

"Okay. How do eggs, bacon, and potatoes sound?"

"Great. I'm starved," Kate yelled from the bathroom with the water from the shower running.

After eating, Nicky quickly showered and dressed. Walking out, Kate thought he was the sexiest member of the band, hands down. She knew she was lucky to be with him, as he could easily have any girl out of the thousands of fans who threw themselves at the band.

"I think we might have just enough time to walk downtown and see the city before the concert. How does that sound?" he questioned.

"Great," Kate smiled, handing Nicky his baseball cap. "Don't forget this."

As they strolled along the streets of Frankfurt, it had an old-world charm. The buildings, both modern and aged, towered overhead. Electric trolleys ran between the tall building making frequent stops along their way. Hearing music, they stopped at a small open-air café for coffee. Drinking coffee while listening to a group of musicians playing accordions was unexpected yet enjoyable. Finally, passing a local bakery, they stopped to check out the delicious sweets on display in the window. Grabbing Nicky's hand Kate pulled him inside.

"Okay. Which one would you like?"

"Wow. That's a hard decision."

Not knowing the proper names for each pastry, Nicky pointed to a tart filled with raspberries. Kate quickly decided on the apple flan. After making their purchases, they continued their stroll along the cobblestone streets, enjoying their pastries. Taking in the sights and sounds of the magnificent city and its surroundings while enjoying each other's company, time seemed to slip away.

"Babe, I think we should make our way back to the hotel. We only have about an hour before the limo arrives. Bruce needs us there early this evening for photos again."

"Okay. This afternoon has been wonderful," Kate smiled, leaning over to kiss him. "Thank you."

"Oh Doll, no need to thank me. I've had a great afternoon as well."

Nicky took Kate's hand as they began the short walk back to the hotel. They had only walked a short distance when Nicky squeezed

Kate's hand as he looked over at her and asked, "Babe, do you know how much I love you?"

Kate smiled, giving him a quick kiss.

"Yes. Nicky, I know," Kate paused, captivated by his blue eyes. "I love you too. We better hurry. Aren't you the lead guitarist in some famous band that's about to go on stage in Frankfurt tonight?" she laughed.

"Oh, the concert," he grinned. Then, grabbing Kate's hand, they ran back toward the hotel.

Getting back to their room, they had just enough time to change before the limo arrived. Hearing a knock at the door, Kate walked over.

"Hey Jeff, come in. We're almost ready."

"Hey, man," Nicky said, walking out from the bedroom.

Looking at Kate, Jeff asked, "Did you guys have a good afternoon?"

"Oh yes, it was great. We walked downtown and spent the afternoon looking through the shops. It was fun."

Walking out to catch the elevator, Randy and Alex joined them.

"Hey guys, are you ready to play Frankfurt tonight?" Randy questioned.

"Yes. I just hope they're as hyped as the fans back in Paris," Nicky mentioned.

"That was a riot, especially with the girls trying to get on the stage," Jeff laughed.

Riding downtown to the sports arena, Nicky became excited just thinking about the concert. As the limo drove past the front of the expansive venue, the line of fans waiting to get in wrapped the entire length of the city block. A giant marquee with brightly lit lettering promoted the concert. It was bright enough to be seen blocks away. The limo proceeded around to the back entrance. Nicky took Kate's hand as they stepped out of the limo.

Walking into the sports complex, they entered a vast labyrinth of concrete tunnels with electrical and heating ducts running the entire length. It was quite a hike walking back to the dressing room. Once there, Kate opened the door. She had a lot of work to do. Entering the dressing room, Bruce was standing next to the catered food, pouring himself a cup of coffee.

"Hey, boys, glad to see you could make it tonight," Bruce teased with a smile. "You'll have just enough time for hair, makeup, and getting changed into your suits before the photo session with tonight's fans," he added.

"Okay. Who's first?" Kate asked as Randy ran over to take a chair.

"Alright. Randy, guess it's you then."

Opening her makeup bags which had arrived with the guy's suits, Kate was ready to get started with hair and makeup. Nicky went over to pick out his suit and tie. The dressing room had only one small changing area, so Nicky quickly grabbed his suit and went inside to change. It wasn't long before the boys were dressed and ready to meet their lucky fans.

"You've got just a few minutes. Better get a little something to snack on before the concert," Bruce suggested.

Opening a Becks and lighting a cigarette, Nicky sat down on a bright red velvet sofa.

"Hey Kate, if you see Mike and the guys, don't forget to let them know that we're on for tonight after the concert," Nicky mentioned.

"Okay." Taking a quick break, Kate came over and sat next to Nicky.

"Alright. Give me a sip of your beer," she laughed.

"You're funny, Kate. You bum drinks of beer, like the boys bum cigarettes from me."

"Okay, boys, let's go," Bruce announced.

"Babe, see you after the concert," Nicky smiled, giving Kate a quick kiss.

"Okay. I'll be waiting backstage."

Walking out, the boys went over to get photos with the few lucky fans who had won the radio station promotional. During the photo session, the noise from the fans filling the arena was overwhelming.

"We're sold out tonight," Bruce stated after the photos were taken."I think it's going to be a great concert, but I've got extra security down front tonight, just in case things get out of control."

The fans went wild with excitement as the guys walked out on stage. The sounds were deafening as Randy yelled as loud as possible, hoping to be heard.

"Good evening, Frankfurt."

"Frankfurt, are you ready for an evening of fun?" Alex screamed.

"We're thrilled to be here," Nicky shouted, raising his guitar high in the air.

In anticipation of the guys handing out roses, unruly fans charged the stage. Girls frantically pushed their way to the front, hoping to get a rose. Security was already in action, trying to avoid a small riot near the stage. It was sheer pandemonium as guys hoisted girls onto their shoulders and shoved their way to the front. Bruce immediately called for extra security to remove disruptive fans from the mosh pit.

Opening with their first song, Nicky watched as chaos ensued. However, despite the disruptive scenario erupting in the crowd, the guys continued the concert. It was always Bruce's call as to whether he would stop the concert or allow it to continue. Finally, after several minutes, it appeared security was able to remove the troublemakers, and the crowd began to calm down. At least to the normalcy expected at a rock concert. Nicky could only hope that Kate was safe and that she wasn't in the mosh pit.

Randy led into their next set of songs as Nicky fed off the fans' energy. The screams were deafening as the guys continued their usual tradition.

They began to loosen their ties and toss them out among the girls who scrambled to retrieve one. Nicky hesitated for the first time before deciding whether or not to choose anyone specific from the crowd. He was afraid he might be pulled down into the mob of fans before he could even reach down to wrap his tie around someone. However, these thoughts didn't last long, as the adrenalin rushing through his veins became intense. Finally, Nicky locked eyes with a young girl and proceeded with David's ritual. Thankfully, as he knelt, placing his tie gently around the girl's neck, it was a success. The fans applauded Nicky's efforts as they screamed, "Nicky, Nicky."

Walking back to take his place on stage, Nicky shouted.

"I love you too, Frankfurt."

Randy was not to be left out. Continuing the process of unbuttoning his shirt, he screamed.

"Are you ready to party tonight?"

The concert took on an ever more powerful moment as the band led into their next big hit, *Without You.* Again, the fans screamed the lyrics. The sports arena was rocking with the music of Black Tie Affair. Security was working feverishly to keep the crowd under control so that no one was accidentally trampled in the mosh pit.

Two girls were removed from the concert as they attempted to pull themselves onto the stage as the band opened with their next song.

Nicky was in his element as the guys performed song after song. His only thoughts were that one day, he would be upfront and center.

As the night progressed, the fans danced in the aisle, screaming out the lyrics to each song. It was pure magic, Nicky thought. He could feel the vibes and energy of rock and roll coursing through his body. Taking a quick look at Jeff, Nicky could tell from Jeff's expression that he, too, was utterly immersed in the music. When an artist connects with their fans in such a heightened state of energy, sharing a moment through their music is like nothing else on earth. Nicky always compared the energy radiating from the fans to how heroin feels to a drug addict. He couldn't get enough. The concert raved on for an hour and a half with no one ready to leave.

At the close of the gig, Nicky felt like he was just getting warmed up. The fans continued to scream and shout out the names of each band member as the guys walked off stage. Finally, however, the guys returned to the stage for an encore. They felt the fans deserved it for braving an unruly mob earlier in the evening. After giving their fans another ten minutes, the guys left the stage. Nicky was in an adrenaline rush after the concert. He felt as if he needed a tranquilizer to bring him down. Without a doubt, he was born to be a rock star.

Walking backstage, Nicky saw Kate with Todd and the boys.

"Damn. What was that about?" Todd smirked. "I've never seen fans get out of control that fast. Thank God for security."

"Oh man, I think it was better than Paris if that's possible," Nicky exclaimed.

"Hey Nicky, this is Michelle," Mike smiled.

"Hi. It's nice to meet you."

"You guys were phenomenal, but I'll have to admit. It did get a little crazy," Michelle laughed.

"Yes. But that's why Bruce only hires the best security," Nicky grinned.

"Well, are you ready to go eat? I saw Bruce backstage earlier, and I reminded him that we're all going out tonight. The limo is waiting to take us anywhere we want to go," Todd added.

"Yes. But first, I want to run back to the dressing room and change. We'll meet you at the back entrance in about ten minutes?"

"That sounds good, just hurry. The guys and I are starved after setting up the venue for tonight's concert."

Running back to the dressing room, Nicky found Bruce, Jeff, Alex, and Randy.

"Guys, I'm genuinely sorry about the concert tonight. That had to be a bit intimidating. Thank God we have well-trained security. Hell, I almost canceled the damn concert. Enjoy yourselves tonight. You've earned it. However, I'm going to turn in early. See you tomorrow," Bruce said, turning to leave.

"Oh, Bruce, Kate, and I are going out with Todd and the boys tonight."

"Yes. I remembered, plus I ran into Todd backstage. Have fun. I just met Michelle. I'm sure she's excited to show you guys Frankfurt," Bruce mentioned.

Quickly changing, Nicky, Kate, and Jeff sprinted down the concrete corridors and outside to the waiting limo. Stepping inside the car, it seemed the party had already started. The guys lit cigarettes as the limo quickly filled with smoke, and a bottle of Jack Daniels made its way around the car as the guys got an early start on their drinks.

"Hey Jeff, meet Michelle," Mike said.

"Nice to meet you," Jeff replied, opening a bottle of Becks.

"So, where are we going?" Nicky asked as he looked at Mike and lit up another smoke.

"Well, there's a great restaurant downtown in Frankfurt," Michelle recommended. "It's called the Heliopolis, and they serve the best Greek food ever," she stated.

"Okay. That sounds like a party to me."

Arriving downtown, Todd asked the driver to park and wait for them. The restaurant was crowded as they walked inside. But they were quickly ushered into a back room before anyone recognized them as band members of Black Tie Affair. As the maître d' came over to welcome them to the Heliopolis, he brought out small glasses of Ouzo which gave off a colorless smoke. Finally, everyone was seated as Mike stood to offer a toast for the evening.

"Here's to an unbelievable concert and my girl, Michelle."

"Here's to Frankfurt," Nicky added.

The night was off to a great start. As the menus were handed out, the guys asked for another round of the strong drink. However, before the food was served, the maître d', as requested, set small glasses of Ouzo on the table.

"Well, it looks like tonight is turning into quite the party," Todd grinned. "Okay guys, oops and girls, here's to a hell of a night in Frankfurt."

Nicky glanced at Kate, who appeared to be having no problem downing the second small glass of the strong alcohol.

"Hey Babe, that's pretty powerful stuff. Are you sure about finishing that?"

"Oh, don't worry, I'm not driving tonight," she said, laughing. "After our perfect afternoon and the concert, which was a bit overwhelming, I think its cause for celebration."

"Okay, Babe, I guess I know where you live," Nicky grinned, leaning over to give Kate a quick kiss to the forehead.

As the meals were brought out, more drinks were ordered by the guys.

"Hey Pete, haven't seen you in a while," Nicky smiled, walking to the end of the table where Pete and John were sitting.

"Hey Nick, that was one hell of a concert," John commented, lighting a cigarette.

"Yes. You guys were in fine form tonight," Pete smiled, bumming a cigarette from John.

"So, how's life treating you these days as the lead guitarist?" Pete questioned.

"All I can say is that it's been unreal getting to perform on stage."

"Well, there's no doubt about it, kid. After watching you tonight and back in Paris, I'd say you were born to do just what you're doing," Pete smiled, lifting his glass to Nicky.

"Congratulations. You're doing one hell of a job, kid."

"Thanks. It's awesome to be with you guys tonight," Nicky replied, walking back to his seat next to Kate.

"Hey Nicky, Michelle and I were wondering if you and Kate might want to hang back for one extra day after the concert is finished and stay with us for a night? Randy and Alex are flying to Rome this weekend, and there's a couple down days between the venues."

"Yes. That sounds like fun," Nicky said, staring at Kate, who now appeared to be getting tipsy. The Ouzo was beginning to affect her.

"Babe, how are you doing?"

"Oh, I'm having a great time," Kate laughed.

"Okay. I'm just checking to make sure you're alright."

The night was getting off to a fun start in more ways than one, as the guys decided after finishing their meals to move the party to another popular nightspot.

"Guys, Michelle knows this great little club, where we can all go and kick back for a while. It's a karaoke bar. How does that sound?" Mike asked, standing so that everyone could hear.

"Yes. We're all on board," Pete replied loudly.

After paying their tab and consuming one last round of Ouzo, the guys moved the party farther downtown to the karaoke bar. As the limo pulled in front of the bar, Nicky helped Kate out of the car. She was now most definitely under the spell of the Ouzo. Walking in, they found empty seats in a dark, secluded corner. The boys passed around a pack of cigarettes and a lighter as each one lit a smoke.

"Man, this is like old times," Mike confessed. "It's good having you out with us tonight."

"Yes, I've missed you guys," Nicky admitted.

As the boys placed their drink orders, Nicky looked at Kate, lying her head on his shoulder. The karaoke bar was filled with locals who seemed to have the time of their lives as they attempted to sing their favorite songs.

Unexpectedly, one young couple got up and tried to perform their favorite song, *Without You*, which just happened to be one of the band's number one hits. Nicky, Mike, and the boys almost fell out of their chairs with laughter. Little did the couple know that band members were in the smoke-filled bar tonight.

"Good thing it's dark in here, and we're sitting in the corner," John laughed hysterically.

"Well, if you don't stop laughing so hard, you're going to give us away," Pete whispered.

"Bruce sure doesn't need us to be the cause of a small riot in this bar tonight," Todd added.

The boys ordered another round of drinks, watching those brave enough to attempt singing.

"Okay, Mike, let's give it a try?" Michelle prodded.

"What are you crazy," Mike choked on his drink.

"No. We're out to have fun, and I love this place. So you're going to sing with me, right?"

"Yeah, Mike, go sing with your girl," Todd urged, laughing.

Nicky roared with laughter at the thought of Mike singing.

"Oh hell. Okay, but just one song, and I'll need another drink first."

It wasn't long before Mike and Michelle walked up to the small stage. Watching as they approached the microphone, John and Todd whistled loudly. Nicky and Jeff tried not to laugh as they sang a song by the Righteous Brothers.

Actually, the joke was on Nicky and the guys. As they began to sing, *You've Lost That Loving Feeling*, Mike and Michelle received a huge round of applause from the people in the bar.

"Damn," Nicky grinned as Mike and Michelle walked back to their seats. "I should let Bruce know. You guys are great," he laughed.

"Well, I wouldn't quit my day job if I were you, Mike," Todd smiled.

As the night progressed, everyone was having a great time. The guys ordered a round of Becks, and another pack of cigarettes found its way around the table. However, Kate was out by this point.

"Wow. It looks like poor Kate isn't going to remember a thing," Mike said.

"Probably, but she really likes you," Michelle mentioned looking at Nicky.

"Yes. I guess becoming the lead guitarist led me to Kate. She couldn't have come into my life at a better time. I've fallen in love with this sleepyhead," Nicky grinned, kissing Kate once again on the forehead.

After another round of beers and more smokes, the guys were finally ready to call it a night.

"Nicky, talk it over with Kate tomorrow and let us know if you both would like to stay with us for a night. Michelle would love to show you her hometown," Mike proposed as they all got up to leave.

"Okay. That sounds good."

After a few minutes, Nicky revived Kate just enough to walk out to the limo with his help. During the ride back to the hotel, the atmosphere was relatively subdued. The guys were falling asleep.

"Okay. Guess this is our stop. It was a great evening," Nicky said as he helped Kate out of the limo. "See you guys tomorrow."

Walking into the elevator, Jeff helped Nicky get Kate inside their suite.

"Thanks, Jeff. See you tomorrow."

"No problem."

As Nicky walked Kate into the bedroom, she began to wake from her stupor.

"Hey Doll, how are you feeling? I think you probably shouldn't have had the second glass of Ouzo," Nicky hinted.

"Oh, I've got a slight headache."

"Well, just rest. I'll get you a glass of water."

Coming out of the bathroom with a glass of water, he found Kate had fallen asleep. Walking over to the bed, he removed her shoes and covered her with a blanket, not bothering to wake her. Slipping into bed next to her, it didn't take Nicky long to fall asleep. It had been a long day and even a longer evening. Nicky was physically exhausted.

The light filtering in the following day woke Kate. Nicky was still asleep. How could she ever repay him for taking such good care of her? It was pretty evident that he did love her. Quietly getting out of bed so as not to wake him, Kate walked into the other room and called for room service. Next, she decided to order breakfast and take a tray to him. After a short time, breakfast arrived, hearing a knock at the door. Kate grabbed the breakfast tray and quietly walked back into the bedroom.

"Good morning Babe, are you hungry?" Kate asked, gently waking him.

"Something smells delicious," Nicky smiled, opening his eyes.

"Doll, really, you've already cooked breakfast this morning?" he teased, kissing her.

Getting back into bed next to him, they enjoyed breakfast as leisurely as two people could. Now, this was living, Nicky thought. After eating, he sat the tray on the bedside table.

"Thank you."

"No. Thank you," Kate said. "Thank you for taking such good care of me last night."

"Oh Babe, I'll always have your back even when you decide to drink a little too much Ouzo," he laughed.

One thing led to another as they sat in bed talking. Before they knew it, another morning had been spent passionately in bed as only young lovers would.

"Well, Doll, it's almost 1:00 p.m. Is there anything special you would like to do today before the concert?"

"No. I'm right where I want to be. So, let's just stay in today and order room service."

"Okay. If that's what you really want," Nicky winked, kissing her.

"Oh, Mike wanted to know if we would like to stay with them after the concert ends. Michelle said she would love to show us around Frankfurt. It's her hometown."

"Yes. That sounds like fun. Do you think Bruce would mind?"

"No. In fact, there are a couple of down days in between the next venue in Rome. Bruce said he was also staying behind for another day to take care of some business. I think Randy and Alex plan to take one of the private jets and fly to Rome early. They've made it quite clear they're not going to spend their free time in Frankfurt."

"Well, what about Jeff? Is he going to stay in Frankfurt or fly down early with the boys?"

"Oh, I'm sure he'll stay here. Who knows he might hang out with Bruce?"

The next concert in Frankfurt was completely sold out, as Black Tie Affair finished their dates at the venue. Nicky and Kate were excited to stay with Mike and Michelle. Kate wanted to shop in Frankfurt and visit Germany's beautiful Mosel wine region. Michelle would be the perfect tour guide being as Frankfurt was her hometown.

After Randy and Alex had made it quite clear they didn't intend to spend one more day in Frankfurt, Bruce allowed them to take one of the private jets along with their latest arm candy to Rome. Bruce knew that Jeff wouldn't want to fly to Rome any earlier with Randy and Alex, so he asked him to tag along on his routine appointments. He owed Jeff some quality time.

Bruce and Jeff remained in Frankfurt for another day as well. All in all, Frankfurt had turned out to be the best venue so far in Europe Nicky felt the energy from the fans in Frankfurt had far exceeded Paris. Finally, all the band members of Black Tie Affair were ready to enjoy a day of respite.

CHAPTER TEN

A Twist of Fate

"Okay, Doll, do you have everything packed? It's almost 8:00 a.m. The limo will be here in about thirty minutes," Nicky said, hurrying to clear their things out of the hotel suite.

They were both anxious to see the apartment Mike shared with his girlfriend, Michelle. They decided to get up early today to fit in some sightseeing with them. There would be no concert scheduled for this evening, allowing them some time with their friends.

The final concert in Frankfurt had been held the night before in front of another sold out crowd. As a result, the entire band had a day off from their scheduled performances. Everyone had decided to stay in Frankfurt, except for Randy and Alex. They were determined to spend their extra day in Rome with their new girls. Being on good terms with them, Bruce graciously agreed to lend them one of their corporate jets to facilitate their romantic rendezvous in Rome.

"Hey Babe, the concierge just called the room and said the limo is downstairs waiting," Nicky urged.

"Alright, I'm almost done packing."

Entering the elevator, they were finally ready to leave the hotel.

"Hope you've got everything?"

"Yes. I thoroughly checked both rooms. I'm sure we have everything."

Nicky was looking forward to spending time with Kate without a nightly concert intervening.

"You look great today," Nicky smiled, leaning over to kiss Kate in the back of the limo.

Driving downtown, the billboards advertising the previous concerts were still in place. Looking over at one of them, Nicky commented.

"Man, Frankfurt has the greatest fans. There's no doubt we are loved here."

"You have a huge fan base, and they love you. Who wouldn't want to see Black Tie Affair's new lead guitarist," Kate laughed. "Of course, I may be a little prejudiced," she teased, hugging him.

It only took a few minutes before the limo pulled up to the entrance of the high rise where Mike and Michelle lived. Setting the luggage in the foyer next to the elevator, Nicky used the lobby phone to call their apartment.

"Hey, we're here," Nicky said as Mike answered the phone.

"Come on up. Do you have a lot of luggage?"

"Just a couple bags, but they're manageable. We'll be up in a few minutes."

"Okay. I'll let Michelle know you're here."

Putting their luggage into the elevator, they pushed the button to the fifth floor. Getting out, Nicky managed to get everything over to the door.

"Hey guys, it's so good to see you. Come inside. Michelle is in the kitchen. She'll be right out."

"Oh, your apartment is beautiful," Kate commented, looking around. A large balcony sat off the living room. The views were amazing as Kate walked over for a closer inspection. The apartment faced one of the most beautiful streets in Frankfurt, Berger Strasse. The busy street reflected bars, restaurants, and the hustle of people below as they went about their everyday routines, shopping in the many stores which lined the Strasse. Traffic and electric trolleys added character to the narrow streets.

"Wow. The view is gorgeous. It's like looking at a modern-day painting of downtown Frankfurt. Everything is centrally located," Kate added.

"Hey Kate, welcome to our home," Michelle smiled, walking out from the kitchen with a warm plate of apple flan. "Come. I'll show you the rest of the apartment," she mentioned sitting down the dessert on the coffee table.As Kate walked into the kitchen, a large window overlooked a city park behind their building. The park was green and lush, with an overabundance of tall trees surrounding it. Kids below played on a merry-go-round and swings. The sounds of laughter and dogs barking was heart-warming and gave you a sense of family.

"Bet you never get tired of such a view."

"Not at all. I spend a lot of time in the kitchen, and I enjoy the sounds coming from the park."

The kitchen was modern, with stainless appliances offering every amenity needed to prepare a delicious meal. Walking Kate into the bedroom, it had a wall of windows on one side which also came with amazing views of the city. There was another bedroom across the hall, which mirrored the other room.

"Wow. I'm sure you never get bored living here, and with the convenience of being right downtown, it offers you so much."

"Yes. Mike and I love it here, and with him being away so much with the band, it helps keep me busy. So let's go back to the living room, and I'll get coffee for everyone," Michelle smiled.

"Nicky, I think we need an apartment in this building. I just love it here."

"Well, Doll, maybe one day, but right now, I see a lot of travel in our future," he said, walking over to put his arm around her.

"Nicky, let me have your luggage. I'll take it into the spare bedroom. Please, both of you, have a seat. Michelle has made an apple flan, and I think she's in the kitchen getting coffee for everyone,"

Mike said as he carried their luggage into the guest bedroom. Nicky lit a cigarette as he sat down next to Kate.

"So, how long have you and Michelle been together?" Nicky asked.

"We've been together almost seven years. We met at a Black Tie Affair concert here in Frankfurt. Best venue I ever helped to set up," Mike smiled.

Michelle handed them each a cup of coffee and sat down next to Mike.

"Oh, is Mike telling you the story of how we met? I won a radio contest and got free tickets to the concert and a photo with the band. I had gone backstage with the other winners, but somehow I managed to get lost. You know how it is back there, just a concrete jungle of long narrow hallways. Anyway, to make a long story short, Mike found me wandering aimlessly and gave me directions to rejoin my group. It was love at first sight, wasn't that right?" Michelle teased.

"Yes. Sweetheart, you're right. Your gorgeous red hair got my attention, and I wasn't about to lose track of you," Mike winked, hugging her.

"Nicky, I almost forgot. Why didn't Jeff come over with you?"

"Well, he decided to hang out in Frankfurt with his Uncle Bruce for a while. I think Bruce had some business he needed to take care of, and I think he also feels like he's ignoring Jeff," Nicky added.

"He certainly doesn't give Jeff any special treatment, considering that Jeff's his nephew."

"Are Randy and Alex leaving today for Rome with the two girls from the concert last night?" Mike inquired.

"Yes, I think they left earlier this morning. Bruce allowed them to take one of the private jets. He's too easy on those two. Bruce called David on the carpet and sent him off to rehab, and I know those guys smoke pot," Nicky remarked, sipping his coffee.

"Okay. Enough talk about the band and work," Michelle interrupted, glancing at Mike. "I've got a lot of places that I want to show you in Frankfurt. Also, I want to take you to the Rhine River and show you the wine country."

"Oh, that sounds wonderful. I would also love to visit the Mosel River if that's okay," Kate asked.

"Alright. I guess we better be going. We have a long day ahead."

Just as they were about to leave, the phone rang.

"Excuse me for a moment while I answer this," Mike said, walking over to the phone. Hearing Bruce's voice on the other end, Mike seemed baffled.

"Hey, Bruce, what's up?"

"Mike, are Nicky and Kate with you?"

"Yes. Do you need to speak with them?"

"Well, not exactly. Hell, I don't even know how to say this, but I've just received a call informing me the boys' plane never arrived in Rome."

"What? What are you saying?" Mike questioned, totally confused.

"I know this is upsetting. But, Mike, I can't believe it? It appears their plane went down.

"Bruce, are you sure? How do you know?"

"Well, their plane never arrived. From the details I've gathered from the airport in Rome, they determined it disappeared off their radar screen somewhere over the Apennine Mountains," Bruce explained.

"Oh Bruce, this is unbelievable. Are you sure?"

"Yes, as much as anyone can be at this time. Mike, I don't know what your plans were for today, but I'll need you and Nicky to standby until I get all the details."

"Yes. Bruce, whatever you need us to do. We'll be at the apartment, and you can reach us at any time. We'll wait to hear from you. One thing before we hang up, I sure hope you're wrong, and this has been a huge misunderstanding."

"Alright, Son, please let Nicky and Kate know. I've got more phone calls to make. I'll be back in touch as soon as I have more details about what happened."

"Okay, Bruce, I'll let them know. Talk with you soon and please don't worry. I think this is all just a matter of some miscommunications."

Hanging up the phone, Mike just fell on the couch, holding his head in his hands.

"What's going on?" Michelle asked.

"Was that Bruce on the phone?" Nicky interrupted.

"I don't know how to say this. I really don't," Mike stated

"What is it, Mike, spit it out?" Nicky demanded.

"The boys' plane never made it to Rome today."

"So what does that mean? Are you saying their plane went down somewhere?"

"Yes. It's hard to believe, but that's what Bruce said on the phone."

Kate started screaming.

"No. No. Randy and Alex were on that plane. Do you hear me? Do you hear me, Nicky?" she pleaded as she fell into Nicky's arms, crying.

Nicky leaned back into the sofa, holding Kate in his arms. She was almost inconsolable.

"Mike, are you sure you heard Bruce correctly?" Nicky asked in disbelief.

"Yes, Nicky, Bruce was pretty specific."

"This doesn't make any sense. How could this have happened?"

Michelle walked back into the kitchen to put on another pot of coffee.

"Kate, sweetheart, everything is going to be alright. I'm sure of it. Bruce will probably call back in a few minutes and tell us it was all just a horrible misunderstanding. But, Babe, do you understand what I'm telling you?"

"Oh, Nicky, I loved those guys. Randy and Alex were the brothers I never had," Kate sobbed, burying her head into Nicky's chest as he held her tight.

"I know. Sweetheart, I know," he whispered into her ear.

"Mike, would it be alright if I took Kate into the guest room and made her more comfortable?"

"Sure, man. Do whatever you think will help."

Michelle walked back in with more coffee.

"Mike, do you honestly believe the boys are gone?" Michelle questioned, handing him another cup of coffee.

"Well, I'm not sure. But Bruce seems to be convinced. Why don't you see if you can help with Kate. Maybe take her some warm towels for her face and a glass of water."

"Sure. Whatever I can do to ease Kate's worries," Michelle agreed.

"I need to call Todd." Picking up the phone, Mike dialed his number.

"Hey Todd, this is Mike. Have you heard the news?"

"Yes. I just got off the phone with Bruce. Can you even believe this?"

"Well, maybe it's just a huge mistake."

"I don't think so, Mike. I'm afraid Bruce seems pretty sure of it."

"How is Kate taking the news? Bruce said they were at your apartment?"

"Not very well, Nicky has taken her into the guest bedroom to lie down, and Michelle is getting her some warm towels and water right now."

"Is there anything I can do?"

"No. We're just waiting on another call from Bruce with more details."

"Well, the guys and I are still here in our hotel in Frankfurt, so guess we'll stay in touch. Before I hang up, how did Nicky take the news?"

"To tell you the truth, I think he's in a state of shock," Mike answered.

"Well, it looks like you and Michelle are going to have your hands full. If you need me or any of us, just call our hotel."

"Will do, man. Take care and talk with you soon."

Hanging up the phone, Mike went to check on Kate. Knocking on the bedroom door, Nicky quickly answered.

"Is there any news yet?"

"No. But try not to worry. How's Kate?"

"She's not taking the news very well. It's going to be really hard for Kate. She was an only child, and the boys had become her surrogate brothers. So Kate was close to them, even though sometimes you wouldn't know by the way they argued."

"Oh, believe me, all of us on the sound crew, hell anyone involved with the band knew that Kate loved those two like they were family. Michelle is getting some warm towels for her and a glass of water. If there's anything we can do to help, just ask. I'll be here waiting for Bruce to call back.

If you need anything, just let us know?" Mike replied sympathetically.

"Thanks, man, sorry all of this had to happen today."

"Yeah, aren't we all," Mike said, closing the door as he walked back into the living room.

Michelle brought in the warm towels and a glass of water. Sitting down on the bed next to Kate, Nicky wiped Kate's face.

"Babe, it's going to be alright. I'm here for you. Michelle is here if you need her. But, please, Kate, you've got to be strong. We're still waiting for Bruce to call."

Pulling her to his chest, Nicky kissed away her tears.

"Nicky, how could I ever get through this without you," she sobbed.

"Is there anything else I can do to help?" Michelle asked.

"I don't think so, but thanks for the warm towels and water."

"Okay. I'm going back to the living room to sit with Mike. If either of you needs anything at all, just let me know?"

"Thanks."

Nicky laid down next to Kate and held her tightly, allowing her to cry herself to sleep. Then, hearing the phone ring, Nicky jumped up and ran back into the living room, leaving Kate asleep on the bed. He could overhear from the other room that Mike was on the phone with Bruce.

"Mike, I just wanted to call. It's officially confirmed. The boys' plane crashed, and there were no survivors. I'm sorry. Please let Nicky and Kate know it's been confirmed."

"I'm sorry. Bruce, I'll let everyone know. So what's going to happen next?"

"Well, Son, I'm going to have to call and inform their parents. God, Mike, I hate doing this. I've never had to make a call like this before. I just need everyone to stay put for the moment. I have a lot of things to get done in a short time. First, I've got to cancel the venue in Rome. Then, I'll get Nicky and Kate a reservation back at the hotel starting tomorrow evening. Please let Nicky know that I'll be in touch tomorrow."

"Okay, Bruce, just hang in there. We're all here for you. Whatever you need us to do, just call?"

"Okay, thanks, Son."

Mike glanced at Nicky.

"Well, it's official. The plane went down, killing all on board," Mike said nervously, lighting a cigarette.

"I need a drink," Nicky replied, with trembling hands as he lit a cigarette.

Mike walked into the kitchen to find the strongest drink in his apartment.

"Looks like it's going to be Becks, that's all I have," he said, handing Nicky a beer.

"Oh, that works for me, at least for right now. But tomorrow, after I've thought about this all night, I'm going to need something a lot stronger."

"Oh, I hear you."

So I know this may sound presumptuous, but since Kate isn't in the room right now, what do you think Bruce is going to do with the band?" Nicky questioned, taking a huge sip of beer.

"Well, Bruce is a fighter, and believe me when I say this, Bruce is not going down because of the regrettable loss of Randy and Alex today. Bruce will bring the band back in true form. Just give him a few days or weeks to regroup, and trust me, Black Tie Affair will finish their world tour. This band has had sold out venues for months. You saw how the fans responded to you last night. Damn, I still can't believe they're gone. Bruce still has Jeff, and he's the best in the business, and Nicky, you are literally his ace in this unfortunate mishap. So don't worry and don't underestimate Bruce. He'll keep the show on the road. Do you even know how much money Black Tie Affair brings in with each concert? Well, I can tell you, Bruce is still holding a winning hand with you and Jeff. He only needs to pick up two additional guitarists, and he's back in business. Nicky, you always said you wouldn't stop until you were the lead vocalist and guitarist with a huge rock band. Well, I think that door just opened," Mike stated, staring straight at Nicky. "What do you think about that prediction? I think fate just dealt you a winning hand as well as Bruce," Mike added, trying to smile.

"Wow. I don't know how to respond to all of that, except I can honestly say if Bruce should offer me the lead vocalist position with the band, I sure wouldn't turn it down. Bruce has been good to me, and it's only because of him that I've even been given this opportunity. Hell, I've dreamed of this my entire life, but I never imagined it would come at such a high cost. So I honestly don't know what to think right now," Nicky said with his head in his hands.

"Nicky, I think you've just gotten a promotion. As unfortunate as this tragedy was, it was out of our control, and you should be thanking God that you and Kate weren't on that flight. But right now, you just need to focus on taking care of Kate."

"How do you think Jeff handled the news?"

"Well, Jeff wasn't exactly close to Randy and Alex, or he would have been on his way to Rome with them. I suppose that fact saved his life today. I'm sure he hated to hear the news, but he's with Bruce, and believe me, Bruce does take care of that boy. So Jeff has nothing to worry about."

"I think I'll check on Kate," Nicky mentioned, getting up from the sofa.

Walking over, Mike placed his hand on Nicky's shoulder. "She'll pull through this with your help. If she wasn't made of a strong constitution, there's no way she could travel with us all over the world."

Walking back into the bedroom, he could hear Kate softly crying under the blanket.

"Hey Doll, how are you doing?"

"Oh, Nicky, I think I'm going to be sick."

"Please just take some deep breaths and try not to think about what has happened. You're going to be fine. I'm here, and I'm not about to let anything happen to you. Do you understand? I took care of you the other night, didn't I?"

"Yes," Kate said, wiping her eyes.

"Okay. Then trust me. We're going to get through this together. You're not alone."

"Nicky, are they really gone?"

"Yes, Babe, Bruce called, and it's been officially confirmed, their plane went down, and everyone on board was killed instantly."

"Nicky, I can't do this. I can't," Kate cried. "They were my brothers. You don't understand. I loved them, even though they weren't perfect."

Where had he heard those words before? For a brief moment, his thoughts took him back to Jenna when she had uttered those exact words to him before he left Middleton. Then, tears began to flow down Nicky's face. Life was hard, and no matter how much you loved someone, there would be times when there would be no words to say.

"Babe, I love you. Please just hang on to that," Nicky whispered, pulling Kate into his arms. "Things will get better. The best is yet to come, I promise."

Hearing the phone ring, Mike went to answer it.

"Hey Bruce, is there any news?" Mike asked.

"No. But Mike, please let Nicky know that his parents just called my office in Frankfurt, and I informed them their son was safe and not onboard the jet which crashed today. Also, please let Kate and everyone know we are in the process of calling all the families back in the states and updating them on the incident."

The crash was later determined to be a mechanical failure, not the pilot's. Bruce flew back to the states with Jeff, Nicky, Kate, and the crew to attend the memorial services for Randy and Alex. It was a quick trip with Bruce's hectic schedule, and they were back in Frankfurt within three days. It was indeed one of the most challenging weeks of Bruce's life. It was hard to say goodbye.

The following week seemed to be a haze of confusion as everyone connected with Black Tie Affair tried in their own way to deal with the loss of Randy and Alex. The other band members remained in Frankfurt while Bruce worked through the logistics of replacing Randy and Alex and rescheduled the upcoming venues.

Mike had been right. Bruce announced the fact that he was replacing Randy with Nicky. Nicky now found himself the lead vocalist with Black Tie Affair through another twist of fate. According to Bruce, *the show must go on.*

CHAPTER ELEVEN

The week of the plane crash.
Quebec

Jenna had just made a peanut butter and jelly sandwich and poured a tall glass of milk as she walked into the living room and turned on the television. She had hardly taken her first bite when the news of the plane crash carrying the band members of Black Tie Affair broke through the airwaves about 6:00 p.m. *"All on board were killed instantly as the private jet carrying members of the rock band, Black Tie Affair, went down north of Rome,"* the newscaster announced. Once again, the newscaster repeated the news bulletin, which was now being aired on the news channels.

Jenna instantly got up from the sofa, dropping her glass of milk, having it spill all over the carpet. Jenna simply froze as the words, *'killing all onboard'* played through her mind like a broken record. Then, finally, Jenna screamed so loud that her parents thought something terrible had happened.

"Jenna, for heaven's sake, what's the matter with you?" Audrey yelled, running into the living room

"Oh Mom, Mom, Nicky is dead. He's been killed in a plane crash," Jenna screamed.

"What the hell is going on in here?" Frank demanded, running into the living room.

"Dad, Nicky's dead. He's been killed in a plane crash."

It took a moment for Frank to realize what Jenna had said. It wasn't exactly bad news, he thought. He had never been fond of Nicky Spade.

"Jenna, get a hold of yourself. What's the matter with you? How do you know this?" Frank exclaimed.

"Oh, Dad, it just came on the television as a news bulletin. Dad, the band members were all killed in a plane crash. They were on their way to Rome where the band was scheduled to perform."

"Jenna, sit down and relax. That boy is out of your life. He doesn't mean anything to us now," Frank insisted.

As soon as he had uttered the words, he knew he had said the wrong thing.

"Dad, what are you saying? I'm carrying his baby, your grandchild, and you're telling me he's no longer a part of my life. How dare you," Jenna screamed uncontrollably.

Jenna had to get out of the house. She bolted for the door with no thought of where she was going.

"Jenna, come back. Think about the baby. What are you doing?" Audrey shouted, racing after her daughter.

Jenna had to get out of her father's house. She was going insane and felt like dying, not giving any thought to her unborn child. Jenna walked down the street as fast as possible, given she was eight months pregnant. Then with no idea where she was going, she suddenly panicked, feeling the amniotic fluid drain from her body.

"Jenna, Jenna, wait. What are you doing?" Audrey yelled, catching up with her.

"Mom, I think my water just broke," Jenna cried.

"Jenna, you're not quite eight months along. What have you done? Why did you do this?"

"Oh, Mom, what am I going to do?"

"Well, we've got to get you to the hospital. Let me help you back to the house. Jenna, I can't believe you would do this to yourself and jeopardize the baby. How could you do this?"

"Mom, I wasn't going to stay for one second longer and listen to Dad telling me that Nicky was no longer a part of my life when I'm carrying his child."

"Jenna, calm down. Your dad was just angry and said the wrong things without thinking."

"Then I guess we can thank him for whatever happens. He's to blame for this."

"We're not going to blame anyone. We've got to get you back to the house and the hospital."

Helping Jenna walk home, Audrey ran inside the house screaming for Frank.

"Frank, Frank, we've got to get Jenna to the hospital. Her water just broke."

"Oh hell, what else is going to happen? Can't a man just watch a baseball game in peace anymore?" he screamed back.

"Frank, how dare you? Have you lost your mind? Your daughter is about to have a baby, your grandchild, and your only thoughts are about a ball game? That does it. Jenna and I don't need your help. I'm driving her to the hospital right now with or without you. It's your choice." Audrey yelled.

With Frank refusing to go to the hospital with his daughter, Audrey quickly put Jenna in the car and drove her to the emergency room. She hadn't even packed a suitcase for the hospital, thinking she had plenty of time.

"Mom, what am I going to do?"

"Jenna, what are you talking about?"

"The baby's room, we haven't gotten a crib yet or set up a nursery."

"Sweetheart, that will all have to come later. Right now, we have to get you to the hospital. The baby is coming with or without a nursery. Jenna, are you starting to have any contractions yet?"

"Some. But I can feel the baby moving."

"Well, I think that's a good sign. We're almost at the hospital, just try to relax and don't worry about anything."

Arriving at the emergency room entrance, Audrey quickly ran inside to get a wheelchair. She stopped the first nurse she saw.

"I need help. My daughter is in the car. Her water just broke, and she's not full term."

"Okay. I'll be right with you," the young nurse said, grabbing the nearest wheelchair.

Hurriedly placing Jenna in a cubicle, the emergency room doctor came in immediately to evaluate Jenna's condition. Determining that her water had broken and Jenna was experiencing contractions, she was admitted.

"We need you to fill out these forms, mainly for insurance," the receptionist explained. "After you complete these forms, the nurse will come down and take your daughter up to Labor and Delivery."

"Can you please hurry?" Audrey begged.

"Do you have health coverage? The receptionist asked, looking at Jenna.

"Yes," Jenna answered.

Jenna was visibly shaking. Hospitals made her nervous, and even though she knew what to expect, she wasn't prepared. She only wished that Nicky was standing by her side. He always seemed to calm her worst fears, and now he was gone forever. Jenna began crying inconsolably.

"Miss, are you alright?"

"She just received tragic news. The baby's father died earlier today in a plane crash," Audrey said, trying to keep her emotions in check.

"I'm truly sorry," the receptionist said compassionately. "It won't be long, and someone will be coming to take you up to your room."

Immediately, Jenna saw a nurse walking toward them.

"Are you Jenna Jones?"

"Yes."

"Hi, I'm Bethany, and I work in Labor and Delivery. I will be taking care of you this evening until my shift ends around 6:00 a.m.

I have a room ready for you upstairs. Is this your mother?" Bethany asked.

"Yes," Jenna said, trying to wipe the tears from her face.

She pushed Jenna's wheelchair toward the elevator.

"Okay. I'm ready to take you upstairs. Just follow me," Bethany said, looking over at Audrey.

Pushing Jenna's wheelchair into the elevator, it wasn't long before they reached Labor and Delivery, which was on the hospital's third floor.

"You're in room, one sixteen," the nurse stated. "Please put on the hospital gown, and I'll be right back to get your vital signs and listen for the baby's heartbeat."

The room was pleasant with pink striped wallpaper. An incubator and rocking chair were off to one corner.

"Mom, I'm scared," Jenna whispered, softly crying.

"Jenna, it's going to be alright. Everything is going to be fine. However, I need you to concentrate on having a healthy baby and no more thoughts of Nicky. This baby needs you now more than ever, and unfortunately, there's nothing you can ever do for Nicky."

Walking back into the room, the nurse came over to Jenna's bed. She smiled after checking her blood pressure and listening to the baby's heart rate.

"The baby's heart rate looks good, and your blood pressure is good. However, because your water has broken and you're experiencing mild cramping, it appears you may be in the early stages of labor. So, I'm going to start an IV drip. I know a lot of this may seem scary, but we'll be keeping a close watch on you. Try to relax. I'm attaching the fetal monitors. So we'll be able to monitor the baby closely. Would you like to hear the baby's heartbeat?" she asked, putting the stethoscope up to Jenna's ear so that she could hear the sound of the baby's heartbeat. "Maybe it will help to ease your fears about the baby."

"Everything looks great. I'll be in and out to check your progress. I know the baby is early, but we're equipped to handle preemies at this hospital. We have one of the largest neonatal units in the immediate area, and you're fortunate to be here. If you have any questions or need anything, there's a call button on the side of your bed. You can also have your mother come out and get me or one of the other nurses who work on this floor."

"Okay. Thank you," Jenna replied

"Oh, one more thing," Bethany added, "Please don't get out of bed by yourself. If you need to use the bathroom, push the call button, and I will come in, or someone from Labor and Delivery will come and help you."

"Try to rest."

Looking at the clock on the wall, it was almost 7:00 p.m.

"Mom, how long do you think I will be here before the baby is born?"

"I have no idea, Jenna. Every baby is different. I think you are in the very early stages of labor, and like the nurse said, first babies can sometimes take their time. Your body has never done this before, so it depends upon many things. So just try and relax. I'm not a nurse, so I don't have all the answers. But, I'm not leaving you, so don't worry."

"Mom, if you want to go down and get some coffee from the cafeteria, please go ahead. I feel okay right now, and it's probably going to be a long night."

"Maybe in a little while, I might go down and call your dad and get something to drink. I'm fine for now."

Sitting down in one of the chairs in the room, Audrey picked up a magazine that had been left.

"Jenna, do you want to read a magazine?"

"No thanks, Mom, not right now."

"Well, then just try and get some sleep if you can, sweetheart."

It seemed like forever before Bethany came in to check on Jenna's progress.

"How are you feeling? Have you felt any contractions yet?" Bethany asked.

"No, only mild cramping."

"Well, the baby's heart rate still looks good, so it's just a matter of waiting to see how things progress. So I'll be back in a little while," Bethany said, walking out of the room.

"Mom, do you think Dad is going to come to the hospital tonight?"

"I don't know Jenna, but I'm going down to the cafeteria for a cup of coffee. I'll call him from the phone downstairs. I don't see one anywhere in your room."

Audrey went downstairs and called Frank. However, he wasn't the least bit interested in coming to see his daughter.

"Frank, what's wrong with you? Jenna is asking about you."

"Well, just tell her that I don't like hospitals. Besides, there's nothing I can do. I'll come over tomorrow after the baby is born."

"Okay, whatever, Frank, you're sure disappointing me. It's our first grandchild, and you're not concerned about Jenna or the baby?"

"Audrey, you know I watched my mother die a horrible death in that hospital two years ago, and you think I can walk back in there that easy? I love Jenna, but I have a phobia of hospitals and doctors. So just tell her that I love her and that I will try to come over tomorrow."

"Alright, Frank, but I'm expecting you to pay her a visit tomorrow."

"Fine, I'll be there," he answered, hanging up the phone.

Audrey knew that Frank could be difficult at best. She knew that he detested hospitals and that his mother had met a tragic end due to kidney failure in that same place. Trying to focus solely on the thoughts of becoming a grandmother, Audrey managed to smile. She went into the cafeteria and purchased a cup of coffee. Wow, a grandmother, Audrey thought. She didn't feel old enough to have grandchildren. She wondered if other women experienced these same feelings. She was anxious to get back upstairs to Jenna's room and see her beautiful daughter.

Walking into Jenna's room, a nurse stood over her hospital bed, and a doctor was being paged.

"Oh my God, what's happening? I only went downstairs for a few minutes."

"I need you to please leave the room. Someone will talk with you out in the hallway," the nurse demanded.

"But that's my daughter," Audrey stated.

As one of the nurses came out of Jenna's room, Audrey cornered her.

"Please, what's happening?" she begged.

"Well, the baby's heart rate has dropped significantly for some reason, and we've had no luck in getting it back within a normal range. So we're prepping your daughter for a C-Section. You know the baby is early, and complications can happen. Please don't worry. We need to deliver the baby quickly to give it the best possible chance of survival. There's a waiting room at the end of the hall. You can wait there. Someone will come in and keep you informed."

Audrey cried, knowing that Jenna had just lost Nicky, and if she lost the baby, it would be too much for her to bear. Audrey prayed, asking God to save the baby and her daughter. She knew that she hadn't been in church in a long time, but she cried for forgiveness and prayed for a miracle.

As they wheeled Jenna from the room and past her, she reached out to grab Jenna's hand for a brief moment.

"I love you," she whispered, barely able to talk.

Audrey watched as they continued pushing her daughter down the long hallway toward the operating room. Feeling a panic attack coming on, she could hardly breathe. Walking into the waiting room, she felt like it was the loneliest place on earth. Frank wasn't there to support her through the emergency C-Section.

Jenna was scared as she entered the operating room. She was visibly shaking uncontrollably.

"I know it's cold in here. We will transfer you onto the table and then administer a spinal shot. You're not going to feel a thing afterward, just some tugging as we try and get the baby delivered," the doctor informed her.

As the nurses pinned a blue sheet in front of her, Jenna felt even more nervous. Then she began talking to Nicky and asking for his help.

"Nicky, if you can hear me or if you're in the room, please don't let anything happen to our baby, please. Babe, I need you so much," she whispered as tears flooded her face.

One of the nurses noticed she was crying and walked over to wipe her face.

"Don't cry. You're about to meet the little person you've been carrying all these months. Where's the baby's father?" she asked, concerned.

"He was killed earlier today in a plane crash,"

Jenna could hardly get the words out of her mouth. Then, looking up at the nurse, Jenna noticed tears in her eyes.

"Oh sweetheart, I'm so sorry," she said sympathetically.

"Okay, Jenna, we've made the incision. You'll feel a few tugs," the doctor explained.

Jenna thought it seemed like forever before the doctor made his announcement.

"It's a boy."

The doctor held him up for her to see. He wasn't crying.

"What's wrong?" Jenna demanded. "What's wrong with him?"

"Jenna, we're just going to support him with oxygen and take him to the neonatal unit," the nurse reassured.

Jenna thought her heart would stop as she heard the faint cries of a tiny newborn.

"Oh, thank God, thank God," Jenna sighed with relief.

The nurse held the baby close to her for a brief second. Jenna finally smiled as she saw his beautiful face. He had Nicky's hair and gorgeous black curls.

"Nicky, he looks just like you," Jenna whispered. Then, quickly kissing his soft cheeks, the nurse rushed him out of the operating room and up to the neonatal unit.

Looking up at the clock in the operating room, it was 9:00 p.m. Jenna spoke to Nicky as if he were there.

"Babe, we have a son. Welcome to the world, Cameron Nicholas Jones."

"We'll be done in a few minutes. Then you'll be taken back to your room," the doctor said. "Congratulations."

"When will I get to see him again?" Jenna panicked.

"Tomorrow morning, someone will bring you up to the neonatal unit."

As Jenna was taken back to her room, she was relieved to know they had both made it through the C-Section. Now she asked God to protect Cameron and give him the strength to survive the next few weeks of his life. Jenna was extremely tired but unable to sleep. Thoughts of Nicky and the close call she had just experienced with Cameron were overwhelming.

"Oh, Jenna, Jenna," Audrey repeated as she ran into her room and gave her a huge hug. "Oh, Sweetheart, you did great. Thank God," Audrey said with tears in her eyes. "Jenna, you have a little boy. Can you even believe it? Don't worry, he's strong, and he will be fine, I just know it. So please don't worry. You should probably try and get some sleep. Your father said he would stop by tomorrow."

"Mom, I can't sleep."

"Jenna, just try and relax. I know you've been through a very stressful evening. Believe me. I know what you've been through. But, Jenna, everything has turned out beautifully tonight. Sweetheart, you have a handsome little boy."

"I know, mom, but I don't have Nicky," Jenna cried.

"Sweetheart, please don't do this to yourself. Do you think Nicky would want you to be upset? Jenna, you may not have Nicky, but you have his son," Audrey reminded with tears running down her face.

"Mom, please don't leave me tonight. Please stay with me?" Jenna begged, wiping tears from her eyes.

"I won't leave you, I promise. But I need you to get some sleep. You need to rest."

Audrey remained by her daughter's hospital bed, softly brushing back Jenna's long silky hair with her fingers until she fell asleep. She knew that her daughter's heart had been breaking on the very day that she had become a mother. There was still a long way to go before they would know for sure that Cameron would be completely alright. Audrey stood proudly by her daughter's bedside and asked God again to give her strength and courage for the days ahead.

Waking up the following day, Jenna felt as if she had just lived through her worst nightmare, except for the fact that she now had a son whom she thought looked exactly like Nicky. It wasn't long before a breakfast tray was brought into her room.

"Jenna, it looks delicious. You need to eat. You've got to get your strength back."

"No. I want to go up and see Cameron."

"I'm sure they'll be down to get you soon, but now you need to sit up and eat breakfast. I'll turn on the television. We can watch a few shows while you wait to be taken up to the neonatal unit."

Audrey turned on the television catching a news broadcast on the local channels.

"It's probably just about the plane crash. I don't think I can stand to watch that again. Mom, please change the channel. Trying to change the station quickly, Audrey surprisingly found the news bulletin was on each station.

"Today, we are reporting there were only two members of the band, Black Tie Affair, onboard the private jet that went down north of the Rome International Airport yesterday. The names have been released: the pilot, James Laird, co-pilot, Steven Smith, band members, Randy Owens and Alex Garrison along with two unidentified women."

"Mom, what did the news anchor just say?" Jenna asked in disbelief.

"Jenna, he just said that only two band members were killed in the plane crash yesterday, and Nicky wasn't one of them. So, Jenna, Nicky is still alive. Thank God he didn't die in the plane crash. Can you even believe this?" Audrey asked as she walked over to hug Jenna. The news was unbelievable.

"Oh, Mom, that's the best news I've ever heard," Jenna said with tears in her eyes. "Mom, I can't believe it. Our son, Cameron, still has a father," she said, struggling to get the words out of her mouth. But, Mom, so what was this all about? Why did we all have to go through this? Why did everything happen this way?"

"I don't know. Jenna. I only know that you, I mean you, and Nicky have a beautiful son. Isn't that all that truly matters?" she asked, hugging Jenna.

"Jenna, did I hear you say, Cameron? Have you decided upon a name?"

"Yes. His name is Cameron Nicholas Jones."

"Well, that's a very nice name. I like it a lot."

All Jenna could think of besides Nicky being alive was seeing Cameron. Jenna felt that hearing the news bulletin, which let her know that Nicky had not died in the plane crash, was a sign that everything would be alright. She knew in her heart, no matter the odds, that Cameron was going to be okay.

"Hi Jenna, I'm Kristy, and I've come to take you up to the neonatal unit to see your son. Are you ready?"

"I couldn't be more ready."

"Great, then let me get a wheelchair."

"Would it be possible for me to see the baby?" Audrey asked anxiously.

"Are you the baby's grandmother?"

"Yes. I certainly am," Audrey answered proudly.

"Well then, I don't think it's going to be a problem."

Following behind Jenna's wheelchair, Audrey couldn't wait to get her first glimpse of her new grandson as she entered the elevator.

"The neonatal unit is on the next floor," Kristy mentioned.

Exiting the elevator, Jenna could see a wall of windows and a sign which let them know they were on the neonatal floor. Looking at Audrey, Kristy informed them.

"You'll have to put on this yellow gown and wash your hands thoroughly before you go in. Then, Jenna, you'll need to do the same. Can you stand up to put on the gown?"

"Yes. No problem."

After completing the ritual of washing their hands and putting on the paper gowns, they were ushered inside. Looking around, Jenna had never seen so many sick babies in her life. They appeared to have tubes and wires connected to every part of their tiny bodies. It almost brought tears to her eyes. Walking over, she knew which isolate contained Cameron before Kristy told her.

"Take a seat in the rocking chair, and I'll open the incubator, and you can hold your son."

Audrey was breathless as she looked at her grandson. He was handsome. She had never seen a more beautiful baby, despite the wires and tubes surrounding him.

"Oh, Sweetheart, he's so beautiful," Audrey said with tears in her eyes.

"I know, mom. He's a handsome little guy, isn't he? He looks just like Nicky."

"Jenna, you're right. He does."

Rubbing her newborn son's hands and feet, Jenna whispered.

"Cameron, Daddy is safe. He loves you."

Even though she knew in her heart that Nicky perhaps would never meet his son, she knew she would love him enough for the both of them. That night at the cabin on the lake, she always knew she would carry away enough love for the both of them.

Watching as she gently touched her newborn, the head nurse from the neonatal Intensive Care Unit walked over.

"He's doing really well. We're keeping a close watch on him. He seems to be a little fighter. We're supporting him with oxygen and treating him with medications to help his lungs develop quicker. Hopefully, tomorrow, you'll both be able to hold him a lot longer if he continues to maintain his oxygen and heart rate.

That was the second-best piece of news that Jenna had heard today.

"By the way, my name is April, and I'll be here in the unit every day until 5:00 p.m. So have you thought of a name for your son? We always like to call them by their name, if you've decided on one?"

"Yes. It's Cameron Nicholas Jones."

"Wonderful. Then know that Cameron is in great hands. We have the best NICU in Quebec," April informed her. "We pride ourselves with statistics that state how many healthy babies we routinely send home. So you can come back this evening and visit Cameron again if you would like."

"Yes. That would be wonderful," Jenna answered, looking at her precious son.

Cameron stayed in the neonatal intensive care unit for about two weeks before he was well enough to go home. It gave Jenna and Audrey the time needed to go and buy the best of everything for this new little man in their lives. Jenna set up a nursery that would be fitting for any little prince. She would raise Cameron to become the type of man his father would be proud to call his son. Jenna vowed that Cameron would always carry the love of two people within him.

CHAPTER TWELVE

Missing Pieces *Frankfurt*

As tragic as the accident was, which resulted in the untimely deaths of Randy and Alex, Bruce did not suffer from a defeatist attitude. He announced a comeback for Black Tie Affair within a few short weeks. The band was a close-knit family that included the immediate members and over sixty people who traveled with the band worldwide. They were a family that heavily depended upon each other for support, both financially and emotionally. Bruce was not going to allow this tragedy to affect even one person. He knew that Randy and Alex would have wanted the show to go on. Bruce would honor their steadfast commitment to the band and their fans by ensuring that Black Tie Affair finished each remaining venue on the two-year world tour.

Black Tie Affair had a considerable fan base, which was never more apparent than when they had recently played in Paris and now Frankfurt. He wasn't about to disappoint their fans by dismantling the phenomenon he had worked so hard to create. They were loved in many countries, and Bruce was determined to keep that love alive in memory of the two family members they had just lost.

Upon returning to Frankfurt, Bruce opened a larger office and worked day and night feverishly regrouping the band. He reset the dates for each venue in every country. Finally, however, he decided to replace Randy with Nicky as their lead vocalist. Nicky had a gift that was nothing less than magic on stage. He was able to hold and capture an audience like no one he had ever seen before. When Bruce first saw Nicky on stage in Middleton, he knew Nicky was destined for greatness. Bruce believed things happened for a reason, and it was not by accident that he had discovered him. He was going to take this young kid and mold him into the greatest rock star the world had ever seen or ever graced a stage. Black Tie Affair was coming back with such a degree of prominence that it could only get better from here.

Now with Jeff still in place, there would only be two remaining slots that would need to be filled. Jeff was by far the best drummer he had ever come across. Bruce was proud to have Jeff working with him and even prouder to call him his nephew. The band was being reassembled as if by divine intervention. However, the most shocking thing to happen was a phone call he received one afternoon in his office.

"Hello, Bruce. How are you?" the voice on the phone said. "This is David, David Simmons. Bruce, man, I was so sorry to hear about Randy and Alex. I couldn't believe the news when I first heard it. I can't believe they're gone. Bruce, I want to come back."

"David, what a surprise to hear your voice," Bruce answered in a state of shock. "You're probably the last person on earth I ever expected to hear from, especially now."

"I know, Bruce. But, man, I just want to thank you for forcing me to deal with problems that I truly didn't want to face at the time. Bruce, I've been clean and sober for months now. I know you probably heard the stories about how I seemed to spiral downward when I lost my girlfriend, but that's all history now. Bruce, what I'm asking for is a second chance. I desperately want to come back on board with Black Tie Affair. I know I would be an asset now, you need me, and I want to come back home. What do you think?"

"Well, Son, I know we've had our differences. However, I believe in second chances, and you're right. I could use another guitarist of your caliber. If I agree and bring you back as a member of the band again, there has to be an understanding between you and me. There will never be a tolerance for hard drugs of any kind. Son, do you understand?"

"Yes, Bruce, I get it. Don't worry. After hearing about the accident, I just knew in my heart that I had to come back. I guess the only thing I'm just waiting to hear you say is that it's okay?"

"Okay, Son, I'll send the plane to pick you up. Just leave your address with my secretary, and we'll make all the arrangements. Welcome back."

"Thank you, Bruce. I promise you. You won't regret it."

Things were falling into place. Bruce felt good about bringing David back. He had been an invaluable lead guitarist up until the drugs cost him everything. Bruce did believe in second chances. He felt everyone deserved a second chance until proven wrong. Now he was only one member short, and he felt sure he knew where that person was. He had a phone call to make. Bruce called over to the hotel where Nicky, Kate, and Justin were staying.

"Hello," Nicky answered.

"Hi Nicky, this is Bruce. I want to stop by your hotel room later this evening if you and Kate don't have other plans?"

"Sure, Bruce, what's up?"

"Well, Son, I would rather come over and talk with you in person if that's alright?"

"Sure," Nicky repeated.

"Okay, I'll see you around 7:00 p.m." Hanging up the phone, Nicky couldn't imagine what was so urgent that Bruce would want to stop by and discuss it with him. But knowing Bruce, he knew it was of some importance. So it was about 6:45 p.m. when Nicky heard a knock on their door.

"Hey Bruce, come in."

"Hey Kate, how are you holding up?"

"Oh, I'm doing better. It's still pretty hard on me letting go of the boys, but each day with Nicky's help, it gets a little better."

"Sweetheart, I know you really miss them. We all do, and that's kind of why I came by tonight."

"Please, sit down," Kate said.

"Thanks. Nicky, I've had something that I've been mulling over in my mind, and I wanted to discuss it with you before I made any decisions."

"Whatever it is, Bruce, I'll be more than glad to help."

"Nicky, I've given some serious thoughts regarding someone I would like to bring on board as the lead guitarist, and I wanted to get your honest opinion first."

"Yeah. Well, who is it, Bruce?"

"Your cousin, Jerry."

"Wow. Bruce, that's quite a surprise. I'll have to admit Jerry would be the perfect choice, honestly. But, man, you've caught me off guard with this bit of news. Jerry is one hell of a bass guitarist, and I'm not saying this because we're related. Jerry can hold his own in any band. He would be quite an addition to Black Tie Affair."

"Well, Son, I value your opinion, and I knew you would give me an honest answer. When I heard your band that night in Middleton at the competition, I had given serious consideration to both of you. Nicky, you were on top of your game that night, and I could see how much you wanted to win. I could only offer one of you the position. Do you think he would be interested in becoming a band member? Does he still live in Middleton?"

"Yes. Bruce, I believe he would be thrilled. I'm pretty sure he's working at the Ford Plant where my dad works."

"Well, how about we call him tomorrow. If he's interested, then we'll fly to the states and talk with him and his parents."

"Wow. I still can't get over this, but yeah, let's talk with Jerry tomorrow. Of course, knowing Jerry as I do, he will be ecstatic about the opportunity."

"Okay. Come over to my office around noon tomorrow, and

we'll give Jerry a call. Oh, do you think he would be able to leave Middleton and fly back with us to Frankfurt?"

"I don't think that should be a problem, even though my Aunt Joyce might not think so. However, I don't think she would stand in his way when he's being offered a chance like this. It's a once-in-a-lifetime opportunity, now isn't it," Nicky smiled. "Bruce, you've sure been good to me, so let's go get Jerry."

"So that you know, David is coming back as the second lead guitarist. He called me today and pleaded with me to give him a second chance."

"So, what did you tell him?" Nicky asked.

"Well, after a little thought, I've decided to give him that second chance. But don't worry, I would never replace Randy's position with anyone but you. You're going to take Black Tie Affair in an entirely different direction. You're going to get that chance to become a famous rock star. Son, I'm going to make sure of that. Jerry will be taking on Alex's position with the band. He'll become your wingman. Okay. I suppose I should get back to the hotel. It's getting late. Oh, by the way, if Jerry agrees to this tomorrow, we'll be on the jet back to the states tomorrow night. So you might want to pack a few things. Guess your mother will be quite surprised to see your smiling face," Bruce said, leaving. "Yes. I'm certain of that."

"Okay, Son, see you tomorrow. Take care of yourself, Kate."

With that said, Bruce left the hotel leaving Nicky and Kate with a lot to talk over.

"Do you think you're ready to go back to Middleton so soon?" Kate inquired.

"That's a difficult question."

"Doesn't that town hold a lot of memories for you?"

"Yes. It certainly does, but hopefully, we'll only be there for a short time. I'm looking forward to seeing my parents and my brother. Too bad my sister and her husband live in northern Michigan. I would like to see them also."

"Would you like for me to come along? I'm sure Bruce wouldn't mind. I'd actually like to get away for a while, and I think it would help. It would be just the diversion which might help me deal with the loss of the boys."

"Okay. Babe, I think it would do us both good. So why don't you go pack a few things too."

"Thanks, Nicky," Kate replied, kissing him.

"Oh, don't thank me, it's Bruce you need to thank."

"I haven't been back in the states in quite a while."

"Well, let's go pack our bags and see what tomorrow brings," Nicky smiled, pulling her into the bedroom.

Morning came quick enough as Nicky looked over at the clock.

"Kate, it's almost 11:30 a.m. The limo will be downstairs in a few minutes.

"I'm almost done," she called out from the bedroom.

Kate was excited about accompanying Nicky on his first trip back to his hometown. Quickly tying her hair back into a ponytail, she was ready.

Walking into Bruce's office, he was ready to make the call to Jerry.

"I'll put the phone on speaker," Bruce mentioned.

"I hope we can catch him at home."

The phone rang about three times when someone answered.

"Hello. Is Jerry there?"

"Yes. Who's calling?"

"Bruce Weber."

"Just a second. Hey Jerry, someone by the name of Bruce Weber is on the phone."

The name sounded vaguely familiar to Jerry.

"Hello Jerry, this is Bruce Weber, tour manager for Black Tie Affair. How are you?"

Jerry almost dropped the receiver when he recognized the importance of who was on the phone.

"Fine. How's Nicky?" Jerry inquired.

"Oh, he's great. He's here with me."

"Hey Jerry, this is Nicky."

"Hey man, how's life going for you?"

"Well, funny you should ask," Nicky laughed.

"Jerry, this is Bruce speaking. I want to offer you a position with the band as lead guitarist. Do you think you would be interested in coming on board with our band, Black Tie Affair?"

"Say that again?"

Jerry couldn't believe what he was hearing. Wasn't Nicky the one they had been interested in?

"I'm sure by now you've heard about the unfortunate tragedy our band endured with our losing two band members."

"Yes. I'm was sorry to hear about that. But just thankful that Nicky wasn't on board."

"I know, Son, we all were. So what do you think?"

"Oh, Mr. Weber, if you're serious, I would be thrilled."

"Great. That's what I hoped to hear. Nicky and I will be flying into Middleton tomorrow. It's not going to give you much time. Still, if you're seriously interested in the position I'm offering you, you'll be on your way to Frankfurt tomorrow night. Things move pretty fast when it comes to Black Tie Affair. Are you ready for a change and to leave Middleton?"

"Oh, you just ask Nicky. When he left Middleton, I was devastated. Our band fell apart, and I was lost. Now working over at the Ford Plant, it felt like my life was over before it even got started."

"Well, Son, this is your lucky day. So welcome aboard. I think you're going to like what being a member of our band can bring to your life. So if you're ready to rock and roll, then we'll see you tomorrow."

"Hey Jerry, please call my mom and let her know she's going to have an unexpected visitor, but don't give me away. I want to surprise her."

"Okay, Nicky, will do, man. See you tomorrow. Oh, thank you, Mr. Weber, thank you."

"Jerry, one last thing, I'll come by to pick you up around 6:00 p.m. to go over the contract. See you then, Son."

Wow, had he just talked with Bruce Weber and Nicky? He found the phone call unbelievable.

"Mom, Mom," Jerry yelled, running into the kitchen. "Mom, you're not going to believe this. I just talked with Nicky and Mr.

Weber, Nicky's tour manager. He's offering me a position with the band as lead guitarist. Mom, can you even believe it?"

"Jerry, how is Nicky? Didn't the band just lose two of their band members in a plane crash?"

"Yes. Unfortunately, they did, but lucky for me, they need a guitarist. So, Mom, I'm going. I told Mr. Weber that I was interested in taking the position," Jerry announced.

"Oh Jerry, are you sure you're ready to leave home?"

"Are you kidding? I'll be playing with Nicky in a band again. It's a dream come true for me too. When Nicky left, our band broke up, and you'll never know how much I've missed him. Now I've got the chance to be on stage with him and be a member of Black Tie Affair. Mom, Mr. Weber, and Nicky are flying into Middleton tomorrow."

"What, Jerry? Are you telling me you that you'll be going back with them?"

"Yes, Mom, but please just be happy for me. Aunt Joan let Nicky go, and I'm asking you to do the same for me."

Bruce, Nicky, and Kate boarded one of the private jets, which now had been methodically inspected for any signs of mechanical problems, twice now. Bruce wasn't taking any chances. For the first time since leaving home, Nicky was going back to Middleton. He had mixed feelings about seeing his hometown again. It held so many memories of Jenna and the last days they spent together. He was glad that Kate had was coming along. He would need a distraction.

As the jet touched down on the runway at the Middleton Airport, thoughts of that day he had left Jenna began flooding his mind. He grabbed Kate's hand tightly as they walked off the plane. He had just gotten Kate through a very rough two weeks and been her strength now he would need her strength to see him through the next two days in Middleton. Stepping inside the waiting limo, Nicky was excited over surprising his mom.

"Nicky, I'm going to drop you and Kate off at your house, and then I'm going over to the hotel to get a few hours of sleep. I've arranged to meet with Jerry and his parents at 6:00 p.m. this afternoon to go over the contract. If you and Kate would like to be there, that's fine with me. I figured since you all were family that you might like to be there as well."

"Thanks, Bruce. I want to tag along. I think it might help to ease any fears that Aunt Joyce would have about letting Jerry go soon."

"Okay. I'll pick you up this afternoon," Bruce said as the limo stopped in front of Nicky's house.

Running up to the door, Nicky couldn't wait to see the reaction on his mom's face. He grabbed Kate's hand as they ran inside, not even bothering to ring the doorbell.

"Mom," Nicky called out, "I'm home."

Hearing her son's voice, Joan almost dropped a hot pan of meatloaf, which she was taking out of the oven.

"Oh Nicholas, Nicholas, you're home," Joan smiled, running toward him. She hugged Nicky so tight until he was almost breathless. Joan held him for minutes, not wanting to let him go. Then, with tears in her eyes, she just looked at him as if she was seeing him for the first time. "Oh Nicky, what a surprise," she smiled, hugging him once more. "I was so scared when I heard about the plane crash. The details were so sketchy on the news channels we really were not sure how many band members were on the plane. I was so frantic."

"Well, Mom, I'm home, but only for a day. Mom, this is Kate. She's a stylist. She does hair and makeup for the band."

"Nice to meet you, Kate," Joan smiled.

"Nice to meet you too, Mrs. Spade."

"Hope you like meatloaf."

"Smells delicious. It's hard to get a home-cooked meal these days," Kate added.

"So, Nicky, what brings you back home?"

"Mom, Bruce has decided to bring Jerry on as a replacement for Alex. He was the bass guitarist."

"Oh, does Joyce know?"

"Well, I'm sure she does by now. But, Mom, who could have

ever known that you and Aunt Joyce would both have sons on tour with a famous rock band such as Black Tie Affair," Nicky grinned.

"Well, that's something to think about now. But, honestly, Nicky, I can't say it surprises me. You both are very talented musicians. I'm not shocked someone finally took notice of your talent. You both spent years practicing in Larry's basement. I'm excited, but I can't speak for Joyce."

"Yes. It's going to be one hell of a ride, playing with Jerry on stage. I can't wait."

"Son, your dad, should be in soon, and Tony will be home around 4:00 p.m. So you and Kate have a seat, and I will get you something to drink."

"Mom, if it's okay, I would like to borrow the car and show Kate around Middleton."

"Alright, Son, have fun," Joan said, handing him the keys to her car.

Walking out the door with Kate, Nicky needed closure on this part of his life. Kate would help him finally put the memories of Jenna to rest.

"Babe, I'll show you Middleton High School, where all my dreams and ambitions of becoming a musician started. Then I have a favorite place I want to share with you."

Nicky knew Middleton never held enough importance to keep him there while driving by the high school.

"Here's the high school. I can't say that I ever took my education seriously. I guess the fact that I didn't graduate says everything."

"Nicky, is this where you met Jenna?" Kate questioned.

He hesitated for a moment.

"Yes. It is. I want to show you a special place where I used to sometimes go after band rehearsals and daydream about my future."

Driving down by the lake, Nicky parked the car. Then, getting out, he took Kate's hand as they walked out on the pier.

"Wow. This is beautiful."

The warm summer sun was shining brilliantly. It reflected a myriad of colors off the water. They walked down to the end of the wooden pier and took a seat on the bench. It held so many memories of Jenna. Kate took his hand and looked into his eyes.

"Something's been bothering me since we left your house."

"Yeah, Doll, what is it?"

"Why didn't you introduce me as your girlfriend to your mother?"

"I thought I did," Nicky asked, confused.

"No. You introduced me as the stylist," Kate sighed.

"Damn, Babe, I'm sorry. I must be jet-lagged. I didn't do it on purpose."

Kate wasn't sure if she believed him or not. Only time would tell. Nicky quickly pulled her in for a kiss.

"I'll make it up to you, I promise."

Holding each other tightly, they sat on the bench in the warm sun. Their last afternoon in Middleton was a busy one. Nicky and Kate joined Bruce, Jerry, and his parents for dinner at the now-famous Rosetta's Restaurant, where Nicky was signed to tour with Black Tie Affair.

Sitting at the table, Nicky began reliving the afternoon when he had sat in those exact seats and watched as Bruce had changed his life forever. Now it was Jerry's turn. Later that evening, Nicky and Kate spent time with his mom, dad and Tony. They had a precious few moments in time to spend together as a family. Nicky caught them up with his career and the many places he had been while on tour.

The limo arrived early the following day to pick them up with Jerry. Unfortunately, due to road construction, the car drove directly past the house where Jenna had lived. Nicky took a deep breath.

"Oh Babe, this is where Jenna lived," he said, squeezing her hand.

As the limo drove past, Nicky was finally able to give closure to this part of his life, or so he thought. Arriving at the airport, they found Bruce waiting anxiously at the steps of the aircraft.

"Okay, kids, are you ready to go?"

Bruce had his missing pieces. He was excited. He finally had everything he needed to make history with the band. Bruce knew that he had a winning combination with Jerry beside Nicky on stage.

As the jet lifted off the runway, Nicky took Kate's hand. He had finally put to rest the memories he was leaving behind. However, Nicky could have never known that these memories would one day walk back into his life.

CHAPTER THIRTEEN

The final pieces.
Frankfurt

It was late evening when the jet touched down in Frankfurt. It had been a long flight. However, Bruce finally had everything he needed. There were no more missing pieces. He could now move forward.

"Jerry, I've booked you a suite at the InterContinental Hotel along with Nicky, Kate, and Jeff. I know things are moving pretty fast for you right now, but we're going to be in Frankfurt for another week. It will give you time to settle in and get used to the time change. I'm going to leave you in the hands of Nicky. He will introduce you to Jeff and the gang tomorrow."

"Thanks, Bruce," Jerry said, trying to take in the views of Frankfurt from the limo.

"I've got a lot of work to do tomorrow. This week is going to be very busy. Rome will be our next scheduled venue on this tour. I've arranged for the band to perform in Rome by the end of next week. I'm also arranging a memorial tribute to Randy and Alex as a way to open the remainder of our tour," Bruce said. "Oh, one last thing, I'm waiting on another band member to arrive. As soon as he arrives, I've made arrangements for everyone to start band rehearsals at the sports arena this week. Hopefully, it will be all the time you'll need to be ready for Rome."

"I can't wait to meet everyone and start rehearsals," Jerry smiled excitedly.

"Okay, kids, think this is your stop," Bruce said as the limo pulled up to the hotel. "Talk with you later."

"Thanks, Bruce, see you tomorrow," Jerry smiled.

Walking into the hotel, Jerry was amazed by its décor.

"Wow. It appears Bruce takes excellent care of everyone in the band," Jerry stated as they walked over to the reception desk.

"Yes. Bruce is awesome to work for, and being part of a band like Black Tie Affair is an unbelievable opportunity. We're like one huge family. You'll see. Your life just got upgraded to first class. Let's pick up the key to your room, get the concierge to have our luggage carried upstairs, and have a drink," Nicky suggested.

"That sounds pretty good to me, but aren't you tired?"

"Oh, you don't even want to know what happened when I arrived in London. The guys took me out to the pubs and introduced me to the English beers, all before my body had a chance to catch up with the time difference. I think you can handle a few drinks in our room. I'll call Jeff over, and you can meet him tonight."

"You'll love him. He's the drummer for the band and such a great guy," Kate added.

After Jerry had dropped off his luggage in his room, he walked over to Nicky and Kate's suite.

"Wow. Cool room," Jerry remarked as Nicky answered the door.

"Come in and sit down. I'll get you a Bitburger."

"What's that?" Jerry questioned.

"Man, you are from a small town," Kate laughed, handing him a beer. "It's a German Beer."

Hearing a knock at the door, Kate opened it knowing that it was Jeff.

"Hey Jeff, come in. Meet Jerry, Nicky's cousin."

"Hey man, I've heard a lot about you."

"Well, I hope it's all been good," Jerry smiled.

"Yeah, well, anyone related to Nicky can't be all that bad now, can he?" Jeff said, reaching out to shake his hand.

"So, you're our new lead guitarist. Welcome to the band. Cool to have you on board," Jeff said, taking a seat.

"Thanks, man," Jerry grinned.

Nicky lit a cigarette sitting on the couch next to Kate. The night seemed to fly by as they brought Jerry up to speed regarding Black Tie Affair. Endless hours of conversation carried on until the early hours of the morning. Sunlight was beginning to filter in through the curtains as they decided they had better get in a few hours of sleep.

The following day at the office, Bruce got the call he had been waiting on. David had arrived in Frankfurt and was on his way over.

"When David Simmons comes in, please bring him into my office," Bruce informed his secretary as he poured himself a cup of coffee.

The paperwork seemed endless as Bruce tried to tie up all the loose ends and reschedule the venues.

"Hey Bruce," David smiled, walking into Bruce's office.

"Hey, Son, how was your flight?"

"Oh, pretty good. However, that flight across the pond never seems to get any shorter."

"That's for sure. Take a seat," Bruce smiled. "Well, David, I'm glad to have you back. Son, you are and have always been a great guitarist. So I'm giving you your old position back with the band. Just need you to sign a few pieces of paper to make it legal, and then we'll be back in business."

"Bruce, I really want to thank you for having faith in me again. I promise you'll not be disappointed."

"You were a valuable asset to the band until you went off the deep end, so to speak. However, we won't revisit past mistakes this morning. Welcome home, son. I've got you a suite over at the InterContinental Hotel along with Nicky, Kate, Jeff, and our newest member Jerry Godwin. I think you're all going to get along great together. One last thing, rehearsals will start tomorrow morning at the sports arena. I've arranged for you guys to practice there this next week. This weekend, we open in Rome with a memorial concert dedicated to Randy and Alex. So I'm counting on all of you to be in top form by the end of the week. Well, I guess that's it for this morning. I'll call for a car to take you over to the hotel."

"Great, thanks again, Bruce," David smiled as he was about to leave.

"Oh, let Nicky and the boys know that I'll probably stop by the sports arena tomorrow morning," Bruce added. "Again, welcome home, son, now go get some rest."

"See you tomorrow Bruce," David said, closing the door to Bruce's office.

Lounging back in his chair, Bruce had his boys back. He finally had all his missing pieces. However, his heart still ached from the sadness of losing Randy and Alex.

It was a beautiful day, as the boys and Kate stepped into the limo the following day to ride down to the sports arena.

"David, please meet my cousin, Jerry," Nicky smiled, making himself comfortable as he sat back in the limo next to Kate.

"Hey, man, nice to meet you," David said, reaching out to shake Jerry's hand. "Bruce didn't mention the fact that you two were related."

"Yes. We grew up together in Middleton. In fact, we were playing together in a band that we formed in high school, The Underground, when Bruce discovered Nicky."

"Well, welcome to the band. We're just like one big happy family, isn't that right?" David added, winking at Kate. Katie, how are you holding up these days? I know you were really close to Randy and Alex. I'm so sorry."

"I miss them every day," Kate sighed.

"It's good to have you back."

As the limo pulled around to the back of the sports arena, the boys were anxious to get inside and start rehearsals. Black Tie Affair was back. The rehearsals couldn't have been going better. Jerry had no problem at all picking up the songs. Nicky and Jerry were the perfect complement to each other. With their incredible musical abilities and handsome Italian profiles, they were destined to become rock stars whom the fans would adore. In the distance, the guys saw Bruce walking down the auditorium aisle toward the stage. He had a giant smile on his face.

"I like what I'm hearing," Bruce boasted, seeing the guys on stage.

"Hey Kate, what do you think?" he asked as he walked past her seat.

"Oh, they sound unbelievably good. I can't wait until we play Rome."

"Well, it's coming up this weekend. Are you boys ready to play Rome in memory of Randy and Alex?" Bruce yelled in their direction.

"Yes, they each responded."

Bruce had all his boys now, and he was ready to take his show back on the road. The boys were in fine form. It was Wednesday night, their last night in Frankfurt. Bruce rented out the best restaurant in town as was usual for him. He made sure there was no one left out of the festivities. The entire crew, roadies, friends, and the band members attended. Drinks flowed freely, along with numerous toasts during the night. They were saying goodbye to the boys and trying to put an end to their sadness. Bruce stood to make one last toast to Randy and Alex at the end of the night.

"Would everyone please stand and lift their glasses in a gesture of remembrance to Randy and Alex.

"Here's to Rand and Alex. You're sorely missed but never forgotten. Always in our hearts, always members of Black Tie Affair."

"Now, let's go to Rome and play some rock and roll."

The following day as the jet lifted off the runway in Frankfurt, Jerry sat back in his seat, glancing at Nicky and Kate.

"Man, do you ever get tired of this. I mean the private jets and the limo service?" Jerry questioned.

"Why? Are we supposed to?" Nicky laughed.

"Damn, Larry and Justin wouldn't believe how our lives have changed," Jerry grinned.

"Yeah. You'd be right about that," Nicky smiled.

Rome

As the plane arrived at the International Airport in Rome, the boys and Kate walked over to the waiting limo. They were soon on their way to the hotel which Bruce had reserved. Jerry was shocked by the passing scenery, noticing the numerous billboards advertising the concert.

"Do they always advertise like this for the concerts?" Jerry grinned.

"Yes. Bruce will plaster a town with advertisements if they give him the opportunity," Nicky laughed.

Arriving at the hotel, it was opulent. Met by hotel staff, who waited for their arrival, they were ushered inside through tall wrought-iron glass doors. The hotel's décor reflected the best of Italian design. Colorful canvases depicting vineyards accented the interior. Tuscan-inspired lanterns lit the walls, and the foyer was encircled with large terracotta pots filled with bright red geraniums. As the guys and Kate walked over to check in, they were stunned by the exquisite beauty of the hotel.

"Amazing," Kate raved as they received their room keys and entered the elevator, taking them up to their suites.

"Does Bruce always splurge on such extravagance?" Jerry once again questioned.

"Well, yes and no. However, I can't remember a time before that we've stayed in such luxury," David said.

They were all anxious to see their rooms.

Walking into their suite, Nicky and Kate found it a bit ostentatious. Each suite contained a balcony, with luxurious red velvet curtains draping oversized French doors leading outside. White marble floors reflected the evening sun and crystal chandeliers hanging above.

"Wow," Kate said. "These accommodations are a bit over the top, but I think it's unique. I guess the old saying is, *When in Rome do as the* Romans do, she smiled. I wonder if Jerry, Jeff, and David's rooms are as elegant as ours."

"Well, from the looks of this place, I'm sure of it."

Nicky took a banana from the fruit basket and went over to the sofa to sit down.

"Come over here, Doll. Let's just sit for a minute.

"Did Bruce tell you about the venue for tomorrow night's concert?"

"No. So what's the deal?"

"Well, it's going to be our first open-air concert. Bruce said there wasn't an auditorium or indoor arena large enough to hold the crowd of fans who are expected to turn out and show their respect for Randy and Alex. The amphitheater seats over twenty thousand people, and we are sold out for tomorrow's memorial concert."

"Are you nervous about performing in front of so many fans?"

"No. Can you even imagine what the energy level will be like with such a large crown?"

"How do you think Jerry will do? It's going to be his first performance."

"Oh, he'll do great. He thrives on attention. It seems to run in the family," Nicky laughed.

"You guys sounded unbelievable at rehearsals this past week. I think Bruce was quite pleased with how well you all meshed together."

"Bruce knows talent when he hears it. He knew what he was doing when he went back to the states and signed Jerry and then allowed David to come back."

"I think tomorrow's concert may even have a bit of heavenly guidance," Kate mentioned, still hurting from the loss of the boys.

"Hey Babe, I think we should call it a night. It's been a long day, and tomorrow is going to be huge for all of us."

Taking Kate's hand, Nicky led her into the bedroom. He just needed to feel a warm body next to him. Nicky was beginning to feel the pressure of his first performance as the lead vocalist. He needed Kate tonight in so many ways. Nicky needed the reassurance that only two people in love can give each other when faced with a unique challenge. Tomorrow was a new day, the beginning of his dreams.

As the sun came up the following morning, they had hardly slept at all.

"Good morning Babe, what a night," Kate smiled, kissing Nicky awake.

Nicky had never looked more handsome, lying in bed with his new unshaven appearance. This man of hers was going to take Rome by storm. After a leisurely day spent in their hotel room, it was almost time to meet the boys downstairs. They had opted to stay in today rather than sightsee in this beautiful city. Nicky just needed to be alone with Kate until it was time to leave for the venue. He didn't want or need any distractions from others, even Jerry, until they were ready for the concert.

Riding over in the limo to the amphitheater, it was quiet. Even the boys were at a loss for words. Tonight, Black Tie Affair was back. There was a reverence to those who were no longer with them. There would be lots of time to celebrate after the concert. Tonight was about homage to the ones they had lost. The limo drove them around to the back entrance of the theater, where Bruce was there to meet them.

"Hey boys, are you ready for tonight? It's going to be a little different than an indoor auditorium. You'll find the lighting and sound is not quite the same, but you should get a feel for it after being on stage for a short while. There will be no rehearsals before you go on stage, as is usually the norm when playing an indoor arena. You will do great, so just relax, enjoy yourselves, and don't get too bothered by the idea this is a tribute to the boys. The fans have come expecting to see the incredible return of Black Tie Affair, and that's just what we're going to give them, all twenty thousand of them.

As everyone walked to the dressing room at the back of the stage, the room was small but filled with roses of all colors, wishing them the best for tonight. The best Italian cuisine and expensive champagne covered a long table against the back wall. Kate immediately began with hair and makeup while Nicky sat down on the sofa and lit a cigarette. Jerry walked over to sit next to Nicky.

"Wow, man, can you even imagine? Tonight we'll be on stage together, unbelievable with you as the lead singer for Black Tie Affair and me as your wingman. We've come a long way since Larry's garage and Middleton. So here's to a hell of a night in Rome. I love you, man," Jerry grinned as he lit a cigarette. Bruce popped the cork on the champagne and began filling fluted glasses to pass around.

"Here's to tonight being a huge success. There'll be plenty more champagne tonight after the concert."

"Okay. I need the two pretty boys sitting on the couch, Jerry and Nicky, over here. Right now," Kate teased. "Let's get done. You need to start getting dressed."

There were only about twenty minutes before it would be time to go on stage.

"Nicky, aren't you going to shave really fast before I do your makeup?"

"Are you kidding? Not tonight," Nicky admitted. "It always seemed to work for Randy and Alex, so why would I break with tradition, especially tonight," Nicky winked.

It wasn't long before it was time to take the stage. Suddenly, Kate walked over and grabbed Nicky, kissing him so passionately the whole room blushed.

"Okay, guys, go out there and make my brothers proud," Kate smiled.

"I'll walk over to the back of the stage with you boys," Bruce said. "Okay, now go out there and make rock and roll history."

The Tribute

Jeff walked on stage first and started playing drums for the warm-up to announce the arrival of the other band members. David walked out second as the fans roared. Jerry was next. He held his guitar high into the night air. Then, finally, Nicky made his appearance. Boisterously, the fans stood to their feet, showing their love for Black Tie Affair. Screams filled the amphitheater and could easily be heard over a mile away.

"Thank you, Rome, thank you," Nicky shouted. "Thank you for coming out tonight to help us honor the loss of our two band members, Randy Owens and Alex Garrison." "Thank you so much," he shouted. "Let me introduce the newest member of our band, Jerry Godwin playing lead guitar, and David Simmons is back with us on bass. Playing drums tonight is our own, Mr. Jeff Weber, and I'm Nicky Spade. We're so happy to be back on stage with you tonight.

"Rome, we love you. We're so happy to be here with you tonight," Nicky exclaimed once more as he absorbed the energy from the fans.

"How are you tonight?" Jerry yelled excitedly. The fans remembered Randy and Alex by screaming even louder.

"Here's to, Randy and Alex," David screamed, holding his guitar high in their honor.

"Thank you, thank you," Nicky shouted as loud as was humanely possible. "Rome, are you ready to rock and roll?"

Nicky thought the screams resonating from the fans could have easily been heard into outer space as he stared into the night sky. The stars appeared like a bright canopy of diamonds sprinkled like dust across the vast universe. He knew without a doubt that Randy and Alex were most definitely watching from above, and he knew they were smiling. Nicky introduced their first song of the evening.

"Rome, here's to you with our love. I hope you like it. It's called *Without You*." The fans once again stood to their feet and sang along. It was pure magic as the fans immersed themselves in the music coming from the stage.

After their first song, the boys walked to the front of the stage, loosened their ties, and tossed them to the girls in front. However, David once again knelt on one knee, placing his tie around the neck of a beautiful young girl, kissing her on the cheek. The girls went wild, screaming out their love for David.

"David, we love you. Welcome back," the fans yelled.

The air was electric, and you could feel it. It was tangible. Nicky, Jerry, and David remained near the front of the stage.

"Here's to Randy and Alex," Nicky shouted as they began to jam on their next hit, *Cruising.* The fans were ecstatic and screaming as girls were hoisted onto the shoulders of guys standing nearby. Staring at the crowd near the front of the stage, Nicky began to think for a second that Bruce should have hired extra security to keep things under control. But instead, two girls fainted and were practically trampled before being pulled from the crowd and safely removed.

"If you know the lyrics to the next song, we want to hear you. It's a night to celebrate the lives of Randy and Alex," Nicky shouted.

Jerry played solo for the first few verses as the fans sang the lyrics, danced in their seats, and even out into the aisles. After that, it was an actual party in ever since of the word. The amphitheater rocked to the music of Black Tie Affair, and the guys on stage were living in the moment.

"Rome, let's rock this place. Are you ready?" Nicky yelled as he led into their next song, *Fade to Black.*

The screams of the fans were deafening as they shouted their love for the guys on stage.

"We love you, Nicky."

The entire arena lit cigarette lighters during their next song, holding them high in the air as the band performed one of their slower numbers, *Falling Stars.* Nicky glanced at the vast audience with thousands of tiny flickering lights. It mirrored the night sky.

"Thank you," Nicky shouted as he led into their next song, *Dreaming.* Nicky quickly captured the heart of his audience. He was a natural, and the fans loved him as they returned their love with screams of affection.

"Nicky, Nicky," the girls screamed in unison.

The concert continued for about an hour as Nicky drank in the love and adoration of his fans. Then, feeling that time no longer existed, the fans' reactions consumed him. He was born to do this.

In front of thousands of adoring fans, he was living his dream under the evening sky.

All too soon, the concert was coming to a close. However, no one wanted to leave. It had been a mutual love fest between the boys on stage and their fans. So how was it possible to end a night like this under the stars in Rome?

"Rome, thank you for coming. We want to close by singing a new song for you that I wrote earlier this week. It's dedicated to Randy and Alex. I know they are here with us tonight in spirit. I hope you like it. It's called *Because of You.*

You could literally hear a pin drop. Then, an unnatural silence fell over the entire amphitheater. Nicky belted out the words to his new song, watching once again as the fans lit cigarette lighters, holding them high into the night air as they swayed with the music.

When the song ended, the guys walked toward the front of the stage. Nicky, Jerry, David, and Jeff all locked hands for a brief moment smiling, and then began saying their goodbyes.

"Here's to you, Randy and Alex," the guys shouted their final salute.

The amphitheater resonated with screams of farewell from the fans.

"Rome, thank you for coming tonight. We love you," Nicky yelled.

Jerry shouted, "Goodnight, Randy and Alex. We'll forever miss you,"

David cried, "Goodbye, Randy, and Alex. You'll never be forgotten."

"Always in our hearts. We love you," Jeff added with a shout, holding his drumsticks high into the air.

"Rome, thank you for celebrating with us," Nicky once again shouted. "Thanks for remembering our bandmates, Randy and Alex. Their memories will forever live in our hearts," Nicky yelled into the night.

As the boys left the stage, the roar from the fans was deafening and seemed to go on forever. Then, a multitude of fireworks exploded upward into the night sky. Fans remained standing in the aisles, not wanting to leave, as the boys disappeared backstage. Bruce and Kate came running up to meet the boys as they walked off stage.

"Oh Nicky, they loved you," Kate exclaimed, jumping into Nicky's arms hugging him tightly.

"Guys, you were brilliant. Unbelievable. Congratulations, we're back," Bruce grinned. "That was an amazing concert tonight, just amazing. Tonight will never be forgotten," Bruce smiled.

Todd, Mike, Pete, and John came running over as soon as the guys walked off stage.

"You guys knocked it out of the ballpark," Todd grinned with a laugh.

"Totally, awesome," Mike added.

"Nicky, they loved you, man," Pete smiled.

"I second that," John replied.

"Alright boys, everyone down to the dressing room. We have some cold champagne waiting for us," Bruce exclaimed.

The evening was about to get started with a night of celebration.

Walking into the dressing room, you could hear the sound of corks popping from the tops of the champagne bottles. Everyone was given a glass as Bruce toasted.

"Here's to the comeback of our band, Black Tie Affair. *But, most importantly, here's to Randy and Alex"*.

"Okay. I've got the best spot in Rome reserved for us tonight. Two limos are waiting for all of us at the back entrance. Before the boys could even get changed, there was a knock on the dressing room door. Bruce found some unusually dressed security standing at the door.

"Are you the stage manager?"

"No. I'm Bruce Weber, the band manager. Can I help you?"

"Yes. We need to come in and secure the room."

Being somewhat confused, Bruce questioned.

"Well, for what reason? What's going on?"

"Princess Alexandria of Spain is waiting. She was in the audience tonight and would be pleased to meet the band members."

Bruce scratched his head in disbelief.

"Yes. By all means, please come in."

"We need everyone, except the band members, to please step outside of the room now," they demanded. "You can stay, they said, pointing at Bruce."

"Wow," Nicky smiled in utter disbelief. Then, staring at Kate. "Babe, sorry, you might have to step out for a minute."

Todd, the crew, and Kate stepped outside the dressing room as security secured the room. Knowing the room was secure, one of the guards stated.

"This will only take a few minutes of your time."

Quickly they returned, followed by a teenage girl. Then, finally, one of the guards announced.

"Princess Alexandria of Spain."

She was beautiful with dark skin, black hair, and piercing green eyes. Nicky thought she appeared to be about sixteen years old. Unsure of protocol, Nicky simply bowed.

"Nice to meet you. I'm Nicky Spade."

She blushed, extending her hand, and then moved to Jerry, David, and Jeff.

"Thank you for allowing me to come backstage and meet you. I'm a huge fan, and I enjoyed your concert. I've come to extend a royal invitation to visit the palace in Madrid. My parents would like to have your presence at a private social event. May I please inform them you will be present?"

Nicky looked over at Bruce as if asking for his permission.

"Yes. We would be honored. Thank you," Nicky stated, quickly glancing at Bruce, who now had a massive smile on his face.

"Arrangements will be made for next month. You will receive a royal invitation. Thank you for allowing me to come backstage. The concert was great.

I look forward to your performance in Madrid," she said, smiling as she was hurriedly ushered out of the room by the security.

The guys stared at each other in shock.

"Damn," Nicky smiled. "Can you even believe it? We've just met an actual princess."

Bruce walked out to ask Todd, the guys, and Kate to return. They were all amazed.

"Well," Kate said as she walked over to Nicky. "A princess, really," she questioned.

"Hey, Babe," Nicky said, kissing her. "Do I denote a little jealousy?"

"No. Not unless you had gone with her," Kate teased.

"With that security. Are you kidding?" Nicky winked.

"Okay. Who's hungry?" Bruce asked. "I think we should leave before someone else wants to meet you," he teased.

"I'm starved," Jerry said, picking up his glass of champagne.

Nicky lit a cigarette, trying to comprehend what had just happened.

"Alright, as soon as you're changed, the limos are waiting."

"Okay, Bruce, where are we going tonight?" Todd questioned.

"Oh, it's probably the best Italian Restaurant in Rome," he grinned.

"Bruce, how would you know? We're in Italy, and they're all Italian, right?" Mike said, laughing.

Later that night in Rome, Bruce had been right. They ate in the best Italian Restaurant. Wine flowed freely all evening. Bruce always took care of his boys after a concert. He took pride in finding the perfect restaurant in every city and having the management close their doors to the public. It was a private affair for Black Tie Affair after each concert.

Returning to the hotel after dinner, it was already early morning. However, Nicky wasn't ready to call it a night. It had been his first performance as the lead vocalist with the band, and he was still reeling from the extraordinary events of the evening.

Unlocking the door to their suite, Nicky popped the cork on a bottle of champagne. Then, filling two glasses, he took Kate's hand and pulled her out to the balcony. Standing under the remaining stars which sprinkled the predawn sky, Nicky pulled her into his chest, kissing her intensely.

"Wow, Doll, I feel like I'm in a dream."

"Well, Nicky, I think what you're feeling is just the beginning. The fans adored you. You connected with them in ways that only a true artist could ever do."

As the morning sun made its appearance over the green vineyards which covered the rolling hills, Nicky held Kate in his arms. The sunrise brilliantly painted the sky in hues of light orange and pink. Kate thought it was the most breathtaking view she had ever seen. Kate felt it was a sign that Randy and Alex were watching over her. She finally had closure.

Holding Kate in his arms, Nicky's thoughts raced back to the morning on the balcony at the lake with Jenna. They, too, had stood together covered only in a blanket, taking in an incredible sunrise. Still, an ember of love remained in his heart for Jenna.

"Babe, let's go in." Taking Kate's hand, they walked into the bedroom. Once again, Nicky needed her now more than ever.

The following day the newspapers carried the events of the concert on the front page. It was evident Rome loved Black Tie Affair. They were in the Eternal City of Love for only one more day before leaving for the next venue in Greece.

CHAPTER FOURTEEN

Touring the Mediterranean

As the plane circled Rome, they were now on their way to Greece. Jerry sat glued to his window, taking in the last views of the Coliseum. Nicky was excited to discover their next concert would also be an outdoor venue. He loved the ambiance of a concert at night under the stars. Kate flipped through the pages of a magazine as Nicky lit a cigarette.

"Doll, guess there's no better way to see the world than with a rock band."

"Yes, especially when you're the lead vocalist. Oh, I forgot to ask about the song you sang at the concert, the one you wrote. I didn't know you had written a song for the boys?"

"I wrote it last week in Frankfurt in-between rehearsals at the sports center. I wanted to surprise you because I knew the boys were a huge part of your life."

"Well, with all the excitement going on in the dressing room after the concert, I forgot to ask. However, Babe, I love that song."

"Thanks. I think the fans loved it. Hopefully, it will become another hit for the band."

Later, as the plane began its descent into Athens, Kate could see the azure blue waters of the Aegean Sea in the distance. She was looking forward to a few days off from their hectic schedule, and she thought this would be the perfect place. She was excited about visiting the Parthenon and the Greek islands, especially Santorini.

Arriving at their hotel, Bruce never managed to disappoint the guys with their accommodations. It was located on one of the busiest streets. Beautiful ocean blue awnings covered wrought-iron balconies, complementing the white-washed stone structure.

"Oh, this is beautiful," Kate said, stepping out of the limo.

Walking inside, Kate was not to be disappointed. A courtyard sat directly in the middle of the impressive lobby. It was open to the air above and enclosed lush gardens adorned with a stunning decorative fountain. The sun streamed inside the Greek-inspired entrance casting its brilliance across colorful mosaic floors. Walking over to the reception desk, Nicky picked up room keys.

"Okay, guys, we're all going to have our own rooms again," he said, tossing room keys to everyone.

Walking toward the elevator, Jerry was amazed by their accommodations.

"We're all on different floors," he announced, catching his key.

As the elevator came to a stop, Nicky and Kate's room was on the second floor.

"Okay, guys, see you tomorrow. Oh, you're all welcome to come to our room anytime for drinks, unless you see the *Do not disturb sign* on the door," Nicky laughed.

"He's just kidding," Kate blushed, pinching Nicky.

"Am I doll?" Nicky winked.

The concert was three days away, and Kate was determined not to waste their time staying inside the hotel, which had been the case back in Rome. She had regretted not being able to visit the many beautiful sites, so she made a list of all the places she wanted to see in Athens and the surrounding Greek Islands. Tomorrow they would go to the Parthenon, and the day after, they would visit the beautiful

Greek island of Santorini. Waking up early the following day, Kate was anxious to start the day.

"Hey, wake up, sleepyhead," she smiled, kissing him. "Are you ready for a day of sightseeing?" she whispered.

"Well, if you keep that up, maybe not," Nicky smiled, returning her kisses passionately. Then, running for the shower, Kate was anxious to get out of the hotel. "I'll order breakfast," Nicky announced as he sat up in bed, lighting a cigarette.

The following two days found them playing the typical role of tourists. Wearing his usual disguise, a baseball cap, they toured the Parthenon and the Greek Islands.

However, they both agreed the island of Santorini was by far the most visually stunning place they had ever visited. The island was beautiful with its steep, narrow paths, which meandered upward through the white-washed village. It offered spectacular views of the deep azure water of Caldera Bay, which sat below.

It was their last day in Athens, as the limo arrived at the hotel entrance to retrieve them for the concert.

"So, how did you two spend the last two days?" Jerry asked, getting inside the limo.

"Oh, we visited the most remarkable place on earth, the Greek Island of Santorini and the Parthenon. By the way, what did you do?" Kate inquired.

"The boys and I also spent the day visiting the Parthenon, and then we went on a walking tour of the city."

"Is that all?"

"Well, we stayed in and played poker one afternoon day," Jeff replied.

"Wow, Jeff, only you guys would sit inside playing cards while staying in one of the most beautiful places on earth."

"What? You had a poker game, and I didn't get an invite?" Nicky grumbled.

"Well, we thought you were tied up, figuratively speaking," David grinned as they all laughed.

Kate always seemed to become the target of their crude jokes.

She figured it was the price she paid for being the only girl. The boys passed around a pack of smokes, each lighting up cigarettes.

"You guys are mean, and you're making it hard to breathe in here," Kate complained.

As the limo parked at the back of the amphitheater, Bruce was waiting by the entrance.

"Glad to see everyone could make it tonight," he laughed. "Thought I might lose you guys by giving you a few days off. Follow me down to the dressing room. We've got a concert to do tonight."

Walking into the dressing room was much the same as the others. The only things which seemed to change were the food brought in by the caterers and the flowers, except for the vase of red roses, which they occasionally used to pass out to their fans.

"Okay, who wants to go first?" Kate asked.

"Guess I will," Jerry said, quickly extinguishing his cigarette.

After pouring a drink, Nicky and David took a seat on the somewhat worn sofa as Jerry sat in the chair while Kate styled his hair and applied a small amount of makeup. Bruce glanced over at Nicky.

"I've been informed there will be another member of a royal family in the audience tonight. I'm not sure of their title, but I believe they are vacationing on one of the islands. So we hired extra security for the concert. Not sure if they'll want a private meeting after the concert with you guys or not," Bruce smiled. "But be forewarned," he said, pouring himself a cup of coffee. "Twenty minutes till showtime."

"Okay, Nicky, your next. Quickly get over here. I've only got a few minutes to finish all of your hair and makeup." Then, styling Nicky's hair, she looked at him in the mirror.

"So, is it another princess tonight?"

"Doll, no worries," he winked. "You know you're my one and only."

Finally, the boys were all dressed and looking stylish.

"Boys, let's go. I'll walk out with you," Bruce stated.

Kate kissed her handsome guy.

"Have a great time."

"Oh, you don't have to worry about that," Nicky grinned, returning her kisses.

Walking out on stage, it was another beautiful night under the stars. Nicky knew he could easily get used to this. But, now, the idea of playing inside an auditorium made him nervous.

"Hello, Athens," Nicky shouted, walking on stage. The fans were already standing as the guys took their places on stage. Looking at the vast sea of people, Nicky knew it didn't matter the venue or the country, Black Tie Affair was loved by their fans. They were blessed with the best fans on earth, who never failed to come out and support them. The concert went off without a hitch. The fans once again adored them. Nicky sang the song he had written for Randy and Alex as the audience lit cigarette lighters and stood to their feet. It was another incredible concert under the night sky. Tonight it had been Athens. The fans openly welcomed Nicky. He was once again living his dream and all that came with it.

After the concert, Bruce whisked them away to another amazing restaurant.

"So, what do you have in mind for tonight?" Jeff questioned Bruce as he relaxed into his seat inside the limo.

"Well, all I can say is that I was informed they have the best Greek food in Athens." Jeff smiled.

It seemed this was always Bruce's answer to the question of restaurant choice, no matter the venue or its location. The funny thing about his uncle's answer was that he was usually spot on.

Arriving at a small quaint bar that sat off the main street, the boys questioned his choice for tonight. The restaurant was small and lacking in décor as they entered. The aged stone interior had signs of visible cracks running along the walls. Lanterns were lit and hanging from wooden columns. Small tables covered with red-checkered tablecloths, glowing candles, and surrounded by chairs with straw seats filled the room. The restaurant's ambiance came more from the beautiful Greek music, which played softly in the background.

"Welcome," the owner smiled, quickly pulling together enough tables and chairs to seat the boys and Kate. Immediately, a waiter brought out a brass tray containing shots of Ouzo, the famous Greek drink. Nicky looked at Kate.

"Hey Doll, honestly, do you think you should go there?" he asked, concerned.

"Nicky, I love you, but you're not my dad," Kate retorted, picking up one of the smoking shot glasses.

As the boys raised their glasses, Bruce toasted the band.

"Here's to our opening concert tonight and three wonderful days in Athens."

Picking up their menus, Kate ordered eggplant casserole. Nicky and the boys ordered braised lamb while Bruce ordered his favorite stewed rabbit with pearl onions, red wine, and cinnamon.

As large wooden platters containing their delicacies were served, the aroma was mouthwatering. Nicky ate fast, afterward thinking he would be sick. The comradeship shared this evening felt like family. Finally, another round of Ouzo made its way around the table. No one failed to enjoy another shot, not even Kate, who was now receiving a rather strange stare from Nicky.

"Well, boys, we are scheduled to play in Madrid next month. We received our official invitation to visit the royal palace after the concert. According to the tour schedule for the remaining year, we will be in Portugal, Morocco, and Africa. How does that sound?"

"Damn, guess we are going to be busy," Jerry exclaimed.

"Well, isn't that what a world tour is all about," David laughed, lighting a cigarette.

"Hey, can I bum a smoke from you?" Jerry smiled.

Passing the pack of cigarettes around the table, Nicky lit a cigarette giving Kate a seething glance as he watched her toss back another shot of Ouzo. The night was getting late. Looking down at his watch, Bruce knew they should call it an evening after consuming the numerous strong drinks.

"Well, boys, I think we should call it a night."

Just at that moment, the waiter brought out another tray of Ouzo. "I suppose we can consider these our nightcaps," Bruce said, taking one of the shot glasses. Everyone took one of the small glasses, including Kate. She had always considered herself one of the boys. So she gave herself a reason to take the glass from the tray by thinking of herself as one of the guys.

As she downed the shot, Nicky gave her another irate glance.

"Kate," he whispered into her ear.

There was nothing he could do. Kate slammed the empty glass down on the table, receiving stares from the guys.

"Okay. The car is waiting. It's late, and we should be leaving."

Everyone pushed back from the table to leave, except for Kate. The moment she stood, the effects of the strong drink instantly brought her to her knees. Anticipating Kate's dilemma, Nicky caught her before she hit the floor.

"Poor girl," Bruce reacted caringly, unaware of her past encounter with the robust drink in Frankfurt.

Quickly picking Kate up, Nicky carried her to the limo.

"Man, I'm sure she was drinking to suppress her feelings regarding Randy and Alex," David reckoned. "She was so close to those two."

"It's been hard on her losing them," Jeff added.

"Yeah, whatever," Nicky vented, trying to get her inside the limo. He wasn't happy with Kate's actions tonight. Nicky knew she didn't have a tolerance for Ouzo, yet she was determined to keep up with them. He could not fathom her reasoning. It didn't take long before the limo dropped them at their hotel.

"Goodnight, boys. See you all tomorrow at the airport. Nicky, take good care of my girl?" Bruce insisted.

"Okay, Bruce, see you tomorrow," Nicky replied, carrying Kate inside the hotel.

Making sure Kate was comfortable, Nicky took off her shoes and covered her with a blanket. But, unfortunately, she would simply have to sleep it off. Walking out to the living room, Nicky enjoyed another cigarette. Finally, deciding there was nothing left to do but get some sleep, he walked into the bedroom.

Waking the following day before Kate, he looked at her, finally finding a little empathy for her in his heart. Brushing back her hair with his hands, he kissed her awake.

"Babe, how are you feeling?"

"It seems like the room is still spinning."

"I'll bring you coffee and aspirin. Then, I'll order orange juice and toast if you feel like eating."

"Thanks," Kate moaned, pulling the covers back over her head. Nicky went into the other room and ordered breakfast. It was almost 10:00 a.m., and they were supposed to meet Bruce at the airport at 2:00 p.m. After spending another leisurely morning in bed, trying to get Kate recuperated, the passing time finally forced them to get ready for their ride to the airport. Kate jumped in the shower, where finally, the warm water revived her.

Walking out, she looked stunning with her black curly hair pulled into a ponytail. She was wearing blue jeans and her favorite T-shirt with the band's logo.

"Well, Doll, I guess you do like that shirt."

"Of course, it's my favorite," Kate smiled.

"It's 2:00 p.m. I think we should go down to the lobby."

Meeting the boys downstairs, everyone walked outside to the limo. They were on their way to the airport.

Arriving at the hanger, Bruce once again spoke with the pilot. He had made it a habit of questioning the safety of the aircraft.

"The plane is in good shape this morning, sir," Robert reassured Bruce.

After losing the boys in the tragic accident, Bruce didn't take any chances. Robert had been with the band as a pilot for many years, and it must have been a miracle Bruce thought that he hadn't been flying the day the boys were killed.

"Good afternoon, kids. Are you all ready to fly to Istanbul, Turkey?" Bruce asked.

For the next four weeks, they played at various venues along the beautiful coast of the Mediterranean, Cyprus, Beirut, Tel Aviv, Alexandria, and even Cairo. Black Tie Affair never failed to have thousands of adoring fans wherever their travels took them on their world tour. Nicky was quickly becoming well known in the world of rock and roll. His name sold out venues faster than Bruce could have it entered on the marques. Nicky and the band had now been introduced to people of prominence and royals at many of those venues. Black Tie Affair was currently scheduled to make a command performance in Madrid.

Madrid

They were now on their way to perform in Madrid by invitation from the royal family. Nicky lounged back in his seat, trying to sleep. He was exhausted from the hectic schedule of the past weeks. However, Kate was determined to keep him awake. She spent the entire flight reliving the details of their two days in Cairo. She recounted how they rode horses at the pyramids and enjoyed a felucca boat ride on the Nile River at sunset.

"Kate, for heaven's sake, you should try to get some sleep. You must have been a travel guide in another life," Nicky complained, putting a pillow over his head.

As the plane began its descent into Madrid, Nicky was still tired. All he could think about was getting to the hotel and catching up on some much-needed sleep. Arriving at their hotel, he was anxious to check in, get their room key and go to bed.

However, what awaited him was quite a surprise. It seemed that by having accepted the royal invitation, their stay in Madrid had come with a complete itinerary, compliments of the royal family.

Entering the hotel, it was beautiful—gorgeous gardens covered the grounds. Ivy had entwined itself on the outer walls and into the greenery of the flower beds, which contained many species of blooming flowers. As they followed the long portico leading to their room, Nicky looked over at Kate.

"Do you think there's any way we could get out of the engagement for tonight?" he complained.

"Oh, are you kidding? We've been given private seats tonight to watch a bullfight, compliments of the royal family, and you would even dare to think of not accepting. So you better jump into the shower and revive yourself after that long flight," Kate suggested.

Unlocking the door to their suite, they found it came with an abundance of fresh flowers and a sideboard covered with trays of fruit, cheese, and entrées which looked delectable. Quickly, opening a bottle of wine, Nicky poured himself a glass along with Kate and walked out on the patio to have a cigarette.

"Man, they've certainly gone to extravagance to show their appreciation."

"Nicky, I think you forget how famous you've become, as well as the band. Bruce has even been asked to add more venues to this tour."

"Now that you've mentioned it, I was going to discuss an opportunity that Bruce threw past me last week. I was just waiting till I had a little time to tell you about it."

"What are you talking about?" Kate questioned.

"It seems I'm being offered a movie contract back in the states after this tour is over."

"So what did you decide? Are you going to do it?"

"Yes, in fact, I'm looking forward to it.

Bruce is going to schedule our concerts back in the states around the time it would take to complete the film."

"Wow, Nicky, first you got the lead position with the band, next you began writing songs, and now you're going to star in a movie," Kate vented, somewhat irritated.

"Yes. Doll, what's wrong? Aren't you happy for me?" Nicky hadn't given much importance to Kate's input on his decision to take the role. He'd agreed to it from the very beginning.

"Everything is beginning to happen so fast now," Kate shrugged.

Putting his arms around her, he pulled her close.

"Babe, don't worry, you're just tired. Come with me. Nicky will make things better," he winked with a wicked smile.

The three days which followed in Madrid were incredible. The band was given the royal treatment during their stay, and the concert was phenomenal. The concerts were sold each night entirely. It was evident Spain loved Black Tie Affair.

However, they loved Nicky Spade even more. The visit to the royal palace was evidence of the love they were shown in Madrid. Nicky's first album with Black Tie Affair had quickly made its way to the top of the charts. His rise to fame as a rock star had happened relatively fast, maybe too fast. Nicky felt like he didn't deserve all the hype and media that followed him. His career had been an easy one, and at times he felt like he had never been required to pay his dues, so to speak like so many other artists. He could only hope to stay on this same path.

The two-year world tour with Black Tie Affair seemed to end too soon.

The band performed at venues in Japan, Taiwan, the Philippines, and Australia. The tour finally ended in the Hawaiian Islands. Nicky, Kate, and the boys, under the loving guidance of Bruce, had toured over thirty countries by its close. Nicky Spade now had worldwide name recognition. He was a phenomenon in the world of rock and roll. He had taken Black Tie Affair to staggering heights as a band. Now, he was set to do something for himself.

CHAPTER FIFTEEN

Hollywood

Nicky's path to stardom had now taken a new direction. From the day Bruce had informed him of his possible role in a movie based loosely on his life, he had found himself dreaming of the day he would arrive in Hollywood. Finally, at last, the two-year tour was behind him. Nicky hoped Hollywood might one day have another star on its famous sidewalk with his name on it.

Arriving at the hotel, Nicky was anxious to check in and then make arrangements to check out the movie set and its location.

"Kate, the limo will be arriving shortly."

"No, problem, I'm almost ready."

Nicky had never visited Los Angeles or the west coast. Instead, he had literally traveled the world without first seeing his own country.

"Okay. Let's go," Kate smiled.

She looked stunning in the cute sundress she had bought in Hawaii. It was summer, and even in Los Angeles, the temperature can sometimes climb above one hundred degrees. The production company had sent a car to pick them up from the hotel.

Due to the intense heat, they were shooting indoors today. The scene took place inside a restaurant, and even though it was air-conditioned, the lights used for filming made it seem hotter than the sun. Bruce had negotiated into Nicky's contract a position for Kate. She was to remain as his stylist and makeup artist. Several times during filming, the director stopped and asked her to reapply Nicky's makeup.

Nicky enjoyed acting. He was a natural. He had never imagined in his wildest dreams that his becoming a famous rock star would lead to an acting career as well. The day seemed to drag on forever as the director demanded numerous retakes. Finally, Nicky's co-star, Renee Ricci, walked over at the close of the day. She was hosting a huge party at her house in Malibu for the cast, and she wanted to make sure Nicky would make an appearance.

Renee was beautiful, in her early twenties, tall, slim, long blonde hair with a glowing, olive complexion. Captivated by Renee's gorgeous blue eyes, Nicky felt an instant connection to Renee the first day they met. She was Italian, and Nicky loved that they shared the same heritage.

"Hey Nicky, are you are coming to the party later tonight?" Renee questioned, walking off the set.

"You bet I wouldn't miss it. Kate and I will be there," Nicky answered. Overhearing their conversation, Kate felt uneasy around Renee.

"Nicky, do we have to go?" Kate asked as soon as Renee left the building.

"Yes. Kate, we do. I'm sure you'll have a great time. I can't afford not to make an appearance. You know how it is in Hollywood. I'm sure there will be other celebrities there as well. Renee's movies are box office hits, so I have to go. Kate, I'm going with or without you?"

"Okay, Nicky, okay." Kate was having a hard time fitting into the goldfish bowl called Hollywood. She was not even an extra on the set, just hair and makeup. Now, she found herself somewhat jealous of Nicky's role in his first movie, *Life in Spades, The Chronicle of Black Tie Affair.*

Reaching the hotel, it was only a short time before the limo arrived to take them to Renee's home in Malibu. Lounging back on the sofa, Nicky opened a beer and lit a cigarette. He needed a few minutes to unwind from his hectic day on set. Kate quickly dressed. She wasn't about to let Nicky go alone.

"Babe, you should hurry. The limo will be downstairs shortly."

Nicky finished his beer and dressed for the evening.

"You look handsome tonight," Kate smiled, watching Nicky walk out from the bathroom. After kissing her guy, it was time to go.

Making their way down to the lobby, it seemed strange to be without the boys in the band. They were now staying at another hotel. Bruce was in the process of setting up venues along the West Coast, where they could easily perform, while Nicky took on his acting role.

Sitting in the back seat of the limo with her arm around Nicky, it seemed odd they were on their way to a party in Malibu instead of a concert.

"Nicky, I'm going to feel like a fish out of water at this party."

"Doll, stick close to me and don't worry. You'll do fine."

Entering the long circular drive of Renee's beach house was exquisite. Tall Queen Palms lined the driveway leading through a massive wrought iron gate which opened into a large courtyard. Two gorgeous oversized oak doors stood at the entrance of the sprawling beach house, giving no hint of the beautiful ocean which sat directly behind it.

"Wow, this place is incredible," Kate remarked as Nicky rang the doorbell.

It was only a few minutes before a stately gentleman opened the door.

"Hello, I'm Nicky Spade, and my girlfriend, Kate."

"Welcome. Please come in. Renee is receiving guests on the patio. Follow me. I'll take you outside and inform her that you are here."

Glancing at the impeccable décor, Kate was impressed. A wall of glass windows revealed a panoramic view of the stunning cobalt waters of the pacific.

"Hey Nicky, I'm so glad you could make it," Renee smiled, failing to acknowledge Kate's presence

Instantly, Kate realized why she disliked Renee. She was egotistical. Adding to Kate's level of discomfort, the numerous people on the balcony, none of which she knew, made her quickly feel alone and adrift in a sea of people.

"Hey Nick, how's it going? Great job today on set," a tall, distinguished man with gray hair grinned. "I'm Brad. Renee and I share this house, and I'm a huge fan of yours."

Walking back inside to find a bathroom, Kate was disturbed by what she saw. People were sitting on a white leather sofa, passing a silver tray filled with lines of cocaine. Feeling very uncomfortable, she immediately went to find Nicky.

"Nicky, we need to talk."

"What is it, Kate?" he asked, somewhat annoyed.

"I want to leave."

"We're not leaving. We just got here."

"Nicky, people in the living room are using cocaine. It's being passed around on a tray," she whispered into his ear.

"Well, what do you want me to do about it?"

"I think we should leave and now," Kate demanded.

"Oh Kate, get with it. You're not in Kansas, Dorothy. That's what the boys told me when I first arrived in England. You're in Hollywood, and things like this happen. It's a lifestyle. Just accept it. You don't have to participate," Nicky answered, being insensitive.

"Nicky, I'm shocked by your answer."

"Well, I'm here making some new connections, and I'm not about to rock the boat, so to speak."

"Okay, Nicky, but I'd rather leave."

"Well, that's totally up to you, but I'm not going anywhere. Guess you'll have to call a taxi."

"Fine. I'll stay, but it's against my better judgment."

Throughout the evening, Kate watched as cocaine was freely used by those who attended the party. Keeping a close watch on Nicky, she stuck to him like glue. Kate no longer wished to be introduced to those in attendance. She had nothing in common with them. Constantly glancing at her watch, the time seemed to drag.

Taking a glass of wine from the bar on the balcony, Kate walked down to the beach. She took off her shoes and walked along the shore as the warm water gently washed over her feet. It felt relaxing and was her only reprieve from the crowd at the beach house.

Moments later, Nicky came running down the beach after her.

"Hey Kate, wait up. What are you doing down here?"

"Well, you weren't going to leave, and I didn't feel like mingling with that group."

"Doll, do you really feel that uncomfortable? Are you sure you want to leave?"

"Yes. I do."

"Okay, then let's walk back up to the house, and I'll let Renee think you are not feeling well?"

"Whatever, Nicky, please get me out of here."

"Alright. Let's go," Nicky reluctantly agreed, putting his arm around Kate as they walked back up the embankment to the beach house.

He knew that Kate would have a difficult time exposed to the lifestyle of those he worked with on the movie set.

Arriving at the hotel, Nicky unlocked the door to their hotel suite. Grabbing a beer, he lounged back on the sofa and lit a cigarette. He began contemplating his dilemma with Kate.

"Hey, can I have a sip of that?" Kate smiled, sitting next to him.

"There's more in the mini-fridge. Go get yourself one."

"What's wrong with you? Since we've arrived in Los Angeles, you've taken on a different attitude, and I must say I don't like it."

"Whatever, Kate. I'm going to finish this movie, and there's talk of another movie in the works after this."

Deciding she'd had enough of his arrogant attitude for one evening, Kate went to bed without him.

Waking up the following day, Kate discovered that Nicky had never come to bed. Instead, he'd chosen to sleep on the couch. As a result, things were subdued between them the next day on the movie set. They hardly spoke during the drive back to the hotel after the day's filming.

"Nicky, I think you need to get back into the studio and record another album. I know you're going to finish this movie, but you aren't needed on the set every day, and it would give you the flexibility to get back into your music. You seem to be happiest when you're on stage, not on a movie location."

Kate had ulterior motives for persuading Nicky to give up his ambitions of remaining in Hollywood. She wasn't going to raise their baby under these conditions. A baby which she hoped would bring them closer and which he knew nothing about.

"Well, I'll think about it. I'll call Bruce and see what he can set up with the band."

Over the next two days, Bruce managed to locate a recording studio so Nicky and the boys could start work on their next album.

One evening, Kate decided to go shopping.

"Nicky, do you want to go to the mall? I've really missed shopping in the states. We've been out of the country forever, and I forgot how much I truly missed some of my favorite stores.

"No, Babe, you go. It was a hard day on the set. There were so many retakes, and after being in the recording studio late last night, I think I'm going to turn in early."

"Okay. Are you sure?"

"Yes. Enjoy yourself, take your time. Besides, the boys said they might come over for poker."

"Fine. I'll just get a cab to the mall. I'll be back around 10:00 p.m."

After calling for a taxi, Kate went downstairs to the hotel lobby to wait for her ride to the mall.

Even without Nicky, Kate enjoyed her trip to the mall. She was a shopaholic and had desperately missed her favorite shoe and accessory stores. Stopping at her favorite lingerie store, Kate decided to go in and purchase something cute and sexy to spice up the evening. Unfortunately, Nicky had not been himself lately, and she needed to get her man back. Surely, it was all stress-related. Shooting the movie and staying up late at the recording studio seemed to be taking its toll on him. She couldn't wait to get back to the hotel and model her latest purchase. Tonight would be the perfect time to reveal her secret. First, however, Kate decided to stop for coffee and dessert at a restaurant in the mall before leaving.

As the taxi arrived back at the hotel, Kate barely managed to gather all her shopping bags out of the back seat. Then, sitting her prized possessions down, she unlocked the door to their hotel suite. It was dark and quiet as she stepped inside. Clearly, Nicky had decided to turn in early because it was evident there had not been a poker game.

Putting down her shopping bags, Kate tried to stay quiet so she wouldn't wake Nicky. Then, slipping into her new lingerie and a hint of her favorite French perfume, she decided to surprise him. Walking over to the bedroom door, it was dark entering the room. Turning on a small lamp near the vanity, Kate gasped in horror. She screamed, catching Nicky in bed with Renee.

"Nicky, how could you. How could you?" Kate vented furiously.

She felt like she had been kicked in the gut and was nauseous. Then glancing at the nightstand by the bed, she saw a vile of white powder and the evidence which let her know that Nicky had been using cocaine with Renee.

"Nicky, how could you do this to us?" she screamed, picking up the first thing her hands touched throwing it at him. The alarm clock barely missed his head as it went flying into the wall. "Nicky Spade, I hate you, I hate you," she cried. "Bastard," she screamed. "I loved you, and now look what you've gone and done."

Quickly sitting up, Nicky stared at her, noticing the lingerie.

"Wow, Doll, the lingerie you're wearing is sexy."

Kate knew that Nicky was high on drugs, and she had Renee to thank for it. Renee just sat in bed and stared at Kate.

"Oh, Kate, you got back early."

"You bitch," Kate shouted. "Nicky Spade, you're a bastard," she screamed.

Nicky appeared oblivious to the situation unfolding around. "I'm out of here. Do you hear me, out of here? You ungrateful bastard," Kate screamed once again.

Walking over to the closet, Kate began packing her suitcase.

Hollywood had been the worst thing that could have happened to them as a couple. It was evident now that even the new life she carried would never be enough to save him. The best she could do now for herself and the baby would be to leave him and Hollywood. He would never know that she was carrying their child.

Hurriedly pulling her clothes from their hangers, Kate took one last look at Nicky, who had fallen asleep. Drugs had definitely played a role in the horrific events of this evening. Hastily, she got her clothes and suitcase into the other room. Then, closing the bedroom door, she overheard Renee.

"Wow. I thought she would never leave."

Kate decided the only thing left to do was call the hotel where Jeff and the boys were staying. Hopefully, one of them would come over and pick her up. Quickly getting changed, Kate went down to the lobby.

After Kate left Nicky, he moved in with Renee at her beach house in Malibu. Renee quickly tossed her boy toy, Brad, to the curb and offered Nicky a place to live. Never one to sleep without a warm body next to him, Nicky moved in with Renee without hesitation. Nicky hadn't blamed Kate for leaving him. He knew that he had let her down with his drug abuse. However, Nicky felt Kate would never fit into his current lifestyle. He was glad that she had chosen to relinquish her job as his makeup artist and hairstylist. Seeing Kate on a routine basis would have been an awkward situation and not been a good idea for either of them.

Renee and Nicky were inseparable, both on set and off. It seemed reasonably safe to say that in Hollywood, many times, hookups occurred between actors and actresses who were starring in movies together. It had definitely been the case with Nicky and Renee.

As a result of their numerous parties and drugs, their notoriety made them the buzz of the tabloids. Their relationship seemed solely based upon their need to remain part of the Hollywood scene.

After working for almost eighteen months on their current movie project, *Life in Spades, Chronicles of Black Tie Affair,* it was set to rap by the end of the week. Nicky was looking forward to the premiere of their new film. He was excited to share his name on a movie marque with Renee Ricci. The movie drew much attention among the millions of Black Tie Affair fans who knew about his leading role with the beautiful Italian actress.

The night of the premier, Bruce and the boys from the band, Todd, and the sound crew arrived with other prominent people. Those who were either part of the motion picture or personally invited to attend.

As the limo carrying Nicky and Renee arrived in front of the theater, the paparazzi were everywhere. The crowd waiting outside to catch a glimpse of Nicky and Renee turned into a mob scene as security tried to keep the theater cleared.

Walking the red carpet to the entrance, Nicky held Renee's hand tightly. The excitement of entering the theater with Renee, the flashes from the cameras, and screams from the crowd, seemed comparable to the feelings he always got when he walked out on stage. The only difference was that he was accompanied by a gorgeous woman on his arm tonight.

After the film was shown at the premiere, the production company gave a huge studio party. Nicky and Renee appeared to enjoy the fame and notoriety they received from the movie.

The movie received rave reviews from the people who were lucky enough to attend the premier. It would open in the number one position at the box office the following week—revenue from ticket sales where the highest ever recorded at all major theaters. There was only one point of sadness tonight. It was the fact his parents, along with Tony and Annie, had been unable to attend.

After the movie was released, it wasn't long before movie producers sent additional scripts to him. However, Renee was no longer a part of the picture or his life. She quickly moved on. They were no more than two ships that had simply passed in the night. Renee's only interest in Nicky had come from the film.

As hot as these typical Hollywood relationships were, they always seemed to burn out fast. Renee was heavily addicted to cocaine at this point and already looking for the next best thing when it came to a lover. Nicky was quickly tossed aside just as Brad had been previously. He now found himself moving out of the beach house and back into the hotel. His living arrangements didn't have a high priority at this time. The movie had now made the band even more famous. They were once again scheduled to make appearances at venues that were quickly selling out months in advance all across the country.

Nicky's life had changed dramatically since moving to Los Angeles and starring in his first major role in a motion picture. He was in the tabloids now more than any other rock star, and his reputation only seemed to work in his favor. It appeared all the publicity from his use of drugs, his torrid affairs with starlets and even prostitutes made him even more in demand. He went on to make three other movies before leaving Hollywood.

Nicky, Bruce, and the boys in the band completed several albums during their time in Los Angeles. Their record sales were well into the millions worldwide. Nicky was at the pinnacle of success. Some of the best songs he had ever written had now made their way into the number one position on the music billboards. In addition, Nicky was selling out more rock concerts than any other artist. As a result, there was a huge demand to take the band back out on another world tour. However, Bruce stepped down from his management position with the band. He had finally had enough of Nicky Spade. Bruce felt like he had lost a son to cocaine. He could no longer stand by and watch the so-called train wreck he referred to as Nicky Spade. Nonetheless, there would be no problem hiring new management for the band.

After spending over a decade in the City of Angels, Nicky was finally ready to move on. This city had cost him a lot over the years as far as relationships. He was now leaving without Kate and Bruce.

However, Nicky now found himself at such a place in his career he no longer cared for those around him. The boys in the band were having a hard time dealing with his ego problem. Jeff and Jerry were the only members of the band that had remained stable. David was again succumbing to the use of drugs. Yet, even with all the personal problems Nicky and David now brought to Black Tie Affair, they were more in demand than ever. When the boys were on stage, they always gave a stellar performance, and the fans loved them.

Now under new management, Black Tie Affair was scheduled to perform for two years worldwide with an option for an additional two years if ticket sales supported it. Their first venue would be Thailand.

CHAPTER SIXTEEN

It's in the Genes. *Quebec*

"Jenna, did you remember to pick up the balloons?" Audrey inquired.

"Yes, Mom, I went to the party supply store right after the bakery."

It was Cameron's thirteenth birthday. He was officially becoming a teenager, and it was cause for celebration. Jenna had always managed to give her only child the best parties ever, and today would be no exception. The only reason for sadness today would be the fact that his grandfather had died just recently and never lived to be part of today's festivities. Frank, Jenna's dad, suffered a fatal heart attack while working only two months previously. He had looked forward to Cameron's thirteenth birthday, and no one could have ever predicted that he would have passed only months before.

"Mom, do you think we'll have enough pizza, or should I run over and pick up two more?" Jenna yelled upstairs to her mother.

"Jenna, I think you're going overboard with the food. The three large pizzas we have downstairs will be enough."

Jenna had taken the day off from work to decorate the house for the party. After Cameron was born, Jenna went back to school to get her high school diploma. She had always been interested in becoming a teacher. It was the one career field that seemed to fit a single mom. Jenna had never married. She hadn't planned her life that way. It just happened that she never met anyone with whom she felt a connection. Nicky had been the one great love of her life. The morning she had left Middleton, her perspective on family changed forever. Her mom and dad had always been beside her, helping her raise Cameron. Together they made an incredible team and her family unit. She felt very blessed to be Cameron's mother and proud of the life she had provided for them.

"Mom, I'm going to pick Cameron up from school. The house is all decorated. I'll be back in a few minutes."

"Okay. Drive safe."

Parking in front of Cameron's school, Jenna could see him walking down the sidewalk with two of his friends. Cameron was tall for his age, and with his black curly hair, he was the spitting image of Nicky. He had Nicky's gorgeous Italian profile and dark skin.

"Hey, Mom, Billy, and Jason are coming home with me today for my party."

"Yes. My mom said she would pick us up after the party," Billy explained.

"Okay, great. Boys, buckle your seat belts."

It wasn't long before they were back at home. Running into the house, Cameron was excited to see what Jenna and Audrey had planned for his special day.

"Wow. I love it," Cameron remarked when he saw the decorations.

He was already into the music scene, and all he had wanted was a new guitar for his birthday. Jenna's theme for his party was rock and roll. So Cameron was delighted when he saw his birthday cake was made in the shape of a guitar.

"Mom, this is neat. I really love it."

"Now, your party doesn't start until 4:00 p.m., so if you boys want to go up and hang out in your room, I'll call you when the other kids arrive."

"Okay, thanks, mom," Cameron smiled, running up to his room.

"Jenna, you've done a great job with the decorations," Audrey grinned, walking into the dining room.

"Oh, thanks, Mom. It's truly hard to believe that Cameron is officially a teenager today, isn't it?"

"Yes. It seems like only yesterday that Cameron was born. Now, look what a handsome young man he has become," Audrey smiled.

"I know, mom. We've been blessed with our little guy. I love him so much."

"I know Jenna, so do I. So where is our birthday boy?"

"Oh, he ran up to his bedroom with Billy and Jason."

The rest of the afternoon passed all too soon as Cameron's friends arrived to help him celebrate. There was more than enough pizza, ice cream, and cake for everyone. The look on Cameron's face when he opened the guitar box containing his new guitar was priceless. His passion, even at the early age of thirteen, was music. Cameron had inherited his father's love of playing the guitar and his passion for singing. He always chose to sing the solo parts with the youth choir at church. Cameron was naturally gifted with a strong voice, and Jenna began to see glimpses of his father coming through in his personality. He loved to sing in front of an audience, especially at church. Cameron had never been into sports, even though his grandfather had desperately tried to involve him in the world of baseball. It was evident that Cameron was destined to follow the same path as his father.

CHAPTER SEVENTEEN

The Hard Rock Years.
Bangkok, Thailand

As the plane landed in Bangkok, Thailand, it was new territory for the band and its members. Bruce was no longer with them as their tour manager, and Kate had been replaced with a new hair and makeup assistant. The band was now under new management. William Kirkland had replaced Bruce. He was easy-going and tolerant, even more so than Bruce. As the boys in the band called him, Bill was very tolerable when it came to the fact that Nicky and David were known to be using cocaine. His stance regarding their behavior was unusually lenient. As long as the boys didn't get caught and ticket sales remained high, Bill turned a blind eye to their addictions. The show must go on, and to replace Nicky at the height of his success would have been suicide. Black Tie Affair dominated the world of rock and roll. Ticket sales were the highest gross per venue than any other band at this time. Thailand's venue had sold out in less than twenty-four hours after tickets had become available. Nicky lit a cigarette in the back of the limo.

"Hey man, can I bum a smoke?" David asked.

"No problem."

The boys were on their way to the hotel. They were tired. The flight from Los Angeles had been long. Nicky simply wanted to get to his hotel room and relax. He had left Los Angeles without a girl on his arm, which was unusual for him.

Arriving at the hotel, the guys discovered they were sharing rooms for this venue. Jerry and Jeff had taken one suite, leaving the other one to be shared by Nicky and David. The hotel was modern and had a piano bar in the lobby.

"Well, guys, you're up on the tenth floor," Nicky stated, glancing at Jerry.

"Yeah, guess this is your stop," Jeff said.

"Are you guys staying in for the night?" Jerry questioned.

David glanced in Nicky's direction.

"I'm not sure yet, but if we decide to leave the hotel, we'll give you a call," David answered.

"Yes," Nicky agreed. "See you both later."

Bangkok shared the notoriety of Amsterdam when it came to its nightlife, the availability of drugs, and the party scene. Knowing this, Jerry was worried about Nicky and David. Jerry knew about their problem with cocaine. He felt if they were going to leave their hotel room tonight, they would definitely need a chaperon.

Without Bruce, there would be no one to oversee any situations which might arise. Jerry also knew if they got into trouble, it could easily jeopardize the concert the following evening. However, Jeff would be relieved later that evening when he went down to check them.

"Hey Jeff, come in," David smiled, opening the door.

"I came down to see if you guys needed anything?"

"No, you didn't. Let's be honest, Jeff. You just came down to see if we had left our hotel suite. Don't worry. Nicky passed out after drinking a few beers tonight. He was exhausted from the flight. So now you can go back upstairs and let Jerry know not to worry about his cousin for the night, okay, man."

"Okay. You've caught me. Have a good evening. See you both in the morning."

If Nicky and David were going to get into trouble, they couldn't possibly have chosen a better city than Bangkok. However, tonight they had dodged a bullet.

Waking up to the smell of coffee from the other room, Nicky rolled over, opening his eyes. Once again, he had slept alone. This was new territory for him. Staring at the empty bed, thoughts of Jenna raced through his mind. Girls like her only came around once in a lifetime, if you're really lucky. He had let her slip through his fingers. He often found himself wondering if she had ever married.

"Hey Nicky," David shouted from the next room. "Are you awake?" he asked, knocking on the bedroom door.

"Yeah, man, what do you need?"

"I was going to order breakfast and wanted to know if you'd like me to order for both of us?"

"Yes, that sounds good. Bacon and eggs will do fine and maybe some orange juice."

"Okay. I'll call down for room service."

After eating breakfast, Nicky thought he would call Jerry and Jeff's suite to see if they would like to take a tour of Bangkok today before the concert. However, before Nicky could even call their room, there was a knock at their door.

"Hey man, have you made any plans for today?" Jerry inquired.

"No. I was just getting ready to call your room."

"Well, Jeff and I were planning on visiting some of the temples today. We thought you and David might like to come with us."

"Yes. I think that would be awesome," David replied, glancing at Nicky.

Jerry, Jeff, Nicky, and David spent the entire afternoon sighting seeing, and taking in the diverse culture of Bangkok. After they visited the statue of the Emerald Buddha, they toured the Grand Palace.

Later that afternoon, as they arrived at the hotel, there was only two hours before the limo would pick them up—just enough time to shower and dress for tonight's concert.

Stepping inside the limo which would carry them to the Bangkok Coliseum, it was evident that Nicky and David had snorted a line or two of cocaine.

"Nicky, man, are you alright?" Jerry inquired.

"Yeah. I'm feeling great." Nicky's eyes were dilated, and he appeared fidgety as he lit a cigarette.

"Man, you do you and let me worry about myself. Okay, Dad?" Nicky vented abrasively.

Jerry glanced at Jeff. He worried the guy's cocaine addiction would negatively impact tonight's concert.

Walking into the dressing room, Bill had arrived earlier with their new assistant.

"Hey guys, this is Jackie, the new stylist and makeup artist for tonight's concert.

Jackie was voluptuous, tall, and blonde with curves in all the right places. Nicky thought she must be in her early twenties.

"Jackie, please meet the guys, Nicky, David, Jeff, and Jerry," Bill said.

"Hi, nice to meet you all. I'm a huge fan of Black Tie Affair. So who wants to go first tonight?" she asked

"Guess I'll be your first victim," Nicky answered, taking a seat.

"I've heard a lot about you," Jackie smiled.

"I'm sure it's all great, right?" Nicky winked.

"Yes. I loved your movie."

"Thanks, Doll."

Having finished with makeup, he went over to light a cigarette and pour himself a drink. It didn't take long before Jackie had finished with everyone.

"I can't wait to see the concert tonight. Todd has offered to find me a great spot to watch your performance," Jackie said, taking a seat on the sofa next to Nicky.

"Great. Then I'll see you after the concert."

"Okay, guys, it's only about twenty minutes before showtime," Bill announced, lighting a smoke.

"Hello, Bangkok," Nicky yelled, walking out to the center of the stage to the roar of the fans.

The massive building had seating for over six thousand people, and the venue was entirely sold for both nights.

"Hello. How are you tonight?" Jerry shouted.

"Bangkok, it's nice to be with you this evening," David screamed, holding his guitar high in the air.

The girls in front began shouting, Nicky, Nicky, before he could even lead with his first song of the evening. The guys walked toward the front of the stage and began the ritual with their ties. The girls went crazy trying to get as close to the front as possible in hopes of grabbing one. David always bent down and tied his tie gently around the neck of a beautiful young girl as the other girls screamed. Security was doing a superb job keeping the mob in front from becoming out of control. The concert lasted for over an hour and a half, as the boys performed all their number one hits. It seemed to go off without a hitch even though Nicky and David were high on cocaine.

After the concert, the boys raced backstage to their dressing room and changed. Unlike Bruce, the new tour manager, Bill, chose not to hang out with the boys after the concert. As a result, he was not as hands-on as Bruce had always been. Quickly getting changed, they were ready for a night of fun in Bangkok. Passing Jackie in the hallway backstage, Nicky thought it would be nice to ask her to tag along.

"Hey Jackie, the boys and I are going out to enjoy some Thai Cuisine. Would you like to come?"

"Sure."

Getting inside the limo, Todd had highly recommended a restaurant and given them the address. Passing around a pack of smokes, Nicky and David lit up their cigarettes.

"So Jackie, where are you from?" Nicky questioned.

"Oh, Los Angeles."

"But, you weren't on our plane coming over from Los Angeles."

"I know. I still had another day of work to finish on a movie set before leaving. Bill flew me in yesterday evening."

"I don't understand how I never ran into you. The boys and I lived in Los Angeles for quite a few years," Nicky added.

"Oh, I've followed your career for a while now. You have quite the reputation back in Hollywood," Jackie replied, reaching for a cigarette as Nicky quickly reached over to light it.

"Well, you're not anyone in tinsel town these days if your reputation doesn't precede you," Nicky winked.

It wasn't long before the limo drove up to the entrance of an ornate Thai restaurant. The detailed trim on the eaves of the steep roof was amazing. The design shared similarities with the temples in downtown Bangkok. Walking in, it appeared busy. Nicky asked for seating in an adjacent room where they could enjoy their dinner without easily being recognized. It seemed odd to be eating after a concert without Bruce. He had always taken good care of the guys by treating them to the best restaurants in town. Tonight, he was undoubtedly missed. Nicky gave a toast to Bruce when the waiter returned with their drinks.

"Here's to Bruce, wherever he is tonight."

After finishing their meal and enjoying the Thai Cuisine, David suggested they continue their evening by going to one of Bangkok's most prominent nightclubs. Jeff and Jerry were unhappy with the idea but figured it probably was best to go if needed. In addition, they thought it would be better than having Bill called out in the middle of the night to retrieve Nicky or David. So the limo drove them to a nightspot which David had read about in one of the brochures.

Walking inside, Nicky took Jackie's hand. It was dark and crowded, which helped keep their identity a secret. Nicky found a small table in a corner. The dance floor was packed and the focus of everyone's attention, which helped keep them incognito. Nicky excused himself to go to the bathroom, which Jerry knew was not a good thing to do if he was recognized. However, Nicky needed another quick fix, and he was determined to get it at all costs.

After leaving for the bathroom, it was only minutes before Nicky came running back to the table, motioning for them to get out of the club. Jerry had

known something was going to happen. He was just relieved to see the limo was waiting outside. He hoped they would make it out before things got ugly, not knowing the circumstances. Rushing to get inside the limo, it left quickly with all of them safely inside.

"Okay. What the hell happened back there?" Jerry asked, staring at Nicky.

"Damn. I only wanted to do one line of coke, and this woman walks into the men's bathroom and tries to put the moves on me. When I turned around to better look at her, she was not a she but a he. As I tried to fight her, or I mean him off, he recognized me and started screaming for help. Hell, I just barely got out of there." The guys and Jackie broke out in a riot of laughter.

"Oh, you're crazy, Nicky," David mentioned, laughing hysterically.

"You almost got everyone into serious trouble, and we have another concert to perform tomorrow night," Jerry added.

"Okay, kids, I think we better call it a night," Jeff remarked, laughing.

As the limo drove back to their hotel, Nicky wondered where Jackie was staying.

"So Jackie, where does Bill have you staying while we're here in Bangkok?" Nicky asked.

"Well, to tell you the truth, it's over by the airport, but I don't feel safe going back there by myself tonight."

"You can room with David and me for the night."

"Oh, that would be great," Jackie smiled.

Taking the elevator up to their hotel suites, Nicky and David was the first stop.

"See you both tomorrow," Nicky said, glancing at Jeff.

"Yes. It was fun, goodnight," Jeff added.

Unlocking their door, Nicky, David, and Jackie were in for the night. Nicky, acting like the gentleman he sometimes can be slept on the sofa, giving his room to Jackie. However, after the incident at the club, he was totally worn out.

Black Tie Affair performed the following night to another sold out crowd. The fans in Bangkok loved them. Nicky and David managed to leave without another incident. They were now on their way to Taipei, Taiwan.

Taipei, Taiwan

As the jet touched down at the international airport in Taipei, the landscape of Taiwan looked similar to Thailand. The band was scheduled to perform for one night only at the largest sports complex in Taipei. The limo drove up, parking next to the private jet as its door opened.

"How do you guys ever manage being in a different country every week?" Jackie questioned as she descended the steps of the plane.

"You get used to it. I find it to be educational," Jeff replied, walking to the limo.

Jackie sat next to Nicky for the ride downtown to the hotel. Sitting in the back of the limo, Jeff missed his Uncle Bruce, who always managed to travel with them. Bill seemed detached from the guys in the band and never accompanied them. It seemed his focus was only on ticket sales and the revenue brought in.

It was only a short distance to the hotel as the limo arrived at an Asian-inspired resort that sat on the banks of the Danshui River. Detailed Chinese dragons were carved into the supportive wooden pillars at the entrance and offered protection. Walking inside, a mosaic mural depicting the local culture covered the walls. Nicky walked over to the reception desk, checked in for the boys, and picked up the keys to their rooms.

"It appears everyone is getting a suite at this venue, and we're all on the tenth floor." Tossing keys to the guys, they walked across the hotel lobby, searching for the elevator.

"Hey guys, over here," Jerry announced. "Around this next corner," he added.

Entering his suite, Nicky found it extremely lavish. The walls contained a mini version of the ceramic murals found downstairs. A large balcony overlooked an oriental garden that covered the hotel's grounds. However, the focus of his attention was the fully stocked mini-fridge and bar. Walking over, he poured himself a shot of bourbon and lit a cigarette. Nicky had just finished a line of coke when someone knocked. Quickly hiding his drug paraphernalia, he answered the door.

"Hey Nicky, I just thought I would walk over to see if you had any plans for this afternoon?" Jackie inquired.

"Come in. I can't say that I've given it much thought. Would you care for a drink?" Nicky questioned.

"That would be great." Nicky poured them each a glass of wine.

"Wow, you have a stunning view from your balcony," Jackie mentioned, taking her glass of wine outside. My room overlooks a parking lot toward the front of the hotel."

"Why don't we sit outside for a while," Nicky suggested, lighting another cigarette. "Would you care for one?"

"Yes, please. I know it's a nasty habit, but I got addicted to cigarettes on a movie set last year. Everyone smoked, and I found it works great to calm your nerves," Jackie added.

"So, what would you have to be nervous about?" Nicky questioned with a smile.

"Oh, I just went through a horrible breakup. I was with this guy for two years, and it didn't end well."

"Sorry to hear that."

That fool's loss would surely be his gain, Nicky thought.

"I was wondering if perhaps you would want to go and tour the Lungshan Temple tomorrow morning?" Jackie asked.

"Yes. That sounds like fun. So Doll, you're interested in temples? The boys and I toured the Temple of the Emerald Buddha while we were in Thailand."

"So, how was it?"

"Oh, it was cool. It contained the largest Buddha that I've ever seen," Nicky explained.

"Well then, I can't wait until tomorrow."

It wasn't long before Nicky found himself once again letting his emotions come into his conversation.

"You remind me of Kate, our former assistant, which you replaced. She loved taking in the sights everywhere we toured."

"Well, I don't know how to respond to that. I never met Kate. But, I do like to have fun. I'm pretty daring. Guess I would try anything at least once."

"Then I think you picked the right group of guys to work for."

"What time will the limo pick us up for the concert tonight?"

"Oh, usually around 4:00 p.m.," Nicky answered, walking inside to pour himself another shot of bourbon.

"Well, it's been nice talking with you. Thanks for the drink. I should get back to my room and take a short nap before the limo arrives," Jackie smiled, following Nicky inside.

"Okay. See you later this afternoon." Nicky hesitated for a brief moment, contemplating kissing her before she left.

Closing the door, Nicky began to entertain thoughts of a possible relationship between the two of them. However, tomorrow might give him more insight into whether they shared any common interests or if he felt a connection between them. All too soon, it was 4:00 p.m. as the boys and Jackie met down in the lobby to wait for the limo. When it arrived, Jackie got in first, followed by Nicky. He made sure he was seated next to her.

"So, did you just sleep the afternoon away?" Jerry asked, glancing at Nicky.

"No. Jackie stopped by for a drink, and we sat outside on the balcony." Jackie looked at Jerry and smiled.

"Nicky's room has the most beautiful view of the gardens."

Jerry knew that Nicky always seemed to attract all the girls. He remembered high school and Jenna. He had been the first to meet Jenna, but she ended up with Nicky as always.

Arriving at the sports complex, they were late due to traffic.

Finding their way through the maze of tunnels, they finally caught sight of the dressing room.

"Okay. Let's get started. Who wants to go first?" Kate smiled.

"Guess I will," Jeff answered, taking a seat in front of the large mirror.

Catering had brought in an array of rice, vegetables, and sushi. Nicky and David walked out to the bathroom, passing Bill as he walked toward them.

"Hey guys, is everyone already here?"

"Yes. Everyone is in the dressing room," David answered.

Nicky and David needed a fix before the concert. Finally, coming out of the bathroom, they both felt a rush of energy from the cocaine.

"Hopefully, this will get us through tonight's concert," Nicky grinned as they walked back into the dressing room to get changed.

It wasn't long before Jackie had finished with their hair and makeup. She thought the boys looked incredibly handsome in their suits, especially Nicky.

"Okay, guys, ten minutes," Bill stated.

Walking out on stage first, Jeff got the attention of all the fans with his intro.

"Jerry came on stage, followed by David, and then Nicky made his grand entrance.

"Hello, Taipei. We are so happy to be here with you this evening," Nicky shouted, staring at a crowd of six thousand screaming fans.

"We love you, Taipei," Jerry yelled.

As always, some of the fans tried to shove their way to the front of the stage. It almost became another mob scene, as security tried to keep the fans back from the stage. Nevertheless, the evening's concert was fabulous. The screaming fans adored them. The fans never knew that Nicky and David were high from their use of cocaine.

Time stood still as Nicky performed one hit song after another. Nicky absorbed the energy resonating from the thousands of screaming fans. He felt connected to each of them. It was like they had become one soul under the influence of a highly addictive drug called music.

"Thanks for coming out to party with us tonight," Nicky shouted as he left the stage. "We're Black Tie Affair, and we've enjoyed spending the evening with each of you," he added.

"We love you, Taipei," Jerry yelled.

"Hope to see you again. Thanks for coming out to party with us," David shouted.

The boys were anxious to get changed out of their suits, walking backstage.

"Great concert," Todd remarked, passing Nicky in the hallway.

"Thanks, man."

Meeting up with David and the boys in the dressing room, Nicky already made plans for the evening.

"Hey, let's go to the *Ta Lat*."

It was the largest night market in Taipei.

"That sounds like fun," David suggested, quickly changing clothes.

"Would you like to tag along?" Jerry asked, glancing at Jackie.

"Oh sure, why not," Jackie quickly answered. She wasn't sure what she had just signed up for, but it sounded interesting.

Overhearing their plans, Bill spoke up.

"That area can be dangerous after dark, so be forewarned."

It wasn't long before they were all dressed and ready to go. Getting inside the limo, the driver had decided not to wait for them this evening. He didn't feel safe parked along the water's edge at that time of night but agreed to pick them up at a later hour.

Soon the limo parked at the crowded marketplace. The guys quickly jumped out, eager to survey the numerous vendors and food kiosks.

"Why don't we get something to eat," Jeff recommended.

Walking past booths displaying seafood, some of it wasn't recognizable.

"Well, let's be daring and try some of it. I dare you," Jackie grinned, tempting Nicky.

"Okay, you point at it, and I'll try it."

Jackie quickly surveyed her options. Finally, choosing a fish she had never seen. It looked more like an eel.

"Okay. That one," Jackie pointed.

For a moment, Nicky had second thoughts as Jackie handed him the aquatic creature. Downing it fast before he changed his mind, it almost came back up. Everyone was amazed at Nicky's determination to not look weak in front of Jackie.

"So, how was it?" Jerry asked, laughing.

"Well, I'll tell you one thing, it sure didn't taste like sushi."

"We better get you something to drink," Jeff suggested walking to the next food booth.

"Here's some warm oolong tea to wash it down."

"Geez, Jeff, I expected something a bit stronger after downing that slimy creature."

The night was off to a great start as they walked deeper into the market. Suddenly, the night air began to feel a bit chilly. Nicky took off his jacket and put it around Jackie, who now seemed to be getting cold. The vendors displayed cheap trinkets, which appeared like cheap, flashy jewelry, and then there were some truly unique finds. A row of vendors near a dark alleyway had an extravagant booth of jade jewelry which caught Jackie's attention. Walking over for a closer inspection, Nicky could see that Jackie was eyeing a particular bracelet.

"Oh, do you like this one?" he asked, picking it up for a closer look.

"Yes. It's gorgeous."

Just as Nicky reached into his back pocket to get his wallet, he could feel a tug at his jeans. A teenage boy grabbed his wallet without warning and raced down the side alley. Nicky hurriedly chased after him without thought of the situation or dangers. Jeff and David shouted for him to stop.

"Nicky, just let the wallet go. Let it go, man."

Without further hesitation, Jerry sprinted down the dark alley after his cousin.

"Oh no. What just happened?" Jackie screamed.

"A kid just stole Nicky's wallet," Jeff answered.

"What are we going to do?"

"Well, we're sure not leaving you here alone to chase after them, that's for certain," David stated.

There was nothing to do but wait. David knew that Nicky had a couple of vials of cocaine on him, and he wasn't about to call for the authorities. So, unfortunately, Nicky was on his own.

"Oh my God, someone please help us," Jackie screamed as David quickly covered her mouth with his hand.

Quickly he leaned close to her ear and whispered.

"Hush. Be quiet. Trust me. We don't want the police involved. Nicky has drugs on him."

It seemed like forever before they saw Nicky and Jerry emerge from the dark alley, both covered in blood.

"No," Jackie screamed in total shock.

Running over to Nicky, they were horrified. Nicky was cut across his face near his left eye. At first glance, it appeared Nicky had possibly lost his eye.

"Nicky, Nicky," Jackie cried just before passing out. David caught her in his arms.

Thankfully, Jerry's cuts were only superficial. Yet, he knew Nicky would need a doctor to close his wounds.

"We've got to get him to a hospital fast," Jerry demanded, trying to wipe the blood which was profusely pouring from Nicky's cut.

Immediately removing his blood-splattered shirt, Jerry applied pressure to Nicky's gash, trying to stop the bleeding. Jeff and Jerry held Nicky up as they frantically helped him back to the location where they hoped the limo might be waiting. David had to carry Jackie in his arms, trying his best to keep up with them. Then, it was a stroke of luck. Jerry could see the long slim outline of a car. Taking a closer look, it was the limo. Hurriedly getting inside, the driver drove to the nearest hospital.

"Nicky, do you have any cocaine on you, man?" David questioned as he propped Jackie against the seat.

"Yes. I've got two vials in my pocket."

"Quick, give them to me," David demanded. "What the hell,

Nicky? Are you just looking for trouble?" David warned, grabbing the vials, he quickly tossed them out the car window.

It now appeared Jackie was conscious as she sat up in the back seat.

"What happened?" Jackie asked, staring at Nicky. Then, finally, she gasped, remembering the incident.

"Oh my God," Jackie freaked, noting the deep cut across Nicky's face.

Arriving at the nearest hospital, Nicky was rushed inside a cubicle. It seemed to take forever while the doctors stitched his face closing the deep cut near his left eye. Jerry hurried inside a bathroom in the waiting room and attempted to clean the bloodstains from his body and clothes. Finally, he had to remove his shirt. It wasn't worth saving at this point. Jackie gave him the jacket which Nicky had given her to stay warm. As they kept waiting for what seemed like an eternity, Bill walked in. Jeff had called him at his hotel and made him aware of the ongoing situation with Nicky.

"What the hell have you guys gotten yourselves into tonight?" Bill yelled. "Didn't I warn you that the market was a dangerous place late at night?

Didn't I tell you?" he ranted.

The waiting room fell silent as he looked at David.

"Did Nicky have any coke on him tonight?" Bill furiously demanded.

"Oh no, Nicky would never do that. He knows better than to carry it on him."

"I hope you're telling the truth. This whole venue depends on whether or not anything is found on him. Do you hear me? Do you understand?" Bill continued to fume.

"I know. Nicky was clean," David said, lying under his breath.

Wow. What had Nicky gotten himself into, David thought. Glancing at the clock on the wall, it had now been over an hour since they had taken Nicky back. Jerry was now distraught that Nicky had possibly lost the vision in his left eye. Jerry rubbed his forehead. Things had escalated so fast, and as a result, Nicky was now being treated in a local hospital. Their decision had been impulsive and now might cost Nicky his eye. They should've never gone to the night market after Bill had warned them.

Jerry tried to be strong for Jackie. She was sobbing as David held her in his arms. The surgery seemed to be taking a long time. Where was the nurse who should come out and let them know something? For one possible minute, Jerry sat there with his head down, thinking the worst. What if something had happened to Nicky and he had died in Taipei? How could he ever deliver this kind of news to his Aunt Joan? Jerry started praying.

"Please, God, have mercy on Nicky. Please let it be your will that he recovers without losing his eyesight."

Jerry needed a miracle tonight for his cousin. Tears began flowing down his face as he began reliving their younger days growing up in Middleton. He knew Nicky's aspirations and dreams of leaving Middleton and becoming a famous rock icon one day. Now it might come crashing down due to one wrong decision. At that moment, the door to the waiting room opened, and a nurse walked in. God must have heard my prayer, Jerry thought.

"Are you all waiting for news about Nicky Spade?" she asked.

"Yes," Jerry said, jumping up from his chair.

"Well, he must have had an angel watching over him tonight. The doctor managed to save his left eye, leaving no permanent damage. The cornea was scratched. Also, the cut looked worse than it appeared. It turned out to be more of a superficial cut to the face. It only took about twelve stitches to close. So he's going to be fine. You can take him home soon. His condition appeared a lot worse than what it was when you brought him in. We had to put him out, not knowing the seriousness of the cut over the eye. He's a fortunate young man," she mentioned.

"Thank you. Thank you," Jerry repeated.

"Oh, are you okay?" the young nurse asked curiously, seeing the drops of blood which had remained on his arms?"

"Yes. I'm fine."

"If you hadn't found him as quick as you did, he wouldn't be alive now. That market is a dangerous place, especially late at night. The kid would have killed him for his wallet. There's no doubt about it. So, you probably saved his life," she informed them.

Jerry now wondered if fate had played a role in him being at the market to save Nicky's life.

"Well, guys, are you going to wait around to take him back to the hotel, or would you like for me to wait and see that he gets back?" Bill questioned.

"To be honest, I would like to wait for my cousin," Jerry said, relieved. "Actually, I think that would be a good idea. I need to talk with hospital personnel and ensure this doesn't make it into tomorrow's newspapers. We've got to keep this incident private and out of the local papers. I don't want this to interfere with the band being on a world tour. Our venues are scheduled for another year and a half, with options afterward. Our ticket sales have never been higher. So, this situation stays here in this room. Does everyone understand?" Bill demanded.

"Yes. We hear you," David answered.

"Okay. I'll leave you all to wait for Nicky. I'm going down to the hospital office and see if anyone's there at this time of night."

As the guys and Jackie sat waiting for Nicky to be released, they couldn't believe the close call they had just encountered hours earlier in the market. Then, finally, Nicky was walked out by the nurse.

"Okay. You can take your friend home now."

She had no idea of the prominence of her patient.

"Make sure he goes straight to bed and gets a lot of rest. Here are some pain meds if he should need them. The stitches will dissolve on their own in a few weeks. So take care of him and, for heaven's sakes, stay out of that market late at night," she said, leaving.

"Damn Nicky, that was a close call, buddy," Jerry exclaimed.

"Oh, I know, man. But, Jerry, you saved my life. That kid would have killed me with his machete."

"Well, let's don't think about it. Let's just get you back to the hotel."

"Wow, Nicky, you're lucky. I've worked in Hollywood as a makeup artist for years. Your scar can easily be covered. Trust me, I would know. Just wait. When I get through with you, no one will ever notice it," Jackie remarked, inspecting his stitches.

"Thanks, Jackie."

"Now, let's get you to the limo," Jerry said, helping Nicky to the car.

"Okay, let's get out of here," Nicky grimaced, trying to feel his face.

Arriving at the hotel, Jerry ensured that Nicky got to his room safely.

"Nicky, is there anything I can do for you before I go to my room and get some sleep?" Jerry questioned.

"No, man, I think you've done more than enough. Go get some rest, and I'll see you in the morning."

Nicky speedily bounced back from the incident. He was lucky as the band wasn't scheduled to perform at another venue until the following week when they would open in Manila. After that, the scar never became a problem. Jackie showed Nicky some phenomenal makeup tricks to keep it hidden, which was a good thing because a week later, she was gone. The boys joked that the incident at the night market had scared her away.

The band traveled extensively throughout Asia for the first year of their world tour. Bill extended their tour after a short hiatus back in the states. It seemed Black Tie Affair would be on tour for a length of two years afterward. Bill had to work hard to keep Nicky from himself. His exploits became well known with the boys in the band and the crew. It became more than a full-time job to keep Nicky out of the newspapers and tabloids. He had reached the pinnacle of success as a rock icon.

Only those who worked closest to him and those who slept in his bed knew the real Nicky Spade. But unfortunately, his rise to fame and fortune that he so desperately chased in time would become his early demise from the world of rock and roll.

Years of using cocaine and the abuse of alcohol would dramatically begin to affect his health and, along with that, his ability to perform on stage. However, he remained loved by millions of fans. He was considered a legend in the industry. Bill figured he probably had at best another year to perform before his body would no longer withstand the rigors of the demanding lifestyle of a rock star. So, bill scheduled one last farewell tour in the states and Canada with Black Tie Affair, starring Nick Spade as their lead vocalist. However, during this tour, Nicky would get some shocking news.

CHAPTER EIGHTEEN

Regrets, Reminisces, Rebirth.
Quebec

"Mom, have you seen Cameron?"

"No. I believe he went to Billy's house to practice with the band."Cameron was now eighteen, and Jenna was worried about his future plans. She was beginning to see a lot of restlessness in her young son. The same familiar traits which she had remembered in Nicky.

When Cameron was born, Jenna had promised herself many years ago that she would never bring Nicky into his life. Her dad had an extreme hatred for him, and her mom had never mentioned his name while Cameron was around. So she felt it would be best for everyone to let him think his father had been killed in a car accident. It was a huge lie, and Jenna had often doubted if it had been the right decision during his young life.

Leaving Middleton, Jenna had chosen to let Nicky off the hook. She gave him the freedom to chase his dreams at the expense of her and their son. She felt vindicated in her decision to keep their son from ever knowing about his dad or having a relationship with him. However, fate would soon give her reason to question her decision.

"Mom, I have a slight headache, so I'm going to bed a little early tonight. Will you please tell Cameron to let me know when he gets home?"

"Yes. Sweetheart, don't worry. Jenna, Cameron is eighteen now, and you're going to have to learn to let go just a little."

"Oh, I know, Mom. It's not easy."

Jenna's whole world revolved around Cameron. She knew she was overprotective but wasn't that how all single moms were, she thought?

Coming in from school the following day, Jenna had a headache. At first, she had not given it much thought and simply took aspirin. However, it wasn't working, so Jenna felt going to bed might be the cure she needed.

However, waking up the next morning, the headache seemed to have reached an overwhelming level. Walking downstairs, Jenna immediately went to the medicine cabinet for more aspirin and over to the coffee pot to pour herself a cup of coffee. Reaching for the bottle of aspirin, the unthinkable happened. Jenna fell to the floor unconscious. She lay there helpless without anyone knowing.

Audrey never slept in. She had already brewed the morning coffee and was now outside working in her flower garden. Deciding to come inside for a moment, she was horrified to find Jenna lying on the floor.

"Jenna, oh my God, Sweetheart," Audrey screamed. She was traumatized by discovering Jenna unconscious. Running over to the sink, Audrey quickly wet a towel, attempting to revive her. Nothing was working.

"Jenna, Jenna, please wake up. Wake up," Audrey demanded, trying to lift her daughter from the floor to no avail. There was nothing to do but call for an ambulance. Cameron had left for school. Typically Jenna would have also left for school. However, she had fatefully decided to call in sick before she came downstairs.

Immediately Audrey called for an ambulance and left a note for Cameron. When the ambulance arrived to take Jenna to the local hospital—Audrey got into her car. She raced to the location where Jenna was taken.

Walking into the hospital, Audrey panicked. What had happened, she worried. She knew her daughter had complained of a headache the night before, but how could something this serious happen so suddenly?"

Audrey ran over to the nurse's station to check Jenna's status.

"I'm Audrey Jones, Jenna Jones' mother. Can you please tell me what's going on with my daughter?"

"They are running tests. I'm sorry. We can't let you back right now."

"Is she still unconscious?"

"Yes. But please, try not to worry. Your daughter is in excellent hands."

"You'll need you to fill out some paperwork at the reception window. Do you know if she's currently taking any medications or has any ongoing health issues?"

"No. She's completely healthy. The only thing I can tell you is that she complained of a headache last night before going to bed."

"Please have a seat in the waiting room, and we'll let you know something as soon as we can."

"Okay," Audrey replied, consumed with worries. She felt as if she was in an unbelievable nightmare.

It seemed like an eternity before one of the doctors came out and informed her they were immediately taking Jenna into surgery.

"Are you Mrs. Jones?" he questioned. "I'm Doctor Sloan.

"Yes. How's my daughter?"

"I'm sorry to inform you that your daughter had an aneurysm, which resulted in bleeding near her brain. She's being taken upstairs to surgery. I truly hate to be the bearer of such devastating news. Unfortunately, her condition is extremely grave. I'm truly sorry. I wish I had better news."

Audrey could hardly believe the words spoken by the doctor.

"Mrs. Jones, are you alright? Do you have anyone you can call?"

"No. My husband, Jenna's father, is deceased. How long will she be in surgery?"

"It depends on the exact location of the aneurysm and the severity of the bleeding. There's a waiting room upstairs. It's located on the second floor. Someone will let you know when she's out of surgery. Afterward, she'll be moved to the Intensive Care Unit on the third floor."

"This is so hard to believe. My daughter is young, and she's been the picture of health," Audrey mentioned, wiping tears from her eyes.

"Do you have a priest or pastor that you can call?"

"No. Is there a chapel in the hospital?"

"Yes. It's also on the second floor. Just follow the signs. You can't miss it."

"Thank you. I'm going to the chapel. I will be in the waiting area afterward. Will someone please let me know something as soon as the surgery is over?"

"Yes. Mrs. Jones, we will keep you informed. But, again, I'm genuinely sorry."

Audrey needed a higher power this afternoon. Finding the chapel, she went inside and kneeled at the altar.

"Oh God, I know it's been a while since I last talked with you. I need another miracle this afternoon, just like the miracle for Jenna and Cameron the night he was born. Please, give her the strength to survive. She has never asked for much in life, just the beautiful son you blessed her with. Oh God, help her beat the odds so heavily stacked against her. Please give her back to Cameron and me, please."

After leaving the chapel, Audrey went to the waiting room. It seemed like an eternity before a nurse finally came in.

"Mrs. Jones, your daughter made it through surgery. However, she's in a coma. You can see her in a few minutes. She's being transferred to the ICU. The doctor will be in shortly for any questions you might have," the nurse stated.

"Thank you for letting me know."

Audrey saw Cameron running down the hallway toward the waiting room thirty minutes later. He must have seen the note which she had left. How would she ever tell him?

"Nana, what's wrong with Mom?"

"Oh sweetheart, come in the waiting room and sit down."

"I don't want to sit down. I want to know what's going on?"

"Cameron, your mom had an aneurysm."

"What does that mean?"

"Well, a blood vessel somewhere near her brain has ruptured. Sweetheart, I'm sorry. It's serious. Your mom just came out of surgery. I'm waiting for her to be moved to a room in the Intensive Care Unit," Audrey explained.

"Does this mean they corrected it with surgery?"

"Oh, Sweetheart, it only means they've managed to stop the bleeding and repaired the ruptured blood vessel. She's in a coma right now. No one knows how long she might stay this way."

Cameron sat down in the waiting room with tears flowing down his cheeks. Nana, we can't lose her. We just can't. We lost Papa. We can't lose Mom," he cried.

"I know, Sweetheart, I know," Audrey lovingly repeated, putting her arms around him. "Everything is going to be okay. Please don't worry."

Together they sat and waited for Jenna to be taken to the ICU. A few minutes later, the doctor walked into the waiting area.

"Are you Mrs. Jones?"

"Yes. How is my daughter?"

"I'm Dr. Wyatt. Your daughter made it through surgery, so that's a good sign. I'm sure Dr. Sloan told you the seriousness of her condition. We've managed to repair the blood vessel and stop the bleeding. But, unfortunately, she's in a coma. The next few days will be critical. She's young, and I must say, fortunate to have survived. We're doing everything possible for her. She's in excellent hands. Do you have any questions?"

"How long before you'll know anything further?" Audrey begged.

"I'm sorry. I can't give you an answer. At this point, it's just a matter of supporting her and waiting. You can go in and see her in a few minutes. Someone will come in and take you to her room."

It was only a short time before the nurse walked in.

"You can go in and see her, but only one person at a time."

Audrey thought Cameron should be the first one to go in.

"Sweetheart, you go first. Please be strong. The nurse said she will be on life support, which simply means a ventilator will be breathing for her."

"Nana, I just want to see her."

"Follow me. I'll take you to the ICU," the nurse said sympathetically.

Nothing could have ever prepared Cameron for what he was about to see. Jenna was almost unrecognizable. Her head was wrapped in a turban of white strips of gauze. Her face seemed pale and puffy, and she was connected to machinery which evidently was keeping her alive.

"Oh, Mom, I love you, I love you," Cameron reiterated. "Mom, can you hear me? Please be strong. You have to fight. Mom, I love you," Cameron cried softly, holding his mom's hand. He had to leave the room. He was becoming too emotional to stay longer, and he didn't want to cry in her presence. Slowly Cameron walked out of Jenna's room with tears in his eyes.

"Oh, Nana, she doesn't look good. I'm so worried about her."

"I know. I'm going to go in and see her. Wait here."

Audrey walked into her daughter's room. It was overwhelming to see her beautiful daughter lying on the stark white sheets of the hospital bed hooked up to various machines keeping her alive. Audrey wiped the tears from her eyes as she stood next to Jenna's bed. She felt helpless. Why had this happened? She had no answers, and she didn't understand. Finally, Audrey gently picked up her daughter's hand and pleaded with her to be strong and fight for her life.

"Jenna, if you can hear me, please, don't leave us. Cameron and I need you. Please be strong. You can do this. Sweetheart, I'm not leaving. I'm going to stay in your room until you wake up. Do you understand? Jenna, we love you," Audrey wept, holding her precious daughter's hand. Walking back to the waiting room, she checked on Cameron.

"Sweetheart, there's nothing you can do. Please go home. There are cold cuts in the fridge. Make yourself something to eat. I'll call you if there are any changes."

"Oh Nana, I can't leave, Mom. I can't."

"Cameron, your mom will need you to take care of yourself. There's nothing to do here. I'm going to stay with her for the night and as long as they'll let me. So please just go home. There's plenty of food in the fridge."

"Okay, but you promise to call me."

"Yes. Sweetheart, don't worry. I'll call you if anything changes."

With encouragement from Audrey, Cameron decided to go home for the evening.

It had been over two weeks, and Jenna had remained in a coma on the ventilator. Although Audrey convinced the nurses to allow her to sleep in Jenna's room most nights, she wasn't leaving. It had now become an ordeal with some of the hospital staff. However, Audrey was determined to be with her daughter if she were to wake up. She read books to her and even played soft music in the background. She talked with Jenna daily and kept her up-to-date with the daily news in the area. Audrey had remained friends with some of their former neighbors who still lived and worked at the Ford Plant in Middleton, Michigan. She called her friends in Middleton, making them aware of Jenna's condition, and asked for their prayers.

As if by fate, one of the ladies who worked at the Ford Plant was discussing Jenna's tragic condition with a friend in the cafeteria. At that moment, Nicky's father, Joseph, who also worked at the plant, walked into the cafeteria, overhearing their conversation regarding Jenna. It appeared a divine appointment.

"Excuse me. I couldn't help but overhear your conversation. Did I hear you mention Jenna Jones? Were you talking about the Jones family who lived here in Middleton? Her father, Frank Jones, worked here several years ago."

"Yes. Why would you ask?"

"Well, my son dated Jenna before he left Middleton. She was almost a member of our family and frequently at our home. Is she alright?"

"I'm sorry to tell you, Jenna is in a coma on life support."

"What happened?"

"She had an aneurysm and is in critical condition."

"Oh no, I sure hate to hear that. My wife and I really liked Jenna. She was like a family member when she dated our son, Nicky."

"Well, you might want to remember her in your prayers and have your son pray for her as well."

"I certainly will. Thank you so much for letting me know."

"What is your name?" she asked curiously.

"Oh, I'm Joseph Spade."

"Well, Joseph, I'll let Audrey know you asked about Jenna," she smiled.

Middleton was such a small town. It seemed, for the most part, everyone who lived in Middleton either worked at the plant or knew someone who did. It was the primary employer for the tiny community. Joseph couldn't wait to get home and let Joan know about Jenna.

"Hey Joan, you're not going to believe what I heard today," Joseph remarked, walking in later that afternoon from work.

"What?" Joan asked curiously, looking up from her newspaper.

"Well, I walked into the cafeteria to get some coffee, and I happened to overhear a conversation between two women, who were standing by the drink machine. They were talking, and then the weirdest thing occurred. I overheard them refer to Jenna Jones. They discussed that they had just found out she'd had an aneurysm. Jenna is on life support and may not pull through this horrible incident."

"Joe, are you sure you heard them say, Jenna Jones?"

"Joan, I even interrupted their conversation to make sure. I asked them for specifics. Yes. It's Jenna."

"Oh my God, Nicky loved her. We all did. What do you think we should do? Do you think we should try to get in touch with Nicky?"

"Well, I don't know, but if she didn't make it through this tragedy and we didn't let him know, he might never forgive us."

"Okay, Joseph, you have to call William Kirkland. He's the new tour manager for the band. Call him at his office. Someone will be able to get a message to him. However, I have no idea where the band is performing this week. But it doesn't matter. Someone can get a message to him or give us the phone number to his hotel."

"Okay. I'll call William right now," Joseph said, reaching to get the phone.

"Hello. William Kirkland's office. May I help you?"

"Yes. My name is Joseph Spade, Nicky Spade's father."

"How are you, Mr. Spade? What can I do for you this afternoon?"

"Well, I need to get a message to my son or either a phone number to his hotel where he can be reached."

"All right. Please give me a moment while I check their schedule. Okay. It appears the band is performing in Seattle, Washington, this week," the receptionist informed him. "I can give you the phone number to Bill's hotel. I'm not sure where the band members are staying."

"Thank you. That would be great."

Quickly writing down the number, Joseph hung up the phone to call Bill.

"Good evening Claremont Hotel. How can I direct your call?"

"I'm trying to reach Mr. William Kirkland. I believe he's a guest in your hotel."

"Hold, please. I'll connect you to his room."

It was only a few seconds before the phone in Bill's room went to an answering machine. He wasn't in. Joseph had no choice but to leave a message.

"Well Joan, I tried Bill's hotel room. He wasn't in, so I left a message."

"That's all you can do for now, unless Nicky happens to call home, and you know how slim those chances are. We've done all we can do for now, except pray. I'll call some of the women at the church who knew Jenna and ask them to pray for her."

Even though it had been over eighteen years since they had last seen Jenna, Audrey had always been fond of her. She had practically lived at their house during her senior year. They never understood why their son had not married the love of his life.

Walking into his hotel room in Seattle, Nicky heard the phone in his room ringing.

"Hey Nicky, this is Bill. I just got a message from your dad."

"Is everything alright?"

"Well, Joseph was calling to let you know about someone named Jenna Jones. Seems as if she's in the hospital and may not make it."

"Say that again, Bill."

"Jenna Jones, do you know someone by that name?" Bill questioned. "It appears she's in the hospital, and it doesn't look good."

"Bill, did my father say which hospital she was in?"

"No, but he did mention that she was in Quebec."

"Bill, I don't have time to explain right now, but I must get to her. I've got to see her. Since we're not scheduled to perform at this venue until the weekend, can I please use one of the private jets to fly to Quebec?"

"Yes, Nicky, that won't be a problem, as long as you're back in time for the concert. So when do you want to leave?" Bill asked.

"As soon as possible."

"Okay. I'll have the plane ready. I hope she's okay. I'll send the limo over to take you to the airport in about an hour. Will that be soon enough?"

"Yes. Thank you so much. I'll call you from Quebec."

Sitting on the edge of the bed, Nicky lit a cigarette. He couldn't imagine anything happening to Jenna. He had always loved her. It hadn't mattered to him who was in his bed at night. Yet, thoughts of Jenna were never far from his mind. Nicky had tried to find comfort by having a warm body next to him each night, but no one had ever filled the spot in his heart that she held. He had always intended to try and look her up one day, even thinking about trying to reach her after the farewell tour ended. Now, he might never get that chance.

Nicky wondered if she'd ever married, but it wasn't important to him. He just needed to see her one more time. If possible, Nicky desperately needed to talk with Jenna and understand what had happened between them. Why had she never responded to any of his postcards or the messages he had left with her grandmother? He just needed closure to that part of his life, and without talking with her, he would never have his answers.

Nicky walked across the hall to Jerry's room.

"Hey man, what's going on?"

"Jerry, you're never going to believe this, but Bill just called and said my dad had left a message on his phone in his hotel room."

"Is everyone back home alright?"

"Yes. The strangest thing is, it's Jenna," Nicky answered, trembling with tears in his eyes."

"Jenna, man, you haven't seen her in years. What's wrong?"

"She had an aneurysm or something like that. I'm not sure. They don't think she's going to make it. She's on life support."

"Oh man, I'm so sorry to hear that." What are you going to do?"

"Well, Bill is going to let me use one of the private jets. I'm leaving for Quebec within the hour."

"Do you want me to go with you?"

"No thanks. I need to do this by myself."

"Nicky, you're still in love with her, aren't you?"

"Yes," Nicky said with tears in his eyes.

"I thought so. Jenna was one of a kind. There was no doubt about it. The boys and I never understood why you so easily let her go. We all thought you would have married her and stayed in Middleton."

"Well, I know it sounds crazy, but look at where we both are and what has happened to us with our careers. I was so young back then. I was chasing dreams."

"So, what are you going to do if she's married?"

"Oh, that's something to think about, but I just want to know that she's going to be alright. I'll cross that bridge when I get to it. I need answers and closure on our relationship. I've always loved her."

"Okay, man, but don't get your heart broken again. Jenna's a part of your past. Wouldn't it be best just to leave it that way?"

"No, Jerry, you don't understand. Jenna and I were soul mates. I sent her postcards and left messages with her grandmother and never understood what had happened. I have to have answers."

"Okay, Nicky, go get your answers, but most of all, I hope that she's going to pull through this."

"Thanks, Jerry. I'll see you in a few days."

It wasn't long before the limo arrived to pick Nicky up for the short drive to the airport. It was a long lonely flight to Quebec. Laying his head back against the seat, he tried to sleep. Memories of Jenna kept flooding his mind. He just needed to see her one last time. He had so many questions, and he needed answers. Nicky knew that he had never found another love in his life like Jenna. He had to deal with the fact that she might now be married or at least have someone special in her life. He could never have expected her not to marry. Hell, she wasn't a nun. He sure hadn't lived the life of a monk either. He had to prepare for whatever would happen when he saw her. It didn't matter. He loved her. He had always loved her. He would be able to walk away if only he could know that she would be alright. Nicky desperately needed to see her one last time.

As the plane began its descent into Quebec, Nicky wondered how many hospitals were located near the address where he had sent the numerous postcards years ago. He would need a phone book.

After the plane landed, he quickly ran inside the airport to check all the hospitals nearest that location. Then, he asked the limo driver to wait. Writing down all the listings of local hospitals near the last address he had for Jenna's grandmother would only be a method of elimination. So, starting with the first hospital, he gave the address to the driver.

As the limo pulled into the entrance of the first hospital, Nicky hurriedly ran inside and inquired about a patient named Jenna Jones. It just so happened she wasn't a patient at this hospital, but there were two more to check out.

The driver rushed him over to the next hospital. Quickly running inside, it wasn't good news again as there was no one listed as a patient with the last name of Jones. Getting back inside the limo, Nicky started to panic. What if she passed away before he got there? What would he do? He was beginning to feel desperate. All these questions were racing through his mind.

As the limo pulled up to the entrance of the last hospital, he prayed.

Dear God, please let this be the right one.

Then, frantically, he rushed out of the car so fast he forgot to close the door. His prayer was heard as he hurriedly made his way to the reception desk.

"Yes. We have a Miss Jenna Jones. She's in the Intensive Care Unit on the third floor. There's a buzzer on the door to allow entry."

His heart was racing. What was he doing? What was he going to find? What if she didn't even remember him, hated him, was married or in love with someone else. Worst of all, what if she didn't want him there?

Finally allowed into the Intensive Care Unit, Nicky stopped for a moment to catch his breath and take a quick look through the window to see if anyone was with her. Thank goodness, she was alone. Glancing around, he hoped no one would see him go in.

Walking into her room, he gasped, noticing her lifeless body and beautiful blond curls wrapped in a turban of gauze. Then, tears began streaming down his face as he saw the ventilator which was now keeping her alive. Taking her hand, he needed to talk with her even though it was evident she was unconscious.

"Babe, I'm here," he whispered, looking down at her with tears in his eyes. Sweetheart, I love you. I've always loved you," Nicky wept, gently kissing her on the forehead. "Oh Jenna, I've missed you so much. Please be strong. You have to come back to me. Can you hear me?" he demanded, wiping tears from his eyes. "I'm so sorry for leaving you all those years ago. Can you ever forgive me? Jenna, fame doesn't mean anything when you're without the one you love. Oh

Babe, can you ever find it in your heart to forgive me? I've loved you from the very first day I saw you in class that morning. Sweetheart, I can't lose you again. I just can't. Please, I'm begging you to be strong. I need you. Jenna, you have to wake up. I'm not going to let you go again," Nicky said with tears running down his face.

"Babe, I can't stay," he said reluctantly, taking her hand. The band is on tour in Seattle. You may not be able to hear me, but I'm leaving a phone number where you can reach me. I'm putting it right here on the table next to your bed. Hopefully, someone will find it and give it to you. I'm praying that you will contact me. Leaning over, he kissed her goodbye. Please call me when you wake up. I have to believe you can hear me. Doll, I'll love you forever," he whispered, becoming too emotional to remain at her bedside.

Gently laying her hand by her side, he noticed she wasn't wearing a wedding band. Oh my God, maybe she had never married either. As he turned to leave, he could only hope and pray that she would wake up and somehow remember him being with her today. Standing in the doorway, he stopped taking one last glance at the love of his life. "Jenna Jones, I love you," he said, wiping the tears from his eyes.

Walking out the door, he stopped once more to look back at Jenna through the large glass window. Catching a reflection of himself, he felt disgusted. He barely resembled the young, determined boy who had left Middleton with big dreams so long ago. He had made it to the top, but at what cost? He felt he had let Jenna down. Hell, he had let himself down.

Taking one last glance at Jenna, maybe she would be better off without him. For a brief moment, he had second thoughts. Perhaps he should go back in and retrieve the note. Hell, if there was any chance of getting Jenna back this time, he had to take it. He just needed a second chance. With tears flowing down his face, there was only one thing to do. He would leave the note hoping that she would find it by some miracle. Nicky left the hospital that evening knowing that he had said what was in his heart. With tears in his eyes, there was nothing more he could do. Now he would have to return to Seattle and wait, praying she would come out of the coma and call.

Audrey walked out of the bathroom in Jenna's room. She couldn't believe what she had just witnessed. Audrey was in disbelief, having just watched Nicky Spade walk back into her daughter's life. Then, with tears in her eyes, she walked over to Jenna's bedside.

"Oh, Sweetheart, Nicky was here in your room. Jenna, Nicky loves you. He really loves you. Can you hear me? He never stopped loving you."

Remembering all the postcards that Nicky had sent to her daughter, she began crying as she recollected how she had hidden them, each one of them. She had never given Jenna one of them, not one. Audrey broke down thinking of how she and her mother had run interference, ensuring that Nicky never contacted her daughter. What had she done? How could she ever live with herself? How would she ever tell Jenna, and worse yet, what if Jenna never forgave her? It was all a chance, but a chance she would have to take. She loved her daughter, and now it was clearly evident that Nicky had always loved her as well. They were a family, Jenna, Nicky, and Cameron. Cameron had never even known his father was alive. Now the possibility existed that Jenna might want to tell him, but first, she had to wake up.

"Oh Jenna, you have to wake up, you have to. You can finally have everything you've ever wished for, but first, you have to find the strength to come back to us. You've had your rest. Now it's time to wake up and put your family back together."

"How is she this evening?" the nurse asked, walking into the room.

"Everything is the same."

"How long can she stay in this unconscious state?"

"Well, there's not a definite answer to that question. It just depends upon your daughter. We are supporting her with everything she needs. Now it is up to her and a higher power. Hopefully, she will be strong enough to come out of the coma. Let me check her vital signs. I know it's hard to see her in this condition. Why don't you take tonight off and just go home and get some rest? There's simply not anything you can do, and we're monitoring her very closely. Her vital signs look great," the nurse added.

"Oh, I don't know. I feel better when I'm with her."

"Well, suit yourself. I'll be out at my desk if you should need anything."

"Okay. Thank you."

Glancing at the bedside table, Audrey saw Nicky's note. Deciding to pick it up, she was determined this time to make sure Jenna got it. Never again would Audrey step in between Jenna and Nicky, trying to force them to live their lives the way she wanted. How could she have ever done that to her daughter? Maybe she had done it more for Frank. He hated Nicky, but now Frank was gone and would no longer be a part of her decisions.

Audrey decided to stay one more night in Jenna's room. Picking up an old magazine, she tried to get comfortable in the hard chair which had been brought in for her. She had almost fallen asleep when she caught something out of the corner of her eye which got her attention. It seemed as if Jenna's fingers had moved. Being so tired, she assumed it was her imagination. She had been rather emotional this evening, and she was sure that her mind had let her see what she so desperately wanted to see and nothing more. First, however, she had to walk over to Jenna's bed for a closer inspection. Then, picking up her daughter's hand, suddenly, she felt the response of Jenna softly squeezing her hand. Audrey screamed.

"Oh Jenna, you're waking up." Then, reaching for the buzzer to call the nurse, Audrey asked the nurse to rush down to Jenna's room.

"Yes. Do you need help?" the young nurse inquired.

"Yes. My daughter just squeezed my hand."

"Are you sure?"

"Oh, I'm positive."

Looking into Jenna's eyes with a light, the nurse smiled.

"Well, I don't know what you've done this evening, but it looks as if she's beginning to wake up," the nurse answered as Jenna started to move her arm. It appears you're going to get the miracle you prayed for," she added, removing the ventilator tube.

Finally, Jenna was breathing on her own.

Audrey knew it wasn't anything she had done in her heart, but more what Nicky Spade had done.

"Oh, thank you, Jesus."

With tears of joy, Audrey walked over to her daughter's bedside.

"Jenna, thank God. Sweetheart, you're going to be alright."

After the medical staff came in and checked her progress, the nurse smiled.

"Will you be staying with your daughter again tonight?"

"Yes. I'm not leaving her, especially now," Audrey replied, wiping tears from her eyes.

"Well, if you should need anything, just use the buzzer.

"Okay. You can be sure I'll let you know."

Audrey walked back over to her daughter's bed.

"Oh Jenna, I knew you would come back to us. I just knew it."

Reaching over for the phone in the room, Audrey called Cameron.

"Hello," Cameron answered.

"Cameron, your mom is beginning to come out of her coma."

"Nana, are you sure?"

"Yes, Sweetheart, I'm sure."

"Oh Nana, it's a miracle."

"I know Cameron, I know. I'm going to stay with her tonight."

"Do you think I should come over to the hospital now?" Cameron inquired.

"Well, honey, it's up to you. She's not fully awake or sitting up, so if you just want to come over after school tomorrow, I think that would be fine."

"Okay, Nana, I'll probably just come by tomorrow since it's so late. Please let her know how much I love her."

"Sweetheart, have a good night. I'll see you tomorrow," Audrey added.

"Love you, Nana."

What Audrey had witnessed in her daughter's room could only be explained with one simple word, *love.* She had witnessed the power it conveyed. Without Nicky being aware of her presence in Jenna's room, she had watched the strong bond of love and affection he had shared with her daughter. There would never be any doubt in her mind that it was his visit that had brought her daughter back. She would never be able to repay him. The only thing she could do was share the postcards with Jenna as soon as she was home and well enough to read them. She owed Nicky this. It was the least she could do. She had to try and right the horrible wrong she had done. She would ensure that Jenna got her family back.

Over the next few weeks, Jenna made a remarkable recovery. She would be one of the rare cases which never gets fully explained. There was no explanation other than the power of love. Jenna continued to surprise her doctors with her remarkable recovery. She had come off life support and was now in rehab on her way back to normal. It had only been two short months since the incident, and today she was going home.

"Oh, Sweetheart, you're coming home today," Audrey smiled.

"I know, mom, isn't it wonderful."

"I knew you would be strong enough to beat the odds stacked against you. If anyone could do it, I knew you would be the one."

"Where's Cameron?" Jenna asked.

"He went to bring the car around to the front entrance of the hospital. The nurse will be in shortly to put you into a wheelchair and push you out to the car.

Jenna was surprised as they entered the driveway of their home. Cameron had made a giant *Welcome Home* banner that hung across the front of the garage. Getting out of the car, she immediately hugged Cameron.

"Thank you, Cameron. Thank you so much. It means more than you could ever know."

"Oh, Mom, it was nothing. Nana and I are so happy to have you back at home finally."

Balloons and flowers were everywhere, conveying good wishes

from the teachers at school as Jenna walked in. She was thrilled to be out of the hospital finally and back home with the ones she loved.

During the first weeks at home, Jenna grew stronger. Then, slowly, she finally made a full recovery and was ready to go back to work and excited about seeing the children in her class.

After dinner one evening, Audrey asked her to come into the living room.

"Jenna, there are things which I need to discuss with you. I was just waiting until you were stronger and the time was right."

"Okay, Mom, what is it that you want to tell me?"

"Jenna, I don't know where to start."

"Well, how about at the beginning."

"Sweetheart, you had a visitor one evening at the hospital while you were still unconscious."

"Okay, was it Reverend Griffin?"

"No, Jenna, it was Nicky," Audrey answered.

"Mom, are you sure? That couldn't be possible. Who would have told him?" Jenna questioned, utterly stunned as if she had seen a ghost.

"Well, I don't know. But yes, I'm sure. Nicky walked into your room one evening. I had no idea he even knew you were ill or how to find you. I had walked into the bathroom and was just about to come out when I opened the door and saw him standing beside your bed. I stayed hidden in the bathroom because I wanted to hear what he would say. Oh, Jenna, he loves you. I'm sure of that now. He poured his heart out to you. But you were unable to hear him, even though I do have to believe that somehow he got through to you. After his visit that night, you moved your fingers for the first time. Oh, Jenna, he held your hand and begged you to be strong. Nicky said he had lost you once and that he wasn't going to lose you again."

Jenna began shaking as tears streamed down her face.

"Mom, do you know how long I've waited for him. Hoping one day, somehow, he would come back into my life. But, Mom, I love him so much. Do you even know how much I love him?"

"Yes, Jenna, I do know that you've always loved him, but did it have to take such a crisis to bring him back into your life?"

"Well, Mom, fate is a strange bedfellow, and if that's what it took to bring him back, then I'm grateful that I almost died.

"Jenna, you don't know what you're saying," Audrey gasped.

"Oh, mom, I do, don't you understand. What else did he say?"

"Jenna, I can't remember every word, but I can say that I've never heard any man pour his heart out to anyone as Nicky did to you that evening. But, Jenna, he was crying. Nicky kept pleading for you to forgive him for leaving. I know he loves you. There's no longer any room for doubt. But sweetheart, I've got to ask for your forgiveness," Audrey hesitated.

"For what, Mom, I love you? You've always been there for Cameron and me."

"Well, Jenna, please, you have to hear me out first, and I pray that you don't hate me afterward. I was only trying to protect you," Audrey wept, handing her a box of postcards.

"Mom, what are these?" Jenna asked, looking confused.

"Jenna, Nicky sent you postcards. He kept you informed of what was happening in his life and a short message saying he loved you forever on each one. They're all here. I saved them for you. You know how much your father hated Nicky. Jenna, I felt like I was doing the best for you and your father," Audrey explained, handing Jenna the box of postcards.

"Mom, how could you? How could you have done this to me? Why did you do this to Cameron and me? How could you?" Jenna screamed.

"Oh Jenna, I don't know. Looking back, honestly, I don't know. All I can say is that I'm sorry. Can you ever forgive me?"

"Nicky also called your grandmother numerous times, leaving messages and trying to contact you. However, she and I ran interference and agreed never to let you know."

"Oh, Mom, I can't believe this. I really can't. Was Grandma in on this before she passed away too?"

"Yes. Jenna, we both were. I'm so sorry. Please forgive her and me as well. I was just trying to protect you. You were so young, and he left you pregnant with Cameron. I guess I just hated him for what he did to you," Audrey related with tears in her eyes. "Plus, your father despised him."

"Mom, I never blamed him for what happened."

"Well then, why didn't you tell him about the baby?" Audrey questioned.

"Because he would have never gone to Europe with Black Tie Affair if I had told him. Mom, Nicky wasn't father material back then. I loved him enough to let him go, so he never knew."

"Mom, I don't hate you for what you did. You and grandma did what you thought was best for me, even though I wouldn't have agreed with you."

"Jenna, there's something else."

"What, Mom, what else have you done now?"

"Oh no, it's nothing like that. Nicky left a note for you the evening he came into your room at the hospital. He left a phone number and asked that you contacted him when you came out of your coma. Jenna, it was almost as if Nicky knew you would be alright. He left this for you," Audrey smiled, handing her the note.

"Mom, he wants me to call?"

"I know, Sweetheart. I guess it's all up to you now."

"Mom, I just want to take the box and go up to my room and read them right now, if that's alright with you?'

"Jenna, you do whatever you feel is best. I'll support your decision. But, what are you going to do regarding Cameron? Are you going to tell him?"

"No. Not right now. I'm going to tell Cameron, but not just yet. So please let me be the one to tell him about his dad. I want to tell him when I think the time is right and in my way. So please promise me that you're not going to say anything about Nicky to him?"

"You have my promise. I'm not going to tell Cameron. That's for you to do. But, Jenna, I love you, and if you want a future with Nicky, I won't stand in your way any longer. I truly feel that he gave you back to me that night in your hospital room. I owe him everything," Audrey cried.

Jenna walked over to hug her mom. Sitting on the couch, they both cried. There were no more words to say.

"Sweetheart, you go and read your postcards. Just know that Nicky never forgot you when he left Middleton. I truly believe it's meant for you both to have a second chance in life and share it with your beautiful son."

"I love you, take the cards and the note and do whatever you feel is best."

"Thanks, Mom, for telling me tonight. I know it was hard. You will never know how much this means to me. I think you've more than made up for your past mistake," Jenna smiled, forgiving her mom and relieving her of her guilt.

Jenna couldn't help but wonder about the years she had lost with Nicky. There was no way to turn the clock back. She could only go forward from this evening. Grabbing the note and the box of postcards, she ran up to her room.

CHAPTER TWENTY

The Son comes up in *Quebec.*

Nicky was back on tour with Black Tie Affair. It was his farewell tour. The band was scheduled to perform in the United States and Canada. Nicky had always wanted to leave when he was still at the top of his game. He had risen to fame faster than any other artist as the lead singer with Black Tie Affair. He had become a rock god adored by his millions of fans worldwide.

With his health now failing him, he was finally ready to step down from the pinnacle of success that he had achieved. There were only a few more venues to play before he would walk away from the only life he had ever known since leaving Middleton. However, Nicky was carrying a huge burden with him. He had not heard from Jenna. Certainly, someone must have given her the note he had left. He held onto the hope that Jenna had not passed away. Surely, if something had happened to her, he would have received a call. He could only assume that she had decided not to have any contact with him. Either way, he was hurting. He loved her, and somehow he had to believe that he would get a second chance. He had to find the strength to go on. There were more concerts before he would finally go back home. He would need time to think about his future plans with or without her.

Jenna was now having difficulties with Cameron back in Quebec. It seemed he would drop out of high school before he graduated. He had become his father's son in every sense of the word without even knowing him. Cameron joined a local rock band and began seriously thinking of going on the road. Jenna and her mom were not able to reason with him. It seemed the more she begged him to stay and finish school, the more determined he was to leave. Cameron was gifted. There was no doubt about it. Jenna knew he was every bit as talented as his father, maybe even better in a lot of ways. He most definitely carried within him the genes of a rock star. However, Cameron had no way to know his father was a famous rock star. Jenna was proud of him, but she wanted him to finish school and put his talents to better use. Jenna had saved every newspaper article and tabloid ever printed about Nicky. She was saving them for just the right time, but she wasn't so sure this was it. Jenna had kept up with Nicky's career from the first day he had left Middleton.

However, she was now worried about Cameron and what steps she could take to keep him from throwing his life away at such an early age. She felt pretty sure the local band he was with now was unsuitable for him. He just needed guidance and direction. Jenna suddenly knew what she had to do.

Jenna sat at the kitchen table, waiting for Cameron to come home. She held in her hand the box of postcards. The conversation she was about to have with Cameron was long overdue. During the past hour, she had replayed in her mind repeatedly how she would tell Cameron about his father. Then, hearing the front door open, she heard Cameron's voice. As he walked into the kitchen, she looked up at him.

"Cameron, we need to talk."

Black Tie Affair was scheduled to play in Quebec at the end of the month. She had kept up with the band along with their schedule during Nicky's farewell tour. She was making plans to see him when the band arrived in Quebec. Jenna was going to need Jerry's help.

Hopefully, she could count on him. Jerry had helped to decorate the cabin the night before she left Middleton. Surely, he would find it in his heart to help her, especially if he knew about Cameron. Jenna couldn't wait for the concert. Her whole life was riding on this one venue.

It had seemed like forever, but finally, the night of the concert had arrived. Jenna had managed to get in touch with Jerry. He promised her that he would not let Nicky know that she would be at the concert. However, Nicky had wished for a miracle that Jenna would hear about their upcoming concert in Quebec. Hopefully, she would see the billboards or catch the news media, which would let her know that Black Tie Affair was performing at the massive Sports Dome in Quebec. Unfortunately, however, since he had not heard from Jenna, Nicky felt she must no longer feel the same toward him. It was time for the guys to leave their hotel and go to the venue at the Sports Dome.

"Bill says we're sold out for tonight's concert," Jerry smiled, trying to keep his secret under wraps.

"Yes. We have the best fans in the world," Nicky replied, lighting a cigarette. He was extremely nervous about the concert tonight. Although it wasn't like him to be worried, he couldn't explain it.

Arriving at the Sports Dome, the complex was huge as the limo drove around to the back entrance, the line of fans waiting to get in wrapped the entire length of two city blocks.

"Man, I'd say from the looks of that line, those are some die-hard rock fans," David exclaimed.

"Yes. It's still over two hours before the doors open to the public," Jeff added.

Walking into the back entrance of the complex, it was just like the thousands of other venues where they had performed. Following one of the long corridors, they finally found the dressing room. It was filled with catered food, fresh flowers, and a fully stocked bar.

"Okay, boys, who wants to go first?" asked Antonio.

After Jackie's departure, Bill had decided to hire a guy for hair and makeup. He hoped a guy would be less of a distraction for the boys, or so he thought. Jeff volunteered to be first at hair and makeup tonight. Looking up at Antonio, Jeff smiled.

"Do you have any plans after the concert tonight? I know the best restaurant in Quebec."

Nicky looked over at Jeff with a wide grin.

"Okay, guys, over twenty thousand fans are filling those seats out there right now," Bill stated. "Should be a great concert," he added.

Nicky went to the bar and poured himself a drink. Again, he couldn't shake his case of the nerves. But, again, it wasn't like him to be so nervous. David came over to sit on the sofa next to Nicky, pouring himself a drink.

"Wow, man, what are you going to do when this is all over?"

"I don't know," Nicky said with his hands shaking.

"Okay, guys, fifteen minutes to show time," Bill always reminded them.

Jeff walked on stage first to the roaring screams of the fans. Jerry came out next and walked up to the front.

"Good evening, Quebec. How are you tonight?" he shouted, holding his guitar high into the air.

David was next as he walked out and screamed.

"Hello, Quebec."

"Nicky, Nicky," the fans began to scream.

Finally, it was his turn to walk out to the center stage. As he walked out, the fans stood to their feet and shouted.

"We love you, Nicky. We love you!"

"I love you, Quebec," Nicky yelled back. "How are you this evening?"

As Nicky led into their first song, the fans went crazy as they yelled out their love and support for the band. Nicky's nerves seemed to calm the second he held the microphone in his hand.

"Thank you, Quebec. We are so happy to be here with you tonight," he shouted. "I'd like to sing a song for you which I wrote many years ago called, *Because of You*, I hope you like it."

Without a single thought or hesitation for what he was about to do, Nicky found himself surprised by what he said next.

"I'd like to dedicate this song tonight to Jenna Jones."

Jerry looked over at him with a surprised smile. Wow, there was no possible way Nicky could have known that Jenna was in the audience tonight. The roar of the fans was deafening.

After the song, the boys began to undo their ties and walk toward the front of the stage. Nicky couldn't help but wonder if Jenna might be in the audience tonight. Unfortunately, there was no way to tell in the vast crowd. However, he found himself looking for her anyways. Walking to the edge of the stage, the guys tossed their ties to the girls standing in front with their arms outstretched. David, as usual, kneeled and gently tied his tie around the neck of one of the young girls, which happened to catch his attention. Then he kissed her quickly on the cheek as the girls screamed. This action always brought out the security guards. If girls were going to faint during the concert, this was usually it, and tonight would be no different.

Next, the boys led into their new number one single, *Don't Look Back,* as the crowd went wild. Tonight was turning out to be a great concert. Nicky finally relaxed and enjoyed the love coming back from his adoring fans. Black Tie Affair had the best fans on earth. There was no doubt about it. Nicky was going to miss the close connection with his audience.

After spending another hour on stage, Nicky knew his fans would not leave disappointed tonight.

"Goodnight, Quebec," Jerry shouted.

"Thank you for coming," David screamed.

"Quebec, we love you. Thanks for coming out to party with us tonight," Nicky shouted. "We are Black Tie Affair, and we've enjoyed being here with you tonight," Nicky yelled as the four of them walked off stage. Nicky was anxious to get back to the dressing room and get changed.

Opening the door to the dressing room, Nicky got the surprise of his life. Jenna was standing right in front of him. She looked more beautiful than he could have ever imagined. He had waited his entire life for this moment. He hesitated, trying to read Jenna's face. Then she smiled at him, the same smile she gave him the first day they met. That was all the encouragement he needed.

Scooping her up in his arms, he held her tight.

"You came, Doll," Nicky exclaimed with tears in his eyes.

Staring deep into his eyes, Jenna was speechless.

"Yes. I love you, Nicky Spade. I've always loved you. I've missed you so much," Jenna smiled as tears streamed down her face. "So this is what you've been doing since I last saw you."

As Nicky put her down to stare at how stunning she was, she took his hand.

"Nicky, there is someone I want you to meet. You have another huge fan."

Turning around, a handsome young man who mirrored his image smiled at him.

"Nicky, this is our son, Cameron."

Without hesitation, instantly, Nicky knew this was his son. Walking over, he put his arms around Cameron.

"You never told me, you never told me," Nicky repeated, embracing his young son.

"I know," Jenna smiled, wiping tears from her eyes. "I know."

EPILOGUE

Six months later

Nicky knew the perfect manager for Cameron. There was only one person which Nicky trusted with his son's career. So, picking up the phone, he placed the call.

"Hey Bruce, how has retirement been treating you these days?"

"Oh fine, I guess, but I've sure missed the excitement as tour manager of Black Tie Affair. How are you doing, son? I heard that you've finally cleaned up your act. I'm so proud of you. How's the farewell tour going?"

"It's been great so far. Bruce, I hope you're sitting down. I've got some exciting news. Jenna and I are finally together."

"Oh, that's wonderful, Nicky. I am so happy for you."

"Well, Bruce, as great as that is, it's not exactly why I've called."

"How can I help you?" Bruce questioned.

"You're not going to believe this, but Jenna and I have an eighteen-year-old son, Cameron. Bruce, he's really talented. Cameron is driven to become a rock star, and he will not stop until he fulfills that itch. Bruce, he's good, real good. I was wondering what you were doing with the rest of your life, besides spending it in some retirement home?" Nicky teased. "I guess what I'm asking is that we need your help. Cameron and I want you to manage his career."

"Son, say no more. I've just been waiting for a call like this. I would be delighted to come out of retirement. Hell, retirement is for old folks," Bruce laughed. "I'll be on the next plane to Quebec. I know the perfect place to get his feet wet. It's one of my favorite places in Quebec. So I'll work on getting him booked to play there by next month."

As Nicky sat in the smoke-filled bar that evening, Cameron was about to take his place on stage. His hands were shaking as he lifted a tall glass of bourbon to his lips. He was nervous tonight. However, tonight was no longer about him but his son, Cameron. He knew his young son's life was about to change in ways that he could never imagine under the loving direction of Bruce.

Cameron received a standing ovation after performing his last song. Now having finished his farewell tour, Nicky looked up at his son. The torch had been passed. His career was now over. It was up to Cameron to continue his legacy.

Trembling as he stood, Jenna grabbed Nicky's arms to keep him steady on his feet.

"Nicky, let's go home. The show is over," she smiled.

www.ingramcontent.com/pod-product-compliance
Lightning Source LLC
Chambersburg PA
CBHW030348200726
48286CB00013B/501